THE
BLACK
DUCHESS

Also by Alanna Knight

Fiction

THE LEGEND OF THE LOCH
THE OCTOBER WITCH
THIS OUTWARD ANGEL
CASTLE CLODHA
LAMENT FOR LOST LOVERS
THE WHITE ROSE
A STRANGER CAME BY
THE WICKED WYNSLEYS

Historical

THE PASSIONATE KINDNESS: The story of R. L. Stevenson and Fanny Osbourne
A DRINK FOR THE BRIDGE: The Tay Bridge Disaster, 1879

Plays

THE PASSIONATE KINDNESS, or THE PRIVATE LIFE OF RLS
DON ROBERTO: The life of R. B. Cunninghame Graham
GIRL ON AN EMPTY SWING: One-Act Occult Thriller

Nonfiction

SO YOU WANT TO WRITE

Alanna Knight

THE BLACK DUCHESS

A NOVEL

Doubleday & Company, Inc.
Garden City, New York 1980

ISBN: 0-385-15326-0
Library of Congress Catalog Card Number 79-7668

Copyright © 1980 by Alanna Knight
ALL RIGHTS RESERVED
PRINTED IN THE UNITED STATES OF AMERICA
FIRST EDITION

For
Giles Gordon

Author's Note

Among the many books and background material consulted in the writing of this book, I am particularly indebted to Garrett Mattingly, *Defeat of the Spanish Armada*, 1959; A. M. Hadfield, *Time to Finish the Game*, 1964; J. R. Hale, *The Great Armada*, 1913; J. S. Corbett, *Drake and the Tudor Navy*, 1899; J. R. Tudor, *The Orkneys and Shetland*; *The Orkneys & Shetlands Miscellany*, vol. i.

The writing of any history of this time was further confused by the use of two calendars in Europe in 1588. The Gregorian (New Style) proclaimed in 1582 was used by Spain and most of western Europe. The English resisted such change and clung to the Old Style, which was ten days behind. I have used the New Style and 29 July in Spain was 19 July in England.

THE BLACK DUCHESS

Prologue

Edinburgh: July 29, 1565

The bed they shared lacked curtains and smelt of mice. Apologies were made. The Palace of Holyroodhouse was severely overcrowded, since by my lord Darnley's wish the entire powerful Lennox clan were to be present to witness his triumph. To see him not only wedded and bedded to the Queen of Scots, but also the bestowal of the ultimate accolade: the Crown Matrimonial, King Henry of Scots.

None had time or patience to spare for Amyas Lennox and Felipe de Montreuse, who moaned of scufflings in the night and spiders' webs in the bed canopy. There were far more interesting and dangerous webs being spun behind every closed door in Holyrood that summer. After all, the cousins were but ten years old and small for their age. And their parents were far down the clan hierarchy.

Thomas Lennox was a minor official at the English court, whose twin sister, Marjory, had married Don Flores de Montreuse, equerry to the Spanish ambassador. Don Flores also possessed a twin sister, Alma, who had married Thomas Lennox. In due course these marriages produced only sons, more like twins than cousins.

Their first meeting had the fascination of staring into a mirror, although Felipe's flaxen hair was curlier and he was the younger by two months. The same hazel eyes were deeper set in Amyas, wider apart in Felipe, while the latter's eyebrows were darker. But the handsome shape of head and face, the curve of lip, chin, and nose were identical. So too was an impish humour which gave rise to infinite possibilities for teasing and tormenting their elders.

"A pair of lovely lads," whispered the fond parents.

"Devil's brats," said those they mischiefed, smarting.

Neither Amyas nor Felipe slept well that sultry evening before the Queen's wedding. The curtainless windows also lacked shutters, and a full moon flooded the small chamber, turning short summer night into day.

"A blood wedding," muttered superstitious Edinburgh townsfolk, shuddering, observing in horrified whispers that the moon was ringed in scarlet.

"The Queen is ill advised, besotted by a pretty lad."

There had been omens aplenty for their heedless, headstrong Queen. On sea, ghost ships off Leith; on land, phantom horsemen clattering down the Royal Mile. Comets in the sky, sea monsters in the lochs. And in the Orkney Isles, the standing stones, those mysterious obelisks left by the giants of long ago, had taken to walking, while a glut of mermaids lured poor sailors to their doom in the boiling treacherous seas. But no one really cared about Orkney, a daftlike place, unchancy—sinister, some had heard, tottering on the far edge of the known world, barely civilised, the realm of wreckers and witches.

"Awake, young masters. Time you stirred."

Felipe moved resentfully. It seemed that he had just closed his eyes.

"What is the hour?"

"Six of the clock. And Her Majesty has been about since dawn," said their servant reproachfully. "Take an example from the Queen."

"It is her wedding, not ours," whispered Amyas as they both yawned, tumbled out of bed, trying to keep their bare feet swinging clear of the chilly floor, awaiting the ewer of warm water.

"Like you my lord Darnley?" asked Felipe.

"Nay, I like not his mouth," said Amyas.

"Nor I." He did not like Darnley's habit of fondling him, and was too shy to ask his cousin if he had similar experiences. "His lips are soft and wet, like a serving wench."

They frowned, silent, pondering this revelation of character. Lacking sisters, womankind, apart from aunts, mothers, to be decently respected, was fit only to be dismissed in amused contempt.

"Aye, and he has a wicked temper."

This too they considered, for both had fallen foul of him in wine, and in Felipe's case, since he could not run as fast as his cousin, had earned a cuffed ear which burned red and hot for an hour.

"Think you the Queen truly likes him?"

Even two children could see that Lord Darnley was weak and vain, a liar too. And he simpered.

"Queens should be cleverer than we are," they agreed.

"I like Her Majesty." Felipe's chin thrust out, rushing to her defence.

"Aye, she is a proper woman."

"And beautiful."

"Kind too."

Amyas tried hard not to sigh. The Queen had given them sweetmeats yesterday, but they were cautious regarding their revelations to one another about their goddess. Each had his own private fantasy about Mary Queen of Scots. Enough to walk the same floor and see her, hear her silvery laugh and admire that long white throat. Enough to merit one single smile for a whole hour's daydreams.

"God's grief, cousin, have you looked at the day?" shouted Amyas, running barefoot to the window.

Felipe peered over his shoulder. Far below, in the grounds of Holyroodhouse its Chapel hidden in mist, the townspeople had gathered to watch the royal wedding. An unseen murmur.

The cousins exchanged glances. Yesterday, returning from the loch, they had seen John Knox delivering an impromptu sermon from the balcony of his house in the Royal Mile.

"Papist harlot," he had roared, comfortably aware of virtue and the true religion upon his side.

Remembering his words, Felipe murmured, "Why is the Queen a harlot?"

"I know not. But a Papist—is what you are, cousin." Amyas chuckled and had to duck smartly to avoid his cousin's descending fist.

"Amyas, be still." A parent's grip tightened.

"Felipe, your manners. Everyone watches you."

A small cheer arose as the Queen's wedding procession approached.

The Queen wore a black mourning gown with the great white mourning hood in which she had buried her first husband, thus plainly declaring she was no virgin but the Dowager Queen of

France. She was seen to stumble, and looks were exchanged. Did dead hands reach out and pluck at the hem of her gown?

The dazzling spectacle of the day was reserved for her bridegroom, magnificent in white velvet and satin. But love, naked in her eyes for all the world to see, outsparkled the diamonds that were her wedding gift to him.

She was attended by the Catholic lords, with David Rizzio and her half sister, the Countess of Argyll. A tall handsome man walked at her side, Lord Robert Stewart, her half brother and another of King James the Fifth's many bastards. His looks were already running to coarseness through constant debauchery, for he had inherited, besides the hot Stewart eyes, the hot Stewart lusts. Court ladies, not over-fussy, whispered of him as a brutal lover, and no woman, not even the meanest serving wench, was safe from his lewd attentions.

Amid cheers, the procession was returning to the Palace when thunder, which had lurked ominously since dawn, turned to heavy rain. The great drops fell like largesse scattered to the waiting, eager townspeople. Another cheer arose, resounding as far as John Knox's ears as he prepared for St Giles, stripped of all idolatrous images, that Sunday morning. Despite his insults and threats, Queen Mary was still the darling of her people's hearts.

As everyone raced indoors to escape a drenching, the Queen retired to her chamber to emerge, radiant in cloth of silver, her eyes brighter than the candles hastily lit to banish the gloom. She had cast aside her mourning and would "with God's help now embark upon a pleasanter life."

"During the space of three or four days there was nothing but balling and dancing and banqueting," grumbled John Knox in a spiteful huff because he liked wine and good living too but had not been invited to the wedding. Sitting up half the night, preparing a daunting speech for the event, he had no option but to tear it up next morning. His statement omitted, since he was not present, that there was considerable bickering. Feuds were begun, love affairs ended, and as Lord Darnley early proved unreliable, with a small head for wine but a large head for debauchery, the seeds of the future were well and truly sown during those first momentous days.

August bloomed and faded, September came and touched the afternoon fields with mellow gold while the weather continued outrageous, as only a Scottish summer could ever be. In their chambers, close to a roaring fire, Don Flores and Marjory shivered, homesick for the heat of Madrid, while Thomas and Alma Lennox rubbed chilly hands and thought of rose-red Lennoxhoe and harvest home.

The nocturnal habits of their elders combined to throw the cousins much upon their own devilish devices. While their parents drank and danced in the great hall until the birds' dawn-chorus outdid the yawning minstrels and put the guttering candles to shame, Amyas and Felipe tumbled like puppies, growling one moment, mirthful the next, their high spirits uncontrollable, their behaviour a trial to everyone. They raced with banshee wails down deserted chilly Palace corridors and laid snares for unwary servants, while behind closed doors their elders slept late and woke grumbling to sore heads, to whispered intrigues or new lovers.

One morning the cousins, rushing like wild creatures, cannoned into Lord Robert Stewart, who was leaving somewhat stealthily a bedchamber which was not his own. All three went spinning, accompanied by the searing sound of tearing material.

Lord Robert seized Felipe, who was nearest. "By God's blood, I should spit you for this." And he brought down his hand hard upon the boy's head.

"Leave him be—bully!" shouted Amyas, diving into the attack. He was also seized, and the cousins' heads were soundly banged together until they were dizzy. At the same time their arms were unmercifully twisted, for Lord Robert's nightly exertions kept him in the prime of condition.

"You may yell as you wish, none can hear you." He leered. "Devil's brats that you are," he added, looking round for other means of prolonging their suffering.

"Stop—at once, Robert," yawned the young man who emerged from the next bedchamber to see what was amiss. The newcomer was a stranger to them. A head shorter than Lord Robert, he had the tough looks of the seasoned military man. "Before God, they are but bairns." His accent was rough.

"Bairns, are they? Look at my doublet—torn—"

"I daresay that the Queen your sister will generously provide another."

Lord Robert scowled. "I will thank you not to interfere, James Hepburn. Keep your peace."

"You likewise, or you will find a ready sword in someone your own match—"

"Yourself, perhaps?"

The young man so addressed unsheathed his sword, slowly smiling. "Aye, me—"

The cousins, forgotten, stared up at the two men in fascinated horror, knowing instinctively that the contempt and hatred they saw depicted on their countenances had much deeper roots than this accidental meeting.

At the end of the corridor a door opened and all were bowing as the Queen strode towards them, faintly dishevelled, flushed with sleep. The cousins exchanged a glance. Beautiful, adorable goddess—

"What is amiss, my lords? You have awakened my husband, and he is ill pleased." Suddenly she saw the children, dropped on one knee beside them. "Ah, *mes petits*—are you lost, then?" They stammered a reply, to be shouted down by her ill-natured bastard brother.

"Nay, they are not. They misuse your hospitality—as a bear garden."

The Queen raised delicate eyebrows and began to laugh. "Surely, my lords, you do not quarrel over these two."

Felipe rubbed his sore head with a grimace and she gathered him into her arms, held out a hand to Amyas. "*Mes adorables*, are you hurt? Tell me." The deep sultry voice had made men and boys her willing slaves. Many were still to lose heads and lives for those caring and caressing tones—

Lord Robert shrugged huffily.

"As for you, my lord Bothwell, you must learn to keep your sword in check, for your temper, I fear, matches your hair."

James Hepburn ran a hand sheepishly through unruly dark red curls. "I am but your servant and your slave, madam."

"Slave indeed. I fear you are too impudent—and too bold—for such a role."

But her look was an invitation, his returning glance a caress, and the interview made the cousins again sharply aware of that adult world closed to them. Where even parents could be—and mostly were —unpredictable and slaps unearned were delivered with alarming promptitude.

"Away, *mes petits*." The Queen smiled. "See now, the sun shines."

Even as the cousins turned to bow, she was walking away and had forgotten them, her hand resting lightly upon Lord Bothwell's arm, leaning a little towards him, swan-necked in her loose gown.

"My lord," they heard her whisper, "before God, it is good to see you again." And their voices were leaves rustling as, heads down like lovers, they disappeared.

In the Palace gardens, where a weak sunlight threatened rather than made rash promise of good weather, the cousins forgot all about Lords Robert and Bothwell as, in the still dripping shrubbery, they held contest of strength over who should be Queen's champion. Equally matched, they emerged rueful and exhausted to examine torn hose and bloody knees, and sitting together on a fallen tree, they swore to fight all tyrants. And to serve the Queen. For after all, they were almost brothers—

"When I am a man, I shall go to sea and sail upon a great ship," said Amyas, whose home, Lennoxhoe, at Plymouth, stared over the cliffs uneasily aware of an alien continent, constantly awaiting its chance to invade and sweep Elizabeth of England from her throne.

"When I am a man, I shall be a pirate," said Felipe, not to be outdone. His hero was one Karim el Raschid, a pirate captain who served King Philip, Felipe's godfather, and who filled his head with highly coloured yarns from strange exotic shores.

"Who knows, maybe we shall meet—"

"I trust not, cousin, since my pirate ship will definitely seize yours as prize."

"Then I shall die fighting," said Amyas proudly.

"I fight better than you—"

And forgetful of their oath, they rolled shrieking on the grass, desisting only when the tall shadows of their parents hovered over them, brought by Lord Robert, the traitor, who had glimpsed them in the garden.

"Come, Amyas—Felipe—hurry—"

"We sail from Leith upon the afternoon tide."

"Leave Holyrood? Now?" The cousins exchanged glances. Nobody, as usual, had told them it was today—or that these past weeks in a magic world—give or take a few fights—should not last forever.

For Felipe childhood ended two months later, when his parents, voyaging to yet another royal wedding in Portugal, had their ship attacked by pirates and all hands lost.

For Amyas childhood lasted until spring, when his mother died of the babe conceived during the Holyrood festivities.

PART ONE

The Most Happy Armada

1

Off Corunna: July 29, 1588

Magnificent, proud, with a seabird's grace, the *Black Duchess* glided out of the harbour's still waters to join the Armada, anchored off Corunna. As she met the open sea, she dipped and bowed, a mistress acknowledging her lover. Her figurehead seemed to take on life, the changing colours of mellow sunlight touching green waves, reflecting her moods, turning her savage negroid face through dark menace into smiling content.

The galleons of the Great Armada, close enough to witness her approach, trembled in their tall sails. With reason, for *La Duquesa Negra* was infamous, the terror of every ship and every sailor in the Mediterranean. A thinly disguised pirate craft, despite respectability conferred by their insignia, the cross of Burgundy, which she flew. As she dropped anchor alongside the flagship, they saw that she was contemptuously small by comparison to their vast bulks. Built to cut and run, to board and take prizes, built for speed. They observed that her figurehead was vulgarly large. A shining brown countenance, huge black eyes, thick negroid lips parted in a smile which showed teeth white and sharp. The jewelled coronet perched upon her black curls was the final insult. Signifying royal birth, it offended the noble captains of the Armada almost as gravely as her enormous breasts, bared, gold-nippled, her round seductive belly.

The *Black Duchess* looked dangerous, fierce as her master, Capitaine Karim el Raschid, "Black Karim," leaning on the taffrail. A giant of a man, his height diminished the tall young man at his side.

"The wind is about to change, Master." He stared up at the sails. "Fortune smiled upon your arrival."

Don Felipe Flores y Lennox de Montreuse smiled. Flaxen hair darker and less curly than it had been during that Holyrood summer, twenty-three years ago, the early promise of good looks had been fulfilled, turning golden boy into well-favoured man. A comely face but wary, a chilling quality about fair hair touched with red. A certain granite determination about chin, hazel eyes, and wide cheekbones, the stubborn line of mouth hinted more at Rufus Scots peasant, the court whispered, than high-born Castilian grandee, godson to the King of Spain.

Their sneers were not without reason. Felipe had suffered—and dealt by return—many a bloody nose on the subject of his imperfect blood, the defect provided by a Scots mother from that cold northern land peopled by prune-faced heretics. In Spanish eyes it was just a shade less detestable than the hated English enemy they waited to fight.

The short velvet cloak he wore, elegant and ermined, bore the insignia of Commander of the Most Holy Armada. His title a mere convenience, since it had not been honourably earned in battle and this was his first command, a deficiency he shared with many of the Spanish noblemen in the galleons around them.

A half-Scots commander who had never put to sea travelling on a pirate ship with an infidel captain. What were things coming to in Spain these days? Experienced old sea dogs—of whom there were few —shook heads over charts and with treasonable disregard for blasphemy, muttered, "What kind of fool was His Most Catholic Majesty to put his faith—and his Armada's fate—into the hands of such men?"

There was worse information to follow.

Don Felipe was a spy.

Commander of the *Black Duchess* was a convenient disguise for the passenger being carried to Scotland and a secret meeting with the Catholic lords led by the Earl of Huntly. Felipe was already late for his appearance in the sheltered cove north of Aberdeen.

He did not travel empty-handed. His powers of persuasion had been strengthened by a king's ransom in gold, to provide an army to march south upon Whitehall. There the bastard English Queen would be subjected to the same axe as she had suffered last year upon the neck of her royal cousin of Scotland. Remembering the vision he had carried through the years of Mary at Holyrood, Felipe regarded his mission as a sacred vendetta, a knight pledged to avenge a wronged queen.

But dogged by ill-luck and worse weather, the Armada was running two months behind the original plan. Nor had the unexpected presence of the English fleet patrolling the Scillies improved tempers. The element of surprise so essential to their expedition was lost.

While the might of Spain awaited "God's wind" to speed them forth to destroy His heretical enemies, the schemes of Felipe's royal godfather to have him betrothed once again had produced a prospective bride in Corunna, a convenient place to join Karim's pirate ship. Meanwhile, in Scotland, the conspirators paced the shore and daily expected the sail of the *Black Duchess;* in its wake a victorious Armada, with fighting men and supplies to reinforce their uprising.

The *Black Duchess* had hardly anchored when she was honoured by a visit from the Duke of Medina Sidonia, Admiral of the Fleet. Following Felipe into the master's cabin, he regarded the treasures gathered therein with distaste. The Admiral was not a subtle man. His thoughts were transparent. Such magnificence paled the opulence of his cabin in the flagship *San Martin* and he wondered, as had Felipe, how much this splendour had cost in ships and men who had gone to the bottom of the sea.

The Admiral ignored the offered chair. "You are aware, Don Felipe, of the supreme importance of the mission entrusted to you. The throne of England. Willed to his Most Catholic Majesty by none other than the late unfortunate Queen." Sternly he added, "And no Catholic prince has more legitimate claim by royal descent—"

Felipe stifled a yawn. Surely the Admiral was not about to solemnly lecture *him* upon his royal godfather's rights to the English realm? No one close to Uncle Philip as he had been for most of his life could hope for a single day to pass without reference to His Majesty's wrongs at the hands of England and his marriage political to barren, unlovely Queen Mary Tudor. She had made his virility the laughing-stock of Europe. And King Philip never forgot an insult.

"We have not a great deal of time for details," continued the Admiral, wishing that Don Felipe would betray emotion or interest. An enigma born of an enigmatic monarch in the cold marble halls of El Escorial. "You are aware—" he repeated.

Felipe indicated the handsome chair opposite, and awareness, by the merest inclination of an eyebrow. "Your Grace will be seated and take wine," he said gently. "There is always time for wine."

Impudent pup. The Admiral sniffed, scenting a reprimand, and was further offended when the cabin door opened with such alacrity that he guessed the newcomer had been lending a sharp ear to the proceedings within.

The giant who filled the doorway dwindled portly Medina Sidonia into demoralising insignificance. The Admiral had not the slightest difficulty in recognising Black Karim el Raschid, the pirate notorious as the "Scourge of the Mediterranean." Contemptuously he brushed aside Felipe's attempted introduction. Don Felipe's lack of aristocratic Spanish blood on all four sides irked him; the captain of the *Black Duchess* was also undeniably mongrel. Part Arab, part Negro, with black curling hair, a handsome curved nose and fierce cruel eyes.

The door closed softly behind him. For all his bulk, Karim moved like a shy forest creature.

"*He* is fully to be trusted?"

"Fully, Your Grace. With all our plans—and with my life." The dark eyebrows twitched in mocking humour. "My life, which is also important—to me. As you have doubtless observed, Karim is my shadow." Felipe knew he eavesdropped and was in no way perturbed. Raising a long, thin hand, he tapped his chin thoughtfully. The gesture sharply recalled His Majesty to the Admiral, who noticed with grudging admiration that the elegant tapered fingers were undoubtedly Spanish. Such hands never belonged to a Scots peasant tilling the earth. He recalled rumour rife upon His Majesty's devotion to Don Felipe. How unhappy, unmanned as Mary Tudor's husband, Philip had sought warmth and affection elsewhere in the English court. Whisper had it that he found consolation and more than he bargained for in the extremely warm and comely small person of the redheaded Scots lady-in-waiting, Marjory Lennox, of that powerful clan who had spawned Lord Henry Darnley. An expedient marriage to a devoted Spanish equerry, Don Flores de Montreuse, failed to supply a reliable answer to why the Queen had been so upset when the young man before him was born remarkably well-formed for a premature infant.

With a sly glance the Admiral decided that rumour, in common with smoke, was not entirely without fire. King Philip was also tall and their bearing decidedly similar, although His Majesty's once golden youth had now faded into tarnished gilt. Embarrassed to come upon royal bastardy in the undoubted—and strong—resemblance, he was temporarily at a loss for words.

Felipe chose the pause to interpose: "I am a little anxious, Your Grace, concerning the young King of Scots."

Medina Sidonia was silent, delicately aware of sacrilegious ground and the divine right of kings. Delicately, he cleared his throat: "We have no quarrel with King James," he said stiffly.

"I am glad of that." Felipe stared out of the great window and his lips curved at another scene oft relived in memory. Of the Queen of Scots kneeling in the corridor of Holyrood Palace, protecting him from Lord Robert Stewart's wrath. "I was acquainted with his late mother."

"Upon whose soul Sweet Jesu have mercy," said the Admiral, crossing himself in pious regard for the unhappy Queen whose demise had given King Philip full justification for his Most Holy Armada. "We expect no opposition from King James, a timid monarch. We understand that naked swords are forbidden in his presence." The Admiral enjoyed such contemptuous gossip.

"I know all that," said Felipe shortly. "Is it not to be expected when David Rizzio was murdered before the Queen his mother's eyes—her own life and his unborn—threatened? To say naught of his father's, Lord Darnley's, untimely end in the mysterious explosion at Kirk O'Fields?"

"We do but come as his mother's avengers." The Admiral's tone was reproachful.

"Indeed? You may find it difficult to persuade Jamie of that." Did the stiff-necked old fool not realise that "canny King Jamie" had shocked even the most cynical by fawning upon the English Queen, his mother's murderess, with the words: "he would not be so fond as to prefer his mother to the title of King of Scots." Aye, Jamie would fight to the death if he saw the coveted English throne being snatched from under his nose and handed over to King Philip of Spain. Not only patience had been required waiting for Queen Elizabeth to die, but he had lived every day in constant terror of treachery, of assassination.

"Once victory is assured," said the Admiral smoothly, "the Duke of Parma will doubtless know how to persuade a stubborn king."

Felipe was aware of Scotland's bloody history and that the victorious Spaniards need not soil their hands with King Jamie's blood.

Scotland had always specialised in breeding warlike lords not unskilful in exterminating their own kings, who would lose no sleep over the divine right of kings and eternal damnation, if the price offered were tempting enough.

Medina Sidonia placed his fingertips together delicately. "We do not anticipate any difficulties. A skirmish merely, for we have heard that the survival of England depends on a handful of ships. Of the captains experienced in sea fighting, only four are noble lords. And one is the notorious Earl of Cumberland."

Felipe smiled at Karim, who had brought in wine. The Arab captain laughed, throwing back his head. He revealed white teeth, enviably sharp and plentiful.

"The English pirate lord, Excellencies. We have ofttimes crossed swords in battle. A fine and worthy opponent," he added, bowing low in the direction of the Admiral, who studiously ignored his interruption. "But El Draque is the man we must watch."

Felipe concealed a smile at the Admiral's outraged expression. "Karim is right, Your Grace. We must do more than keep an eye on El Draque. We must remember Cádiz."

Medina Sidonia winced. He needed no reminders of the catastrophe which had befallen the first Armada. On April 19, 1587, two months after the Queen of Scots had laid her head upon the block, Sir Francis Drake had sailed into Cádiz harbour at five in the afternoon, accompanied by twenty-three ships, conveniently mistaken for Spanish merchantmen.

Helplessly the Spanish captains watched their Armada blazing, their victuals and plans for the English invasion going up in flames which soon transformed the harbour into a gateway to hell. El Draque, the Dragon, the Devil incarnate, had once more displayed his uncanny powers of invincibility. His "singeing of the King of Spain's beard" had cost them two dozen ships, a million ducats of supplies. Fifteen months it had taken to rebuild and restock, but the fresh wood, which had replaced seasoned timber, warped or was full of worms. Victuals had gone rotten, water was too foul to drink. With the present delays the crews were back on wine, biscuit, and weevil with full knowledge that these also would be finished before the fighting began. Cursed by delays, bad weather, and worse living conditions, Medina Sidonia knew there was discontent aboard his ships. Desertions were plentiful—despite rigorous guards and heavy punishment.

The Admiral was in no danger of forgetting. And if Mary Tudor had Calais engraved upon her heart when she died, then Cádiz was definitely engraved upon the heart of the Duke of Medina Sidonia. Preparing to leave, he said, "As commander of this ship, Don Felipe, I trust you to maintain stern discipline at all times. No slackening of moral fibres—daily prayers—we must never forget this is a holy war we fight and that Almighty God is on our side and will give us victory over our heretic enemies. The men must go as saints into holy battle, pure in heart and thought. No daggers drawn except against the foe."

He paused, allowing his stern gaze to drift from Felipe around the opulent cabin. "And no public nor private harlots are to be accommodated. Remember that the severest sentences will be carried out upon officers or crew known to be harbouring such individuals. Whatever the rank," he added, his voice heavy with accusation since officers were known to ignore such orders.

Many a night of solemn darkness in his cabin had been broken by smothered female laughter as a pinnace was rowed stealthily back to harbour. Most captains regarded the harlots who sailed with every ship as a necessity of long sea voyages. Some loyal women came with children to be with the man they loved, others for the immemorial reasons of a profession more ancient than the sea trade itself. Captains would argue that these women faced the same perils as camp followers on land and were useful in nursing the sick and wounded.

Don Felipe made no comment, but, bowing, led the way out to the deck.

"It is His Majesty's wish that you remain in contact with the flagship at all times, that you stay out of danger, and do not act in any manner likely to imperil the success of your mission."

Felipe knew a moment's fleeting gratitude to his godfather. He had little desire to live—or to die—in the role of hero.

"Which means that unless we are boarded by the enemy—which God forbid—you are not to seek combat other than in self-defence."

Felipe nodded assent and accompanied him to the rail, where Karim watched the sails being hauled.

"Excellencies, do you not feel it? A change in weather—"

"God's wind—at last," said the Admiral as if Karim had not spoken. "Have a courier report of your well-being daily, Don Felipe." And as the young man inclined his head in silent acknowledgement, he continued; "You need have no fears; we will see you safely to Scotland, if God wills it." He gestured towards the galleons and galleasses, the transport urcas and zabras, already shaking out their sails, displaying their colours in a fiesta-like touch. "You see before you the greatest armada that ever put to sea," he added reverently. "What chance has the English Jezebel with her handful of ships? Would that Almighty God had given us a foe worthy of His holy work—and of our might."

A signal gun was fired from the Admiral's flagship. With a flourish of trumpets the Great Armada was on the move; the creaking in its forests of masts and timbers was like a thousand round shots, transforming its lofty towers into a fantasy city threatened by seaquake. Unreal as a bright tapestry from some draughty castle wall, blowing in sudden draught, Felipe thought. At any moment it might vanish—

As the decks strained under his feet, fascinated, he watched the shouting crew tramping round with capstans, chains rattling on anchors, while above his head the mighty painted sails of the *Black Duchess* were unfurled, shaken into the wind. At last the heavy yards braced round to catch the northwest wind on the starboard tack, and with a great creak of timber, a rustle of sails like a lover's moan, she was released from her shackles and sped in the wake of the *San Martin*, out to the open sea.

For a while Felipe continued to watch the sailors' activities as if he understood their tasks. Then frowning, hands behind his back, he walked among them, trying to appear confident and knowledgeable, their commander and well able to sail this ship—or any other—single-handed should the necessity arise.

He suspected there were few Spaniards among the half-naked brown and black men already sweating at their labours. Moors, Africans, Arabs, were prevalent, some deeply scarred as if from earlier engagements of battle. Tattooed from head to foot, bone or gold rings through noses and ears, feathers in their hair, they were nonetheless a desperate crew of the best and most fearful of the sea's fighters. After that first glance they were no sight for any man's derisory amusement, and Felipe would not have cared to face any single one of them in hand-to-hand fighting least of all the mulatto Mahmoud, Karim's second-in-command.

Karim pointed to the ships alongside. "Pray that this voyage will be short, its outcome victorious, Master, for they are ready to mutiny. A few more days in Corunna—" He shook his head. "They daily fear another Cádiz."

Felipe guessed from the crew's sullen glances in his direction that they were discontent with the bargain Karim had made with the Spanish King. These men owed no allegiance to any mortal and called no man sovereign; the *Black Duchess* was their home, Karim their ruler because he was stronger than they. Felipe could only guess at his power over such men, at what riches they had been promised, what bribes and threats, to take their place thus docilely in another man's war.

As if he read Felipe's thoughts, Karim smiled. "My *Duchess* has not suffered from the earlier delays, the rotten food and foul water. My men are skilful at securing supplies while we are in harbour." He grinned. "They also make admirable spies. We have our own thieves' kitchen, here upon the seas."

"What of this meeting with the Duke of Parma?"

Karim frowned. "With due respect, Master, for he is His Majesty's nephew, none trust him. He is known to be fickle, self-seeking. If the ships had not lingered to meet him—a delay which was fatal, since he chose not to arrive and they were forced by storm into Corunna—"

Above their heads the cloudless blue was now threatened by great cumulous clouds building fast from the horizon.

"Take not that as any sign of comfort, Master; we are in for more bad weather."

Felipe groaned silently, since he was keeping uneasily abreast of his own threatened seasickness.

"The last storm had those galleons capering about the sea like whores at a revel, as they tried not to smash into one another." Watching the young man's sober face, he laughed. "My *Duchess* cares little for drowsing in stinking harbours. Men grow restless—and dangerous—during such inactivity."

Returning to the cabin, Karim spread the charts. To his cheerful "There is no turning back now, Master," he received a bewildered shrug which he mistook for apprehension. He put an arm heavy with gold bracelets across the shoulders of Felipe, whom he loved better than the multitudes of his own flesh, spawned upon a hundred wives in too many harbours on too many nights of his long life.

"My *Duchess* is built for speed and bad weather too. Have no fear, Master. She can cut and run before her enemies, whether man-sent or God-given." Karim smiled. "We are to expect few of either if His Grace is to be believed."

Felipe had turned pale, leaning against the gilded chair.

"My *Duchess* will get us out of any tight corner," he added soothingly.

Felipe yawned.

"My Master is tired—a rest—"

Felipe shook his head, frowning. "My ears feel strange—ringing—"

Karim recognised the all too familiar signs of approaching seasickness. In a few hours Felipe would be helpless, sick as a dog, if rough weather came—

"My *Duchess* will fare better than these galleons," he said consolingly. "They were built for sheltered waters, the leisurely pace of the Mediterranean. If ever they have to face into the teeth of an Atlantic gale—" He shrugged expressively, and Felipe followed him to the window, where the galleons swayed, a magnificent sight on a blue shining sea, each bordered by the white frivolity of lace from the waves breaking against their sides. "Those bow and stern castles are already top-heavy, Master; see how they lean—they were never meant for ships of war."

The sight of the great moving, creaking world outside, the feel of the floor shifting beneath his feet made Felipe's head ache abominably.

"We will get you safe to Scotland, never fear."

Felipe abruptly returned to the table, where he sat in the gilded chair, glad to avert his eyes from the scene beyond the cabin window. He longed to be alone, to creep into the handsome canopied bed, "rescued" from a captive Venetian galley.

He gestured around the cabin. "Can I not persuade you to return here, Karim, for all this is yours?"

"Nay, Master, the cabin is for leisure and I expect none. It is an honour that you occupy it upon the voyage. Here you will be comfortable and reasonably safe."

At the mention of comfort Felipe weakened. "What of these orders the Admiral left us?"

Karim unrolled the parchment. "The flagship is to be kept under careful observation at all times; during bad weather we have a series of watchwords for the nights. At sunrise and sunset the men in the tops will count the ships, and should they discover more than the given number a gun will be fired, the nearest ships alerted to inspect the strangers. If there are more than four strange ships, then two guns—"

"Enough, enough," groaned Felipe. "Let us thank God that I command in name only, for I would be sure to get my signals in the wrong order."

Black Karim grinned. His unpretentious young master had retained the humility and gentle shyness—and the stillness that was the legacy of his parents' tragic death so long ago. Manhood had added regal bearing, good looks which those earlier days had presaged, and if Felipe would never make a sailor he would never lack courage to do what was right. He would have put his own life into those inexperienced hands now clasping the arms of the gilded chair. And yawning again—

"There will be little to do for the next hour or so, Master. Perhaps a rest—"

"Nay, order a tub for me, if you please." He stretched his arms above his head. "Perhaps I can soak out the weariness—"

Karim raised scimitarlike eyebrows. The young master had scarce arrived on board than he had demanded water to bathe. He felt certain that Don Felipe must take more baths than anyone in Spain, including His Most Catholic Majesty.

"Afterwards we will share a flagon of Burgundy. I feel it is time we relaxed a little."

Karim bowed, delighted at what the Admiral would have called this loosening of the moral fibre. "First I must inspect that all is well—"

"Then I will accompany you. To be seen at least modestly interested, if not in full command—"

Karim grinned. "You shall inspect them, Master. They will be honoured."

Felipe doubted that, and after some time of negotiating the swaying decks he parted thankfully from Karim. His head ached abominably, his stomach heaved. As he was about to close his cabin door and sink upon that inviting bed, scream upon scream rent the air outside.

A fatal accident—the English— Racing towards the sound, he found Mahmoud struggling with a dervish-like figure.

"A stowaway, Master," the man gasped.

The stowaway was a woman. As her screams continued unchecked, Felipe groaned. A woman was all he needed to earn Medina Sidonia's further displeasure.

Felipe regarded the stowaway with disgust. She was hardly recognisable as female, the dense black hair tangled, her features distorted with screams and curses. What little remained of her garments was scarcely less black than her face and skinny arms.

The men were looking at him, awaiting his command.

"Place her in the women's quarters," he said, and turning on his heel, hoped that was the end of the incident and the first order he had been called upon to give the crew.

The woman's screams continued to rend the air. "Let me go, you devils."

Again the men stared at Don Felipe Flores y Lennox de Montreuse.

Much to his relief, Karim appeared, hurrying along the deck. He rattled out some command in Arabic to Mahmoud and then bowed low to Felipe.

"Master, that you should be so affronted Do not concern yourself—a matter of no importance— We will take care—"

"I know your care, you black scum," shrieked the stowaway. "Rape!"

Felipe sighed, wishing only to rest his aching head. "Explain, Karim," he said wearily.

"Master, the men, finding her hiding, presumed her to be one of the harlots. They intended no harm to her, but were interested in a little sport." He grinned. "They wished only some proof of her abilities and that she was able and willing to please them—"

"Tell them they have my permission to proceed."

The crew needed no second bidding, and descended upon the new female with shouts and scufflings, like dogs with a juicy bone, each trying to drag her away, to be first in line to sample her charms, now inadequately covered.

"Sir—oh, please, sir, help me," she screamed, the sound followed by a yelp of pain as the nearest man had his hand bitten, and added his curses to the woman's cries.

Karim laughed. "'Twill take several to hold her down, Master; the woman has sharp claws—and sharper teeth—"

"Save me, please, sir—help, in God's name—"

Felipe turned his head away and made to enter his cabin, ready to close the door upon the crew's sport. The stowaway was not to be silenced, her screams continued to pierce the air, the continued noise reminding him that the *Black Duchess* was within hailing distance of the Admiral's flagship. What if the Duke of Medina Sidonia were taking the air on the *San Martin*'s deck and heard this female caterwauling—despite his express orders that harlots were forbidden?

"Karim, do something, for sweet Jesus' sake—"

"What shall I do, Master?"

"Anything—to keep her quiet. That noise must cease— Slit her throat if necessary." And as Karim drew out his knife, Felipe shuddered. "Nay—nay—bring her to me."

Karim sprang into the fray, scattering like ninepins the men who were set upon ravishing as a suitable afternoon's entertainment. Pushing them aside, he swept up the stowaway in his arms and advanced towards Felipe with a triumphant grin.

"Put me down—you great black bully. My father will have your head—"

"Shut up, bitch, or I'll have Karim strangle you," said Felipe, closing the cabin door. "The Admiral will have us in irons for going against his orders."

Karim had set the stowaway upon her feet, but held her tightly. She struggled to escape, panting.

"Don Felipe—the saints be good to you—for helping me—"

"I am not helping you. Why should I? You deserve all you get, stowing away on a pirate ship—"

"I did not—"

"You hardly came aboard with the provisions. What sort of treatment did you expect—what think you men are made of?"

"Pigs!"

Felipe opened the door, motioned to Karim to take her out.

"No—please, Don Felipe. You'll not stand by and see a princess of Ireland—and a virgin—raped."

For the first time she was speaking to him in English. When she was pleading instead of screaming, her voice was soft, gentle, and beguiling. He wondered why the accent was familiar—not Scots—but Irish. Karim held her firmly, and Felipe took a step nearer, daring those flashing talons.

He saw beyond grime and tangled hair, the tawdry gown in tatters, that her eyes were deep green, sooty-lashed, almond-shaped. Skin white and soft, lips curved, red and shining—an alluring face with a child's gold dust of freckles. His eyes dropped to bared shoulders, rounded breasts, small waist. He could imagine the rest, since that shapely body made him acutely aware— Sweet God, how long had it been since he had a woman?

Felipe was unlucky with women. He had been betrothed at seventeen, to a girl of fifteen, who died of a strange sweating sickness a week before the nuptials were to take place. Two years later his second betrothal was solemnised in the Church of San Lorenzo de Escorial, King Philip's private chapel of prayer and devotion, more suited to monastery than royal palace. Isabella proceeded to spend a considerable amount of their brief marriage either in prayer or regarding his supplications for a little of the conjugal love that the meanest bridegroom might expect with long-suffering sighs and fawn-like terrified eyes. His lovemaking was reduced to undignified fumblings in the dark curtained bed, which had miraculously produced a child on his chilly bride but scarcely warranted the description of anything so improper as carnal love.

Isabella had died of that stillborn child and now lay in the chapel of El Escorial, a marble effigy, hardly less mobile than he had seen her in her short and saintly life, as complete a stranger to him in death as she had been in life. He wondered if she had chosen death to escape his attentions. As well as his pride being hurt, he felt guilty. Since Almighty God clearly did not intend that he should marry for breeding purposes, he settled instead for a mistress—or rather for a series of mistresses. Here, too, fortune frowned upon him. Not for him the happy undemanding relationship. Instead he soon tired of easy conquests and listened, stifling bored yawns, to sighs and hints for a more permanent union.

Finally His Most Catholic Majesty Uncle Philip decided that a political marriage was expedient and, casting about for an eligible pawn, considered his godson would fit the role. In Corunna, despite Uncle Philip's assurances that the lady had royal connections as well as childbearing hips, Felipe trembled before a rather aged virgin with a booming voice, who looked tough as an old hen. He had rallied eagerly to the call from the *Black Duchess*. Even the meeting with the Catholic lords in Scotland could not be more doom-laden than the prospect of such a marriage.

Small wonder that he now regarded the stowaway with renewed interest. A little dalliance, a pleasant half hour—

"She may stay, Karim. My bathtub is at her disposal."

The Arab's eyes flashed with delighted realisation. "Aye, Master."

"Nay, Karim. Your services will not be required. I presume she is able to bathe herself. But lock her in and be brisk." He indicated the documents he carried. "There are certain items mentioned by His Grace—" At the older man's glum expression he smiled. "There, there, Karim—you may have her later. Tell the men—commander, captain, and officers—then the crew may have her. That is an order."

The girl opened her mouth wide and began to struggle, filling the deck with piercing screams. Thrusting a hand over her mouth and trying not to be badly bitten thereby, Karim thrust her back into Felipe's cabin.

"I will have Abdul guard the door until you return, Master."

Abdul was a giant negro, almost as tall as Karim and considerably more villainous in appearance. As he came forward and stood, back to the door, arms folded, Felipe grinned.

"That should persuade her not to attempt an escape. Now, may we proceed with the inspection?" And pleasantly anticipating his return to the cabin like a starving man with the prospect of a hearty meal, Felipe accompanied Karim to a vantage point which afforded a fair view of the Armada.

The description Most Happy or Most Fortunate Armada seemed well chosen at that moment. The first fighting line contained the Portuguese and Castilian squadrons, ten galleons in each, moving across the water like swans asleep. Alongside were four Neapolitan galleasses, half galleon, half galley, heavily gunned and capable also of reverting to and manoeuvring with oars, if necessary. In the second line another four squadrons of large and formidably armed merchantmen. These were the wings of the force; the body contained thirty-four small galleys, like the *Black Duchess*, built for speed and deadly aim. The innermost core, the great heart's blood of the Armada, twenty-three urcas, or "hulks," freighters, supply and hospital ships, valuable but vulnerable.

Karim sighed with pleasure. "Master, is this not a sight to gladden every Spanish heart and strike the fear of death and damnation into the King's enemies—and Allah's?" he added hastily, to Felipe's amusement, as he led the way below deck. In the armoury Felipe was gratified by the close-packed arms store with its powder and round shot and by a plentiful store of cannonballs.

"Each gun is capable of firing fifty rounds of these, Master. However, the chances of hitting our target are very slight—or of doing lasting damage, our vision hampered by much smoke and little fire." He shrugged. "I prefer the boarding party, the grappling hooks—and the sword."

Felipe left him, thoughtful upon the matter of the ships' stores. Food must be constantly replenished and a standard of cleanliness maintained. Already there were bad odours, and a galley like the *Black Duchess*, with its crew of two hundred and fifty, would be unspeakably foul if the battle with the English was not over and all safely home within the next two weeks. The fouler the ship, the unhealthier its crew, the weaker its fighting strength.

Absorbed not only by the well-being of the ship but also giving thought to the safer storage of those chests of gold he was to deliver into the hands of the Earl of Huntly, he was grateful that his designation of Commander was unconnected with provisioning or directing the fighting. He felt moderately safe in the hands of Black Karim, and looking across the sea of masts, the gilded painted cabins, and the full sails, he found it hard to believe that this Armada gliding peacefully through calm waters went to a destination of shot and smoke, blood and death, under an azure sky.

His contemplation was so deep he hardly noticed Abdul unlock the cabin door for him and was astonished to see inside a rope draped across from one wall to the other, festooned with an assortment of garments drying, or rather dripping, into pools upon the polished floorboards.

He was even more surprised to see a strange youth in white frilled shirt and velvet breeches sitting in his gilded chair, cushion-padded for comfort. The youth had straight black hair tied back by a ribbon—

It was the shirt he recognised first. His second-best, and expensive, too. And those were undoubtedly his breeches under the thick leather belt.

The stowaway—that damned girl—

Before he could remonstrate, while he was still gathering breath, she smiled.

"I am grateful to you, Sir Captain—for the bath. Most Christian of ye. And me wondering when I would ever have the welcome sight of water again. My gratitude also—for rescuing me—"

"Rescuing you be damned," he exploded. "Harlots know the score when they take on a ship's company. Do not expect favours—"

But now that the grime was removed, he was pleasantly surprised by the girl's appearance. Pretty, she also had a look of breeding about her. Before God, a high-born harlot—now that would be something of a novelty. Perhaps he would be fortunate enough not to catch the pox, one excellent reason which normally killed any lust, any temptation.

Again his blood kindled, and even as she began to protest her innocence, he strode over and put a hand on her mouth. "Nay, señorita, that was not my reason for rescuing you. Come—we will have off that shirt," he added not ungently. "I have never undressed a youth before—"

The green eyes widened. "Do not—dare—touch me—"

As she shrank from him, Felipe's hand fell to his side, obedient to memories—and the behaviour required—of his past. He groaned inwardly, another Isabella. Sweet Jesu—he had suffered more than enough of unwilling virtuous women, and now even a harlot spurned him.

"If you know some tricks by which I will not tire of you," he began gallantly, "then perhaps you may stay here—"

"Tricks—"

"Come now, we delay the bedding," he said impatiently, and the girl's lips moved, but no sound came.

"Bedding," she hissed at him. "Bedding." The green eyes had changed into narrow slits. "And me thinking you were a hidalgo—you only half a Spaniard—"

"I am wholly a man, I assure you."

"But no gentleman, that I assure *you*."

Felipe fought back anger since every passing moment made the prospect of the girl more desirable. Her voice, even rasping in anger, enchanted him. The siren song of the Celt. It twitched at long-ago memories of Scotland, of glens and heather and great shining lochs. Of Holyrood, of the Queen of Scots—of Amyas Lennox and laughing careless boyhood—

To think that one day he should meet an Irish harlot and feel sentimental about the blood his Lennox mother had bequeathed him. He smiled. This one need have no fears for her future; she would be extremely popular with the crew, who must weary of dark-eyed Spanish, Moorish, and gypsy women. Perhaps if she stayed with him, he might negotiate some suitable marriage for her—when he tired— for she was young and pretty still. *When* he tired of her—

"Let us proceed." And he laid aside his leather doublet carefully and unfastened the points of his shirt, while the girl's startled gaze followed his actions. "Come along, señorita. I am not sure that I approve of you wearing my second-best shirt," he added indulgently. "However, we will remove it—carefully. I do not want creases or tears—"

Even as he stretched out his hand, she retreated until the tall chair was between them. "You will get more than creases and tears if ye take another step, Sir Captain—"

"Be not so coy, señorita." He seized her arm. "Come along now, you will find the bed to your taste—there are no fleas," he added proudly, ignoring her resistance.

"Let me go—help—"

Felipe shook her, held her struggling against him. "Be silent or you will go back where you belong—to the stews in the women's quarters—"

Her screams faded and she stared at him, lips quivering. Again he groaned, for those great green fawnlike eyes were an unhappy reminder of his chilly departed bride.

"You should feel flattered, señorita," he said stiffly. "Public harlots are rarely selected by those in command." And he found himself reeling back, cheek smarting, from her stinging blow.

"Public harlot—flattered— I am no harlot. Rape me and I will have your name blackened in every court in Europe. And I will tell them all that Don Felipe Flores y Lennox de Montreuse—to give ye your full fancy name—is a spy. And not a very good spy at that."

Felipe's hands dropped, as did his jaw. Sweet Jesu, did the entire world know of his assignation in Scotland? He swore with fervour and such eloquence that even the girl paled. "And who in hell's name are you?"

She drew herself up proudly. "Maeve O'Neill. Me father was cousin to the Earl of Tyrone," she added carelessly.

So the story about being an Irish princess, although a slight exaggeration since Tyrone merely considered himself King of Ireland, was based on truth.

"Was your father Connor O'Neill?"

"He was."

"I am sorry. I heard of his unfortunate—"

"Save your commiserations. A madman, a lecher throwing away his life— God spit upon his memory."

Felipe was shocked at her vehemence. "Surely—"

"Ach, save your breath, for he never was father to me. A piece of valuable merchandise to be sold to the highest bidder, that's all I ever was."

"A common situation— Do not mistake the advantages of a good marriage, señorita. The only solution for a motherless daughter—"

"Is that so?" She surveyed him, hands upon hips. "You seem to know a lot about it. Are you a married man yourself?"

"I am a widower."

"Children?"

"None."

The girl seemed mollified. "You should have known me father."

"I met him several times."

"Did ye now? Then you doubtless were acquainted with his purpose of selling me to a bald old lecher while he chased a hot bitch of twenty-one—"

Connor O'Neill. Felipe remembered the scandal of the Irish mercenary and his affair with a remote cousin of King Philip, a "respectable" Spanish matron. At least so she claimed to be when they were surprised in bed together by her husband. She had been taken against her will— The King's straight-laced religiosity was affronted, his erring cousin threatened with exile although adultery was a normal pastime in the court.

O'Neill had died in the duel of honour with the lady's husband; honour had been satisfied. Between the floridly handsome man he had met, under forty but rapidly going to seed on the effects of drink and loose living, and his daughter, who could not be past eighteen, there was little resemblance, except in the Celtic colouring. She looked little more than a child, despite her forceful tongue.

She stabbed a finger at him. "As for yourself, Sir Captain, it is common knowledge that you are a spy."

He laughed, but the sound was hollow.

"The court say they would not trust King Philip's godson even if he does have good Spanish blood—and respectable, too—from his father, Don Flores, when the other half from his Scottish mother is heretic." She nodded as if approving of the court's discernment. "They expect Spain to be betrayed by anyone who is cousin to that vile race of England. They say His Majesty must be mad, besotted—"

Any pity for the girl before him was swamped by the information that everyone at El Escorial—including the English spies who masqueraded as refugees from the Huguenots—were discussing his secret mission. All desire for her left him in the sickening realisation that someone had blundered.

She laughed scornfully. "Everyone knows you meet the Scottish Catholic earls—and that the *Black Duchess* carries gold to finance the expedition."

Felipe cast a melancholy glance towards the locked chest. His spying activities might as well be signalled round the entire Armada. The Admiral had wasted his time with his suggestions and precautions.

"It is also known that an army awaits to march south into England, to be paid for with your Spanish gold. They say the English Queen is to be slain and King Philip proclaimed—"

"Enough, enough." The girl was repeating this story parrotwise, as if it was some oft heard tale. Guessing that his mission was freely discussed in every council chamber and boudoir the length and breadth of Spain—and God only knew where else—shattered the last shreds of his confidence. He wondered how many English spies had already alerted the English court that Don Felipe was on his way.

The girl's smile was triumphant. "And I might as well tell ye, Sir Captain, that I also left a message regarding our destination in Scotland, to be forwarded to the Earl of Tyrone, me father's cousin—should anything *unfortunate*"—she stressed the word heavily—"befall me."

"And may I ask why you decided to honour the *Black Duchess* with your charming company?"

"Sure, and I have told ye—that pig of an old man, Don Diego de Martinez—the wedding was all fixed for Sunday."

Felipe stifled a desire to laugh out loud, wondering if Maeve O'Neill would be sympathetic if he told her of his own disastrous betrothal arrangements and the skinny old virgin he had escaped in Corunna.

"When I saw this ship it was like a gift from God, for I remembered that the *Black Duchess* was taking Don Felipe to Scotland. So I decided to stow away, seize the chance of getting to my own folk in Ireland."

"Scotland is a long way from Ireland."

She shook her head. "Aye, but not so far as Spain. Once I set foot on Scottish soil, there are Highland friends of the O'Neills. From the east coast I can head west, to the MacDonalds of Skye—"

"You make it sound easy as a bird in flight. Did you not stop to realise the dangers of travelling in a ship going into battle?"

She shrugged. "Battle? A skirmish against a handful of English ships and a few fighting men hardly worth the name. That is what I have heard—the Spanish noblemen complaining about unworthy opponents, a disgrace to their honour—"

"There is always El Draque," he reminded her softly.

"What is one man against the whole might of Spain?"

"He did exceeding well against the Armada in Cádiz."

"Just because the Spaniards were unprepared."

Felipe realised she talked about Spain as a foreigner, and said, "When did you leave Ireland?"

"When me mother died, me father put me into a convent until I was old enough to be of use to him."

"You are not too late to seek refuge from a disagreeable marriage in a convent."

"I have no vocation for good works, nor the mind to be a nun."

"So I realise—or the company of ship's harlots would never have appealed to you."

"Ship's harlots, even death itself, Sir Captain, would be better than warming the bed of Don Diego. I made my plans well, slipping aboard with the women—knowing nothing could be done once the ship sailed—"

"Except save you from the crew's attentions," Felipe reminded her sharply. "I fear you relied too strongly on my chivalry, señorita."

"Nay, Sir Captain. I relied upon my own bargaining power. Something me father taught me."

"What is that?"

"We all of us have something to sell and someone to buy."

"In your case, señorita, it might be regarded as something to take —by force if necessary." His appraising glance was meaningful, as he added softly, "And if you refuse, there are despatch ships keeping in touch with the mainland—"

"If you try to send me back there, I will never reach the shore alive—that I promise you."

"You are but a child; you have hardly begun to live."

"Long enough, long enough." She shook her head sadly. "I suspect that I shall never make old bones, that God did not equip me for long life. Rather the quick death from round shot, the snuffing of a candle, Sir Captain, than the slow death of capering to the tune played by Don Diego."

"He offers you marriage, señorita. Many women settle for such arrangements and patiently await other means of gratifying their desires. In Spain purity is essential before marriage, but society does not wince when married women cuckold their husbands."

"That is not for me. When I give myself to a man, in marriage or out of it, it is not for politics or gain, but for love alone—and for the rest of my life. No buying, no selling, no betraying." She looked at the stern still face above her and shrugged in embarrassment. "But I would not expect you to understand—or any man. I shall put my faith in God's good grace to give this Armada a speedy victory. I have heard—"

"You have heard too much," he said shortly. One thing was clear. He could not afford to let this human gunpowder keg further jeopardise his mission, and he cursed the day O'Neill had ever been drawn in the plot to woo his Irish relatives, and in particular the Earl of Tyrone, to provide sanctuary should the Scottish landing miscarry and an early escape, with treasure intact, be necessary, around the Scottish coast. Connor O'Neill, he groaned, whose drunken confidences had reached every salon in Spain—and beyond.

He looked upon the mercenary's daughter with sudden loathing. Had she been a man, he might have asked Karim to get rid of her, as he would an unwanted litter of kittens or pups, closing the door and his imagination on whatever methods Karim used. But he could not take this innocent but infuriating creature's death on his hands. The alternative looming swiftly into his mind was bleak and unpalatable. He would have to keep her safe by him, a hostage, on the off chance that if all went wrong in Scotland, the Earl of Tyrone's niece might be valuable currency indeed among treacherous Irish bogs and treacherous Irish lords.

Thankful that knowledge had killed all desire for her, he bowed, cold but polite. "You are welcome to share this cabin—it is large enough for two."

"Nay, Sir Captain," she replied, eyeing him doubtfully. "I am much obliged, but I would prefer the safe company of the harlots."

"Safe?"

"Aye, safe. I know where I am with women," she added primly.

Felipe laughed. "Sweet Jesu, if you consider that your virtue is in any danger from me, then you do yourself too much honour. I would never force my attentions upon a respectable maid—"

"Is that so?" Her eyes mocked him. "My impression was, Sir Captain, that she might not have time to explain that respectability until it was too late. If you remember—"

"Yes, yes," he said hastily. "A regrettable error, but if you will associate with such women—er, they have their own devices to put a man on his mettle."

"So I have observed," she said drily.

"As a matter of fact, señorita, I have never cared for women who ape men, in their clothes and bearing, wearing breeches, with their hair tied back like any common sailor."

As he spoke she carelessly untied the ribbon and, shaking her head obediently, regarded him through a dense black cloud of shining hair. Taken aback by her sudden unexpected beauty, he looked away, said stiffly:

"Rest assured, señorita, no harm will come to you—from me."

She curtseyed, very much a woman despite the male attire. Then seeing the fleeting lust in his eyes, she eyed him warily, a gazelle cornered in deep forest.

"You will not have to fight off my advances—or any man's—while you are under my protection on this ship."

In the short silence each assessed the other, suspicious as fighting dogs.

"Very well, perhaps I might make myself useful—keep the place tidy—"

"Jesu forbid, a woman being useful at sea—and in my cabin— that is more than my already overburdened soul can countenance. Your servant, Señorita O'Neill."

And he bowed himself thankfully out of her presence. On deck he found Karim, who regarded his approach with the amusement and sly interest of age and experience for a younger man who has just enjoyed an attractive girl.

Felipe decided not to tell the Arab captain that he had shirked his pleasure with the stowaway. He acknowledged Karim's knowing look with a chill bow which defied further intimacies or questions.

"Well, Master," said Karim, "we are now well under way."

Leaning on the taffrail, Felipe decided that he felt better in the open air watching the pilot steer into the breeze that had awakened the sleeping *Duchess*. With timbers groaning like a woman in love's ecstasy, her sails a lover's sighs, she moved, leaping swiftly across the sea, small but exquisite by the side of the vast swaying Armada, floating upon the waters, a dream city threatened by the sea gods' wrath.

Aye, he felt much better. And as he narrowed his eyes against the glare of shimmering waters, each breath he took was heady, as sparkling wine—each wave held a million stars.

"Pray that the wind holds, Master, that the enemy watchdogs sleep and bark not."

"We will be safe in Scottish waters before the week is out."

Karim frowned. "Master, I would urge you against overconfidence in this matter. The English might be small in numbers, but they will make up that deficiency by the fierceness of their spirit."

"I cannot believe they are better fighters than our Spanish soldiers, Karim. After all, they serve a weak, vain queen."

"Whom they worship—aye, like the Virgin Mother you Christians claim—"

"Come, you exaggerate. She cannot compare to His Majesty as a ruler."

Karim was silent. "Believe what you wish to believe, Master. After all, your bonds are deep— But remember that you are also a mongrel." He thumped his chest. "As Karim el Raschid here—in the heart—"

"His Majesty has treated me like a son. Spain is my home," said Felipe sternly.

"Is it truly, Master?" Karim grinned. He bowed and, aware that a change of subject was advisable, asked:

"What think you of my *Duchess*, Master? Is she not a superb creature?"

"She is indeed." In the short time Felipe had been with the ship, he realised she had some mystic existence of her own. A sea-Eve, mother, mistress, wife, and child. What was the secret of her power over the brutal men who made up her crew? What strange fascination made these savage creatures eager to serve on her, with Karim as their master? Felipe could see scant reward for any of them, allied with the strong possibility that should the Armada fail, their own lives might be forfeit.

As for Karim, no woman would ever touch or rival his devotion to *La Duquesa Negra*, thought Felipe. The Arab captain regarded women as fit only for an hour's dalliance, the sweet or bitter necessity of appetite indulged, forgettable as last week's wine.

In youth Felipe had been awed when about to take a wife; he had learned that Karim had not one wife but many. "Too many to count, Master Felipe—in forgotten ports and lost islands the world over, in places I could never find again had I the notion to do so. Black, white, brown, red, yellow—" He laughed. "All colours, and as many shapes and sizes." He sighed. "A woman's vow, Master Felipe, is fit only for writing upon the water."

Felipe remembered that other time when Karim now asked, "What woman could compare with my *Duchess*? A goddess, is she not? Carrying live men in her womb, their lives at her whim or command."

"A fickle goddess, Karim," said Felipe, remembering the lives lost, like those of his parents in a sudden storm.

"True, Master, but is that not the case with all women we men want most? Man has always loved the woman who treated him worst. Is that not so?"

Whether it was or not, Felipe could not tell him. Although he was past thirty, he had truly loved only two people, and for both of them he would have gladly died.

His first love had been Mary Queen of Scots. The only other person he had loved was his cousin Amyas Lennox. He had never met man nor woman with whom he could establish such depths of mind and being as Amyas. Expecting the intimacy between man and woman to replace the friendship, boundless and complete, between children, he had been bitterly disappointed. Through the years he had waited hopefully for the woman who would be his soul mate and companion, satisfying needs of body and soul. Despairing, he wondered if the young women of Spain were incapable, because of their background and social position, of anything but breeding. Betrothed and married, a lover many times, still the barrier remained.

Dissatisfied, lonely, he found himself retreating into a place in his mind, where he had mentally kept Amyas alive through the passing years, where he talked to him as he had done in boyhood, sharing intimate thoughts, frivolous and profound, dreams and desires. Knowing that the face he beheld in the mirror was also his cousin's face, he talked to that mirror image, consulting him through the years, sharing with him that first beard and moustache, since Amyas might have such hair—or lack of it—upon his face. As his voice broke and his body changed, so, far away, did Amyas share the same pride in growing manhood, the same fears and uncertainties.

In Amyas he had more than cousin, more than brother. Amyas was his other self, and some days he felt that by closing his eyes he should drift into that other life across the sea at Lennoxhoe. He visited Amyas often in dreams in the house he had never seen but knew from description. Amyas was always overjoyed to see him; they would rush towards each other with excited talk and laughter. He would awaken miserable, reluctant to shake off the dream of Lennoxhoe for the reality of El Escorial and another interminable day with the royal children, with whom no intimacy of any kind was possible. Believing themselves to be divine, they were stiff, formal, and careful in their associations, hedged in by piety and solemn from the day they were born. Only the very young romped, but they too soon acquired dignity, rigid as the formal court clothes which they were forced to wear, even at play.

For all his royal godfather's affection, protocol made Felipe accept his position in the court as somewhere between poor relation and trusted servant.

At some point in the corridors of his mind, and his dreams, that love for Mary of Scotland and Amyas met. The late Queen still walked, a radiant bride on Darnley's arm, in a sunlit memory. If by laying down his life ten times over he could have restored her life, given her back her throne, then he would have considered such sacrifices small indeed.

He knew of the many plots emanating from El Escorial and begged to be allowed to take part in the many rescues planned. But King Philip shook his head, insisting that he could not allow any person so near to himself to be implicated in such dangerous political machinations. When Felipe heard of the death by torture, the confessions wrung at such cost from those golden young men who gave their lives for Mary of Scotland, he closed his mind against the horror. But had he been Amyas Lennox, would he have declared his allegiance to the English Queen? Idly he wondered what fortunes had befallen his cousin. Was he still a dreamer of dreams, a searcher lonely and loveless?

3

Amyas Lennox was neither lonely nor loveless. He had looked into his mirror with scarce a thought in years now of his Spanish cousin, whose face he wore.

At first glance they were still identical, but Amyas wore the fashionable narrow beard and moustache. His countenance was slightly more rugged and weather-beaten than Felipe's, as befitted a prosperous sea captain and merchant who spent more time facing into the elements than into fashionable Plymouth society. He was heavier in the shoulders and more given to ready laughter than his solemn Spanish cousin. His obvious good humour and well-being were tributes to the happy marriage which had absorbed seventeen of his thirty-three years. With a wife who worshipped him, his adoration untarnished by the passing years, their union was also blessed with two charming children, Barbara and Francis.

The years had dealt kindly with Amyas and his fortunate marriage to Sir Francis Drake's niece Jane. He had Lennoxhoe and its estates, while in the harbour of Plymouth Sound the *Warlock* was at anchor. Armed for battle, but with sails folded, decks empty, she rocked gently in the swell which presaged the storm already gathering upon the horizon, a storm which had mightily abused the heavy Armada galleons and sent them capering across the waters, trying to avoid collision with one another.

As Amyas Lennox paced the quayside, he was joined by his commander, Sir Francis Drake, and the other captains and officers of the *Revenge*'s squadron. All were anxiously scanning the horizon in the now hourly occupation of those who sailed the Queen's ships. Despite constant assurance from pulpits throughout the land that God was on the side of Elizabeth of England and would give answer to their prayers in resounding victory, the men chafed at this non-action.

Who but the Devil ruled such capricious weather, sending King Philip's Armada scurrying for shelter without a shot being fired? That same accursed wind which forced the Queen's ships back to port, but for a few fast ships left on patrol. Seriously short of victuals, since they never carried more than a three-day supply, there was little point in wasting good battle time in the Scillies and Ushant, awaiting an enemy who refused to appear.

However, no sooner had they dropped anchor in Plymouth than a despatch ship caught up with them, breathlessly imparting the information that the Armada was once more under sail. Rumour was apparently also at the mercy of bad weather, for no Armada sails were sighted, and despairing of a fight, they had been pondering the next move when a Cornish merchantman, thankful to be safe home out of troubled waters, rushed up the quayside steps, crying that great ships like castles had given him chase—

Cutting short the preamble, Sir Francis demanded their position, already unrolling the chart he carried.

"They were drifting back towards the French coast, out of the lee of the wind—just there, Your Lordship."

Sir Francis beamed. "You have done well to reach us in such timely fashion." And to his captains: "Our quarry is taking shelter, it seems, near Bayonne—here." He indicated the chart. "And, gentlemen, we may as well settle ourselves in like manner," he added, indicating the horizon, where great thunderheads already gathered, the sails of a phantom navy. "There will be no sailing for any of us before morning tide, if and when this storm has blown itself out."

Dismissing them with a warning to lodge within call of the signal gun from the *Revenge*, he put an arm about Amyas's shoulders. "If you have a stoop of ale in your kitchen, nephew, I will gladly accompany you—and my officers too."

Amyas's expression was black as the gathering clouds since he longed for this inactivity to be at an end, to be back with his beloved family. Most of all, he longed to have his beloved ship trading again —in her normal peacetime occupation. He bowed. "It will be an honour, sir."

Sir Francis chuckled. "Perhaps so, perhaps not. My dear niece might take it amiss having hungry men thrust upon her household for food and beds at short notice."

"Sir, you are always welcome at Lennoxhoe. We see little of you at the best of times—and there are beds aplenty—and victuals too."

The little troop mounted and rode quickly ahead of the storm, across bosomy downs, whose bright emerald, overburdened by the glowering sky, was fast diminishing to the olive of a much-faded tapestry. At last Amyas saw the distant chimneys of Lennoxhoe, a modest manor house built in the E shape to flatter his Queen. Rose-red brick, dwarfed by the strange light, it seemed to huddle against the approaching storm.

It reminded Amyas that he had other troubles besides bad weather and an elusive Armada. "I wish to Almighty God that we could come to grips with the Spaniard."

"There is no opposing God's wind, lad," said Drake, smiling. "It teaches a man humility to sit and wait—aye, and patience too. One learns to use the waiting time to make plans and perfect strategies. You are unused to war, nephew."

Amyas said nothing. He found himself tongue-tied in the presence of Jane's uncle. Hard to realise that this very ordinary Devon seaman with his pronounced dialect, his almost unprepossessing appearance, was the terror of the seas. Many believed he had sold his soul to the Devil in exchange for a magic mirror which gave him powers to watch over his enemies. El Draque—the Dragon, or the Devil—the Spaniards called him. Amyas had never seen Drake in action, but guessed that the homely face hid a soul capable of great courage, the thickset yeoman's body concealed swift action and a mind rapier-sharp, which belied his slow and often halting speech. Heroes should look the part, but rarely did so.

"You are young yet, lad. Time will change all that."

Amyas did not contradict him. He was past thirty, yet on some days he felt old as a Biblical Methuselah. Especially when he was on land. Land seemed to slow down his actions, his thoughts. Land people confused him; they were sly and devious, lacking the simplicity of the men who sailed the *Warlock* with him. He seemed to be a man divided, for when he was at sea he belonged to a different world. He felt that God had given him two distinct lives to live. One as captain of the *Warlock* and one as master of Lennoxhoe, husband, father.

It was in the latter role that he had more worries than most. The south coast of England lived under the shadow of a rumoured Spanish invasion, and many feared more the Duke of Parma and his army waiting at Dunkirk than the Great Armada itself. All men, except the very old and very young, were under strict orders to bear arms should the invasion become reality. Although the wealthy landowners had retreated from homes close to the sea, leaving them stripped of treasures, abandoned, Amyas did not despise their actions. He would have done likewise since Lennoxhoe lay close to Plymouth, a danger area, and he had a young family at risk.

Jane refused to leave. Not from ill-advised courage or stubborn pride, but because their unborn child would be in peril should she travel at this time. Frail pretty Jane, whom he loved more than life itself, determined to safeguard this last pregnancy—her fifth—since the last two were stillbirths. Already the familiar ominous signs were present, plus the pains and constant nausea. Both guessed that all was far from well, and Jane had reason for concern. She had almost died when Francis was born, nearly fourteen years since. She had been advised against further children, and at the time both had resolved that there should be no more.

They had wed at sixteen, and after seventeen years of marriage were still deeply in love. Abstinence was cruel upon them, separated for long periods while Amyas was at sea. Had Jane been unwilling, he would unselfishly have refrained from any lovemaking between them. But lying in his arms, Jane would whisper that there were ways and means of not begetting children, there were herbs and simples; a wise woman in the village—

"This time, dear love, there will be no babe."

But returning from that next voyage, he would find her pregnant again. She did not blame or reproach him, not even for his own crude and unsuccessful methods, whispered by more worldly wise seamen, for not begetting children. There was nothing anyone could do if it was God's will that a child should be made.

"God's will." He realised he had not heard a word of Drake's optimistic conversation on the subject of England's superior fleet and fighting men.

Sir Francis asked for the health of his niece.

Amyas said she was far from well, adding, "This accursed Armada could not have come at a worse time—" He stopped. Could Drake understand a man like himself, who put wife and family first, before the sacred person of Her Majesty Queen Elizabeth? Amyas avoided his own dread, that he would die in action, leaving Jane a widow and his children orphans, undefended in the face of a Spanish victory and subsequent invasion. Nightmares presented pictures of the cruel fate which surely awaited his wife and their unborn babe, let alone his son Francis and fifteen-year-old Barbara.

Rumour already ran rife. The Spaniards would hoist all babes upon their swords, then roast and eat them, especially since they had been deprived of fresh meat for so long. The women too old or ugly to become public harlots for the soldiers' use would be slain, while sturdy lads would go as slaves in the galleys. As for maids like Barbara— The fate of his lovely daughter, already rushing across the lawns to welcome them, terrified him most.

Seeing the distinguished company, she curtseyed first before running forward to kiss her father, then her great-uncle. Drake swung her up into his arms.

"Maid, you get bonnier by the day. How in this drab world do you grow so beautiful?" And chucking her chin, he laughed, "How many men's hearts have you broken since last we met, eh?"

Barbara blushed and dimpled as Drake held her at arm's length. "I think we shall have to ask for you at court, seeing that Her Majesty enjoys the company of pretty blossoms around her."

"Oh, Uncle Francis, would you do that for me—would you really?" squealed Barbara, clinging to his arm. "Oh, Uncle Francis—"

"Aye, maid, I will see to it."

Almost as tall as he, she kissed his cheek and, aware of the officers' amused glances, drew herself up proudly and announced, "As my lady mother is indisposed this evening, I have arranged that preparations be made to refresh you, gentlemen. Please be kind enough to follow Jem into the house."

Jem, the old steward, gave her a delighted grin and bowed the men in the front door. Amyas made to follow, his arm about her waist.

"Nay, Father, not yet," she whispered, her voice urgent. "I need herbs—"

"Your mother—" he began anxiously.

"She is well. She sleeps. Do not worry, Father. I take good care of her."

"And of the house?"

She curtseyed. "Aye, sir, I am mistress in her absence."

"You are indeed," said Amyas approvingly, tucking her hand

warmly into his arm. "My congratulations upon your prompt dealings with our unexpected guests—"

"Father, will you give your permission that I go to court, as Uncle Francis suggests?" Seeing his rueful expression, she added hastily, "After all, I am a woman now."

"That is true." And Amyas thought, Would that it were not so. I liked my Barbara as a child, perhaps so do all men with daughters. Perhaps we as fathers are a little jealous that soon, all too soon, other men will darken their horizons and we will cease to be the one beloved in their lives, suffering many rivals, our overthrow inevitable as life—and death—itself. There was no point in pretence, his Barbara was blossoming into a woman, and a beautiful one, the gold of her hair touched with a redder shade than his own, the same deep blue eyes that were her mother's. He realised with a pang of fear that although he thought of her as child still, she was but a year less than Jane had been when they married.

"Perhaps I might meet the Queen. It is rumoured that she comes to Plymouth to review her fleet. As she reviews her soldiers at Greenwich. Is that true?"

Amyas shook his head. "Alas, dear one, it is but rumour to put heart into the men who fight."

"I thought all men had heart to fight for their Queen and country. Had I been a boy, none should have kept me at home," she added scornfully. "And there is Francis in Oxford, praying that the Spanish wars will last another two years so that he will be old enough to go to sea with you. It is so unfair." And stamping her foot, "To be a maid is a dreadful infliction."

"I am glad. I am glad that you are a maid," said Amyas, and caught her in his arms. The frown left her face and the dimples returned as she kissed him fondly.

"Why will the Queen not come to Plymouth?"

"Because we leave as soon as this storm which approaches blows itself out. With God's good grace we will leave on the morning tide. Now, what about those herbs?" he added, longing to go inside and see Jane.

In the walled garden Barbara gathered basil, rosemary, thyme and returned with them in a tiny sweet-smelling bouquet. "About the Queen," she insisted. "Bessie told me she heard she was coming for sure—"

Amyas took her hand. "Bessie is an old gossip." Bessie, who had been wet nurse to both children and stayed on at Lennoxhoe, watching over them through the passing years, to serve his household with love and devotion, was quite capable of promising Barbara the moon on a silver salver, should that please her young mistress.

"Will you let Uncle Francis take me to Greenwich?"

"Nay."

"But I want to see the Queen. You heard him say I could, that she would like me."

"I like you more—and I need you here. So does your mother."

She seized his arm, skipping a few steps as she had done in childhood, smiling up into his face. "Then dear, dearest Father, please will you take me—someday? The Queen likes you—you told me she did. Oh, please—please— I so want to see her. And I want a place at court," she added, thrusting her small chin into the air.

"You are too young." He knew it was a lie, an excuse.

"But in a year or so? She will not forget me if I make a favourable impression. She never forgets a face—or so I am told."

Amyas smiled wryly. He knew from personal experience that a man's face, his name, and the fashion in which he was made, if comely, would remain long in the Queen's mind. But women, especially pretty maids, were creatures she had no wish to remember. They recalled all too frequently and painfully that she was neither young nor beautiful, and that even the Queen of England had no command over passing time. She could not put back the clocks, although she might remove every offending mirror in the Palace.

"Why will you not let me go?"

"My dearest," he said, hugging her to him, "be happy whilst you may. You do not want to leave us for that nest of intrigue at Whitehall—" Her sigh said she did. He ignored it and continued, "The rich and the famous are seldom happy—" Her smile and raised eyebrows betokened amused disbelief. "Often, my love, if you followed them to their great houses, you would find a very different story once their doors closed."

But he knew he could not convince her and that by depriving her of a chance at the Queen's court he also deprived her of the possibility of some excellent marriage, perhaps to a duke or an earl. After all, the English Lennoxes were simple folk, and Sir Francis had been knighted by a grateful Queen not for his noble blood but for the treasures with which her palaces were filled, thanks to his wily piracy —or so men whispered in envy.

If Amyas had a wish for his daughter, it was that in marriage she remain in the ranks of yeomen and merchants, and simple, honest seafaring folk, among whom she had been reared. There true happiness lay. He had no desire to see his beloved Barbara a victim of the corruption and dangerous intrigues of court life, the broken hearts and broken lives, the adulterous brief unions—and the heads that went to the block. He thought of her gentle, compassionate heart, how she could cry for days at the death of a pet dog, mourn for a fallen sparrow. Such tenderness was not for his sharp-tongued, bitter sovereign.

As if she read his thoughts, Barbara said, "I once saw a painting of the Queen, and she looked like a princess from a fable, riding on her great white horse, like the tapestry in the Long Gallery, she was. You have oft told me she is gentle and kind," she added reproachfully.

"Very well. Promise you will take good care of your mother and the new babe—"

Eagerly, eyes shining, she seized his hand, pretending not to notice his solemn face.

"And when this Spanish war is over, I shall take you to Whitehall. Only a visit, now—"

The laughter died from her eyes. "And what will happen," she whispered, eyes closed, as if afraid to breathe life into the thought, "if we do not win?"

He looked into her face, uncannily like his own, and wondered uneasily if it was a mirror whereby she read his mind. Trying to veil his misgivings, to sound hearty and confident, he said, "I daresay that your father and the *Warlock* will go on as before. I am no traitor, I am fighting for my true country, like any humble honest sailor. But if we should lose, then perhaps the King of Spain will be just as eager for an honest merchantman—"

"Oh, Father—you could not— You would never do that!"

"And what would I never do?"

"Trade for King Philip—*wicked* King Philip," she added in a horrified whisper.

Flushed and angry, she had entirely forgotten that there was bad blood in her father, he thought sadly, Spanish blood in the loyal English captain fighting for his Queen. She had forgotten her Spanish grandmother, that strange marriage of twins to twins.

He wondered if Cousin Felipe still lived, since of those four happy parents only his father, Thomas Lennox, remained, and he had returned to Scotland and the court of King James the Sixth. Sometimes, but not often, he recalled that childhood visit to Holyrood Palace. But as a loyal Englishman, true to his Queen, he preferred not to dwell upon his boyish devotion to Mary Queen of Scots, who had been every bit as bad—so he was told—as John Knox ever prophesied. Within a year of that marriage in Edinburgh she had connived at Darnley's death and had proceeded to marry Bothwell, his murderer. There were letters between the guilty pair produced during the Queen of Scots' trial which proved her adultery and complicity beyond a shadow of doubt.

Amyas was not surprised by those revelations in the Casket Letters, since he carried in his mind down the years a picture of Queen Mary and Bothwell, heads conspiratorially close, disappearing down a Holyrood corridor. It took little time to fit the incident into the story of this vile Scottish Queen and her plots to murder his good Queen Elizabeth, to steal the English throne and relight the fires at Smithfield for more Protestant martyrs.

Yet, had his mother lived, Felipe would have come from Spain and they would have been reared as brothers, the twins they resembled. Amyas recalled bitter disappointment when the plan failed, baulked by King Philip. However, he soon rallied since he met Jane in the following year. Three years later, at fourteen, they were betrothed, married at sixteen. Since that day, Jane had filled his life and he needed no other, for she was sister, mistress, comrade, mother, wife. Jane and the children she had given him—and the *Warlock*—encompassed his entire world. He rarely looked beyond its narrow confines, except to wonder anxiously what the pattern of his present life would have been had Jane not also been Sir Francis Drake's niece. In these troubled times, with Spanish and Scots blood flowing in his veins, since neither was popular in England, he doubted whether Her Majesty would have considered him a fit person to command, in her name, one of the precious few fighting ships at her disposal.

Aye, the Queen of England had a prodigious memory for what a man most wished to forget.

Elizabeth of England had growled at him, "One of my captains—with a Spanish mother and a Scottish father, indeed. Are many aware of your disastrous begetting, Master Lennox?"

"Not many, Your Majesty."

"Then keep it that way." The bird-boned hand she had placed

upon his arm was still beautiful, even if she was gap-toothed, growing ugly, and old beneath the paint which grew thicker by the year but still failed to hide wrinkles, sagging contours. Yet her smile was still charming, alluring, despite the few blackened stumps of teeth which she fought to conceal. The mob's prospect of Her Majesty might be gallant and young, but she needed distance these days to add enchantment, Amyas thought. Nearness brought the smell of age, of musty garments, stale perfume, and unwashed hair. Did anyone ever see her naked, even a lover, though there could have been few such in recent times?

He recalled with guilty enjoyment that there had been a time when, with little encouragement, he could have followed the long line of young men the Queen found desirable. Amyas Lennox had lost not his virtue but his nerve, knowing that Jane would not be as other women, pleased and flattered for husbands to be the current royal stud, in fervent hope of their own ultimate gain. It was well known that the Queen soon tired of all but Robert Dudley. Lecherous as her father, Henry the Eighth, from whom she had inherited most of the Tudor lusts, her restless eyes soon sought, found, another. The erring husband was despatched, sheepishly, back to his manor, pensioned off with a dukedom, to his patient—and ofttimes greedy—dame's considerable satisfaction.

Alone in the royal bedchamber, Amyas had purposely misread the signals that the Queen of England had flown. When her attempts at seduction by innuendo and coquetry failed, she studied him, frowning. Tapping his arm with her diamond and feather fan, sensing that he feared her royal displeasure, she had grinned up into his face like a street urchin.

"I doubt I have found the ultimate rarity, Amyas Lennox."

"Rarity, Your Grace?" He inclined his head, pretending puzzlement.

"Aye, Master Lennox. A man who cares more for his pretty dame than any honour his Queen is ready to bestow upon him."

"Madam, I fail to take your meaning."

"Do not lie, Master Lennox," she had said sharply. "If you do, I shall presume that you do not find me attractive." And cutting short his protests, "Enough, enough—I respect integrity, too—never forget that."

A week later the carter struggled across the Downs to Lennoxhoe, bearing with him a great postered bed. A gift from Her Majesty.

"For my use when I come to Master Lennox's house," the message read. And she could not resist the final barb: "Once it belonged to thy Scottish Queen, who no longer has use for it."

Amyas had never liked the bed, nor had Jane. For them both it stirred unhappy associations, and was banished to the guest chamber.

Amyas realised he had not heard a word his daughter was saying, so engrossed was he by his own thoughts. Somewhere nearby, a blackbird's song pierced the heavy air in an ecstatic requiem to the dying day, and the first raindrops, huge as coins, spattered the terrace at Lennoxhoe.

Together they rushed for the house, and leaving Barbara in the kitchen, Amyas ran swiftly upstairs to greet his wife, pausing to admire the paintings by Marcus Gheeraerts and Cornelius Jansons and the new miniatures of Barbara and Francis by Nicholas Hilliard, completed during his last absence at sea. Thanks to his successful trading with the Netherlands during the past years, he had added many treasures to Lennoxhoe, but none gave him more satisfaction than the fine Hoefnagel which covered the entire wall of the parlour. Appropriately, it was called, "Family Celebration." His trading had added Flemish tapestries and Persian carpets upon the walls, but the fine moulded ceilings, the rooms panelled in pine and oak, had been there already. The handsome windows added abundant light, so that each room seemed to overflow with warmth and colour.

The Long Gallery, adjoining the master bedchamber, was fit for a queen with linenfold panelling, wall paintings, and decorated frieze. Fireplaces at both ends decorated by the enjoined Lennox and Hawkins arms ensured warmth and cheer, for this was the heart of Lennoxhoe. Here were its treasures enshrined, on display. Pewter, pottery and glass, stoneware bellarmines and majolica ware brought from the Low Countries. Here the ladies and children could exercise when the weather was inclement, and there were handsome padded and gilded chairs, not only for heads of the family, but for their guests too. Benches had been long since relegated to the servants' quarters. There were also large Persian rugs scattered upon the highly polished floor, adding further comfort and colour, shocking more frugal friends and acquaintances, who considered rush mats good enough even for palaces.

Jane agreed with her husband's "newfangled ideas," and so did the Queen. When she visited them in 1580, eight years past, she had been royally entertained, and her three days had incurred household expenses amounting to over three hundred pounds. Her gratitude had been overwhelming, and for a normally parsimonious guest she had been extravagant with embroidered gloves, pendants, and earrings. She had also let it be known that her entertainment at Lennoxhoe, "did lycht such a candle to the rest of the county that they were glad bountifullie to follow Master Lennox's example."

Amyas and Jane felt that this example must have set a costly precedent to neighbours, who felt it their bounden duty to present an even greater spectacle of hospitality. This had been assured by the crafty Queen's statement. Many noble houses were beggared by the sovereign's visit with her followers. A royal progress and plea for hospitality—rather a command than a begging—could not be ignored. Considerable shaking of coffers and borrowing went on behind the unruffled scene presented to her. The pride of bragging of a royal visit was an honour dearly bought.

Amyas opened the door of the bedchamber quietly and walked over to the bed where Jane slept. He stood looking down at her as she lay, eyes closed, pale and exhausted, and his heart went out to her. He loved her, so much, more than she could ever understand—

She stirred at his step, and her eyes flickered open.

"Did I waken you, love?"

Attempting a reassuring smile, she took his hand. "Nay, I was but resting." She drew his face down to her. "My dearest," she whispered as they kissed, more like lovers than staid wedded folk, "it is good to see you home again."

Stroking his cheek, she thought that his presence once again filled the mellow pine-panelled chamber, as it had filled her life these past years of marriage, with the same golden light. He was to her the most beautiful man in the entire world, a spun-gold Adonis with his bright hair, and she often wondered at her extreme good fortune in winning him, since she considered herself truly "plain Jane."

"What news? I thought I heard several horsemen—"

"Aye, love, they are at this moment being refreshed in the parlour." As she made an effort to sit up, to rise from the bed, he put out a restraining hand. "Nay, this time our daughter plays hostess—"

"Dear Barbara." She lay back against the pillows, breathing heavily, and he saw anxiously how exhausted she was by this small effort. "Dear Barbara—she is a woman grown already—industrious, reliable—"

"And she wants to go to court."

Jane clasped his hand. "Nay, Amyas—I do not want that for her."

"Nor I, dearest, nor I." How grateful he was that Jane also shared his own lack of worldly ambition. "It was your uncle Francis put the foolish idea into her head, telling her how the Queen likes pretty young maids around her, petals of a flower."

"Uncle Francis—is he here?"

"Aye. Waiting for a wind and the morrow's tide."

She listened silent as he sat upon the bed and, still holding her hand, related the most recent events concerning the Armada. She was glad of an excuse—any excuse—for a few extra hours of his company in these troubled times, for she had spent all her married life longing for his footfall on the stairs, still the dearest sound in life to her. Every parting to return to the *Warlock* was like a little death, and her heart seemed to ache with emptiness for days after he had gone. Even the children, dear as they were, never compensated for his absence, and she was ashamed that she loved Barbara more than Francis, because in her golden way she was Amyas again.

Although he assured her that the months at sea were lonely without her, she suspected that he said so out of kindness, since Amyas could not exist without the seafaring life he had enjoyed since boyhood. She still remembered with delight their first meeting when, prenticed to her uncle Drake, he rode in with him to her home one mellow summer's eve. The illusion of a golden youth born at that first meeting had remained with her. To her astonishment and gratitude, her secret joy was mutually shared. They fell in love at a single glance.

Wistfully in those early days of marriage, she had hoped to woo him from the sea, for Uncle Francis had influence at court. But Amyas shook his head and obstinately refused to discuss a post ashore. He was not even tempted by one at court, although Jane guessed that the Queen, who loved handsome young men, favoured him. She also guessed with some satisfaction that Her Majesty was little better off than herself when, within weeks at home, Amyas turned to daydreaming, staring out of Lennoxhoe's windows like a man in prison, staring towards the sea with his heart in his eyes. Restless, frowning, he paced the garden, staring at the sky, interpreting the cloud's formation.

And Jane knew now the measure of her rival. If it were possible to be jealous of an inanimate object, then the *Warlock* was her equivalent of a hated mistress rivalling Amyas for her affections. She recognised that there would always be competition between wife and ship. Even the figurehead seemed to radiate a malign and scornful disregard for this frail mortal woman who owned but half of her master's soul. But today, as always, she thrust aside her feelings of resentment, determined not to tarnish these precious hours by feeling sorry for herself, by fighting against what she knew to be inevitable. Instead, she asked the question whose answer she most dreaded:

"What news from London?"

"Naught I hear but talk of the Queen's decision to remain there with the court, whatever befalls. She rides out each day, a brave woman on horseback, her gallantry applauded not only by men of courage but also by the humblest citizen. All of them throwing their bonnets in the air, overjoyed at her refusal to seek safety in the shire, to run from the hated Spaniards. She knows her way to the common folks' hearts, thus being one with them, to sink or swim, through adversity. Aye, and not a man there among the crowds who throng around her each day who would not consider it an honour to lay down his life for her."

"She is a remarkable Queen."

"And a remarkable woman, never forget that, my dear. For she refused the protection of the personal army that is her right, saying that such brave men are needed in the fight against the Spaniard."

Amyas was aware that the sky had darkened considerably, and amid the noise of the rain he distinguished the first growl of thunder which crackled across the rooftop of Lennoxhoe.

If the sight depressed him, then it did the opposite for Jane. She watched it unmovingly, with inward rejoicing. Let the storm rage forever, if it would, so that she could keep Amyas by her side, safe from danger. As the next brawl of thunder shook the windows and Amyas lit the candles, she thought wistfully that perhaps the storm presaged another Biblical flood which would wash the Armada back to Spain. When she said so, Amyas laughed.

"What, wife, and do our noble captains out of the fight they itch for? I beg you, do not mention such treasonable ideas to your uncle Drake or he will disown you as no true daughter of the Hawkins tradition." Kissing her, he said gently, "Do not fear, love, you will be safe here in God's hands. And in the Queen's. All crossroads are guarded night and day against surprise from the Spaniards—"

"Aye, and householders have their instructions to have arms and fire precautions at the ready. I saw to it myself, for Jem and Bessie fully understand these matters and can instruct the other servants."

"I noticed a plentiful supply of leather buckets and hoses when we rode into the courtyard. Not, of course," he added hastily, "that it will come to such calamity."

"Bessie tells me of a rumour that foreigners, particularly Catholics, are advised to remain indoors, and secret, during these troubled times—"

"'Twould be better if Bessie held her tongue instead of setting herself up as oracle for the shire," said Amyas wearily, wondering how much fear and despondency the well-intentioned Bessies of this world helped spread in times of peril.

"God's sake," he said angrily, "Bessie and her like are more natural allies to the King of Spain than any treacherous winds."

Jane smiled. "She firmly believes every man who speaks in a foreign tongue to be a spy—and a Catholic. I try to assure her that there are Catholics who are good folk—and loyal to the Queen."

Both were silent, remembering that Amyas had been born a Roman Catholic, but that his father, Thomas, had changed his church with great alacrity to suit the new Queen when Mary Tudor died.

"Bessie has heard that the Catholic lords in Scotland are for King Philip and that the Earls of Morton and Huntly are set to meet the Duke of Parma's invasion from Dunkirk, with plans to open the Scottish ports to the Armada"—Jane swallowed—"after they have defeated the Queen's ships."

"Foolish nonsense," said Amyas with a conviction that he did not feel.

Jane shook her head. "And there is also a rumour that there will be no lack of Catholic supporters ready to march down into England with the Spanish—to subject our Queen to the same fate which so justly befell the treacherous Queen of Scots. Is that not terrible, husband?"

Amyas laughed at her shocked countenance. "If it were true—but it is only rumour, with a hundred hungry mouths to it—"

"They say that the Catholic lords await only Spanish gold, in payment for their services," Jane whispered.

"And from what magical source is this gold to materialise?"

"From a ship in the Armada—"

"Which will find its way not to Scotland, but to the bottom of the sea," said Amyas grimly. He too had heard such rumours and thought of the army of spies and counterspies at this moment busily penning reports, coding and decoding letters for that master spy, the Queen's secretary, Sir Francis Walsingham.

He laughed. "Our mastermind of ciphers himself would be charmed to know that his work, so highly secret, his intelligences, are the gossiping point in every inn between Greenwich and Plymouth Hoe, where each man and woman know the exact state of affairs and make it common gossip of the servants' hall."

Jane giggled too, and the discussion fell to Francis and his progress at Oxford. Amyas was shocked that the lad had been fighting again, according to his tutor's report. The cause, they had delicately ascertained, was his grandmother's Spanish blood.

Amyas thumped his fists together. "The lad cannot help that. Surely it is what a man is and becomes, not who were his ancestors. Do I seem any less an Englishman because my parents were born the enemies of England?"

"Nay, you are the truest Englishman God ever made," said Jane indignantly.

"Because I chose England and to serve her Queen—because I have lived here at Lennoxhoe all my life and my dear wife and children are wholly English. These are the matters to decide a man's loyalties, not his birth, over which he has no choice."

Their talk was interrupted by Bessie curtseying. "The gentlemen are assembled to sup, Captain Lennox sir, and await your presence."

As he followed her downstairs, she said, " 'Tis good to have you home again, sir. Would to God you were safely back and my darling mistress over her trouble, the babe safe born. Do not concern yourself while you are from us—Bessie knows much of childbearing—"

"I know that too, Bessie. My wife is in excellent hands."

Bessie nodded eagerly. "You may rely on that, sir."

"You will take care of Mistress Barbara when I am away?"

"I will that, sir. It is the greatest joy of our lives—Jem and me—to serve your dear family. Be assured, sir, no harm will come to them."

Amyas was so reassured by this big strong woman who had truly served through the years as part of the family that he forgot entirely his promised reprimand upon the matter of rumour-spreading.

In the parlour, with supper laid and the candles lit, he found Barbara sitting in her mother's usual place at the table.

"I trust, Father, that all will be to our guests' liking," she whispered nervously, "for it was short notice."

Besides Bessie's rich potage there was rabbit pie, followed by quinces and conserves from the garden. If the pie was colder than comfort, then the Lennoxhoe ale and the pretty face across the table soon made the *Revenge*'s captain and officers eager to warmly compliment their young hostess.

Through the murmur of talk the candlelight shivered, as rain drummed on the windows and a gale seeped through the stone sills, ruffling the Flemish tapestries into mysterious life. Even the cheerful log fire was occasionally put to shame by gusts of smoke belching out upon the diners.

"Such a storm," said Barbara, apologising for coughs and smarting eyes.

"Aye, and unlikely to abate before morn."

"We are in for a couple of days of unsettled weather, I fear," said Drake.

And lighthearted conversation ended abruptly as the threat of the Spanish invasion loomed large in each man's mind. "The torture of the Inquisition— Have you heard that one of their galleons carries the Inquisitor and his helpers, armed with all the latest equipment?"

"Aye, a hold full, ready to deal swiftly with all English and heretic traitors."

"As a child I lived near Smithfield," said one of the older men. "We could see the smoke of Bloody Mary's burnings, and it hid the sunshine; all around us it was."

"Aye," said another. "Not only within Smithfield but for miles around the city, where the smell of roasting flesh hung upon the air like the aftermath of a grisly banquet."

The men shook their heads in agreement. Never again must Protestant England risk the horrors of Papist rule. Then someone noticed Barbara's frightened expression and hastily turned the conversation to lighter topics, the garden at Lennoxhoe and her brother, Francis, at Oxford.

At the head of the table, Amyas longed for an excuse to be quit of his guests. Upstairs Jane waited for him. It was time Barbara retired too, left the men to their sombre talk and ale.

At last he escorted her upstairs, where they found Jane already fast asleep. Stealthily closing the door, Barbara linked arms with him, rubbing her cheek kittenwise against the velvet of his sleeve. The gesture from childhood reached out to his heart, and he drew her head close, kissing her fair curls.

"Let us talk for a little while, Father."

"It is late—"

"And I shall never sleep after all the excitement—with my head full of horrors." As he opened the door of her bedchamber, she asked, "Was that true about Smithfield?"

"Aye. But it was a long time since. Such things are best forgotten, love."

"Do you believe what the men say about the Spaniards? After all—" She hesitated and glanced up at him uncomfortably.

"After all, Grandmother was Spanish, is that what you mean, my dearest?"

"Aye, Father, and it gives me cause for concern. They say that bad blood will out no matter how many generations—"

"Dearest child, that is foolish nonsense. You must not believe such things." And sitting on the bed beside her, he told her as he had argued with her mother earlier that blood has little to do with men's loyalties.

Barbara sighed. "But you were jesting, Father—you would not really fight for King Philip—would you?"

"If the worst should happen—aye, I would offer any king my services, for men must live—especially family men, with others dependent upon them. And lives, ordinary lives like ours here at Lennoxhoe, must continue."

She looked at him and said softly, "Seeds must be planted and harvests sown. Mouths must be fed and new babes born."

He smiled, hugging her to him. "Aye, daughter. And whoever sits upon the throne of England, these things must continue, the ways of nature—of the seasons. This was man's plan given by God, to survive until Judgement Day."

"What could be worse than wicked King Philip with his torture racks?" she asked doubtfully.

"Tomorrow—by God's will—King Philip could die in his bed, or be replaced by some change of fortune. There have and always will be those who rule over us, oft decided by blood spilt, by death in battle or the executioner's axe. But, dearest child, you will look back upon this day—upon this moment sitting here with your father—when you are older. You will see then your own life like a woven pattern with a thread running through it."

He touched one of her bright curls and let it spring like a living thing to wrap itself around his finger. "All this—will be white. You will be an old lady huddled over a warm fire. But you will know from your own life by then that the fortunes of rulers change little in the lives of ordinary folk, like ourselves—whichever king or country they were born to serve."

"And if we lose," she demanded sulkily, "what if the King of Spain does not want the services of the *Warlock* and Captain Lennox?"

"Then we shall go to the Americas. Escape by moonlight from the harbour and with a good wind steal away across the ocean to the New World, join the many colonies being founded there. Or if I lose the *Warlock*, then we shall go north over the border to Grandfather Lennox at the court of King James."

There was no answering smile to his bright picture painted for her. "That barbaric land. I should hate to leave the river and the house here, so pretty. I read that Scottish folk live in hovels—at least the colonials have forts to protect them from their savages," she added with a shudder.

"Rumours again, my chick. Let us say our prayers that we never need to find out the truth." Stretching his arms above his head, he said, "I must retire, for I am sleepy—you too, daughter." And kissing her good night, he returned to the bedchamber where Jane stirred drowsily as he crept in beside her. At his warm presence she gave a great contented sigh and all night long slept like a child cradled in his arms, untroubled by the storm raging like a fierce dragon back and forth across the frightened land.

Prediction had proved true, and the rain continued unabated until two days later, on the morn of July 30, the sky calmed and the burdened trees and greenery of Lennoxhoe moved gently in a faint breeze. There was summer warmth in the air, and Sir Francis Drake and his officers, frustrated and made restless by the inactivity, wished for exercise.

Amyas was prevailed upon somewhat reluctantly to leave Lennoxhoe and accompany them to Plymouth for a game of bowls. He put a good face upon it, for he would rather have stayed with Jane and Barbara. However, he had gained some expertise in the game and felt it would be churlish to refuse Sir Francis' challenge.

"Your uncle," he told his wife wearily, preparing to depart, "shines forth at every pursuit. It seems that all the talents were bestowed liberally upon him at birth and—God's love—how he does enjoy displaying them!"

"The Spaniards say that he has a wizard's mirror and can summon up weather to suit himself."

"So I have heard," said Amyas drily. "Then we need not complain, since Drake's weather has given us a little time together that we might not have had otherwise." Pulling on his riding boots, he grinned at her. "As for his mirror, he may well need to summon a storm at very short notice if the Armada rides up to Plymouth Sound and finds him playing at bowls."

When they reached Plymouth, the promise of good weather continued. The sky, though indifferently blue, held some fretful drifting clouds, through which a dazed and waterlogged sun put in an occasional welcome appearance. As the game proceeded, Amyas observed Drake's deceptive serenity at close quarters. His movements were slow, calm, and leisurely, yet there was a deadly ruthlessness in each action and a very shrewd fast-moving brain at work behind that slow speech with its marked Devon accent. Small wonder the Spaniards feared him, for he knew the oceans as other men know roads and footpaths. He knew too the strategy of war, and was quick to respond when one of the captains proudly boasted that England, as an island, was invulnerable.

Drake shook his head slowly. "Mistake it not, sir, the watergates of England are the ports of the enemy. The frontier of England runs not through Dover but across there, through Calais," he said, pointing to the distant horizon. "And what lies between is neither French nor neutral territory. It is our own land. Mark it well, gentlemen, England's western frontier in a war with Spain is not the Cornish coast, not Devon, but Corunna—Lisbon—Cádiz. Our best means of naval defence must therefore always be attack."

Halfway through the third game, their scores even, Amyas and Drake's activities were interrupted by raised voices. A man Amyas recognised as Captain Fleming of the *Golden Hind* broke through the rank of watchers.

"Sir," he said, bowing to Drake, "the Armada is at this moment sailing up the Channel. I came as fast as I could," he added breathlessly.

"How many ships did you see?" asked Drake, still weighing the bowl in his hand.

"Sir, I did not wait to count—let us say a great number of sails— off the Scillies. It was like a town of great castles and sails moving forth," he added to the captains who crowded round him. He sounded frightened.

Drake nodded slowly. "You made good time then in reaching us, Captain, and doubtless England will one day properly express her gratitude." As the captains clamoured for orders, he held up his hand. "Orders, gentlemen—be not hasty. Let us proceed with the matter in hand." He laughed. "We have time enough to finish the game and beat the Spaniards too. Pray move aside." And leaning forward, he released the bowl and watched it slide along the green. Surveying the completed move with satisfaction, he dusted his hands and, turning to Amyas, grinned. "Captain Lennox, I think I have you. The game is mine." Straightening his shoulders, he swung round to face the waiting captains. "Now, gentlemen—to orders—and let us be brisk."

The ships were to be made ready for immediate sail. There was little time to spare if they were not to be trapped in harbour at the mercy of a southwest wind with the might of the Armada riding upon it. The captains exchanged worried glances. All knew that from three o' the clock until nine, the flood tide rode into Plymouth and no ship could move until it turned.

Amyas sniffed the air. "The wind favors the Spaniards, sir," he whispered.

"Aye, but they have a fair distance to travel first before they sight Plymouth. Much can change," said Drake, his voice so calm and unhurried that Amyas wondered if tales about that magic mirror could be true.

He found that the captains shared his unease. "Sir," said one of them, "if any of the fleet be caught outside harbour and attacked under adverse conditions—"

"Aye," said another, "the Spaniards could force a fight at close quarters—"

"And we stand to lose by our lack of numbers—"

Again Drake held up his hand. "Have no fear, gentlemen; we will be ready for them. That I promise you. Aye, armed and ready." To Amyas, at his side, he added, "Go you and say your farewells to your good dame—"

"But—"

"Go—you can be spared for an hour or two since you are so near home."

Back at Lennoxhoe, Jane behaved bravely although this hour was for her the hardest parting ever. She clung to him wordlessly. Silently resentful of his departure, this time she was afraid, afraid of the burden she carried of this unborn child, who threatened to murder her and daily sapped more of her remaining small strength. What if Amyas too died by a musket bullet and the children were left alone but for Jem and Bessie? She had a thousand questions to ask as a thousand fearful pictures darted through her mind. Oh, dear God, she needed reassurance of his love, of his return, as she had never done in the past!

If—if—if— She must not beg him to stay. She must send him away with a smiling memory of her to carry into battle. She must not make it more difficult for him. He had done all he could to ensure the safety of his family, the defence of his house. Barbara and she would be defended by loyal and trusted servants who would serve with their own lives if necessary.

To the death, a voice inside her whispered, and she shuddered convulsively.

God was good. He was on their side, the ministers said so and they should know. All would be well; she had only to place her faith and prayers in God to make it so—to keep the Spaniards at bay and bring Amyas safely home.

She blinked back tears and drew the golden head of her husband to her bosom, closing her eyes, trying to make this moment last as she wondered if she would ever look into his eyes and see his dear smile again. At last she released him, thinking bitterly that from this time onwards his life belonged to the Queen and to her old and hated rival, the *Warlock*.

"Go in safety—and God speed you back, dearest love."

"God keep you, sweetheart."

He was gone, her world emptied of its golden light as the door softly closed.

As he rode swiftly to the harbour, the signal was hoisted upon Admiral Lord Howard's flagship, *Ark Royal*. As he approached, the crews were already hard at work moving the ships out of harbour. As the tide was still against them, the ships had to be towed, pulled by boats and smaller craft, and frantic rowing men. Sheer brute strength was needed now—there could be no more delays, no more waiting for wind or tide to help them.

On the *Revenge*, Drake walked the deck, shouting orders, a happy man at last, Amyas thought, watching him from the *Warlock*. Drake

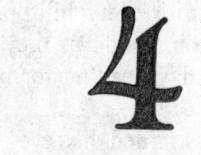

At that precise moment aboard the *Black Duchess* Don Felipe Flores y Lennox de Montreuse was also a very unhappy man.

As Karim had predicted, the great seas rolling in from the Atlantic Ocean had proved too much for the top-heavy galleons, built for calmer seas. The sudden storm with its squally winds had also proved too much for Felipe. He lay sick as a dog, helpless as a babe, tossing and cursing in his great canopied bed. Under the vast royal arms of Spain, swaying creakily above his head, he prayed only that the cabin would stay still for a few moments so that he could die in peace.

His previous experiences of the sea had led him to believe he was a tolerable sailor, liable only to transient bouts of nausea in extreme weather. Such extremes as he had imagined resembled more a millpond than these raging seas. As for His Majesty Uncle Philip's Most Happy Armada, Felipe would have cheerfully accompanied it to the bottom of the ocean, considering as he did so that such a disaster was naught but a happy release from his miseries.

Once, he thought his prayers had been answered. That drowned, he had encountered a mermaid as an enchanting face with translucent green eyes and drifting long black hair gazed down on him.

I am dead at last, he thought with a great sigh. Thank God, it is all over—I am free—

"Come, Sir Captain. Drink." The mermaid's hand was gentle under his head. "Here—a wee sip of wine. You will feel the better of it—"

could always rely on his men in a crisis, knowing they worked best with the odds against them and the Spaniards breathing down their necks. Disciplined loyal men; he was proud of them.

During the dark hours of the night they saw the first warning beacons glow like angry stars from every hilltop, God's eyes and His blessing upon this holy mission. By dawn they were clear of the harbour, and on a warm sunny day heading for battle over a calm and peaceful sea.

On the *Warlock*, Amyas strained his eyes for a last glimpse of Lennoxhoe's tall chimneys, shrouded by the mists of a summer morn. It was like some omen, he thought, pacing the deck, while his mind drifted to the hours of decision which lay ahead. Had he seen the last in this mortal life of those beloved to him, whose existence meant more than life itself? If only he could have seen once more his only son, Francis, who at thirteen would become head of the family —in the event of his father's death. Francis, little more than a child—

At last a warning cry from the tops; the guns fired and whistles blew, and Amyas saw that they had come upon a distant city, vast and holding the horizon. His heart misgave him when he realised the truth, that the distant city of shadowy spires and turrets forming the horns of a crescent moon was the Armada—at last. As it shivered and moved in the shimmering light, he heard far away a flourish of trumpets. Their enemy had observed their approach and was waiting, ready and proud.

At the now familiar accent of Ireland, the sprite into whose hands he had relinquished his weary, aching body and feeble spirit became the mocking face of Maeve O'Neill, kin to the Earl of Tyrone. A thorn in his suffering flesh—a plague upon her and her powerful relatives. Angrily he thrust her hand away.

"Let me be. Leave me alone."

"Come, just a sip now." Her voice, like the wine, was cool and gentle. Obediently he drank, closed his eyes. Slept and woke again, his mouth dry as a bone, croaking, "Wine, for God's sake—wine."

The goblet was again held to his lips. He drank deeply, greedily, but his head had hardly touched the pillow again when the black bile rose in his throat. A basin was thrust before him.

"Sir Captain, in truth you must eat. It will make the sickness easier."

"I want nothing—let me be, for pity's sake."

When next he opened his eyes, it was to behold lines of garments moving above his head. Where was he? Had the Armada been a dream and he was back in El Escorial? Nay, he had never seen washing hanging on a line in those marble halls—

Scotland. That was it. Scotland and the royal gardens of Holyrood Palace. He had wandered into the kitchen with his twin cousin, Amyas Lennox, intent upon mischief, tormenting the maids with their seeming ability to be in two places at the same time. It sent the silly creatures screeching away in superstitious terror, clutching their beads. Aye, a very good game indeed, until they were both soundly whipped.

Holyrood. The green summer garden, how it swayed and moved. If only it would stay still for a moment— The vision faded. Blinking, he found the drying garments remained, their violent gyrations coinciding with the heaving cabin of the *Black Duchess*.

A shadow moved near the bed, hovering. He pointed an old man's quavering hand towards the garments, croaking:

"Remove them from my sight, for pity's sake—"

"Awake, Sir Captain? Good, here is nourishment for you."

That accursed Irish girl was forcing nauseous gruel and saps of biscuit soaked in wine, down his throat. He tried to fight her off, but had need of all his strength to swallow and not to choke.

The effort was endless. He dozed. Later he awoke to hear singing and raised himself on one elbow, hopeful for the siren's song of the deep, token that this time he was indeed at the bottom of the sea.

Instead, there was his tormentor, curled up in the padded window seat of the cabin, plying a needle as she sang.

He groaned. What was she sewing? His shroud— In a weak moment he had given her the key to a chest of bright materials, velvets, satins—

She heard him and walked across the swaying cabin effortlessly on dainty bare feet. Her cheeks were rosy, her eyes bright with laughter. Her obvious excellent health was a personal affront to his misery.

"And what can I be getting ye, Sir Captain?" she asked, patting his pillows. "Are ye quite comfortable?"

"Comfortable. I am in hell, damn you."

Unconcerned, she smiled. "Even a man in hell should eat now and again to keep up his strength." The thought made her merry, and he growled:

"For further torments, that is what you mean." He turned his face from her smile, her hand on his brow. Then finding the hand cool and almost comforting, he closed his eyes.

"You will live, Sir Captain—if God so wills—"

"God in His goodness, forbid—"

"Come now—seasickness is common to most folk—and few ever die of it—"

"Stop your silly prating—I need no lessons from you. Karim— where is he?"

"Too busy to spare time for a sick passenger."

Felipe struggled for his last shred of dignity. "You will please remember," he said coldly, "that I am commander of this ship. Bring Karim to me."

Karim brought a solemn tale of the storm's damage. Although the *Black Duchess* had suffered little, three of the great galleons were casualties. There were other problems than weather:

"Should the English fleet reach us now, Master, only the experienced seamen are capable of fighting."

"How so?"

Karim avoided his eyes uncomfortably. "The soldiers who make up the crew—like yourself, Master—they are sick. Unable to stand, most of them, let alone fight."

It gave him scant joy to learn that his miserable plight was shared by the meanest soldier, the pikemen and musketeers—like himself, landsmen all.

"The whole of Don Pedro de Valdes' squadron—forty ships—have drifted away in the storm—"

Felipe waved aside a chronicle of disasters, and the Irish girl, staring over Karim's shoulder, said reproachfully:

"It is not good to depress your commander with bad news at such a time. Besides, he is ready for his gruel now," she said, thrusting Karim aside, grinning at him, spoon in hand.

Karim watched this operation in amazement, until the girl, wiping the corners of Felipe's mouth with a napkin, carried the empty bowl to the table.

Eagerly Felipe seized Karim's arm. "For sweet Jesus' sake, send that bitch away."

Karim's scimitarlike eyebrows arched. "Master, in what way does she offend?"

"Her vile presence is enough—"

"But you need to be cared for—she has looked well after you—"

"Then get one of the men—"

Aye, that was what he wanted. Some menial he would not be forced to look upon in every waking moment. So at home in his cabin she was with her singing and sewing, her hearty good health humiliated a man, an affront to his virility.

He tried not to listen to Karim's whispered advice. His head ached. He wanted to be left alone. Just to die in peace. It was not too much to ask—

The seaman Karim spared from the crew was delighted to take up the position of body servant to the commander, mostly because of the possibilities it offered an ambitious fellow.

Felipe lay inert in the canopied bed, apparently asleep. No sooner had the man closed the door than he made plain his first duty. He advanced stealthily towards Maeve, his meaningful leer proclaiming that he had other ideas than merely serving Don Felipe.

Maeve yelled, struggling away from his exploring hands, his stinking breath on her face. Suddenly from the dark cavern of the bed they heard the click of the pistol which Don Felipe kept under his pillow.

"Take your hands off her or I will have you flogged. Do you hear? That is an order." The hand that held the pistol never wavered, despite the pale unshaven face, the burning eyes under the unruly matted hair, its gold sadly tarnished.

"Get your filthy hide out of my cabin. At once."

The seaman needed no second bidding, and Felipe sank back upon the pillows, exhausted by his efforts. Wondering, Maeve went over to him. For sweet Jesus' sake, and now he was defending *her*. A hidalgo after all, she thought with pride.

When she stammered thanks, he eyed her coldly. "Be quiet, wretch. All I did was to save myself from being the helpless observer of your sordid couplings. My life is a sorry enough burden without my cabin being turned into a brothel."

Speechless with rage, Maeve could have slapped his face, except that he swiftly turned on his side, presenting the back of his head. However, when Karim entered, he turned over, jabbed a finger in her direction.

"*She* can look after me. At least *she* has the beginnings of finesse. I want none of your unwashed villains in here." And he cut short Karim's apologies: "Enough. It will keep her out of mischief, and she can make herself useful— Oh, God—"

And Maeve was just in time with the basin as he was again violently sick.

Behind them the cabin door swung open. "Masters—the flagship—we have been signalled."

"Landfall," breathed Karim. "The coast of England at last—"

From the bed Felipe murmured weakly, "Thank God." Scotland could not be far off. He looked at the girl, saw the same thought upon her brow. Only another few days—with luck, a week or less—and each would be rid of the other's odious company. Felipe felt better. However, staggering to the window, he discovered that landfall in the gathering dusk was only a long straight line, faint above the sea, thin as rising cloud. At dawn he looked again, saw that the line had grown into the Lizard, a land mass containing an army of angry red eyes. Increasing steadily, these bright eyes continued to march with them from every hilltop as the invasion beacons signalled that they were expected. England was ready.

All that day, the *Black Duchess* sailed majestically onwards, staying close to the flagship. To their left, the coastline with its white cliffs gleaming in sunlight, but the Narrow Seas were empty, deserted, with never the sight of an English sail to challenge their progress. The crews, in battle ranks, lined up uncomfortably close upon the decks, grew restive, uneasy, as the sun rose higher, beating down upon them. They were hot, tired, their nerves frayed by the continued inaction.

Felipe was summoned by a pinnace containing other captains, rowing past the *Black Duchess* to an interview with the Admiral, aboard the *San Martin*. Felipe declined. "Still too indisposed" was his excuse. Karim went instead, to return later with exciting news.

"The captains—and I with them, Master—urged His Grace to head straight on, attack Plymouth, taking advantage of the absence of the English ships, and with a wind in our favour." Karim shook his head sadly. "Alas, His Grace is a stubborn man, Master. He could not take such action without direct orders from His Majesty at El Escorial. The captains—all of us—argued in favour of taking Plymouth—but he would not listen."

And so that day, the Duke of Medina Sidonia threw away his one chance of a successful Armada. Fortune was not prepared to give him or his Armada another chance.

Felipe was not in the least disappointed at such news. Fighting was the last thing he desired, only a safe and smooth voyage to his destination, with as few encounters with the English as possible. The wind with them, the ship no longer bucking, leaping at the waves, his stomach had ceased to heave. Return to normality brought human feelings and desires.

"Is bad weather expected?"

"Nay, Master, my *Duchess* has settled to an even keel."

"What do we now?"

"Wait. There will be no action until the English are sighted."

"Will there be plenty of warning?"

"In clear weather like this, Master—aye, plenty." And the Arab captain was considerably taken aback at Felipe's request for bath water once again. Orders were given, and the men dragged in the deep tub, filled it with ewers of water. However, a slight change in course caused the cabin to sway, and Felipe discovered he was still too weak to climb into the tall tub unaided. Karim assisted him, offering the services of one of the men to help bathe him.

"God's grief, nay. I want not their filthy hands on me. I am here to get clean, not soiled again. *She* can wash me. God knows I have no secrets from her any longer."

Maeve came in obediently from her contemplation of the cliffs. She washed his back and chest, his feet, arms, shoulders, her modesty appeased when he seized the soap roughly from her and washed those other parts decently covered by water.

"Now get me clean linen." She seemed to interpret his needs since such had been laid over the chair, and she was already changing the bed's soiled linen.

Grunting, he stood up with effort, cursing anew when he discovered he had to call upon her assistance with the leather garments and cuirass of battle that Karim insisted upon. Even as a passenger he was told he must be so attired, since it was the commander's duty to be prepared for action and the crew might think his behaviour odd otherwise.

As Maeve buckled him into the leather jacket, the ship heaved and water sprayed from the tub across the cabin floor. Felipe's weight threw Maeve off balance as he grabbed the bedpost to steady himself.

For a moment as they wavered they clung together in the close embrace of lovers, his arms around her waist, hers encircling his neck. His nearness, the sweet smell of herb-scented fresh linen, overwhelmed her. Bare throat, fair hair curling damply into gold tendrils were at odds with the stern face. She felt like a drowning woman, as though her stomach had departed from her body long since. Staring into the bright hazel eyes above her, she thought for a moment she saw tenderness, only a glimmer—a light at the end of a long journey through the dark. It bade her welcome—welcome home—

Then she was reeling back as he thrust her roughly aside. "God's grief, señorita, stand on your own two feet and not upon mine. And clean up this mess." Springing away from her, he walked to the cabin window. Hands clasped behind his back turned upon her, his voice cold. "And when you have done that, get Karim."

"My *Duchess* is fast losing all hope of an encounter with the English," Karim told him. "If it were not for those accursed beacons, ever increasing, I would swear there were no enemy ships anywhere in readiness for us."

Felipe greeted this news with secret jubilation. "All the better—then we sail along the Channel, and straight north for Scotland."

Karim smiled grimly. "I should like to believe in such a happy fable, Master, but alas, I fear there is some sinister purpose behind the English ships' nonappearance. Which we will learn presently—and to our cost."

But it seemed that Karim was wrong, for all that day they sailed, under watchful cliffs upon a sea empty of all but small fishing crafts which vanished rapidly at their first sight of the swaying galleons. Those shining white cliffs made Felipe uneasy. Too far off for evidence of life, were they empty also? Had the population of southern England fled? Would they sail into deserted harbours? Would the Duke of Parma's invasion army find no resistance in cities, villages deserted of all life?

Felipe shared his thoughts with Karim, who frowned. "You are too fanciful, Master—we fight a wily foe. There is good reason for these delays—of that I am certain."

Felipe too found the inaction wearisome, and wandered back and forth between his cabin and the ship's rails. Once he tried to compose a long letter to his uncle King Philip, but threw down the quill in disgust. He was lonely and would have welcomed company, even the Irish girl with her abominable singing. She had apparently deserted him, and aware of hunger, he summoned Karim.

"Master, we believed the stowaway to be taking care of you."

"She is not here," he said huffily.

Where was she? He had forgotten his rage with her.

Maeve was not far away. She had found a shady corner hidden from the crew's attention—and his—where she could enjoy her own thoughts. After she had stormed out of his cabin she swore she would never go back to this arrogant bastard of a Spanish don, whom she had nursed through the long days and nights. Such was his gratitude, ill-mannered lout that he was.

She would find a place in the women's quarters, abandon him and his foul nature. At least it would be pleasant to have women's talk for a change.

The wild gypsy girls, the Arab and mulatto women, greeted her entrance with scowling faces. Although she spoke Spanish, their coarse dialects were beyond her—however, the lewd gestures which accompanied their words were graphic indeed.

They advanced towards her, scowling, menacing. She guessed they hated her and would have enjoyed seeing her raped by the crew. Panic seized her, but from their midst an older woman came forward, sternly motioning the others to keep back.

"We wish you no harm, señorita, but consider that you do us a disservice by taking our livelihood from us. We are aware that the Commander Don Felipe rescued you for himself and think it a great shame that a man high-born should favour you—who are not one of us—when so many talented harlots would be glad of his patronage—"

"You are all welcome to him."

"It would add to our prestige—one who has entertained a Spanish nobleman can charge a higher rate—"

"You are mistaken," said Maeve. "He is not my lover."

The woman looked hard at her, and under that careful scrutiny Maeve felt uncomfortable. At last the woman nodded. "Good, so be it. For when this battle is over, business among us will be brisk. It is then that men who survive need a woman most." Turning, she spoke in some rough dialect Maeve could not understand, and the women, who were eyeing Maeve with apparent surprise, shrugged and wandered back to their places.

"If you wish, we will make a place for you here."

But Maeve hesitated. These dark quarters were hardly more savoury than the vomit-smelling cabin she had left. The woman offered her food and wine, but she declined, saying that although she did not serve Don Felipe as a woman, he had been ill and she was taking care of him.

She was glad to escape. The air was ripe with foetid unwashed sweating bodies, stale perfume, and soiled linen. And another smell she associated with the animals on that farm in Ireland. The mating smell of coupling animals—

Memories of her home brought again the stab of fear. That Don Felipe might discover it was a lie she had told him. Ironic that when occasion demanded she could be as good—if not better—a liar than her despised parent, with his boasts of being first cousin to the Earl of Tyrone.

First cousin, God save us, and him naught but one of the ragged tribe of O'Neill retainers, mostly of remote and bastard relationship, the spongers who hung around the Earl. The nearest Connor O'Neill had been to the castle was as kitchen boy. The rest of his story was fantasy, but he had sworn to have the skin off her back if she ever breathed a word—

O'Neill and the kings of Ireland. She had told Don Felipe she was a princess of Ireland. The truth was so different; she laughed out loud, remembering their hovel of a farm. Her mother had not lasted overlong either, with her randy, brutal husband. Seventeen children in thirteen years—and Maeve the eldest. She could not mourn the poor slattern her mother became, the derelict skeletal creature who regarded death as a privilege to escape her hellish brute of a husband. God only knew what became of that tribe of brothers and sisters or why her father should have chosen to send her as serving maid to the nuns.

One day there had been a scandal. A travelling priest promised her reading and writing, urging her first to visit his cell that night. He would hear her sins, confess her. Aye, and he would teach her great things, he whispered, fondling her in a manner unmistakable even to the green girl she was.

He was handsome, young, and she was intrigued as well as a little frightened by his suggestions. However, the chance of some excitement to break the monotony of life with the nuns was too rare to be missed. What the priest had in mind was soon obvious but thwarted by the appearance of Mother Superior, who delivered some very harsh words to him, while Maeve was dragged, still mercifully undeflowered, from his bed.

Curiously enough, the holy man's behaviour seemed to establish a pattern—or perhaps she appealed only to carnal lusts normally suppressed. Another priest, fondling her, was set upon by a watchful nun, and then two friars, visiting, tried to kidnap her and carry her from the convent. Mother Superior shook her head regretfully. Maeve O'Neill, although industrious, was undoubtedly possessed by an unclean spirit, a temptation to mankind—and priests. Connor O'Neill was asked to kindly remove his daughter when convenient.

Expecting a beating, as was normal, on the mercenary's rare visits to his native heath, and a scowling face—the only one she ever saw upon him—Maeve saw that he actually smiled. She discovered that her father was not displeased by the nuns' story. Joking about her experiences in a heavy-handed manner, he eyed her thoughtfully, asking some searching intimate questions. He took her back to Spain, and in Madrid purchased several gowns, beautiful but immodest in appearance. He then established her in his lodgings as hostess, singing prettily with the lute to his strange and varied friends.

When the elderly, decrepit, but enormously rich Don Diego offered for her, Maeve realised the truth. That she was being sold to the highest bidder. That had all along been her destiny. To her father filial love was laughable and respect meant nothing. Even his death did not release her since he had squandered on the gaming tables—and his mistresses—the money for her sale to Don Diego. The old man was determined to retain his possession of her, and virtually a prisoner, Maeve was abducted, transported to Corunna, there to await the hastily planned marriage.

Trapped, with her wedding day fast approaching, by a miracle she had seen the *Black Duchess* at anchor and remembered its destination with Don Felipe the Spy. She had not exaggerated the story, since her father's drunken carousings were notoriously indiscreet. She had given all her jewels to a servant with a grudge against Don Diego to leave open the back gate. The rest, although heart-stopping in contemplation, was easier than she had expected.

Once the ship reached Scotland, Ireland did not figure in her present plan. She wanted no place in Tyrone's filthy rat-infested kitchens or in the family hovel with whatever brothers and sisters still remained alive. She would travel to London, seek her fortune. But she must be cautious. Should Don Felipe learn the truth, that he had been told a pack of lies and had nothing to fear from the Earl's wrath— Maeve shuddered. Doubtless he would have her thrown over the side, or to the crew's entertainment. And harlotry did not figure in her immediate plans. If her father could make a profit out of selling her maidenhead to the highest bidder, why then, so could she—

Returning to the cabin, she had all but forgotten Sir Captain's ill temper and his base ingratitude. He was attired in a cambric nightrobe, wide-sleeved, his ruffled fair hair diminishing dignity and transforming his scowl into that of a rebellious schoolboy. Remove a man from his breeches and you divest him of all authority, she thought almost maternally. But he gave no answering smile to her greeting and clambered swiftly into bed, turning his back towards her. On the window seat he had vacated she curled up and was soon asleep.

At two in the morning a commotion alongside the *Black Duchess* revealed a captured fishing boat. Terrified for their lives, impressed by encountering not only the Spanish Armada but also a pirate ship, the occupants were only too pleased to volunteer the information that would save their lives.

"Aye, masters, they had seen with their own eyes Lord Admiral Howard and Sir Francis Drake beating out of Plymouth Sound last night."

Then where the devil were they? And the answer was in every man's frightened eyes. Since they could not be ahead of them, they must be following in their wake. The situation Karim dreaded had come to pass. The hunters had become the hunted, and somewhere out of sight in the moonlight the trap was closing.

He did not have long to await confirmation of his fears, as lookouts from the tops reported fifty English ships on their landward side. From the flagship came the order to drop anchor, await first daylight, and prepare to give battle.

Daylight came and revealed that they were surrounded.

Karim cursed. Never would he have allowed his *Duchess* to be caught in such an obvious trap. Ships to their seaward side and another group to windward, while the English flagship, *Ark Royal*, and her squadron bore down upon them, closing straight across the *Black Duchess*'s bows in their eagerness to get to grips with the *San Martin*.

Karim, at anchor, fought his every instinct to cut and run, to take command of the situation and find some means by which his *Duchess* could still weave a channel of escape. No orders came, no signal. Looking at his sails, Karim groaned. The stubborn slow-thinking Admiral's indecision had now lost them the wind. They would have to do battle where they stood.

The signal everyone waited for was hastily flown from the flagship, and every man went to his post.

Felipe joined Karim on deck and together they watched in amazement as, in accordance with the old laws of chivalry, which had nothing to do with the despicable behaviour expected from pirate ships, Lord Admiral Howard of England sent his defiance to Lord Admiral Medina Sidonia of Spain.

Fascinated, the *Black Duchess*'s crew watched as from the English ranks a pinnace headed straight for the *San Martin*. When almost upon it, she hauled up and discharged a piece into the galleon's hull. Too small to inflict damage, this was intended as an insult or impertinence, the sea challenge, equivalent to the thrown-down glove. Appropriately enough, as she withdrew, Felipe saw her name: *Disdain*.

There began a short leisurely exploration, rather than a battle, as each ship tested her opponent's mettle. Chivalry and honour were observed throughout, since, following the rival admirals' exchange of fire from their flagships, exchanges continued between ships of equal rank and tonnage down the line.

Karim was impatiently waiting for the *Black Duchess* to take her approaching place against a small armed merchantman when, quite suddenly, the wind changed, taking with it the last vestiges of a dignified sea-jousting tournament.

Smoke from the cannons drifted away, revealing scattered ships listing heavily, their crews feverishly at work hauling sails and, where they had oars, frantically using them to little avail. All over the sea, and in no kind of order, the galleons ran, trying to get behind the weather.

Felipe, to whom the passing hours had been of interest rather than fear, now walked unsteadily to where Karim was yelling orders. Returning sickness obliterated any pangs of duty which might have troubled him, and he would have given a king's ransom—those treasure chests in his cabin earmarked for the Scottish Catholic earls—to be safe back in El Escorial, his aching head resting upon a cool pillow.

"What is happening, Karim?"

The Arab captain scowled. "Our present course up channel will carry us far from any embarkation port, Master, since our speed is regulated by the heavy transport and supply ships in our midst." He bit his lower lip angrily. "His Grace our Admiral is a fool, and I care not if my displeasure reaches his ears. We had them here, in the palm of our hands"—he banged his fists together—"their vigilance relaxed; the sea was ours. We could have sailed into Plymouth with the wind behind us."

Staring at the scattered ships on an already boiling sea, Felipe shuddered.

"What now?"

"His Grace has a choice—run before the wind or stand and fight. Look—" From the *San Martin* alongside, a signal was being hoisted.

"What does it say?" asked Felipe eagerly, praying that it was to run—anything so that he could return to his cabin—and die—in peace.

"We are for a fight, Master."

Crowded by the English ships in the area, strung out in a long line and closing rapidly, heeling over under the great presses of sail before an ever freshening breeze, all chivalric order was abandoned.

Grasping the rail, Felipe realised that to hurry out of sight would suggest cowardice, aye, the cowardice he felt. But what little pride remained in his weak and miserable body fought against such instinct. Not only heartily sick but dazed, he remained at his post.

The pomp and show of those first shots had been mockingly unreal, a game for the nursery which had little to do with blood and death, the spilled guts of broken men and burning ships.

At his side, Karim groaned. "See, Master—see their plan—"

Felipe saw nothing. His stomach heaved; within minutes he would be violently sick again. He kept close to the rail.

The *Black Duchess* was being swept aside from her place in the fighting line by a large disdainful galleon, the *Rata Coronada*. Eager to come to grips with the English flagship, she cut across their bows and they were suddenly trapped between the crossfire. Karim had expected such an issue, and due only to his crew's experience and his ship's smallness and speed did they escape with little damage, leaving the huge galleons to hammer away at one another with cannon and culverin.

"Well done, Karim," said Felipe.

The Arab captain grinned. "The English are fighting loose and large—see how it is—avoiding at all costs any chance of boarding and hand-to-hand fighting. And that, Master, is our sole hope with such crews—pikemen, musketeers—" He spat contemptuously. "What use are such? Before Allah there is hardly an experienced seaman among them."

Karim's fears were right. They watched from a safe distance the *Rata Coronada*'s shot fall wide of the target, the foam splashes revealing a too short cannon range, while the English round shot crashed with deadly accuracy onto the *Rata*'s heavy timbers and made havoc of her crowded decks with the close-packed ranks of waiting soldiers.

"Why does he not move, for Jesus' sake? He is letting the men be slaughtered like animals," cried Felipe, turning away in sickened disgust and closing his ears to the screaming of men and shot on the crowded gun decks, where they waited their chance to close and board.

The *Rata* mercifully drifted out of range and hearing as three more English ships joined the fray.

"The *Revenge*—El Draque's ship, Master."

Those members of the crew who believed in the Devil made the sign against the Evil Eye, and Felipe saw that Karim's eyes had closed momentarily, his lips moving in a prayer to Allah. Next minute, the three ships were passing and repassing the Spanish galleons in clouds of fire and smoke, sending a furore of iron into their tall castles. The *Black Duchess* was immune from their attentions, she was too small and insignificant to be worthy of them, despite the fact that like an angry terrier, she took every opportunity to attack.

Her shot destroyed only English spars and rigging. She used her skill to cut and run, manoeuvring lightly through the mass, as other English ships moved in firing on the now confused mass of galleons that lay between them and their ultimate target—the valuable urcas and zabras, the supply ships which were the Armada's lifeblood.

Even through the smoke from the deck of the *Black Duchess* it was obvious that the trap was closing in once again.

"Before Allah," said Karim, "does not His Grace see danger when it spits into his very face? Why gives he no signal? Slow old tortoise," he groaned. "Men die like flies all around while he consults the orders that were given him before he left Spain—"

Among the ships now closely engaged, there was confusion of purpose. Signalling in the best of wind and weather was of a rudimentary nature, but after much expenditure of shot both fleets lay huddled in a fog of smoke. Felipe realised that each captain's field of vision must have dwindled as completely as their own, to the exclusion of all their squadron. With only the vaguest idea of the course the battle was taking, each captain was left to his own inclination on what to do next while he awaited signal guns from his flagship.

On the *Black Duchess*, Karim was thankfully able to issue orders from experience and instinct rather than being led by the performance of the smoke-obscured ship next to him.

Felipe learned in those first interminable hours the folly of campaigns planned upon parchment and studied with such care upon desk and table in pleasant rooms where the walls stayed still and peace reigned in the quiet garden. Such measures had no relation to reality, where victory was more often due to intuition, luck, prayer. All were more reliable than those neatly written orders and charts.

Sickened, he observed crowded decks and scuppers running with blood. The air hideous with the screams of wounded men. The fortunate dead unidentifiable as slaughtered meat—

"Break off fighting."

The signal given, the bulk of the Armada made for windward and safety under heavy fire while those nearest tried to rescue two beleaguered galleons, listing heavily, with spars and masts shot away, fighting off the English ships that were intent upon taking them as prize.

It was a question of who would reach them first, when sky and sea were shattered by an explosion—

In Plymouth they heard it, shaking the windows of those houses fortunate enough to have glass in them. Terrified citizens who had remained safely indoors rushed out to see if the world had come to an end. Had God turned a deaf ear to their entreaties and allowed the Spaniards to land? For some time past the town had shuddered to the echoes of gunfire, while the braver souls gathered along the cliffs to watch the battle's progress. When it passed slowly to the east, they rushed back to report, while in every hamlet the air was heavy with rumour.

The watchers had been dismayed by the vast number of the Armada and what appeared to be a mere handful of English ships. However, as the battle progressed, they were able to see even from a distance gratifying damage to the Spaniards. Sails flapping, masts broken, fires on board, but the English ships sailed past, proud, unruffled, and apparently intact.

Among the watchers on the cliff top was Jane Lennox. Lennoxhoe's vast estate led directly onto a steep track along the cliffs and a shortcut to the town. Although Bessie and Barbara had fussed and scolded, saying it was dangerous for her to walk so far, she insisted on going. In an agony of terror for Amyas and the *Warlock*, she could no longer lie in bed listening to the sounds of battle shaking her window while her dear one was somewhere out there in the fighting.

Now the three women stood on the narrow path, arms linked for comfort and security, staring out to sea.

"What will happen if our ships are defeated and the Spaniard sails up the Sound?" asked Barbara in a small voice.

Jane shook her head; her mind was full of woollen rags, but somehow she had to make a plan. "A plan to get Barbara north to Oxford to join Francis," she had told Bessie before her daughter appeared. "I have a sister in Northumberland, near Jedburgh. The Spaniards will never go there; they will surely concentrate upon the south—not that wild land," she added hopefully.

"Mistress dear, fret not. 'Twill never come to that," said Bessie, but with a sidelong glance at her tearful face Jane realised that the old servant's confidence was severely shattered by the nearness of the battle.

"Mistress, you are shivering—you have not eaten this day. Bessie will run back to the house, fetch you some nourishing soup. Will you not come with me? See, the ships have gone."

"Nay, I must stay here for a while. Fetch my cloak, too, if you please."

"Shall I go with her, Mother?" whispered Barbara as Bessie struggled back up the path, grumbling as its steepness squeezed the breath out of her and pausing to ease the strain on her stout body.

"Aye, precious—help her."

Jane watched them, and once out of sight, she sank down on the grass verge and gave way to the tears their presence had restrained. Seaward nothing remained of the fighting ships; only the faint echoes of gunfire denoted that the battle continued out of sight.

Jane shivered with more than the chill sea breeze. She had never been so afraid in her life. The paths beyond her were empty now, the townspeople tiny dots no bigger than insects, moving along the cliff top, trying to follow the battle's progress. Would she could be with them, but the walk from Lennoxhoe had brought an ominous pain in her side. Rubbing her swollen belly gently as if to placate the angry child, she wondered how fared Amyas, for she had been unable to distinguish the *Warlock* in the smoke-wreathed ships locked in combat.

"Amyas, oh, Amyas—please come back to us. God keep you safe—"

She blinked. Had her prayers been answered? The rattle of pebbles above heralded an arrival, and she saw a tall familiar figure hurrying towards her, half hidden by shadows, with the sun behind him dazzling her eyes.

"Amyas!" But even as she held up her hand, she saw it was Francis. Francis, who should have been in Oxford, safe with his tutor. He ran the last few yards and gathered her into his arms. As she clung to him, she fought back tears through an unsteady smile of welcome and kisses exchanged.

Dear God, how he had grown. Just past thirteen and almost as tall as his father. Francis, a man already. She could hardly believe he had matured so in six months. He was less like Amyas than was Barbara, with only a fleeting resemblance in the turn of his head, strong chin, and that slow, endearing smile.

She could hardly believe her eyes.

"I was intending sending your sister to you—should the worst happen—"

He squeezed her hand. "Which it will not, dearest Mother. Besides, I am here to look after you and Barbara until Father returns. I could not stay away when I heard the rumours—"

"But Master Fowler—"

"Master Fowler agrees that my place is with you," he said gently, squaring his broad shoulders with a man's pride. Then, stifling a yawn, "I have ridden all night and I *am* hungry," he added wistfully, a boy again. "Let us both go back to the house and eat something, Mother dear. Bessie and Barbara—I met them—Bessie said I should persuade you, instead of staying here all day, catching your death of a fever." His sympathetic grin reminded her that she was not the only martyr to Bessie's mothering.

She gave one last longing look out to sea, glittering now grey and empty. Francis put an arm around her shoulders. "They will not return this way today. The wind will have taken them miles away up channel."

As he supported her, leaning heavily upon him, back through the grounds of Lennoxhoe, she breathlessly outlined her plan for him to take Barbara to the border country, and in the library she handed him detailed instructions of how to reach his aunt's house.

"But what of you, Mother?"

She patted her stomach. "I cannot travel without endangering the babe here. I will be safe enough," she added with a carelessness she did not feel, and handing him the Bible, said, "Swear, Francis, swear that you will get Barbara to safety. Swear that you will take no more risks—"

Bowing his head, he gave her his solemn oath.

Alone, she prayed that God would guide him. For all his bragging about how he could handle sword and pistol—so that Bessie had been lost in admiration for her onetime baby, murmuring constantly, "I knew it, I knew it"—Francis was but a green boy.

"But what of you, Mistress Jane?" wailed Bessie.

"I must remain here at Lennoxhoe until the babe arrives."

Bessie looked at her, knowing it was true. To travel, so heavy with child, would be dangerous for one expecting a normal confinement, but certain death for both her mistress and the babe. "Then Jem and me—we remain here too. We will take care of you, heart's darling. And the other servants are loyal—my Jem has put them through their paces, turned them into a regular army." Tucking the covers around her, she smiled. "Never you fear. The Good Lord is on our side. Wicked King Philip and his inquisitors are naught to God—"

Jane lay awake in the darkness, sleepless still, her hands across her stomach. There were now few movements from the babe who had been so lively at the fourth month. She thought of those other stillbirths and wondered if, like them, this babe was already dead, mortifying within her, to be taken away shrivelled, blue as a monkey. Stretching out her hand wearily, she touched the empty pillow beside her. Would Amyas's dear golden head ever rest beside her again? Oh, God—where was he? Help us, dear God—help us both.

As the night hours limped slowly away, her sombre thoughts were increased by the wind restlessly calling through the tall trees outside the window. Grateful when dawn touched the lovely room with its golden light and she knew the long night was over, she thought how she loved this house, so dear to her—and this, her bridal bed. She hated to think of her house in Spanish hands, greedy, rapacious talons stripping its treasures, ransacking closet and chest, the heartless smash of precious furniture and glass that could not be carried away—the house filled with the derisive laughter of its looters.

She must not think of it, see that scene in such vivid colours, for with the children gone she would be no witness to the rape of Lennoxhoe. By then she too would be safe.

She would be dead. Her own plans were carefully made. At the first crash of wood as the door splintered she would know the faithful servants were dead, or fled. At the first sound of heavy footsteps upon the great staircase, across the Long Gallery, she would take the pistol, Amyas's pistol, from under her pillow, trusting that somewhere out beyond the dark, he would find her again.

5

Maeve O'Neill had never been so afraid in her life. Not even the sweating, screaming clutch of childhood's nightmare touched upon the reality of the Armada's first battle after the explosion which shook the windows of Lennoxhoe.

The *San Salvator* had been sabotaged by a disgruntled Flemish gunner throwing a firebrand into her powder keg. She carried most of the King's money, the military chest of the expedition.

Maeve watched her float helplessly by, a hulk full of dead and dying men, scuppers running red with blood, abandoned to the English with the stench of death heavy upon the air. "A fine feather" abandoned to El Draque's plucking.

What she expected afterwards was another polite skirmish, a few shots interchanged in courtly chivalrous manner, with the English ships yielding to the Spanish might and disappearing like whipped curs, to leave the seas open for Spain's invasion. That was what she had been told to expect, like every other soul aboard the Armada.

She had not been prepared for the intensity of those merciless battles with no quarter given, the air filled with the acrid smell of gunpowder, the scream and thud of shot, the cries of wounded and dying men, of galley slaves trapped at the oars, of horses and sheep trapped in the holds—forlorn, piteous, and doomed.

When the fighting was fiercest, it seemed that the *Black Duchess* sailed towards the gate of hell, open and waiting to swallow them. Afterwards when the smoke cleared, to reveal crippled ships swaying on an empty sea, Maeve found it hard to believe that she had survived, she was still alive upon this frail ship. Alive too, thank God, were Felipe and Karim. Superstitiously, she felt that as long as they both lived she would be safe.

Once the ship fell into the hands of Mahmoud, then her own days would be numbered. Perhaps guessing his repugnance and terror for her, Mahmoud took an evil joy in tormenting her. Soft-footed as a cat, he possessed the ability to appear without warning, a dark shadow falling across her path. She stifled a cry, for his grinning face was so scarred and evil it was enough to strike terror into friend and foe alike.

She tried to slip past him, but he barred her path, seizing her arm playfully and leering down at her. Although he spoke no English, his gestures were explicit. She ran from him choking with fear, his coarse laughter at her heels. He grew bolder, springing out upon her and pinning her with his body against the cabin wall. Sickened, defiled by his vile touch, she cried out, but when Felipe poked his head out of the door the deck was empty.

Shuddering, Maeve wondered how Karim managed to keep his strange crew in check and from what hells he recruited men to his service, striking enough terror into even their savage hearts to give him obedience. Was it only sheer physical strength? As the fighting continued and casualties mounted among the crew, Maeve doubted that heroic idea. It was the privilege of pirates to take their victims by surprise, not to be targets for an entire enemy fleet. It was also their privilege to choose the place of battle according to its merits and to their advantage, since their superiority lay in speed and attack. Not by any stretch of imagination could she believe niceties of patriotic fervour or religious zeal influenced Karim's men. Whether King Philip or Queen Elizabeth were victorious, the *Black Duchess* and her crew would still be feared by both.

They knew only one allegiance—gain. That was it—the King's gold, contained in the chests in Felipe's cabin. Maeve shivered. That was why Karim's men had followed him so loyally. For a moment, eyes closed, she fell into the other world, the Place of All-Knowing, and saw the future unroll.

Mahmoud would take the gold and vanish into the morning. Karim, Felipe, and she would go to the bottom of the sea, where dead men and women can be relied upon to tell no tales.

She tried to warn Felipe, but sulky and sick, he shouted at her not to be more of an idiot than she could help.

After the screaming, the deafening roar, the acrid death, when the smoke died away and the enemy ship curled away from them, before the next ship appeared, she went on deck. With the other women she helped bathe and bandage the wounded, comforting the dying as best she could by holding wine to their lips, while watching their comrades throw the dead over the side, into the sea. Unshriven, with all their sins upon them. At first this brutal end horrified her, but she began to accept it, feeling pity for these poor heathen savages with their shaven heads, their tattoos and pitiful face ornaments. No doubt they had a god of their own who had their souls in his keeping—perhaps Karim's God, Allah. She felt compassion for her erstwhile tormentors, attending their terrible wounds as they watched her with great pathetic sad eyes, wounded creatures whose gaze reflected the same mortal agony as a deer dying in a forest glade.

Whether the *Black Duchess* was hunter or hunted, riding under the flagship's tall shadow, one battle was much like another as the Armada fought its way, mile by weary mile, along the Channel. Sometimes riding in stately formation, or breaking, running on the wind, the English fleet closed in, tearing at them like an angry wolf pack.

Maeve hated and feared the green and white spectres of the English ships, appearing here, there, and everywhere, bustling and brisk, expected and unexpected. The sea would be empty, then like a shadow thrown by the wind, the enemy ships bounced towards them on unreal waves, with puffs of smoke and slashes of light, straight across their bows. And when it was over, it was hard to believe that the doll-like figures she had seen reeling back, falling into the sea, had once been flesh and blood, torn and dying men. The very seabirds mocked their end, hovering in the skies, for they were never far from the sight of land. And how she hated those accursed white cliffs, unending, lining the path from the world to the gates of hell.

When the weather changed, as it did constantly, the sea too became the *Black Duchess*'s enemy, and Maeve began to think of the ship as having a soul of her own. She hated to see her wounded. The now sadly chipped face of the bold figurehead, the battered masts and spars, the broken windows of the cabin. She thought the sea hated them; its strange stirrings and whisperings suggested the presence of a monstrous being writhing under those endless green sea pastures. A hideous soul composed of shades and shadows, of lost, drowned dreams and ancient cities, of men and strange ships. Sometimes the monster pretended gentleness, turning a shining face, translucent and inviting, but Karim—who had the measure of his enemy —warned her:

"It is but a trick to deceive mortals. The sea never changes and cannot take kindly to men since all its being is wrapped in mystery. Lions and men do not make bargains, wolves and lambs have no compact. Nor do the fishes of the sea and the men of the earth."

Sometimes Maeve tried to plot their course on the charts in the cabin, as Karim pointed out some distant landmark. She was eager to learn, and he was surprised, for he did not expect females to have interest in such matters. He talked to her more than Felipe ever did, relating in his strange singsong voice tales of places he had visited and his long, happy life with his *Duchess*. He also talked of his death —but not from the Armada.

"Allah does not will that I shall spill my blood in this battle between Christians," he said, and Maeve was comforted, hoping that he too had the gift from the Place of All-Knowing.

"I fear no enemy ship, only a black-sailed unfamiliar, who carries in her wake the silence that is death, the call and signal that each man must obey, laying aside his joys and his sorrows to board her."

An unlikely friendship developed between the girl and the Arab captain, who could have crushed her frail bones in his strong hands. Even his villainy did not offend her, for in it there were shapes and grades, a semblance of integrity.

Once when Mahmoud had her cornered, Karim appeared. For a moment, without a word being spoken or a hand raised, red murder blazed across the eyes of both men, then Mahmoud walked away with insolent indifference, whistling between his teeth.

Karim put a hand upon her arm. "Have no fear, señorita, no man shall harm you on this ship while I live. And if, when we reach our destination in Scotland, you wish to remain with my *Duchess*, then it will be my privilege to sail around the north coast and take a princess of Ireland back safe to her own people."

Although her own secret plans to go to London and begin a new life there remained unchanged, she was grateful to the Arab captain, and it gave her a pleasant feeling of security against Felipe's rages that she had found one man she could trust.

As well as the fighting, the weather continued to take its toll of them. Two galleons had been disabled, and the captains rallied round Don Pedro de Valdes when the Admiral refused to wait for his damaged *Rosario*, another casualty from storm damage.

"The slow old tortoise was fast enough at abandoning his captains to their fate," said sympathetic commanders, and such treatment as Don Pedro received did nothing to improve the Admiral's rapidly growing unpopularity. However, sending word that his orders were to be obeyed at all times and without question, he reinforced his remarks by having the sergeant carry a halter ready to hang on the spot any officer, whatever his rank, who stepped out of line.

The Admiral's inability to make fast decisions was becoming notorious. At the Isle of Wight, almost a week after they had first sighted the Lizard with such glorious hopes, they found land so close the soldier crews begged for a chance to show their mettle in invasion. But the slow old tortoise delayed and frowned and lost the wind, which swung round to favour the English.

The *Black Duchess* saw the English ships on their flank headed by *Revenge*, proving once again that El Draque had recourse to his magic mirror.

Karim laughed at such an idea. "He needs no magic mirror to guess that morning land winds tend to veer into sea winds later. This is a common weather condition in these waters and well known to every experienced mariner."

Grimly the *Black Duchess* joined the other ships of *San Martin*'s squadron, tacking north against the wind trying for a better position —to find that Drake, taking full advantage of the initial smoke of the warning guns, had worked his way out to sea and was waiting for them.

When the battle was over, Maeve dreaded finding Felipe or Karim among the casualties.

The fierceness of the fighting had spurred on Felipe to take part, against the Admiral's express orders. He had been in no condition to walk, much less to fight, far gone in sickness, so weak Maeve had to buckle on his heavy sword.

"What Godforsaken idea of chivalry takes you out there? You will be more trouble to Karim than a dozen English ships."

"Shut up, bitch," he said, and tried feebly to slap her. She hoped his aim would be better should he face an English soldier. "Am I to be a coward to sit and watch men die, skulking in my cabin?"

"You might show some grains of sense. You are a sick man still—"

"There are others more sick—and dead—in their thousands. You have seen them like piles of slaughtered meat drifting past—"

"Which does not make your arm stronger to carry a sword—or your legs—"

She stepped aside and his blow descended on thin air. "Bitch, I would have killed a man who cast such a slur upon my honour." As he almost fell, she seized his arm to support him. "Stay away from me— Stay away—"

Maeve accepted his ill nature with good-humoured toleration of mother for fretful sick child, smiling at his tantrums, stroking his forehead, and laying on cool hands and compresses. She no longer hated him. Nor did she fear this poor sick creature whom she could have pushed over with one finger, so weak he was. In the days since they left Corunna, he had changed from an arrogant Spanish don who thought all women were there for his pleasure into a tired, frail lump of a babby, pathetically dependent upon her. Grateful for the varied materials at her disposal and always handy with a needle, she was filling in the idle hours making a new petticoat and kirtle. She would be glad of a replacement for that old cambric night-robe of his, which she wore girdled to her waist—

Hate him? Nay—no more than the poor heathen brown men. Except for Mahmoud—

Felipe had hardly left the cabin to fight than he was back again. He had hardly tasted the wine she offered than the signal was again flown: "Close and fight."

In a last desperate attempt for the victory he saw each hour carried further away, the Admiral ordered a series of attempts to close upon the wily English ships, in the forlorn hope that for his remaining soldiers the pike and sword might be brought into play. The arquebus and musket with their covering fire, sweeping from the tall castles, might yet cause havoc to the lower-built decks of the English ships.

But those ships were ready for them. Squadron engaged squadron, and such rapid firing had never been precedented in sea battle. Within minutes Felipe counted fifty shots lodged in the *San Martin*, breaking masts and rigging, while all around the Spanish ships were filling with dead and dying men, crowded on the decks for the boarding, which was now only a forlorn hope.

Crouched in the cabin, Maeve watched until the round shot grew heavy and pierced the window, sending clouds of glass and splinters of wood across the floor. Wiping blood from her face, her cheek grazed, she ran on deck, where there was utter confusion.

Neither Karim nor Felipe was visible through the dense smoke and fire belching from the guns. She had never been on deck during action before and, horrified, watched an English ship roll gently, lazily, towards them across a sunlit sea, meadow-green—

As she approached, tiny puffs of grey smoke broke prettily from her decks and both sea and sky reverberated to the roar of her cannons. Shaking the entire universe like a tapestry on a castle wall, thought Maeve, and so close she could have stretched out her hand and touched the enemy ship.

There were men staring across the *Black Duchess*'s bows, their words lost, their faces angry, contorted with rage. Maeve had never seen the hated green and white geometric pattern of the Queen's ships this close, and noticed the crudity of the painting, the tar-smelling surfaces—

She saw Felipe on its deck.

He was leaning toward the *Black Duchess*, sword upraised, shouting—

This was witchcraft—like the ship's name—drifting past:

The *Warlock*.

Felipe. In God's name, what foolhardy prank was this?

Now she saw him full face, and although he was Felipe's image, he was differently dressed, the shadow of a beard, not just an ill-shaven chin.

But he was still Felipe.

Felipe.

At that moment she turned and saw him leaping up the steps. She looked again at the *Warlock*'s deck. She was seeing Felipe's shade reflected, a sure sign of death.

"What do you here?" he demanded. "Get you under cover—go—"

Holy Mother, this was witchcraft indeed! She crossed herself quickly.

"Go—I say—" And he dragged her by the shoulders, putting his body shieldlike between her and the open deck.

"Nay, Sir Captain—look—"

Startled by her white face, her pointing hand, her whisper:
"Over yonder—look—"
Through the smoke he saw himself clearly on the enemy deck.
And Felipe knew that he had come face to face with Amyas at last.

Karim was a brave man, but a superstitious one. He knew that the spectre leaning across the rail of the English ship, the *Warlock*, meant death.

"Allah be merciful," he prayed. For this was his second meeting with the One who bore his beloved master's face. A year ago his *Duchess* had chased an English merchantman to board and take as prize. A lively battle, and when victory seemed certain for the *Duchess*, the treacherous wind changed, carrying the prize beyond her reach.

Karim's last sight as the cannon smoke faded was the captain of the English ship. He was no stranger. He was Don Felipe. Karim could have killed him, his pistol raised. He was near enough to see the man's expression, thus faced with death. As thoughts trickled through his head, like sand through glass, he noticed one difference. The man before him was bearded, and unless Don Felipe had the power of sorcery, he could not have left him two weeks ago clean-shaven in El Escorial and now find him so on an English ship in the Mediterranean.

Karim let his arm holding the pistol fall to his side. It was death to see such an image. He had told no one; to speak the words would give power to the Evil One to make them come true. He swore he would never tell Don Felipe; he would forget the encounter, pretend it belonged to the world of nightmare.

Now instead of falling upon his knees and praying to his God for deliverance, he saw Felipe rush forward onto the exposed area of the deck. Regardless of the thud of shot, the breaking splinters of wood, he waved his arms, yelled a name:

"Amyas."

"Keep back, Master, keep back," yelled Karim.

The ships were passing broadside in a roar of cannons. The English ship was slipping away. Karim called again, but his words were lost in the screams of the wounded who fell on both sides. His beloved master had lost his reason, a madman shouting, yelling one word:

"Amyas—Amyas—"

He saw the Irish girl wrestling with him, heard her scream:

"Nay, Sir Captain—stay—"

Karim waited no more. Leaping across the deck, he seized Felipe, who with superhuman strength fought him off, cursing, and raced ahead, into the thick of the fighting.

"Amyas—Amyas—"

But Felipe's words were lost in the thunder of battle roar, and of Amyas only a profile remained, a glimpse of golden head and beard under the helmet—

"Amyas—"

"*Master!* Look to your right!"

But he never heard Karim's warning as in the next instant the air all around was torn apart with red sharp knives which lifted him into the air and hurled him down into space. He saw Maeve's horrified face and that she was spattered with blood—his blood.

Even then he did not believe what was happening. Disappointment was stronger than fear, more bitter than death.

Amyas had gone without seeing him. Not one word, not one glance—

Oh, what an empty, sad place, this world—

And if this was death, then it hurt less than he had expected.

Unaware of aught but the necessity of saving his ship, rapidly being cornered by the approaching galleons, Captain Lennox gave the order to break off the fight and extricated the *Warlock* from the clutches of the nearest galley.

His second-in-command, a young man named Peter Hawkins, raced to his side.

"Captain, Captain, we saw you fall! We saw you die!"

"You see me safe," said Amyas, but his smile changed to concern as Hawkins poured out a story that he, aye, and the whole crew, had seen a man they thought to be himself walking the deck of the Spanish ship.

"His dress, the leather doublet and cuirass he wore, was of the enemy style—but in all other aspects, Master, he was cast in your image."

"The name of this ship?"

"*La Duquesa Negra.*"

"The *Black Duchess*. God's love, man, we met her once before."

"Aye, Captain. Never will I forget. Black Karim."

Now Amyas had the answer to why the Arab pirate's savage hand bearing the pistol had been lowered. The expression Amyas had taken for mercy had been fear.

Fear that struck memory's chord and brought similar recollections. The power of superstition. Maids flying before him and his cousin Felipe de Montreuse in the kitchens of Holyrood Palace.

"What became of—this man—you thought to be me?" Even as Amyas asked the question he knew the answer.

"Dead, Captain. He fell to one of our men. Shot through the head."

Amyas saw little of the hours that followed. He hardly noticed that there was cause for jubilation that the Battle of the Isle of Wight had been won, the Queen's ships victorious.

As he inspected damage to the *Warlock*, encouraging the wounded—praising God there were no deaths—his thoughts were with the pirate ship that had long since quitted the scene.

So his cousin had served with the Armada. He forgot the present, which turned them into enemies, and remembered that they had once been close—as brothers—a long time past.

Guilt of his own omissions in those promises of eternal friendship came to him as he paced the deck. Not only had he ceased to write to Felipe, but he had almost entirely forgotten him over the years, and had finally been the instrument of his death, since he had died of a bullet from the *Warlock*.

The *Warlock*'s sails were empty as she joined the remainder of Drake's squadron, and he, like the other captains, oversaw repairs to damaged masts and sails. He learned with gratitude that throughout the squadron that day the human casualties had been few so far. A handful dead, a score injured—

Peter Hawkins informed him that they were gravely short of

powder and shot. Like the rest of the squadron—and the entire English fleet—they required reinforcements urgently. The *Warlock* received the same curt message: As all ships were in like state, they must guard their supplies against further engagements until such time as they were furnished with replacements.

"We must put on a brag countenance," said Lord Howard sourly, since his flagship was in similar plight.

Conscientiously, no matter how tired was Amyas at the day's end, he wrote up the log of his ship: "Our ships are more workmanlike than the splendid Spanish galleons, but less impressive. This day the fleets were well in sight, and action continued from morning until darkness made it impossible to see our targets, with such expenditure of powder and bullet that it might have been judged a skirmish with small shot rather than a fight at sea. The rate of our fire astonished everyone, since all were used to laborious slow cannon fire. At one stage the sea was so calm we could see the cliffs and the onlookers on the Isle of Wight. One ship after another brought their guns into action, and when it cleared we saw the Armada poised hard against us had been carried away. The fickle wind proved again my lord Admiral Howard's greatest ally in adversity, mocking the Spaniards' hopes.

"We were so beleaguered by a pirate ship . . ." he began, and carefully crossed out the sentence. He wished to forget the encounter, for he had a superstitious feeling mounting to terror that he had been the unwitting cause of his cousin's death and that by committing such an event to paper put upon it the final seal.

The battle of the Armada was now a week old, and as the fine weather remained with them that following morning as they awaited reinforcements, they had the satisfaction of knowing that the Spaniards too were becalmed, their distant sails also empty. Many of the ships were keeled over while the shot holes, evidence of the superior marksmanship of the English, were plugged near the waterline.

But blue skies and seas and gentle calm remained. On that Friday, August 5, Admiral Lord Howard summoned his captains to the *Ark Royal*, bedecked with flags as suited a festive occasion. He greeted them as Her Majesty's lieutenant and exercised the ancient privilege of bestowing immediate rewards upon those who had borne themselves so in battle as to deserve the highest honours.

In the ceremony which followed, knightly accolades were given. One of the astonished recipients was Amyas Lennox, who had considered his *Warlock's* performance "but part of the day's work, and for my own share undeserving of any such high honours. Beseech you be glad, dear wife," he wrote to tell Jane, who would be pleased for her family's sake. "Care for our unborn babe and for thy dearest self, which is the greatest treasure to thy Adoring Husband . . ."

From the deck a cheer arose, and he discovered that reinforcements had arrived at last. They had been taken from the *Rosario*, seized as prize and towed into port with its angry Captain de Valdes, who was now a most happy and illustrious prisoner.

Amyas added a note to Jane's letter: "I hear that the Queen is presently at Richmond and showing great courage, not one whit dismayed. All at Lennoxhoe should be resolved to be of similar heart at this example set by Her Majesty."

Sealing the letter, he stared at the backs of his hands, so rarely idle. His fingers were long and tapered, elegant hands from the painting of a Spanish grandee rather than an honest English merchant captain's. Guiltily he remembered they were also Felipe's hands.

When Felipe was carried into his cabin and laid upon the bed, Maeve did not doubt that he was dead.

The scene before her was already familiar, as if it had been played out over and over in the dark depths of her soul. In the Place of All-Knowing there were laws other than those dictated by sweet reason. Upon that strange shore time ran backwards, forwards, surging like the tides of the sea.

Relieved to see the mirror came from his lips still misted and that he lived at least for the moment, Maeve staunched the blood from his head.

To Karim's anxious "Will he live?" she answered, "Perhaps so. The shot is not embedded."

"Perhaps the fall did more damage, señorita—twice a man's height—"

"We will soon know. If he recovers, he is not likely to make light of any injuries, I assure you."

Karim bowed. "Take good care of him, señorita. He has much to be grateful for—many men would envy him so gracious a nurse." He smiled and laid a hand lightly upon her shoulder. "Myself among them."

"Would to God he had your patience, Karim."

"He had many lovable qualities," said Karim sadly.

"Then I never saw them." Suddenly Maeve threw up her hands. "What are we saying? We are talking of him as if he was dead already." She shook her head, her smile mocking. "I daresay Sir Captain will survive to plague us all—he would be a torment to the angels in paradise, this one."

Two days passed before Felipe wearily opened his eyes. Two days of vicious unabating storm, which had wiped away the fine weather like a smile from a man's eyes and, tearing at them with daggers of wind and sleety rain, had the entire Armada fleeing before it to seek refuge on the French coast, at Calais.

At least Felipe had not been troubled by seasickness this time. He had lain unmoving, like a dead man. Maeve had never seen so much blood, but still the feeble guttering candle of life remained.

Raising a hand, he touched his head and winced. The cloth Maeve removed was bloody.

" 'Tis but a scalp wound, but they do bleed."

Had he been hurt by the fall? Cautiously he moved arms and legs, found that naught troubled him but a mightily sore head.

"Another fraction of a metre, Sir Captain, and you would be finished with sore heads forever," she said grimly.

"I was indeed fortunate." And he smiled on her, apologising for being so much trouble, a great babby.

Karim was greatly relieved to see his master conscious and taking sips of wine—and in moderate spirits. In reply to his question regarding their present position and how the battle had fared, Felipe was pleased to learn that he had missed the storm.

"Fearing that the currents would carry us out of the Channel and into the North Sea, His Grace gave orders that we head for Calais and seek the protection of the Governor for our ships until the weather changes. With a town so near, Master, we would do well to send out one of our boats for fresh water, bread, and fruit. His Grace need know nothing," he added with a grin. "My men know where to look; they are good at finding fresh victuals, good wine, fresh-baked bread—"

Felipe's mouth watered at the thought. He took a bag of coins from under his pillow. "These for their silence, Karim. Now I know nothing of your plan and have quite forgotten you discussed the matter with me."

"There is one other matter. Under cover of darkness the men will be rowing into harbour with empty boats. The harlots expected that we should be victorious by now. They grow bored with delays and sea life. They wish to seek more congenial company." Karim nodded towards Maeve. "Perhaps the señorita should accompany them."

"If she so desires." Felipe almost hoped she might refuse. "Well, señorita?"

Maeve shook her head. "Nay, I continue to Scotland"—and with a flash of a secret smile to Karim—"thence to Ireland?"

"Perhaps we have little more to fear from the English," said Felipe.

"Master, our troubles are not over yet—it is doubtful indeed if they plan to let us calmly sail back to Spain without a fight."

A noise on deck had him leaping out of the cabin, to return a minute later, replacing his drawn dagger with a sigh. "Would to Allah, Master, that we were under sail again. I fear this place. I do not enjoy being in Calais with the entire English fleet to my seaward side." He sniffed the air like a hound at bay.

"El Draque?" queried Felipe.

"Aye, and his fire ships, for we are a sitting target, inviting disaster."

During the hours of darkness Karim and Mahmoud led an expedition into Calais and returned with fresh capons, fish, bread, fruit, and some excellent vintage wine. Karim also brought the latest gossip.

"Cádiz and the fire ships are also occupying the solemn thoughts of the Governor. He was unimpressed to find his harbour occupied by the ships of the Armada—uninvited. To His Grace's personal message of goodwill and plea for succour he suggested politely that His Grace should not tarry long in Calais without endangering the fleet, since a further change in the weather might make the Armada's position unpleasant, not to say downright dangerous."

Karim also reported that throughout the fleet Drake's fire ships were occupying most men's minds and the talk among the captains was mutinous. "Where was the glory of hiding in port? Where were the sweet fruits of victory which the Duke promised at the beginning of the campaign, the skirmish with a poor inferior foe, hardly worthy of their steel?"

"He has made us appear in the world's eye as a flock of sheep, Master," said Karim grimly. "Herded up and down a tortuous long sea lane, led by an efficient shepherd boy."

They had further cause for alarm at dawn, for under cover of night the English ships had approached and lay anchored at full strength, little more than a cannon shot from the nearest galleons. As the day brightened the sea remained empty of the flyboats His Grace had begged the Duke of Parma to despatch in all possible haste from Dunkirk. Fortune and the notoriously fickle Duke had both deserted them.

Gloomily the beleaguered Spaniards watched the English ships firmly anchored to their east and heard their captains' signal across the smooth waters. Soon bold hymns drifted across to them as Communion was celebrated throughout the fleet and upon every deck knelt noblemen in best ruffs and velvets, captains in steel and leather, alongside half-naked sailors, while the sun gleamed like a benediction on bare heads reverently bowed as the Host was passed from hand to hand.

The Spaniards were not to be outdone in the matter of piety. Soon the English heard during their silent prayers the sound of ships' bells tolling the solemn moments of the Mass from the enemy ships. This put ministers on their mettle, assuring the men they had nothing to fear for Almighty God had proved Himself to be of the Protestant faith, while friars addressed similar assurances upon the Spanish ships that His Holiness the Pope and the saints were on their side and God Himself could not abide a heretic.

To Maeve, at the cabin window of the *Black Duchess*, there was a certain irony in the situation of English and Spanish alike impertinently imploring God for His assistance to slaughter their fellowmen, whom God had also created.

She said so to Felipe, who laughingly said he should have been to Mass but was not yet strong enough to go over to the *San Martin* and did not want to alarm the Admiral by his present appearance.

Maeve surveyed him critically. There was little to complain of in his present appearance. He had bathed and, with her assistance, dressed and shaved. He was strong enough to do full justice to the banquet Karim had set before them on the cabin table.

Sucking a bone reflectively, he said, "Our little drama is now almost complete. Soon we will be in Scotland, with the sounds of battle just a fleeting memory." He paused, watching Maeve. The green velvet kirtle did pretty things to her eyes. Astonishing that a princess of Ireland could be so good with her hands in fashioning such a garment. A domestic creature, indeed, different from the maidens of Spain, he thought regretfully. She had been most useful to him—

"I have been thinking—the matter of your journey to Ireland."

She shrugged. " 'Twill be an easy one—do not concern yourself—"

"Indeed I must. You must remain under my protection until I can make arrangements for some reliable escort back to your uncle of Tyrone." He unrolled a map. "See, here—the Scottish coast and our meeting place, north of Aberdeen. To the west—here—Inverness, from whence you might take ship to Ireland. I will see to it personally that you reach Inverness—"

"Nay, Sir Captain, it is not necessary—"

He shook his head. "A princess of Ireland cannot clamber about unreliable heath country and uncharted lanes like a gypsy."

"I am grateful—"

He was disappointed. She did not sound as grateful as he had hoped.

After all, he would be putting himself to considerable inconvenience.

"Let us worry about the journey once we reach Scotland, Sir Captain. I do not like to cross bridges thus—"

So that was it, a childish superstition. He smiled. "Please, no more Sir Captain. I have a name."

Karim entered with several more trays of the freshest, most succulent food they had seen since leaving Corunna. When he bowed himself out again, Felipe poured her a goblet of wine.

"To our success—Maeve," he added, using her name shyly.

"To our success, Philip."

"Philip?"

"I have a fondness for the name. 'Twas my brother's—"

"This brother—"

"Dead, long since. A sweet babe, I loved him dearly."

The word *love* brought awkwardness between them, and Felipe, raising his goblet, said with undue haste, "Then Philip I shall be from this day forward, if it pleases you." He paused before adding, "What of your family back in Ireland?" And when she shrugged: "You are alone then? No brothers to protect you—no sisters?"

"Sweet Jesus." Her laughter was an explosion. "Brothers and sisters by the dozen." At his surprised look: "If they still live; all were babes when I left." And she spared a shuddering thought for the wild, ragged tribe of snot-nosed screaming urchins, trained to be thieves from their earliest days, cruel, vicious, verminous. God forgive her, but she had never felt blood bond for such creatures—except for Philip, gentle and doomed. But at Felipe's shocked glance she said:

"Everyone has swarms of brothers and sisters."

"I had not." There was envy, and a touch of reproof. "I had no one."

How glorious—how pleasant to be alone, she thought. Not to have to fight over every crumb, share every shredded, tattered garment, not to have responsibility as eldest to every screaming brat one's mother bore, to watch one's treasures snatched to placate a yelling sibling, then broken in its cruel, greedy fist.

"I had only one cousin," said Felipe.

"One cousin." Maeve choked. "Jesu, I never counted mine. Hundreds there were—"

Felipe did not smile. "Aye, a cousin—and a twin too." And leaning over, refilling her empty goblet, he was telling her:

"Remember the man you saw," watching indifference change to interest as the story impressed her imagination as the people in Holyrood had been impressed long ago by two people who shared one face but were not brothers from the same womb.

How proud he was, she thought, of his English captain cousin—and how afraid that they would meet again in battle.

Aye, he was proud. And she saw that he was lonely too, the loneliness that is a sickness and fear deep in the heart. She wondered why, studying him with a woman's critical eyes.

When he was not sick or whining and arrogant, he was a comely man. She assessed a face tanned gold, small ears set behind the wide cheekbones, hazel eyes, friendly and intelligent, and above them a long forehead with hair like tarnished gold. Had she met him in different circumstances, she knew she would have been attracted by such a face, the fine features sculptured into a warm and sensuous whole. The effect was pleasing, for although he belonged to a social class and order where she would be forever serving in the kitchen, she could see that he was strong and handsome right enough, and that to a woman who loved him he would be a golden man indeed. For even the hairs on his hands, his arms, legs, and body, were golden. Only eyebrows and eyelashes were mysteriously dark, and the stubble of an unshaven beard. She thought idiotically that should she marry, a husband's body would have more secrets from her than this wilful and stubborn stranger.

He was old to be unmarried, young to be a widower—

"Have you no thought to remarry, begin a dynasty of your own?"

"My efforts have not been spectacularly successful." He refused to go into more details which unmanned him, these puny, laughable attempts at matrimony.

"Your wife—"

"Dead," he said sharply, forgetting that he had told her some time ago. She was silent. Let her think he mourned her still, chose celibacy. It was better than the truth, that he had never in his whole life known a woman's love.

"What ill luck you have had."

"Aye, and I hope that it ends with this pesky voyage."

Maeve felt hurt, staring into her goblet. And then she found that it was not her company, but the ever present threat of sickness, he dreaded.

"You have never been at the sea's mercy. I wish you would impart your secret to me. I am no sooner over one attack than I feel another stealthily approaching. To be a fighting man and thus hampered—it is so ignoble—"

Maeve sympathised with pride humbled by such a confession. "There is no secret. I belong to an island race. We have had to learn the secret of friendship with the sea in order to survive. My grandfather was—" And she stopped just in time, having been about to say "a simple fisherman."

"Your grandfather was Tyrone—I know that. But I did not realise he had attachments to the sea."

"On my mother's side—a sea captain," she said hastily. She would have to do better than that if her deception was to last until they reached Scotland. If he found out now—the town of Calais was just across the water. "The sea gets into a man's blood."

"Then I wish it would get into mine." Smiling, "Tell me about Ireland, since I do not expect ever to go there."

As she described Tyrone's castle and the pretty countryside, making it sound inviting, he noticed there was a cautious reserve too, as if the matter were painful to her. This he dismissed as the stirrings of painful memories at her mother's death, her sojourn in the convent before her rascally father took her to Madrid.

How pretty she was. He found himself caring what became of her when they once landed in Scotland. He doubted she would reach her destination in Ireland unaided. Such a pretty wench would have as little chance as a brightly coloured singing bird escaping into the golden afternoon, the target of every predator, of every great ragged crow and hawk between Aberdeen and Inverness.

He was sorry, because the wine had a strange effect. It was making her almost beautiful. Such a waste that she would never survive that Highland journey. Aye, so pretty, soft, and warm. He let his mind dwell for a moment on the hidden and forbidden charms of this princess of Ireland, niece to all-powerful Tyrone.

He took a deep breath. "Now you shall sing for me." His voice was sharp, and she gave him a wondering look. Was he bored with her already? Smiling, he was refilling her goblet. "If you would be so kind?" he said gently.

She sang of Ireland, the songs of exile, first, then the songs of the heroes, of Conchobhar and the Children of Cailidin, of Cu Chulainn, and Genann of the Bright Cheeks. But when she sang of Deirdre of the Sorrows and her wild, passionate longing for Noisiu, their brief tragic love, her eyes were full of tears, her voice unaccountably sweet and seductive—

Felipe listened politely, unable to understand that any man or woman could be foolish enough—except in a fairy tale—to throw away the world and life itself for love. Still he applauded the song and she curtseyed, smiling, her glance almost coquettish.

"More wine—then sing again."

Her black hair was a cloud about her shoulders, soft and shining. Her eyes were green, dark and bright as emeralds, but unlike jewels, they were inviting— What was that she was saying?

"To our friendship." Holding up the goblet towards him a little unsteadily, he thought. Aye, friendship, that was what he wanted. He had never had friends except Amyas and Karim. Friendship with a wench was a new and not unpleasant experience. Mind you, he was in the mood for a little more than friendship—

Enough. Enough to have a friend; he could not ask for wonders since it was his ill fortune to appear unlovable to women. Oh, worthy, worthy friendship— Shared laughter too, with no possible regret lurking around tomorrow's dawn—except for the effects of this damned good wine.

"Have some more."

"Nay."

"I insist you drink with me—Maeve." Smiling again.

Maeve smiled back, stretching her arms above her head, shaking out her cloud of hair. Such excellent wine and good food had put her into a fine mood, where it seemed that the future must be all rose-coloured, soft as a feather bed, with no cruel, sharp corners to snag upon her happiness. The sad bad old days were gone. Tomorrow was overflowing with good fortune. There would be joy for the picking.

Aye, it was good to be alive for a day like tomorrow—and with such a handsome comrade to share it. Singing, talking, had taken away her last fears of Don Felipe. He was now Philip, the brother whom fate might have spared to her. Nay, she would never forget these moments in this great cabin, not even when she was an old woman; she would remember how once he had saved her from the crew and how a very special devotion had grown between them out of their first dislike, how danger bound them to each other—

She was conscious of his eyes across the table. "That is a pretty gown and well becomes you."

"And that is a handsome doublet."

"But not so pretty as your gown."

They both thought that was uproariously funny and fell to a rather childlike giggling. How like a man, thought Maeve, to take hours to notice her gown. How shyly to compliment her—but she liked this quality in him, no idle throwing off of dazzling compliments. He was no man for needless ingratiation—proud, arrogant. Looking into that face usually so stern, but at this moment transformed by smiles so rare as to be specially radiant, she thought he would be a devil if you met him on a bad day, but would move mountains to keep a promise made. His tender concern for her welfare, now that was remarkable.

She closed her eyes. A deserted shore—he ran towards her, arms outstretched, calling her name—

"Maeve?"

Automatically she held out her goblet for refilling. "I thought you slept and I had lost you," he said.

She smiled reassuringly. But she had been dreaming. She looked at the goblet with distaste and sighed. Wine haze was doing strange things, turning Don Felipe into a proper man, kind and chivalrous, a hidalgo. There were few his equal in the whole world and when you met them they were to be treasured like Holy Miracles—

And suddenly it was all over.

Although she blamed him, it was not entirely Felipe's fault, since wine had led to danger. He had gone in search of Karim and more wine. Alone in the cabin, Maeve decided to stretch her legs and found that they behaved in a somewhat unreliable manner. She was glad to lean on the carved bedpost and stare down upon that inviting bed. Her head was spinning—just a little rest to close her aching heavy eyelids—

Felipe came in carrying more wine, and the picture she presented was both graceful and provocative. Edging past her, he placed the wine firmly on the table, and as he did so the *Black Duchess* gave a sudden lurch.

Maeve put out her hand and the next moment, clasped in his arms, they staggered together off balance, and when he fell on the bed he carried her with him. For a moment they giggled helplessly, both apologising. Maeve was still laughing when he released her. Suddenly he seized her and kissed her in a very methodical way which made nonsense of any ideas she had that he was indulging in brotherly horseplay.

Embarrassed, she struggled to sit upright, to be free of him, laughing still.

He kissed her again, and she felt her body slacken under his hold. Fighting off the wine haze, she said:

"Nay, Philip." Her voice was not as firm as she hoped, and she was alarmed to see his face stripped of laughter, his countenance set in firm, stern lines. Even as he seized her roughly, pinning her shoulders hard against the pillows, she knew there was no plea—nothing—she could think of that would make him change his mind and release her.

She was trapped under him. "Nay—please—"

In answer he shook his head, pulling the kirtle aside, his hands on her breasts. Shivering convulsively, she fought to wriggle free of his body.

"Nay, Philip—for dear Jesu's sake—you promised—"

"I promised nothing—"

"Nay—nay—"

"Aye."

When it was over, the pain and the grudging recognition that her body had somehow betrayed her, that need had turned intended rape into seduction, she looked at his golden head resting on her shoulder, one bare arm imprisoning her.

Where was the tenderness, the sweet words of love, that her own daydreams and the old Celtic legends had promised when she gave her body to a man for the first time? Already he slept. She was forgotten—a thing of the past. Mother of God, he had ill-used her. Even his comradeship was a lie while all the time he schemed to have her, willing or no. He had robbed her of her most priceless possession, her maidenhead, that gateway to a rich, successful life via the highest bidder. All her plans for the future were set at naught, and she hated him—hated him.

And so she cried herself to sleep, to awaken to a signal gun from the *San Martin*. He was already standing by the cabin window, dragging on his shirt. There was a bright glow on the sky, although the day was far past sunset.

"What has happened?"

"El Draque and his devil ships have arrived."

Dragging on her kirtle, she followed him onto the deck, where the night already disgorged eight dark masses sweeping towards them at great speed. Each ship was defined by a strange flicker of light, and before their horrified eyes this flicker burst into red flames, blazing high into the dark sky punctuated by gun after gun firing itself as theS metal of their armament grew hot. Each flash and roar suggested a crew aboard, eager for a fight.

Karim had joined them at the rail. To the question in Felipe's eyes he shook his head. "They are not mere fire ships, Master, but *maquinas da miñas*, mining contrivances which will explode in volcanoes of destruction among our anchored fleet."

"What do we do then?"

"Be away with all possible speed before they reach us. I have already given orders—I stay for no slow old tortoise this time."

Karim had given orders to up anchors and bear away eastward a minute before the same order issued from the flagship, with an additional clause that once the fire ships passed they should return and recover the same position.

Perhaps other captains like Karim gave a derisive gesture in the direction of the flagship. Perhaps some loyal captains did not see or hear the Admiral's orders. With two anchors down and leaping flames threatening to engulf them, most captains were busy cutting cables with all possible speed and scrambling to unfurl heavy sails.

As each great galleon began to waver and shift, trying to avoid the gates of hell ablaze before them, within thirty minutes one hundred and twenty disordered ships had fled without direction into the night. Confusion reigned on every deck as ships fell rapidly leeward, with wind and tide destroying their last hopes of ever returning to their original anchorage. Disobeying the Admiral's orders was the smallest of their problems, with more pressing issues of collisions, shallow water, fire, and El Draque at their heels.

As the Armada ships scattered out of their way, the fire ships ground one by one onto the shallows along the shore east of Calais, to burn out harmlessly like great spent torches flickering by the water's edge. Daylight revealed the flagship standing guard over the *San Lorenzo*, pride of the galleasses, who had fouled her cable and lost her rudder. Helplessly, she lay aground the Calais beach. As other ships sheepishly reassembled, they were confronted with the full extent of the disaster, for there, protruding forlornly from the mud of Calais, lost beyond all hope of resurrection, were over two hundred anchors and as many cables. Although Drake's fire ships had not destroyed a single Spanish ship they had inflicted catastrophe without precedent by depriving the Armada of its disciplined formation and any hope of skilful battle order.

"The least of those anchors is worth five hundred ducats," murmured Karim, reluctant to leave the scene of such a prize. But with the English ships bearing rapidly down upon them, among the outlying ships, another battle had already begun. A pitched battle, this Gravelines, lacking organisation since the Spanish were in no tactical form and even the English had long since lost theirs. Confused, they remembered only to keep with the wind, hammering the enemy with every piece of round shot available, keeping them to leeward, forcing them along the dangerous seaward fringe of the shoals and ever closer to the shallows—

San Martin made the first stand, placing herself squarely in the path of the four English squadrons. But the English were no longer after "single feathers," and the Admiral saw that not even his flagship would be worth sacrificing if he let the other enemy ships pass. Windward of his fugitive Armada, he fell back fighting, acting as cover for the rest while trying to induce any ship able to see or hear his distress to rejoin.

His call was heard by the *Black Duchess*, who, thanks to Karim's skill, had remained close to the flagship's side throughout the campaign. She now tacked toward him with pleasing promptitude, and the Admiral was grateful that she looked remarkably trim and had sustained little but superficial damage. He was further gratified that of the eight ships lost so far, five were by weather, one by collision, one by internal sabotage, one by boarding. But by English gunfire there were none. God obviously watched over them still, and he prayed that His divine protection would endure.

He was glad of the *Black Duchess*'s support as together, with all guns blazing, they faced an apparent unending stream of enemy ships. At one stage Karim reported from the tops that most of the Armada had fallen too far leeward to resume any serious part in the fighting. They quivered like frightened dowagers at a safe distance, their heavy guns silent as in each ship the round shot dwindled and failed.

As if this were the signal the English awaited, they closed in and the Admiral sent a last, despairing "Rally and fight if you are able. If not, then haul up and beat away from this fatal coast with its threat of imminent shipwreck."

The fight had turned close and hot. Though it had begun at musket range, there were times when the ships were within a pike's reach of one another, within hailing distance, despite the din. The galleons, separated from their squadron consort, were battered by a dozen English ships at a time, choosing their own stations, moving around their prey at a leisurely pace, and giving broadside after broadside at close range.

The battle continued all that day, and as afternoon changed into a drizzling evening, the Admiral, who had ignored the English signal to surrender to Queen Elizabeth with honour, sailed to rescue yet another of his distressed galleons.

Crippled, the *San Martin* was leaking badly; and the loss of twenty-nine ships had been counted, with at least six hundred men killed and eight hundred more wounded in this one day's action alone. The English had not lost a single ship, and all sailed on proudly and moderately unscathed.

So too did the *Black Duchess*, either by some miracle or by Karim's excellent handling, although twenty men had been killed and another twenty injured. At one stage when the action was fiercest, the ship was surrounded by English ships. There was only one gap to leeward, and Karim decided to take it and chance not being rammed as he did so. Leaving the steering to Mahmoud, he leaped forward, sword in hand, and found himself cheek-by-jowl with an English ship whose decks were shrouded by a curtain of mist.

The signals to draw alongside and prepare to board were given, and Karim was gratified to see that he had a well-matched adversary, for the English ship was of similar tonnage to his *Duchess*. Already he felt the excitement, the blood-mounting delight, the stretch of each nerve and sinew. Here was his *raison d'être*, the gamble with life and death which made him a pirate captain without equal in the Mediterranean.

Now holding to the rigging, he saw the English sailors shouting: derisive faces, some afraid, some bright with blood lust equal to his own. Mahmoud had joined him, and in a solitary glance they assessed the situation, each knowing clearly the other's mind, for they had faced many such actions.

To Felipe, with pistol ranged, on deck and ready for action, the mettle of such men was admirable. The battles of the Armada had been to him a few hours of intense fear followed by long stretches of intense boredom. He envied men who knew not fear, the agony of certain death—or worse, to be maimed, forever unmanned. He knew that there were men who, wounded seriously in battle, did not feel the pain until afterwards, staring at broken bleeding limbs in surprise. *Fear* was a word uninvented by God or the Devil for men like Karim and Mahmoud, he thought, feeling his dry mouth and listening to the hammering of his own heart. If he must die, then he would try to do so with courage. But oh, it was such a great waste of the life he felt today was about to begin. He had wakened to the dark head of Maeve so close to his own, for the first time with hope—

Hope— He glanced back to where she remained hidden in the cabin, wishing he could have found words to tell her that he was grateful. But for this new experience the old tarnished words of love he had used in so many other women's arms were not fit to describe the rapturous joy. If die he must, then it was as a man happy and fulfilled—and she would never know—

In the rapidly fading light the smoke cleared, and Felipe saw that the scene before him was already familiar. There a few feet away was his cousin Amyas, so close they could have leaned over and touched hands.

This time there was recognition. From Captain Lennox's eyes the tense anger faded and delight took its place, delight and disbelief. His lips moved—something like "Alive," he said, then he lowered the pistol as, for a second from eternity, between the two men the battle faded.

The wind was changing. Even as Karim yelled an order to board, the *Warlock* began to slide away. The two men smiled at each other across the growing distance.

"Be damned if I'll kill you—cousin," yelled Amyas. "Thank God ye live."

"Aye, cousin-brother. God keep you."

He saw Amyas's head move in agreement, although it was not certain he heard the words, for the moment's indecision was fatal. One of the *Black Duchess*'s crew, seeing the two captains facing one another from his position above Felipe on the rigging, considered the English captain an excellent target. Afterwards he maintained that he thought the English captain was about to put a bullet through Don Felipe's brain and therefore, raising his own musket, fired.

Felipe saw the smile freeze upon Amyas's face. Then he plunged like a broken doll from the rigging into the sea.

Felipe turned, swore at the sailor, and plunged in after his cousin.

Surfacing, he saw nothing, then a head, with hair plastered tight to the skull. He recognised Amyas, and as he swam towards him recognised the irony that once before he had dragged his cousin out of the loch near Holyrood.

Drowning men were popularly supposed to see their pasts floating before their eyes and he wondered, Had all time swung backwards? Would they find that death was reality, life but a disordered dream? Would Amyas awake to find himself back in that boyhood loch with youth restored to him and life stretching ahead? If such a thing could happen to him, then Felipe recognised that would be paradise indeed.

But Amyas was dead. He neither moved nor struggled, his eyes were closed, his face cold and corpselike. "Oh, God, take pity—" cried Felipe.

"Master." Above the noise of battle and of the sea was Karim's voice. He saw the *Duchess* above him, his tower and strength. If only he could get Amyas aboard, perhaps Maeve could restore him to life. She was a witch, that one—

Thoughts tumbled through his head, sharper, more vivid scenes than the battle, the smoke from the guns still blazing across his head. Then he saw that Karim and the ship were slipping away from him on the tide. He could not keep up, swimming alongside with his burden. A spar drifted by. He seized it, thrust Amyas's limp body across it. For a moment he thought he heard a groan from the silent lips, but guessed it was but the scrape of body upon wood. He found other hands were helping him—Karim was beside him in the water, a dagger between his teeth.

"Master—come back to the ship or we are both lost—"

Felipe looked at the limp figure of Amyas drifting on the spar.

"Help me get him back—"

"He is dead, Master."

"Nay, Karim."

"Aye, Master—and so will we be— Look."

An English pinnace was fast approaching, the water around them peppered with musket shot. "Come—if he lives, they will take care of him."

And with a last despairing glance at the body of Amyas Lennox, Felipe ducked under the waves and followed Karim back to the *Black Duchess*. When they clambered aboard, he ran to the rail, but the sea was empty where the spar had been and of the English pinnace there was no sign through the smoke.

"Come, Master," said Karim, "for the battle is lost and the signal has been given. We are to make all haste for Scotland."

At that same hour when Felipe struggled to keep his cousin's limp body afloat above the waves, a struggle of yet another nature was taking place at Lennoxhoe.

Jane was dying.

The child had been born, long dead and mortifying in her womb. The labour, long and bloody, was over. Now she lay close to death, white as the pillows upon this, her bridal bed. Holding her hand and weeping sat Barbara, while old Bessie tried to make comfortable her dying mistress for the last time upon this earth, sobbing noisily as she did so.

Jane was glad the ordeal had ended and grateful for a pain-wracked body peaceful at last. In common with those who sail near the shores of eternity, she found her mind already remote from the sufferings of her dear ones, trying as they did to keep her near them in a world whose doors had already closed upon her.

She could not return to them, nor had she any desire to do so. She longed only for the silence of oblivion, the boon of sleep everlasting. She longed also to tell them not to grieve so, for she was beyond emotions of love or hate, drifting away on a cloud of indifference, to a shore where sorrow and human agony were unknown.

Yet strangely into those last moments on earth there glimmered a dream. An intrusion, for she thought of Amyas. Beloved Amyas, and there came a longing to see him so strong that it brought her drifting back to the noisome disturbing world she sought to leave, of weeping women gathered around her bed.

Opening her eyes, she looked towards the door and heard above her daughter's sobbing a footfall—

Amyas.

Then it seemed that the door opened and the bedchamber was flooded with golden light as Amyas ran towards her with outstretched arms. With her last strength she called his name.

"Amyas."

And as her spirit fled, Francis Lennox, who had just entered, closed his dead mother's eyes, her face still radiant, smiling upon his father's name, while all over England bells rang out their glad tidings and the last of the Queen's ships whitened the horizon with their sails.

As the English captains sped for home, the *Black Duchess* turned northwards and like a small forgotten planet riding the cruel cold North Sea, made for Scotland and the Catholic earls.

7

They were alone no longer. Into the eternity of sea, steel-grey and storm-swept, hooded by a dour sky, crept other Spanish ships. Battered, broken, listing heavily, they fled before the memory of the might of the Queen's ships. Flung helplessly in the unknown northern waters, with rudders and anchors lost at Gravelines, they fought to hold some sort of course while in every captain's mind there was but one thought: to escape back to Spain by the one clear way left to them—around the Scottish coast and Ireland. For, they argued, neither country was friend to Elizabeth of England.

The *Black Duchess*, under Karim's skilful seamanship and foresight, had fared better and was under the Duke of Medina Sidonia's direct instructions to proceed to her destination with all possible haste. His "God speed" to the *Black Duchess* had been somewhat ironically received, since their last glimpse of his compassion, as they swung away to the north, was a boat bearing from its yardarm the corpse of Captain de Avila. A grim reminder of the fate to be expected by those who disobeyed orders or conveniently forgot that the Duke in defeat was still Admiral of the Most Holy Armada.

Felipe was weary beyond sleep. Against his eyelids pressed the vision of Amyas plummeting from the deck of the *Warlock*— He was thankful for a diversion from this indelible scene when Maeve entered carrying into the cabin a tiny blue and yellow songbird, which had come to rest on deck from some flock of migrating birds disorientated by the gunfire at Gravelines.

"Poor mite," she said, resting her cheek against its tiny head.

It looked half dead, and Felipe said so. "Let me put it out of its misery."

She sprang back from his outstretched hand, clutching the bird to her breast, her eyes full of anger. Anger, yes, and hatred too, he thought uneasily.

"Don't you dare harm him. No one put you out of your misery when you were wounded," she added scornfully. She wasn't sorry when he looked ashamed, for he had a charmed life, this one. God was obviously saving him for other things than death on the Armada. Twice he had escaped death by a hairsbreadth—

Against all Felipe's gloomy predictions the bird Maeve called Sweetling survived. To his own surprise, because he wanted to please her, he had Karim bring up a small wicker basket and with the aid of a sharp knife and some twine he adapted it into a cage—

"Not a cage—a home," said Maeve stubbornly. "I cannot abide anything to be caged. When we reach Scotland, I shall let him fly away to be with his own kind."

Alone Felipe stared sourly at the bird, who disturbed his rest with its rapturous song. Wearied by the sight of the struggling ships whose tossing motions affected his uneasy stomach, he had retired to the cabin, whose handsome glass windows had long since vanished. The once luxurious cabin was now a sodden ruin, furnishings and tapestries unrecognisable, the canopied bed with hangings stained from the spray of heavy seas. As he closed his eyes, that accursed Sweetling dared to sing joyously, as if the world were newly born in all the innocence of Eden—

"Quiet—quiet, I say—" His request for silence ignored, he threw a rolled-up chart at the cage, but after a reproachful squawk and a flutter of wings, Sweetling reinstated both balance and song once more.

Maeve must remove it from his sight. "Maeve?"

Why was she never there when she was needed? Groaning, he staggered over to the cage and opened the makeshift door. He must be rid of the stupid creature. Just an ounce of feathers he could crush in his hand. He seized it and found little resistance, only the bright bead of an eye watching him curiously. How soft and trusting, not even an attempt to peck him. His fist tightened—

There was a sudden convulsive struggle of protest as fear darkened the bright gaze. Hastily Felipe thrust it back into the cage. That moment's fear had been almost human. In it he had also seen Amyas's face as he plunged headlong into the sea—and Maeve's face when he made a sudden movement in her direction—

Terror was akin to all creatures. He shook his head. He could not strangle that maddening noisy bundle of feathers. He wondered—Should he leave the door open as if by accident? But instead of seizing the chance to fly away, Sweetling merely stood on the threshold puffing out his feathers importantly and, as if near-death had not occurred, continued to sing in a determined manner.

Grumpily returning to his bed, Felipe heard the sound of cheering from the deck. That could mean only one thing—land had been sighted.

Racing on deck, he found the crew staring down into the sea, yelling encouragement. In an attempt to lighten their cargo one of the great transport urcas had jettisoned the animals, including horses and mules, which would not now be needed for the English invasion. The beasts floundered in the heavy sea, which did not, however, drown their piteous cries.

The cheering crew found this excellent sport and now laid wagers upon the frantic animals that swam alongside, trying vainly to keep pace with the galleons. The agonies of sheep were soon over since the weight of sea-soaked wool pulled them down beneath the waves. The mules swiftly followed until only the great heroic Spanish horses remained. The white-maned stallions, swimming with determination and strength, trying desperately to stay with the ships, wild-eyed and terrified, but stubbornly, gallantly, refusing to die—

The crew of the *Black Duchess* and every other galleon in sight urged them on with curses and praise, until a merciful fog descended, hiding the remaining horses and turning the other ships into uneasy ghosts drifting in a queasy sea. The strange horse race at an end, the crew departed glumly, quarrelling over who had won and who had not.

At Felipe's side, Maeve dried her tears. He put an arm awkwardly around her shoulders, trying to comfort her.

"They are God's noble creatures," she said indignantly. "And they have life and beauty—feelings too, the saints help them." Her rage was as great over the drowned animals as for the luckless Captain de Avila. She amazed Felipe that amid so much mortal suffering she could find time to cosset a singing bird and weep over the fate of dumb beasts.

"I must feed Sweetling," she said, and Felipe followed her reluctantly, lingering outside the cabin expecting her shrill cry of despair at finding the bird flown. He was astonished to hear only her gentle cooing, and found Sweetling perched on her finger pecking at crumbs. The joy on her face, the tenderness and love moved him, and he was thankful indeed that he had not strangled the silly creature.

"Thank you for letting him stay," she said.

Did she know she was smiling at him almost tenderly? Felipe went forward, and pretending to admire Sweetling and approve of his cleverness, he put his arm about her and, shyly drawing her head against his shoulder, kissed her cheek. He thought he heard a fluttering sigh, but her "Nay, sir, have done," was firm enough. Pushing him away, she became busy about nothing.

Felipe was furious. So that was how she showed her gratitude. She need expect no more tenderness from him.

Sweetling proceeded to show his gratitude by enjoying his new life to the full. The broken window did not interest him as a gateway to freedom. He hopped about the floor, or sat on the edge of Felipe's chair and sang. Maeve was delighted, while Felipe dourly restrained comment upon the droppings which she appeared not to notice, so proud was she of her singing bird.

Sighing, he stared out of the window. If only the sun would shine again, with perhaps a drying wind. For the past few days when he was not sick he was always cold, his clothes damp. Hungry too—like everyone else on the *Black Duchess*.

There was one way to forget. And sometimes Felipe would have enjoyed making love to Maeve, but he knew no words to tell her, to shyly explain his need. If he touched her during the day, she sprang from him, and friendliness evaporated; she regarded him with the apprehension of a forest creature at bay.

Ill at ease in her company most times, he decided he would be thankful when their paths divided, if ever they reached the Scottish coast. But after Sweetling came, was it only the need for bodily warmth and comfort which drew her close to him as they slept? He remembered how once she had lain shivering as far away from contact with him as possible, with no alternative to sharing his bed since the window seat was now fully exposed to the elements. However, it made no difference now. All desire for her had fled since he was plagued by returning seasickness.

When his head was not too sore, they parried careful conversation, like duellists, and the little bird's well-being became their one vital interest. Yet sometimes Felipe fancied that she sighed, her face wistful as she looked at him. And meeting those wounded eyes, he felt that she awaited some development, comment or apology, but he could not think of what he had done to displease her recently, or summon the healing words for their sad relationship. Which suggested a lifetime's marriage, soured by boredom or infidelity. Inescapable, but with everything said between them long ago.

Damn this ship—damn it to hell—and Maeve O'Neill with it.

He slept little, and she cried in her sleep as if the self-imposed silence during the days erupted in nightmares of grief. He took her in his arms and made gentle love to her as the only way he knew of expressing the emotions she aroused in him. Next morning, because she had no longer fought his will, he hoped for smiles and received instead sighs and sorrowful glances from those bruised eyes, hurt beyond human comfort.

"An enemy ship, Master—"

He followed Karim on deck and saw drifting towards them out of the fog the green and white of England's navy.

Karim hailed her with a warning shot across her bows while the crew at gun positions awaited a returning blast. There was none. Another salvo. Again they waited. Now they could see her name: *Rosie* —her decks weirdly empty.

"Looks as if she's been abandoned," said Karim, "unless this is some trick."

With grappling irons they brought her alongside, the crew boarded her with drawn swords, Mahmoud in their lead. Moments passed before he reappeared.

"Only a few men—dead ones, Capitaine. But she's in good shape, seaworthy. And there are victuals—bread, wine, meat—"

Following Karim across, Felipe found Maeve at his side.

"You stay—"

She shook her head. "I am coming too. I can make myself useful for once."

Cautiously they opened cabins modest and tidy which spoke of the merchant mariners of England. "She has been recently armed with guns and cannons. Undamaged except for a few shot holes," reported Mahmoud. "Her crew—seven dead men, scattered around the ship. Not killed in action—no blood—"

Karim returned from his inspection with a hand to his nose. "Bloated, they smelt vilely—as if they died with some sickness," he told Felipe.

With no opposition to fear the crew gleefully ransacked the ship, eager as small children. Maeve found the captain's quarters and gathered dry bedding, warm blankets. At least they would sleep more comfortably, she thought gratefully. Opening a chest, she found fine cambric shirts, breeches, and in a closet a black woollen cloak.

The silence was broken by a footfall, a shadow in the doorway behind her. Stifling a scream, expecting to see Mahmoud's grinning face, she beheld Felipe.

"Must you always walk like a cat stalking prey?" she demanded angrily, thrusting the garments into his arms. When Felipe disdainfully fingered their coarseness, she said, "Perhaps not the fine clothes you are used to wearing in El Escorial, but they will keep you warm and dry."

Ignoring her presence, Felipe was already stripping off his garments, since everything he possessed had been ruined by contact with the sea. The English captain had been short and stocky. Only his shirts would fit tall Felipe— The moment's laughter was an infinitesimal bond—

"As for this," he said, wrapping the cloak around her, "you shall have it. You will need it for your journey. I seem to remember that summers are treacherous in Scotland."

Fastening it, his hands close to her chin, he saw the terrible child-like fear his nearness brought had been replaced by an expression older, wiser. Moving his hands to her shoulders gently, he clasped them firmly and kissed her forehead. Mutely she raised her face and he kissed her gently, so as not to frighten her. Then, taking her hand, cheerfully he led the way back on deck.

Karim was waiting. "We have come to a decision, Master. Allah has been merciful and has given us a worthy prize. Mahmoud will sail her close to the *Duchess* until we see you safely to Scotland." He looked at his crew with satisfaction, their arms full of spoils, clothes, and draperies grotesquely worn. Perhaps this would make them forget the misery of this cruel northern weather, disastrous to the survival of southern men, Arabs, negroes, mulattos. Used to working almost naked, they possessed no garments worthy of the name against such weather. And he knew that fearing Black Karim, they took their grievances to Mahmoud's ever willing ear—

As for Maeve, the encounter with the *Rosie* had increased her instinctive distrust of Mahmoud, his smile, his unctuous presence. She felt she must warn Felipe, risking his scorn. However, the headache threatening her since the return from the ship finally broke and like a storm engulfed her. Shivering, she wrapped herself in one of the purloined blankets and crawled into bed, welcoming oblivion. She awoke, in the dark, from a bad dream about Mahmoud, and the feeling of danger was everywhere. She stretched out her hand, touched Felipe, who groaned and moved away from her. Should she risk his anger? She felt ill, her head hot, aching, her mouth dry. She was in no condition to face Felipe's scorn. The warning must keep until morning. Perhaps the sickness would have passed and she would feel stronger then—

Morning came too late. Felipe awoke to Karim shaking him awake. The *Rosie* had disappeared under cover of darkness, with Mahmoud and half of the *Black Duchess*'s crew. There was worse to come.

"The King's gold, Master, they have taken the chest with them," whispered Karim.

Although he cursed, Felipe was almost relieved by this turn of events. Without the gold, which was his passport to the Catholic earls, his mission to Scotland was useless. Without gold he need not delay his return to Spain, he would be rid of ships and sailing—he hoped—for the rest of his life.

Karim agreed with his decision. "There will be no invasion of England until another Armada can be prepared. Lingering in these waters, Master, we are greatly at hazard."

"Very well. Set a course for the north of Scotland—and home."

He was aware of Karim's occasional glance at Maeve, huddled in the bed beside him. Turning to arouse her with the news, he was surprised that she had not wakened earlier. He knew her modesty, how careful she was never to be found in his bed in the morning by any member of the crew who might enter.

He touched her bare shoulder. She did not move. Thinking she was heavily asleep, he leaned over and discovered the reason for her passive acceptance of Karim's presence—

Body rigid, face bloated, Maeve was burning with fever.

His exclamation of horror brought Karim hurrying back.

"So—our little stowaway, too—"

"There are others?"

"Aye, Master. Several already this morning." He shrugged. "That accursed English ship must have been fever-ridden. There is little hope—"

He could not let her die. "Somewhere to the northwest of us is Scotland?"

Karim shrugged. "Aye, Master—a day, two days away." Already the seabirds' circling lament betrayed what their eyes could not see.

Felipe seized his arm. "Change that order—make for land with all possible speed."

The scimitarlike eyebrows rose. "Master, we may be still in English waters. To turn west would be to deliver ourselves into the hands of the Queen's ships. His Grace's order—" he added reproachfully.

"To hell with His Grace—obey *my* orders. You have dying men. If the sickness spreads, we will never reach Spain—let alone Scotland—alive."

Felipe was saved from treason by a capricious change in the weather. Out of the horizon black clouds leaped towards them, bearing an eldritch wind. Karim gave the order to shorten sail, but powerless before this new calamity, the *Black Duchess* drifted helplessly north—east, back once more into the ocean.

He explained to Felipe that the torn and damaged sails were unable to cope with the worsening situation:

"The wind has us by the throat, Master."

Expecting rage, he found only docile acceptance as Felipe anxiously hovered by Maeve's bedside.

"Do what you think best, Karim. But get us to land with all haste. For I fear she has little time—" Deathbeds are notorious for arousing conscience pangs in their beholders, and Felipe was no exception. Bewildered, he regarded this girl he had ill-used. The conscience he had not counted among his virtues drove daggers of remorse into him. She was going to die. Perhaps every passing second tolled her death knell—

Karim bowed. "As you wish, Master. And when the storm dies we will steer due east. Allah grant that we will land in waters where the Scottish earls will be ready to receive us with kindness—"

"Indeed, Karim—and succour for your sick crew," said Felipe encouragingly, with a wry smile at his own hypocrisy. Of course he must save Karim from the sickness, but most of all he must save

Maeve. A recompense to his conscience for taking the girl against her will, stifling her struggles, and using her like a harlot until at last she protested no more and lay in his arms, flesh to his flesh, bone to his bone as no woman, wife or mistress, had ever been before. And all the world's sorrow and glory had stared back at him from the depths of those sad, wise eyes, green as the sea, overflowing as the mortal storm.

There were no more protests, only resignation and the melting of flesh, of soul, this oneness he had never known encountered but that was like the end of a lifetime's quest. Far beyond the mere gratification of lust, the limits of his previous experiences, it brought a sense of completion, of hopeful thoughts that there might be more to bedding a woman than a pleasant hour's relaxation or the necessity of breeding.

And now she was going to die, he thought angrily, resentfully, cheating him of his newfound glory, the promise of shared joy, closing the gate upon his one bright brief glimpse of paradise. Gently he touched her limp hands. He had seen death before on the faces of two other women, his betrothed struck by mysterious sickness on the eve of their wedding and the wife who with his son lay dead in childbed. Even in El Escorial death was the constant companion of slave and courtier alike.

Now even the gross swelling of her countenance was fading, and he saw how death's shadow brought beauty again to the half-moon of eyelids, the crescents of sooty eyelashes, and a dainty nose dusted with the gold of freckles, the gentle humorous mouth.

Stroking the long black hair, he implored, "Maeve—Maeve—"

Waxy eyelids trembled, opened wide for an instant, revealing, like some enchanted sea cavern, a dark green microscopic world. There was an emerald flash of sheer joy, then slowly they glazed over, the white lids descended, taking her away from him—

"Maeve—Maeve—" He seized a mirror, put it to her lips, saw by the faint moisture that she still breathed. Frantically he touched her flesh, found it turning cold—cold—

Karim, hearing his voice, came in and stared at the girl with a sigh. "Ah, Master, she is dead then." His voice was sad, for he had truly liked this unusual female with her fine spirit.

Felipe turned upon him savagely. "She is not dead—see her lips. The mirror—here—her breath—"

"Permit me, Master," said Karim gently, and placed a hand upon her cheek, her throat, one bare arm. "She is already growing cold, see how like wax—" He shrugged. "Master, believe me, her spirit has fled—"

"It has not. I tell you she lives." Felipe's mind was full of anguish, alternating with daggers of pain from his stomach as the renewed heaving of the ship threatened to bring back his own devil of sickness again. "Go, Karim, for Jesu's sake," he said weakly. "If you cannot help—"

"None can help—"

"Then don't stand prating like a fool."

Felipe staggered over to the window, dragged down the heavy velvet curtains; opening chests, he withdrew fustian, furs, heaping them on the bed.

Karim returned bearing a phial. "Master, I brought this potion from the Indes. It was given me by a chief for whom I did some small service." He held it to the light, revealing an opaque liquid. "It is a reputedly magic potion taken from the bark of their sacred trees and to be swallowed only if all else fails and Allah turns his face from us."

Felipe smiled wryly. "So you would toy with blasphemy?"

Karim shrugged. "Its magic belongs to the gods of their country, gods who have many strange powers. Perhaps it can help the sickness from the English ship, which is already raging amongst us. Already several of the crew—" He spread his hands wide.

"Dead?" queried Felipe.

"Aye, Master. And our potion is too late, I fear." He nodded towards Maeve's still figure. "However, there is enough for us both, and I am honoured to share it with you. Drink, Master; may those alien gods protect us. We cannot be more than one day's sailing from the Scottish coast once this accursed wind drops," he added with a reassurance he did not feel.

But Felipe took new hope. Keep her faint spirit alive for one more day—once they reached Scotland, there must be help. He grasped at land as a man believing in miracles.

"Permit me, Master." Karim began to remove the covers from Maeve, gathering her body into his arms.

Felipe sprang at him. "What in hell's name are you at?"

"She is dead, Master," said Karim in grieved tones. "I shall put her to rest in the sea with the others—"

"No—no. She is not dead—"

"Master, I have seen death many times—"

"Not this time—not her. Go—please, Karim, leave us."

Wondering if he now had a madman on his hands, Karim needed no second bidding to depart. In the cabin, Felipe stripped off his clothes. He had to put warmth into that cold, still body. Surely nakedness would engender more heat than any weight of clothes. Stripping Maeve of her thin night rail—one of his old cambric shirts—he gathered her close. About to pull the covers around them, he considered the phial Karim had left.

Dare he risk this unknown potion? From the Conquistadores he had learned of the Peruvian Indians' magical remedies for sickness, taken from herbs and the barks of trees.

The liquid tasted bitter, but was not too unpleasant. Turning, he looked down at Maeve, her head limp against his chest. Already her face had a luminous quality, as if he gazed on the beauty of death. With a groan he lifted her head and through her gently parted lips he tried to force some of the liquid, which dribbled unheeded down her chin. Frantic now, he took a mouthful and putting his lips against hers, he ejected the potion deep into her mouth. There was a faint convulsive gasp, and joyfully, knowing that a flicker of life remained, he kissed her cold lips.

She was still alive. Whether Jesu had answered his prayers or the heathen gods who made the potion, he was quite indifferent. At that moment he would have cheerfully sold his immortal soul to any deity powerful enough to keep her from slipping through the gates of death, he thought, wrapping himself about her, arms and legs entwined. Time passed slowly, and at last he felt Maeve's body damp with his sweat under the weight of the bedcovers. For a long time he prayed, then somewhere he slept.

Karim entered and looked down on them. Although the Arab captain's face betrayed no surprise, he was shocked by what he apparently beheld. Carnal knowledge of the dead was a low and vulgar taste. Karim sighed. He would never understand these Christians, taking only one woman and for life. Women, he reasoned, were like horses, though less reliable and strong. Easily come by, easily forgotten, and the last one a man enjoyed was always the best. Nor could he understand how Don Felipe, indifferent to the Irish princess in life, preferred her charms in death. He had not expected such bizarre taste from the godson of King Philip, the young man for whom he felt a father's affection.

The scene offended him, and he left the cabin hastily, too embarrassed to awaken the commander with the news that the *Black Duchess* had sighted land.

Clearly visible in the fading light was a jagged ill-shaped landmass, a broken pattern of islands or rocks faintly emerging from a vast greenness. Karim tempered the crew's jubilation with caution. The instinct for danger which had kept him alive and his beloved *Duchess* afloat through many campaigns hinted at something amiss in the tranquil scene—

"Scotland, Capitaine?" said the pilot.

Karim nodded. "I trust so." A million curses upon Mahmoud's black soul for stealing those precious charts—

"See, Capitaine," the pilot said eagerly, "there are beacon lights. It must be Scotland ahead. We are expected."

The *Black Duchess* was indeed expected, and Karim's instinct for danger had been faultless.

It was not Scotland they approached but the isles to the far north. Isles which lay, according to ancient charts, at the world's end.

The Land of the Simmer Dim, the Orkney Isles, were as yet no part of the civilised world. Despite a lip service to the Christian God, they belonged to an older worship of Odin and Thor, their scanty human population outnumbered by trolls, hogmen, mermaids, Seal People, and sea monsters.

In this sinister fairy tale land, where wrecking and murder were considered respectable occupations, a tyrant ruled before whom the ogres of legend paled into insignificance. This evil genius was Lord Robert Stewart, Earl of Orkney. He and Don Felipe Flores y Lennox de Montreuse were already old acquaintances.

Sweetling trilled happily in his cage. Uncaring of the seabirds' noisy competition or approaching danger, he watched over the motionless pair in the cavernous bed.

Unable to arouse his master, Karim rushed back on deck as the first submerged rock pierced the *Black Duchess*'s side and brought forth a screaming agony of protest from her every sail and spar.

Too late to give the order: "Turn, fly from this accursed land." Another new anxiety gnawed deep at Karim as he threw overboard the empty phial he had snatched from Felipe's bedside.

In his enthusiasm and desperation had he also succeeded in poisoning his young master?

PART TWO

The Isles at World's End

8

"Poison, you say, madam?" Lord Robert avoided his daughter-in-law's eyes and glared down from the high window across the sea. The horizon was beset by the seabirds' cries. It was too much to hope for a wreck and must therefore betoken an approaching storm. He hoped that he wouldn't be stranded overnight in this accursed castle with its wind-wracked, rock-infested shore.

"Yes, my lord, that is what I said. Poison."

Lady Sibella watched Lord Robert's heavy countenance purpling with rage. She hated him only a little less than her husband, Lord Henry, and feared him a great deal more. The vast family and few friends he possessed warned anxiously of an end by apoplexy, while his numerous enemies warmed to such an exceeding pleasant prospect. As for Lady Sibella, she knew that her survival depended on how long she could retain his compassion, hold his anger at bay. She always thought of him as a hound on an uneasy chain, barking wolfishly and showing teeth with few gaps. He was proud of them and suffered agonies of toothache, since pride would not allow him to see a chirurgeon, in case extraction was advised.

He leaned towards her in threatening attitude and pushed a grubby fingernail at her chest. For all his gorgeous attires, his furs and velvets, he always looked and smelt dirty, she thought, turning away from him with a fastidious tilt of nose.

"Poison administered by my laddie, eh?"

"Yes, my lord. That is correct."

He sucked in his lower lip. "Evidence, madam—where's your evidence?"

"A pet dog, my lord—"

"A pet dog might have died from sundry causes," he shouted.

"And a servant. Both died in agonies after eating sweetmeats sent by Lord Henry on two separate occasions. And I wish to appeal to your protection—I have that legal right," she added desperately.

Lord Robert stared out of the window. Jesu, the girl sounded more like her mother every day, with more than a hint of her rascally father in her. She'd make fruit right enough for the executioner's sword too if she didn't watch her step.

He picked a dirty fingernail, playing for time. "And you're ready to swear my laddie's to blame?"

"Who else would wish to be rid of me—saving—" She stopped, and he nodded as if she had said, "saving yourself." Hech yes, but no' yet, ma lassie, he thought. Not until you have served my purpose in keeping you alive all these years by bringing me a few steps nearer yon rickety Scottish throne, occupied as yet by that spindle-legged, whey-faced oddity, Jamie the Sixth.

Again he regarded Lady Sibella. She was a cold fish, this niece of his. He sometimes wondered uneasily if he had been tricked.

He squared his oxlike shoulders under the furred robe. He wasn't beaten yet. Disappointed, maybe, but not beaten. As for that snivelling brat of a son of his, skulking out of sight, he'd given him a lugful. Why in God's name had he been given that weakling, that blundering fool for a firstborn, and not Patrick, flesh of his flesh, bone of his bone—a son to make any father proud? If Pate had been poisoning his wife, he would have made a smooth, swift job, hech yes—he would never have bungled and given the game away.

"I can do naught without evidence, madam."

"Next time then I shall save the corpses for you, my lord," she said sweetly, "although since your visits—and my lord husband's—to Burray are infrequent these days, they may tend to stink a bit in the keeping." Not that you'd notice, she thought, eyeing his slovenly stained finery with disgust. "I think, my lord, you have your evidence—"

"I have?" he asked cautiously. Hech now, what indiscretion had the bitch discovered?

"I understand," said Lady Sibella primly, plucking at a seam in her somewhat shabby but neat gown, "that my lord husband has made yet another mistress pregnant and has loudly declaimed to all and sundry that he wishes to wed her and be rid of his barren wife."

Damn the wench. She heard everything. It was true, Harry was desperate for a legitimate heir, biting his fingernails and getting all the serving wenches with child while his brother Patrick's amiable and fertile wife produced a legitimate child at regular intervals. And every screaming nephew or niece further diminished Harry's hopes of inheriting as Earl of Orkney.

Lord Robert shrugged. It was enough to drive any man to desperation, hech yes, especially from a wife who had never loved him and who had been forced into the marriage bed—

"After all," said Lady Sibella, uncannily interpreting his thoughts, "the union between us was not of my making."

He had thought she would be easy to manipulate. The power she would give him to yield made him dizzily able to forget his own bastardy. If he could but prove that King Jamie was Davy Rizzio's son, or the child of Lady Reres substituted for the stillborn Prince— Not that he believed such stories, but they gave him comfort. Hech yes, there were other rumours in plenty, easily fleshed by bribes. And where the silver failed, he had found the hot steel of torture was remarkably effective in making men eager to please him.

"I implore you, my lord, for a safe conduct for myself and my household—all at Burray Castle—to the mainland."

A safe conduct. Was this to be all his thanks for rearing her, he thought, disgusted, this cold viper in his bosom and with even colder parts in his son's bed if Harry's grumbles were to be believed?

"I will happily renounce all claim to lands and estates," she added, ignoring the fact that he had appropriated all the St Clairs' possessions long since.

Let her go to King Jamie's court with all her tales of woe? Hech no, he couldn't risk it. "Out of the question, madam. You remain here."

She knew by his eyes' hard glare that she need not hope for mercy and her last gamble was lost since she thought despite his villainy that he had a sneaking fondness for her—

"You are sentencing me to certain death—you realise that, my lord," she said sadly.

Lord Robert cleared his throat, a trumpeting sound of embarrassment. If only she would stop looking at him through her mother's eyes—

"You know full well I have wished ever for a simple, peaceful life," she continued. "Never had I the slightest desire for—for such a future as you envisaged; despite my birth—"

Hech yes, her words reminded him she was too valuable to release, too dangerous to fall into the hands of others who might use her. He squared his shoulders, thrust out his jaw. One of the best-hated men north of the Tweed, he had torture chambers full of ingenious weapons to prove that though none loved him, by God, they would fear him. And he had maimed men and women to prove his point, mercilessly walking or crawling the streets, living examples to any who set themselves up against his rule.

"There is a solution," he said.

How eager she looked. "I will do anything, my lord—anything," she added, clasping her hands in supplication.

"Give my son the heir he needs—then you may go."

She looked away. "I cannot, my lord."

"Then you are barren indeed, for he has proved himself—hech yes, over and over," he said proudly.

"I am aware of that—every serving wench in the parish claims to have been got with child—"

"Then you are not intending to blame him for your lack of success. Is your womb so different that it rejects his seed?"

"I have tried—I swear to God—I have tried—"

"There are potions and the like," he said, embarrassed. "Women's geegaws for your condition, madam."

"You mean Baubie Finn's witchcraft—"

He winced. "Herbs. They have succeeded with others. I suggest you pay Baubie another visit if you wish to remain in my laddie's good graces—and for your continued good health, madam. I cannot help you. This household is under my son's care." The afterthought was a threat.

"Care? Is that how you describe our life here—as prisoners?"

"You have my advice. Do something about your barren condition."

Leaving her, he clattered down the turnpike stairs into the rowdy hall, sparking with laughter and wine. Girls shrieked, dogs barked, someone tried to sing to a lute above the din. He looked fondly, proudly at his brood making merry—all the fruit of his loins, nineteen bairns he had sired, legitimate and otherwise. They formed a small army which he was proud to have accompany him everywhere.

He pushed his way through the gaily clad mob. The satins, doublets, velvet hose, the cloaks and bonnets, all had been out of fashion for the past fifty years. They would have aroused derisive laughter in the English court, even in Holyrood, not noted for being up-to-the minute, thanks to King Jamie's canniness over money. But this was his kingdom, and if his lads looked grand and proud and bonny none dare laugh. Hech no, he'd have a man's eyes picked out neat as a corbie would do the job for laughing at one of his lads.

As for that bitch upstairs— She deserved to be poisoned. He scowled. There must be something deformed in her, unable to carry Harry's child, an affront to the virility of his vast clan.

"Make way—make way. Harry!" he roared. "Where's Harry?"

"Over there," said Patrick, his second son, a handsome mirror image. "Behind the arras, Father," he added primly.

Lord Robert stormed over and found Harry taking a little light entertainment in his wife's castle on the person of a serving wench pressed hard against the wall.

"Put her down, Harry. We're leaving."

Harry, startled, relinquished his hold so quickly she stumbled and fell to her knees, gathering her garments modestly around her.

Lord Robert averted his eyes. "Pay your respects to your lady wife. She thinks you're poisoning her," he added shortly.

The Master of Orkney's face was long and pale, only the eyes with their slight squint made him undeniably his father's son. He had the grace to blush.

"Poi—son," he stammered. "I know—nothing—"

So it was true. Harry had never been a good liar. "Hech yes, you've bungled the job like the bairn you failed to beget on her. You've bungled it as you've bungled everything since the day you were born," he added viciously.

Harry matched his mincing step to his father's long stride, stuttering denials, trying to keep up with him.

"It's not my fault."

"Hech no, since you've managed it on every other slut you've lain with. I'm sick of having to pay for your bastards when you're not man enough to get a legitimate heir." He regarded his firstborn with distaste. God knows where he'd got those wan and womanish looks from.

"What shall I do, Father?"

"If you cannot get a bairn on her, she's no use to me," said Lord Robert brutally. "She'll have to go."

"Go? Where?" Harry's eyes widened. "Escape?"

"Hech no, you dolt. If she escapes it will be the worse for all of us. Choose your own way of getting rid of her, but think of something a little more subtle than poisoning. And don't bungle it this time. She must never leave here alive— Oh, come on, laggard—we'll lose the tide. I don't want another night in this damned draughty rat-infested hole."

From her room high in the tower Lady Sibella watched them ride across the hill and disappear towards the ferry. She was under sentence of death—doomed—unless she could escape.

But how? If only a ship would come— She watched the wreckers' beacons pierce the night like candles lit to God to answer her tearful prayers—but she slept less than usual, aware of movements, of voices and the slither of footfalls on the rocky shore below.

At dawn she stared down from the window and saw the ugly squat shape of the witch Baubie Finn climb to Wreckers' Point and stare out to sea.

Sibella sighed. She was long past Baubie's potions, and suspected that the old woman's powers were similarly impotent. She had not been able to summon up storm or shipwreck for some time, and the people were becoming discouraged. Even the gentle minister prayed regularly each Sunday that God would send them a wreck before his flock starved to death in the coming winter. "A rich ship, Lord, well supplied, would keep thy people happy and healthy, better to do Thy will."

Lord Robert robbed the people, and Baubie robbed the sea to replace the effects of his thieving.

Baubie Finn sniffed the air. She could smell a ship in distress, and for the past week had hardly left her cooking pot, stirring, stirring the foul contents, summoning up a fierce tempest with attendant shipwreck. Today she had a feeling in her bones, a trembling of excitement and longing, and for several days the beacon lights had been patiently tended, day in, day out. Several galleons had appeared and as rapidly disappeared again across the horizon. Crippled with broken spars and rigging, they hinted at a sea calamity in the southern world. Listing badly, none came near enough for the trap ready baited— A disappointment to the patient beacon keepers, for theirs was chilly work—

Baubie possessed, as well as second sight, eyesight which many a predatory creature would have envied. Now she did a little dance of glee, observing the sails of a stately galleon bobbing across the wild waters and clearly making for the trap.

It was listing wearily, with its masts broken spars, its sails limp and torn; there would be plenty of pickings for all. One Burray man who had sailed in better days told her excitedly that the earlier ships were Spanish galleons, probably at war with England's Queen. Could this be another? The grandest, the wealthiest ship in the world. Tales of treasures from the Indes, worth a king's ransom of gold and jewels—

Baubie did not often smile, finding little in life worthy of amusement, but as she looked across the sea, her face was transformed into a veritable gargoyle of delight. A simple woman, her mouth watered more on thoughts of wines and victuals since most times the islanders' bellies were too empty for comfort.

Already the rocks were alive with racing figures bounding towards the shore; great ragged crows prepared for a long vigil. Eyes bright with jubilation, they watched the galleon approach labouring through heavy seas into the trap, the Trow Cavern with its roaring hungry waters, its fierce needle-like rocks. Nods of satisfaction were exchanged, and mothers clasped the hands of hungry children, for these were the first sails seen this year. Ten long months since the last wreck— God in His mercy—how long *that* had been. And a miserable poor Swedish merchantman too—peedie-little spoils for starving folk.

Patiently they squatted on the rocks to await tide's turn, which would deliver the crippled ship into their hands.

"What a ship—" The cry was taken up, echoing from one group to the next.

"Not as large as some of the Spaniards I've seen," said the knowledgeable ex-sailor. "Peedie-like in fore- and sterncastle."

"Beggars canna' be choosers, Andro. We must thank the Good Lord for His mercy—"

"Stand aside there."

Baubie Finn needed no second request. Respectfully they made a path for her.

"Fine day's work, Baubie."

"Aye, Baubie, best pickings ye've brought us lang syne."

Baubie acknowledged their gratitude with a queenly grace quite out of keeping with her grotesque appearance. A true member of the Finnfolk, small and squat, broad as she was long, her thick black hair fell past her shoulders. A long nose, close-set squinting eyes, the picture of ugliness was completed by disproportionately large hands and feet. Some whispered that she could take on the form of a spider at will. Children were taught in their earliest prayers to ask God to bless Baubie and to keep them from falling foul of her.

Holding up a hand for silence, she hovered dramatically, arms outthrust to the sea. Climbing on a flat rock, she called:

"Do thee, spirit of the deep, bewitch the seaman's eye
Call upon the rocks to seem smooth as milady's silken gown
Spill out upon our beach treasures untold of gold and wealth—"

The cheering crowd did not hear the final whispered line of this remarkable spell:

"And send my man a good catch—and a mermaid—in his nets."

Baubie's man was lazy and never to be found when he was wanted, a suitable father for the son he had begotten on her, she thought, looking with distaste at Boy, who had wandered out after her. A handsome, well-set-up man, except that the Creator had forgotten a brain to complete His handiwork. But what the Creator had omitted Baubie Finn believed she might yet provide. Earthly help was beyond curing Boy's idiocy; she knew from bitter experience that all her most powerful spells were useless. Only a mermaid as mate could now turn him into a real man.

She regarded her followers with affection, their air of excitement, of good humour tantamount to a Holy Day as newcomers came from every direction to join the tattered, gaunt throng, scrambling over the rocks to some vantage point where the richest spoils from the approaching ship might possibly land. Jostling each other for the best places without signs of ill temper, since they were still united in the common need, exchanging quips and pleasantries, they crouched behind rocks in the hope of surprising whatever members of the Spanish crew managed to survive the breaking up of their ship.

Aye, they would receive all gratefully, all that the Good Lord sent them. And there would be no questions asked when the bodies of drowned or slain men disappeared. The savage folk, barely human at all, who lived away to the north, in terrible caves adorned with human bones, greedily accepted meat that was not always of slain animals. The Reverend Erasmus Flett had remonstrated with his congregation since the graveyard had been violated by body snatchers in search of fresh corpse meat. Flesh was a token of survival, keeping at bay the ever threatening starvation whose grip grew tighter under Lord Robert's regime.

Baubie had no such qualms. She could have told him—aye, and so could many a one of his seemingly prim and pious congregation—that such flesh tasted remarkably like suckling pig—the reason why King James of Scotland, never overly famous for his delicate table manners, had nervously barred it from the royal kitchens.

She watched the scene with satisfaction. To the general air of excitement were added the ringing sounds of knives being sharpened on rocks, while others brandished clubs skilfully wielded to cull the young seals each year, without marking their hides. On every face she saw joyful anticipation. The wreckers knew no compassion for the alien sailors and thought them therefore deserving of no more humanity than the seals themselves, or a whale beached upon the shore.

Baubie was pleased by the timing of the wreck. They would have the pick of the spoils since the tide which separated Burray from the mainland also kept the Earl's troopers, frustrated on the other shore, until they could ride across at low tide.

She glanced towards the castle and saw the light burning in Lady Sibella's window. Poor barren wife, nothing could help her, bonny though she was. Even an idiot son would have been better for her, thought Baubie, looking at Boy. An idiot was safer than no bairn at all for a husband who was getting desperate for an heir—

Aboard the *Black Duchess*, Karim also welcomed the dawn with the remaining members of his crew who had survived the sickness, and scrambled aloft the rigging for a better look at the land ahead. Night, or what passed for darkness in this bewitched area of the globe, was a time of trial and superstitious horror among the men. Instead of growing decently dark the sky was pierced with leaping eerie green tongues. Karim had heard mariners speak of phosphorescent fire. This added another dimension of fear to sinister navigation problems and the echoes of subterranean caverns all around them.

It was too much for the forty crew who remained. They had suffered from starvation, sickness, and the intensity of cold rain and shrill blast upon bronzed skins used to gentler clime and which under adverse weather conditions were taking on a sickly mauve appearance. Now they were faced with the supernatural. Brave men with swords or knives, endowed with the cunning of sheer brute strength over their enemies, they could be merciless and expected no mercy at the hand of their enemies. Brave in the face of danger and treachery from mortals like themselves, the terror of the unknown, the suggestion of immortal souls in peril when the body perished, had them down upon their knees on the deck. Cowering under the flashing lights, they screamed upon Allah to deliver them, for they had fallen into a land where sorcerers awaited them.

Karim had seized a whip and applied it freely, knowing that the ship's only chance lay in forcing his men back into the semblance of right-minded, sensible sailors. Fortunately, the weather itself delivered them. A land wind threatened to carry them far out to sea, followed by a sudden calm in which sails hung limp. Fog mercifully dimmed the Northern Lights. The first gentle light of dawn brought a fresh wind which threatened to hurl them onto rocks now clearly revealed, shining like jet upon the sea. Daybreak also revealed an oblong of greenland—a safe haven—

Karim took the helm, and from the rocks came an almighty roar, as if an enraged sea serpent were about to emerge.

The *Black Duchess* staggered, shaking in her tracks as the tide encountered shallows which Karim had never dreamed could stretch from the still far-off cliffs. He cursed his lack of charts, with only one experienced man, the pilot at the bows calling the depths as best he could. Now the outlines before him speedily dissolved and like a stage upon which the curtain has descended, Karim found he was steering into nowhere. Only the boom of echoing depths, the occasional glimpse of a mighty rock, arising whalelike from the side of the ship, brought warning of danger.

The sudden roar of waters was followed by the scream of timbers torn apart, as with a sickening lurch the *Duchess*'s side ripped open against a submerged rock.

After helplessly standing by his side Felipe rushed back for Maeve. Thanks to the potion or the warmth engendered by his body and the covers, she still lived and was now conscious. Hastily wrapping her in a thick fustian cloak, he carried her up on deck, where confusion reigned as the ship listed heavily, her masts already breaking, snapping like branches under the strain.

Karim shouted, "We can do naught now, Master. Save yourself."

When the burden Felipe carried groaned, opened her eyes, Karim thought the Christian God had worked another miracle.

"We are wrecked, but do not fear, love. I will save you. We are close to land, and our friends await us," whispered Felipe.

"I can stand," she said weakly. "Put me down." She clung to the rail for support while Felipe stared over the side of the ship and discovered a flat rock which would make a suitable landing place for them both. He wished he could see some signs of life on land, but all vision was obliterated by the heavy seas and the spray. He prayed they were not entering some deserted region of the coast. For Maeve must have help—and soon—if she was to survive.

"Come now, I will carry you to safety, love."

Even as he spoke, the ship gave a groan of dying agony and listed heavily to port.

"Sweetling—my little Sweetling—where is he?"

Maeve tottered back towards the cabin.

"Master, save yourself, we are sinking fast," shouted Karim.

Felipe seized Maeve as she fell, thrusting her bodily into Karim's arms.

"Sweetling," she gasped. "Please save him—"

"I will, stay you with Karim."

Felipe leaped down the steps, opened the cabin door, seized the cage, where its silly occupant still sang as if unaware of danger. Halfway up the steps again he heard Karim's warning shout and saw the mast hurtling down towards him. Thrown back, he felt an agonising pain in his leg and saw staring down at him the faces of Karim and Maeve, the latter now clutching the bird in its cage. Karim had set Maeve on her feet and was trying single-handedly to dislodge the mast. It was of no avail. He called to passing members of the crew to assist him, but intent upon making their escape before it was too late, they did not pause in their flight to give the trapped man a second glance.

"Go with the rest, Karim—go—you are wasting your time, and I think my leg is broken."

"Master, I cannot leave you thus."

"You must. Save yourself and the girl—take her to safety."

Karim took out a knife, cut off a length of rope from the sail, and clambered down beside him, binding Felipe's body to the mast. "When the ship breaks up, perhaps you will float ashore with the wreckage. It is your only hope, Master. Allah be with you."

Far above, Maeve's face, pale and ghostlike, stared down at him.

And she was weeping, weeping for him, he thought with amazed gratitude. Then there came a thunder of noise as if the very gates of hell itself were opening. A roar of crumbling, splintering timbers, and as the green waters enveloped him, his last sight was her imploring hand stretched out towards him.

Water was everywhere, in his eyes, his throat. He struggled for a while to keep afloat. Then a floating wine keg danced towards him. Unable to avoid its impact, he realised with pained surprise that this was death. He heard a faint sound like cheering, and looked in vain for angels. His last thought was that he had been taken quite unprepared, believing that death was for others, his own life immortal. Too late he realised his own human frailty, and angry, resentfully struggled no more as the long night of the dark engulfed him.

Seabirds circled the sky above his head, and the air was full of their cries. He wanted to go on sleeping peacefully, but the shrill screaming cut into his skull. He opened his eyes painfully. All around him, black rocks, shining like polished leather. Had he died and gone to hell?

Hell? No, he was too cold to be in hell—cold and wet too. Purgatory, more like, as his faith promised beyond the gateway of death. Purgatory or hell— He would not have cared too deeply if only those seabirds would cease their unending cries.

He tasted salt upon his lips, and grains of sand. He was alive. His face resting on sea wrack. By a miracle he had been washed ashore. He was safe—

Safe? He listened again to the screams in the air, and knew sickeningly that no birds made them. They were human—and dying. He tried to stand, but found himself anchored to the spar of broken mast by the cord Karim had tied around him. Taking out the knife from his belt, he cut through the rope with numbed hands. Free at last, he attempted to get to his feet and almost swooned with agony. Touching his left thigh, he found it grotesquely swollen, bruised, perhaps broken by the falling mast. Crawling upon his belly towards a gap in the rocks, he beheld a busy morning's activities. First the soft thud of club upon bone, a scream, and then merciful silence. Over and over it was repeated as the wreckers moved into the shallows and seized the men who were swimming ashore. They were efficient at their business, skilled in the seal culling. One swift blow was enough—

Felipe lay back sick, knowing there was nothing he could do, an injured man with no weapon but the knife at his waist. He willed himself to watch the sickening scene, not out of compassion since the crew meant little to him, a faceless mass. But Karim—and Maeve— He watched as bodies were hauled onto the beach, stripped, robbed. Here and there a knife flashed and came away red, as a ring from finger or ear proved stubborn and was taken in a more expedient manner.

At the sight of such butchery he retched, burying his head in the soft sea wrack, then forcing himself to look once more, afraid that each new haul would reveal the tall Arab captain, the long black hair and white nakedness of Maeve. As clubs and knives continued to be wielded and the air grew heavier with the screams of the dying, Felipe realised that Karim and Maeve must indeed be dead. Perhaps they had died at the hands of the wreckers before he regained consciousness. An hour ago he would have prayed that they escaped drowning; now, helpless to go to their rescue, he prayed only that they had received the merciful oblivion, the clean death by drowning.

None would be spared, he knew, the blood lust of this orgy of slaying. Ironic, he thought, that he should have struggled to keep Maeve alive for such an end and that God in His mercy had not seen fit to take the gentle creature by kinder means. Angrily he stared at the sky. The God who had remembered fallen sparrows might have been moved to compassion for Maeve's tears for the drowned animals of the Armada, for little Sweetling's plight. She had told him that the meanest slave or felon had a soul. He thought uncomfortably of servants in El Escorial and his indifference to their lives. He wished that he had not chosen this ill-advised moment in his career to remember her words.

At last silence had descended on the beach hidden by the rocks. He drifted in and out of consciousness from his leg's agony. His head wound had reopened and blood dripped into his eyes. Time ceased. A fitful sun blazed into a warm-breezed day. Gratefully he removed his shirt and laid it on the rocks to dry. By moving as little as possible he found that his wounds ached dully, at worst like a toothache, and bearable. The scene on the shore had changed into busy silence.

Now that human opposition was at an end, the bodies pushed back into the sea, the wreckers scrambled across the rocks to where the *Duchess* lay stranded on her side. They had to work fast before flood tide finished off the broken ship. Felipe found his terrors recurring. What if someone emerged carrying a small human bundle wrapped in fustian with long black hair? But his fears were groundless, as like human insects the wreckers swarmed over the decks, their only cries of triumph for swords and wine casks and finery. Occasionally he heard the grind and smash of glass, of furniture which proved resistant to removal, and he almost expected to see Karim rush to the defence of his despoiled *Duchess*. Karim, he concluded sadly, must be dead, or he would have died nobly fighting such desecration of the ship he loved.

The tide was gaining on them steadily when a shrill whistle pierced the air. The wreckers looked anxiously towards the cliffs, shading eyes with hands. Whatever they saw caused concern, for immediately they vacated the ship, racing, scrambling to the shore. They were eager to keep their activities secret, for as the wreckers disappeared from the scene, a lone rider dragged brushwood across their tracks and, satisfied with the result, galloped after them.

For a while it was as if the terrible scenes he had witnessed were of a disordered brain, caused by his injuries. At last the gentle sun gleamed upon an empty wave-lapped shore. About to leave his hiding place and head towards the *Duchess*, driven by some impulse to make certain Karim and Maeve were not still on board, Felipe heard the horses' hooves just in time and saw the troopers lining the cliff top. At the same moment the air was rent by a great explosion from the *Duchess*. She burst asunder, the air full of broken timbers, rigging—and long before the troopers reached the shore, she was mere splintered wood floating away on the tide.

Felipe studied the horsemen who were riding anxiously back and forth along the shore. Although they wore no uniform they were clearly in authority, enemies of the ragged wreckers. He would throw himself upon their sympathy. A moment later he was glad of the instinct that had kept him in hiding.

He was not the only fugitive. Two members of the crew had also escaped the wreckers. Now they sprang out from the rocks away to the right and ran along the sands towards the troopers, falling upon their knees, obviously pleading for mercy. In answer to this they were seized and apparently questioned—or threatened—about the *Duchess*. They pointed excitedly to where only floating fragments remained.

Their revelations did not please the horsemen. Again the men knelt, begging for mercy. There was no mercy forthcoming.

Horrified, Felipe watched the butt ends of muskets descend, heard the crush of skulls cracking like eggshells, and saw the two still bodies kicked into the sea.

Another cursory investigation of the shore and the troopers with a shout that echoed over to him began to ride swiftly towards his hiding place. As the sound of the horses grew nearer, he realised that the men had betrayed him in a last effort to save themselves. Knowing full well there was nothing he could do to save himself, he leaned back against the rocks, heart thumping, but determined to sell his life dearly. His hand tightened on the dagger in his belt. All that remained was to die with dignity. He said a last prayer, and opening his eyes, beheld a miracle—

The troopers were riding back up the steep cliff path, away to the left of the rocky shore. The men had not betrayed him and had probably been unaware of his survival. Now he remembered how God had held him in the palm of His hand. If he had not been injured saving Maeve's Sweetling, he would have suffered the same fate as the crew of the *Black Duchess*. Sweating now with relief, gratefully he recognised the inner voice which had also saved him from being caught on the shore, limping towards the ship when the troopers arrived.

Relief brought feelings of hunger, cold, and thirst. But he was alive. Even pain was worthwhile, to be alive when so many others had died that day. He decided to remain in his hiding place until darkness, acquainting himself with the terrain in preparation for his slow and clumsy nocturnal travel. He doubted that the troopers would be about, the wreckers too gloating over their secret spoils. All he could hope for was to steal a boat and land on some hospitable part of the coast. Somehow he must get a message to the Earl of Huntly. Surely the Catholic lords would have means to smuggle him back to Spain

He wondered where were the honest Leith fishermen, the Fife crofters he recalled from his early visit. In truth this treeless landscape visible from his hiding place did not resemble any part of Scotland he remembered, although one shore probably looked much like another. But Scotland must be in a perilous state indeed under young King James if its people were reduced to wrecking.

He studied the castle which dominated the headland, half hidden by a high wall and crowned with turrets. Did it contain the troopers' garrison? In any case he would head to the left, where a pathway wound past a hilly field crowned by a mysterious mound, like a giant beehive. It intrigued and puzzled him, for he had not seen either wreckers or troopers head in that direction. To his right lay the sea, with all of the once magnificent *Black Duchess* reduced to floating spars and an occasional shape unhappily resembling a bloated corpse.

Time seemed interminable, but despite hunger and pain the sun's warmth soothed him into a fretful sleep at last. As shadows gathered, marking the long day's end, and wisps of smoke emerged from the castle's chimneys, its gaunt severity bore little resemblance to the handsome Scottish castles of his youth. Were they too an illusion left over from halcyon days with Amyas Lennox? He closed his eyes in sudden pain, seeing his cousin plummet down from the deck of the *Warlock*, knowing he would carry that picture printed in his mind's eye until his dying day—which might not be far off. Perhaps, so alike in life, the cousins were both fated to be victims of the Spanish Armada, to die within days of each other, each indirectly causing the other's death despite childhood's affection and solemn vows.

"Aye, cousin," he addressed the brooding sky, "you are not so far from me. We'll meet again soon."

The fast deepening twilight was accompanied by a fine drizzle and fog, which Felipe welcomed since the dismal prospect might keep the curious indoors.

At last he cautiously arose from his hiding place. The movement had him crying out in agony. His injured leg had stiffened during the day and he could barely stand unaided, let alone clamber over rocks and search for shelter, food, and a boat to take him from this accursed shore.

He groaned as his head throbbed anew and the gash across his forehead reopened, the blood trickling down into his eyes. But he wasn't beaten yet. Nearby was a piece of wood roughly the right height. Setting it under his arm, he hobbled a few exploratory steps and began his tortured progress towards the shore, while under his weight each stone and pebble rattled through the silence like musket fire and each clumsy step set his teeth on edge with pain. An hour later the short distance across the pebbled shore became a sandy and uneven slope.

He had reached the cliff path. The first part of the nightmare journey was over, and pausing for breath, weak with pain and exhaustion, shivering and soaked to the skin, he thought of his bleak hiding place longingly as a place of luxury and warmth. The cold wind which had arisen turned his exertions into a teeth-chattering ague. To survive the night he must have shelter and rest.

Against driving rain, with a moaning gale as companion, he stumbled on, the makeshift crutch sinking into the sand, each step more agonising than the last. Far across the field to his left he glimpsed the beehive mound. Perhaps some primitive farm shelter—but whatever its function, his heart rejoiced. The rain had taken care of his thirst, but he was constantly assailed by weakening pangs of hunger. As he leaned against the dyke, gathering strength for the final effort to cross the field, the air was split by the growl of thunder, and a lightning flash dizzily cut across the mud-coloured sky.

It revealed a black oblong at the base of the mound. A door, thought Felipe gratefully. Shelter from the full force of the storm. He cast aside the rough crutch, which had ripped open his shirt, rubbing the skin from his armpit, one more agony among many as he crawled along the wet field. The dark aperture was not a door but a narrow tunnel, and all his instincts rebelled against entering upon hands and knees. This was no sheep pen, of that he was certain, and his scalp prickled in fear. However, even as he hesitated, pinpoints of light on the cliff top, the sound of horses denoted the troopers' return. Hurriedly he scrambled into the tunnel, wriggling through the darkness into what he prayed would not turn out to be his own tomb.

Sitting with his back pressed hard against a wall, rubbing his injured leg, he considered his surroundings. An eerie emanation issued from the dark and silence, an awareness of shapes fluttering stealthily beyond the dim confines. Small whisperings of movement had him tense as a coiled spring as he waited for a hand to descend heavily upon his shoulder—

None came, only the faint slitherings continued, soft as a robe dragged across a marble floor. After a while they too ceased, as if the unseen occupants were satisfied, and as the ground was reasonably soft, his lodging otherwise tolerably warm, Felipe slept.

Amyas haunted his dreams. Amyas was alive; he felt his warm breath as he gripped his hand, laughing. Thank God they were both safe. In that return to the lost days where they had shared childhood's eternal summer without threat of cold winds or mortal tragedy, Amyas's death on the *Warlock* became foul nightmare. A dream within a dream.

But he awoke knowing Amyas was dead. Maeve too was dead— although she was taunting him with gentle arms, her warm and seductive body. She was running away from him along a dark tunnel. He heard her footsteps and knew she ran to her death. He tried to call out—a warning—but no voice came, nor would his limbs move to obey him—

The footsteps grew louder—

He opened his eyes. They were outside his shelter. A faint sunlight filtered through the tunnel and his shelter had become a snare. He cursed his lack of vigilance. Doubtless the troopers had followed his tracks along the field—

"Hey, ye—inside there. Oot ye come. Ye canna' escape." The man's voice was rough, angry. Felipe did not answer.

"We ken ye're wounded. Ye'll no' escape alive, we can tell ye." Another man's voice. Playing for time and inspecting his surroundings, Felipe remained silent, fingering his dagger and wondering how many more of them waited for him.

He took stock of his surroundings. The faint light revealed all around him shelves made of huge stone slabs. He guessed their purpose for each was coffin-wide. How ironic that he had chosen to meet his death in some prehistoric burial cairn! Troopers or wreckers, the end would be the same.

"Are ye coming oot like we tell ye?"

The second man again— Were there but two of them? Could he lure them inside one by one?

"Why don't you come in and we'll talk about it?"

Silence, then some whispering. "Ye're no' a Spaniard then?"

"Of course I'm not a Spaniard. I am a Scotsman from Edinburgh way. I was taken prisoner. I'll be glad to tell you all about it if you will guarantee my safety."

Silence again.

"I saw what you did to the crew when they swam ashore," Felipe volunteered.

"That wasna' us, Master, that was the wreckers."

"Very well, then you are no better than they, since I also saw what you did to the two men who begged for mercy—"

"Nay, Master, we havena' killed any man."

So they weren't wreckers or troopers—if they spoke truth.

"What ye saw must have been—" the man continued.

"Shut up," interrupted the second man. "Ye tell him too much."

"I'll no' shut up. Her leddyship'll be wanting to see him," the man whispered.

"Unless you can tell me who you are, I am not leaving this place," said Felipe.

"We mean ye no ill, Master. What ye saw was either wreckers or the Earl's men—"

"In which case ye're lucky to be alive," said his companion.

"Are ye coming out? We havena' all day to wait on ye."

"I am giving the matter some little thought."

"Master, we mean ye no harm. There's only two o' us—"

"Aye, an' we're no' a' that anxious for yer company, to have our heads blown off, coming in to seek ye," said his companion.

Two of them. Neither Earl's men, troopers, nor wreckers. Perhaps a few honest men did exist upon this alien shore.

"You mentioned her ladyship. Who is she?"

"The Lady Sibella Stewart."

"And where does she live?"

"In Burray Castle, on the hill yonder. Just a step away."

"The castle on the headland. Does this land belong to her?"

"Aye, Master—or at least it did until the Earl stole it—"

"Hush, man," said his companion. "Ye speak treason. Now, Master Scotsman, are ye coming out or no'?"

"I'm coming out. But it may take me some while, so I beg you to be patient."

When at last he emerged into the light, blinking like a mole in the sunlight, he saw the two men in rough but tidy garments, leather-aproned, unarmed, obviously servingmen.

Felipe realised that his own appearance was much more terrifying. They stared at him, the blood congealed upon his forehead, his face and hands black, his hair matted.

"Yon's a gory mess," whispered the elder man in tones of awe.

"Aye, and he chose the richt place to die. I dinna' ken it would be worth whiles carrying him back to the castle—"

"Hold your tongue, man—and give me some of that wine you're carrying. And is that cheese too?" As he stretched out his hand, the men took a backward step, protecting the vessels they carried.

"Nay, Mr Scotsman, these are no' for ye—"

"They are for *him*." And both nodded towards the mound's entrance.

"Him? But the place is empty."

He saw the looks of terror as both hung their heads. "Nay, Master, there is the Hogboy; he lives in there."

"'Tis a mercy ye came to no harm," whispered the younger.

"Do you feed him regularly?"

"Aye, Master—regularly. He needs his food."

Felipe shivered. Whatever dwelt in the mound was obviously no friend to the people. He recalled the stealthy scraping sounds. Sweet Jesu; it was as well he had not known about Hogboy, whoever he might be, or he would not have slept at all.

The two men stretched out their hands to help him to his feet.

"Take care, I beg of you. I think perhaps my leg is broken after all."

He looked up, beheld a blue and cloudless sky alive with lark song, and as they leaned over him the same sky abruptly fell upon his head. The summer sunshine was doused like a candle as he fainted clean away for the second time in his life.

9

The cart's jolting, the nauseous odour of the seaweed under which he had been buried, brought him back to painful consciousness. His groans and attempts to move were greeted by a warning whisper:

"Keep yer head oot of sight, Mr Scotsman, if ye want to keep it on yer shoulders."

Why didn't they kill him and be done with it?

"The Earl's men ken the cart from the castle and are less apt to ask us questions, especially after that—hrmpph—unfortunate episode with the wreckers."

The bone-shaking agony of wheels on rough cobblestones came to a merciful end.

"Ye can come oot now, Mr Scotsman."

Groaning, he needed their assistance to rise from the bed of kelp. A quick glimpse of a small grey courtyard dismally populated by fretful and bedraggled fowls. Then he was bundled through a door and supported down a dark corridor, smelling of long disuse, of lichened stone whose walls oozed, regrettably moist. This was hardly the cheery welcome he had expected, and his ominous thoughts prompted the opening of a door into a stone-vaulted chamber with high barred window.

So much for their promises, he thought, glaring around his prison, too weary to accuse his captors. The elder pointed to a small table. "There's kale broth for ye, barley bread, and ale."

"Aye, and yon bed's a bit more comfortable than the troll-house," added his companion, indicating a pallet of straw.

He forgave all in his delight at seeing food again. Not even feast day banquets in El Escorial had yielded food as delicious-tasting as this simple prison fare. And the rough bed was like floating away on a plump cloud. Grateful for food and warmth, he curled up, and indifferent to a dubious future, fell heavily asleep. He opened his eyes to a tiny candle left burning to greet the evening. There was more kale broth, bread, and ale. This time he fell asleep with the spoon in his hand, and that was how he awakened to the sun of another day streaming through the bars, with birdsong in an azure sky.

By his bedside more food and wine had appeared, and the floor was occupied by a large but crude wooden bathtub. Stiffly he left his bed and limped towards it. The water was warm, and someone had thoughtfully provided clean linen, drawstring shirt, and rough breeches. His most joyful discovery as he bathed was that his leg, though badly bruised, was not broken. Rest and sustenance had brought a sense of physical well-being out of all proportion to his imprisonment. He had donned the garments, which fitted moderately well, when the door opened and a large red-cheeked countrywoman appeared to remove the bannocks and cheese.

"What is this place called?" he asked. The woman shrugged.

"Is your mistress Lady Sibella?"

The woman stared at him, shook her head.

"Speak up—are you dumb?" he said sharply.

She came forward and opened her mouth. The dark empty cavern among decayed and broken teeth indicated that she had no tongue. She beckoned to him to follow her, and ashamed of his rough words, he would have had considerable difficulty ascending the turnpike stair had there not been a thick rope to act as balustrade and the woman's strong arm under his elbow. At last, sweating, panting with effort, he reached an ill-lit draughty stone corridor. Obviously the owners of the castle were poor indeed, since there were no luxuries of furnishings or tapestry to relieve the gloom or adorn the damp and chilly walls.

The woman ushered him into a large chamber containing a canopied bed of handsome dimensions. On the walls a solemn tapestry denoted some violent epic from Greek mythology. Indicating that he was to occupy the bed, she withdrew.

Stretching his hands to the blaze of a fire fragrant with peat, Felipe wondered why he had been removed from the dungeon. The window looked across the shore in the direction of his hiding place, but when he tried the door it was locked. Taking stock of his surroundings, he decided this new prison cell was an improvement upon that he had just left, so resolving to be of good cheer about the future, he lay down to rest his aching leg and await events with patient fortitude.

Without any idea of how long he had slept, he opened his eyes to sun streaming through the window, to blue skies, birdsong, and a day so beautiful it hurt to be alive. Touching the soft pillow, he felt he would never again be ungrateful or take the simple things of life, such as good food and a warm bed, for granted. The nightmare from which he had awakened of sea battles and shipwreck seemed distant and unreal. There was but one part he regretted losing. An Irish stowaway called Maeve O'Neill—

She was not the beautiful woman who gazed down upon him— A cloud of dark auburn hair, a heart-shaped face dimpled into a smile touching brown eyes and warm curving lips. She was like some half-remembered vision from his past—but where? The square-necked velvet gown was out-of-date, but the white coif and ruff denoted the well-to-do matron. She was young, he thought, perhaps not yet twenty, but those wide-spaced eyes with their uneasy darting glances hinted at unhappiness, lurking tragedy—

Who the devil was she? Impossible that they had met before, but the sense of the half-forgotten remained—

"Marie Jamesina Sibella Stewart," she said, bobbing a curtsey. "Wife to Lord Henry Stewart."

The names meant nothing to him.

"This is my home, Burray Castle."

"And which part of Scotland is this, pray?"

"Scotland, sir? Scotland!" She laughed, throwing back her head and showing small and excellent white teeth. The gesture touched again that elusive memory chord. "Sir, you are not in Scotland. This is Orkney, the isles to the north."

"Orkney," he repeated slowly, nervously recalling barbaric tales whispered by returning ships about the horrendous customs of the inhabitants. Some of the remoter islands were cannibalistic too. Rumours of course; they could not be true in this civilised world— But Orkney— What infernal misfortune—

"Our winds are fickle. Our weather this year is worse than usual," she added with an apologetic shrug. Did she thus dismiss the wreckers' activities, he thought angrily, as a whim of weather? He only half heard her explanation of the rough channels and shipwreck, considering this new disaster to his plans.

Orkney, what a place to land! The islands at the end of the world, sailors used to call them. Small wonder the barren treeless coastline had little in common with the Scotland of his childhood, the dreams he had carried of peat fires and warm hearts— A traveller to El Escorial had described this land where the centuries had slipped by unrecorded, leaving the markers of a strange race mysterious as legend. They had disappeared without trace, leaving their burial cairns to be Viking-plundered, their stone circles and megaliths feared and superstitiously avoided as the home of magic. The Norse sea kings came and founded an island race of peaceful farmers, owning their lands under the ancient Udall law, their only enemies the gods of sea storm and land wind, whom they learned to propitiate.

For saints and sinners alike in this humble paradise all went well until the coming of Lord Robert Stewart, created Earl of Orkney by his half sister Queen Mary of Scots. In a reign of terror he had used sword, fire, torture, murder to bleed the island and place its people in thraldom. What he could not take by tax he would steal by stealth, or by threat of treason. Oh, there were tales in every court of Europe about the infamous Earl of Orkney, and Felipe remembered childhood's loathing of the bullying braggart and lecher he and Amyas encountered to their peril in the corridors of Holyrood Palace—

"My husband is Master of Orkney."

Felipe had scant hopes of mercy from the eldest son of such a father. Small wonder the servingmen who rescued him were so fearful.

"Lord Robert Stewart rules the Orkney Isles? And Zetland too?"

"And everyone in them," she whispered, her fingers playing with a loose thread on her sleeve.

"Including yourself?"

"Myself—and the members of my family and household. Am I to be told your name, sir?" she asked firmly, changing a dangerous subject.

"Philip—Philip Lennox."

"A good Scots name." Her smile was mocking. "Are you certain sure that is your name, Master Mariner?" So the sweetness had a cutting edge. There was shrewdness bred by necessity for survival. He recognised this was no foolish woman who would accept the slight story he had prepared—

"Let us try once more," she said pleasantly. "The truth would save time—"

"Would I lie to you?" He spread his hands wide, trying to sound hurt.

"You have already done so." She pointed an accusing finger. "No Scots sailor speaks Spanish in his sleep. I have been here for some time—"

"And you are so well versed in Spanish that you would recognise a sleeping man's mumblings?"

"Aye, sir. Besides French, Latin, and a little of the Scots tongue—Gaelic—I also speak Spanish," she said modestly.

Felipe laughed soundlessly. Here at last was a woman worthy to be his enemy.

"You waste my time," she continued sharply. "You are no captive Scotsman. You are from the Armada. A spy, in all probability. The story you told John and James will not do for me."

"Truly, lady, my name is Lennox, my mother was—"

"Enough, sir, of your protestations. Why are you here?"

"You have a convenient memory, madam. I am your prisoner."

"You are my guest," she said, smiling. "If you will speak truth, then perhaps we may be of service to one another."

"Very well. Don Felipe Flores y Lennox de Montreuse, commander of *La Duquesa Negra*, late shipwrecked on your shore. But my mother *was* from Scotland and I am familiar with the country. After our recent troubles with the English ships I was under orders to return home again when—"

"I know the rest of the story," she interrupted. "The wreckers are not of my making. I am powerless—"

"Your husband's troopers took over from the wreckers, lady," he reminded her.

"Devils." Her eyes overflowed, and Felipe guessed that his wild shot in the dark had reached its target. His concealment suggested a lack of harmony between Lady Sibella and her husband's family. This was a second sword which an otherwise unarmed man might find worthy of the wielding.

"How came you to the troll-house?"

Troll-house. He remembered being told that such marked the burial of the fairy people, who ruled the isles in the shadows of history before the Seal People returned to the sea. And for any human to desecrate their cairns by entrance or other violation was to court dire sickness, misfortune, and grief. His prickling flesh had recognised that uneasy pervading atmosphere—

"You would shelter safe there," she said grimly, "for none will set foot where the spirits of the dead still walk."

Felipe decided not to mention those small noises and whisperings, but shuddering at the fate he had escaped, said, "Surely men recognise they are but empty tombs—"

"Empty, but cursed still. Tombs of great princes violated by robbers, some ancient power lives on, my lord. Even the wreckers avoid them, although there are tempting stories, hints of treasures secretly hidden by the Finnfolk."

"Your servingmen left gifts for—what was his name—Hogboy?"

She shivered. "We don't take chances on earning the ill will of the trolls. God in His mercy knows we have enough natural misfortunes without courting the unknown—"

The door opened to admit the servingwoman. "I must go to my mother, who is ailing," said Lady Sibella. "You will meet her anon. Inga here will attend your needs. You will not be able to carry on any conversation with her since she cannot talk. However, her hearing is excellent."

Even inhibited by the pillows, Felipe's bow was courtly. "I am your grateful servant, lady—"

"Nay, Master Mariner, you are my guest. For a little while." She smiled. "And Burray Castle is yours to command."

Why such compassion for his comfort? Felipe guessed that his lodging in my lady's chamber was the best that this poverty-stricken castle could provide. Surely his place was rightly in the dungeon he had just left. For what reason was he, a presumed shipwrecked Spanish sailor and a probable spy, so regally entertained since Lady Sibella could not have known when he was brought to her that he was a Spanish nobleman?

When Sibella returned, she found him asleep. She envied his capacity for rest, in his delicate and dangerous position, doubting whether she would have dared to close her eyes so trustingly upon an alien land.

Her foster-mother, Lady Mary St Clair, had tearfully insisted she hand him over to the Earl's men. "You take too great a chance—with all our lives—should he be found under the protection of Burray. Give him to the wreckers then; let their gentle mercies be his comfort."

"I cannot give an innocent man into certain death," she said.

"Would you rather give all who have served you to certain death when he is discovered?" wailed Lady Mary. "And our home to the fire? Have we not enough misfortunes of our own without caring what becomes of a Spanish don? I beg you—reconsider. And who knows? There might even be a ransom," she added temptingly, with a sad look around her empty walls.

Strange sentiments, thought Sibella sadly, from the woman who had dared all through the years to protect her. Lord Erland St Clair's tragic death had utterly vanquished his wife, and drained her of humanity too.

For some time she stood looking down at the Spaniard's golden head, the handsome but chilly face untroubled, innocent even, in sleep. Suddenly she longed to see his heavy eyelids open and again that gentle smile break up the stern, blunt lines of mouth and chin. His good looks did not move her, but she had best beware of that beguiling smile. It was as though two people lived inside that comely exterior. The man cold and mature, uncaring and inclined to cruelty where women were concerned. And the boy, who could be teasing, jesting clown or earnest schoolboy, sensitive but ill armed against adversity, facing the world with only a butterfly net in which to catch sunbeams.

She decided he was at least a decade her senior, but there was the stardust of youth upon this man whom age would never trouble with a bald pate, a great belly, and jowls. The passing years would merely mellow and garnish. Even when he became an old man, women would still desire him.

Desire. The word hung upon her mind. Desire was something she had never experienced. And looking down at the sleeping face, she allowed her imagination to wander—to awaken in those arms, her head pillowed on his shoulder. Was desire that curious flood of awareness, of warmth, the illusion of falling from a great height? She caught in rein her dangerous thoughts, since her purpose now was to use this newcomer, this stranger, to her best advantage—in escaping the Earl's clutches.

She was aware that his eyes had opened and were upon her, green-gold under dark eyelashes. There was mockery in his glance, sliding down face and neck, until she became warmly aware of the cleavage between her breasts emphasised by the stiff busk, the low neckline of her gown.

"I trust you rested well, my lord?"

"Well enough." Lazily the eyes raised to her own.

"Well enough to dream up more lies?" She tried to sound stern, realised she had failed.

He laughed softly. "I only lie with a lady, never to her."

Sweet Jesu, did the man have power to read her intimate thoughts?

Her blush pleased him. "You have a plan for my escape, lady?"

"Only to have you out of Burray before my husband returns."

Was her motive to make an erring husband jealous? The thought interested Felipe since those tragic eyes in one so young suggested ill-use at some man's hands. From what he knew of the Earl of Orkney, it was feasible that the Master might also have the makings of his infamous father. He looked at her sharply, in time to surprise an expression more fitting to the face of cat upon the arrival of particularly opportune mouse.

The Lady Sibella would need careful watching—

Behind the sweetness lurked the cold steel of reason marked by shrewd glance and careful question. All proclaimed that this lady was neither foolish nor vain, and his presence in her bed had been carefully calculated.

If only he could remember where he had seen her image before. It hung upon the threshold of memory, taunting and tormenting, refusing to be summoned—

She turned from the window. "The Earl's men search the shore for the treasure they believe was carried in your ship."

Was it Spanish gold the lady yearned for? Was that the reason for his cherishing? "There was no treasure, madam," he said bluntly. "They waste their time. Anything worth the taking has gone with the wreckers. All else went to the bottom of the sea or drifted away with the tide and their gunpowder."

"You speak truth?"

"I do, lady."

Again she stared down at the shore. Silent for a few moments, she came quickly to the bed in the manner of one who has come to a decision. "My lord, I cannot keep you here for long. A few days at most, then you must be gone, well or ill, lame or whole." Her voice and trembling hands indicated fresh terrors.

"Do you fear your husband's displeasure at finding me here?"

"Fear? I loathe my husband—and every member of his vile family."

I was forced into marriage at thirteen. The Earl hinted to my parents that refusal would be regarded as treason, punishable by confiscation of their property—death. They are monsters of cruelty."

"Does your husband not love and protect you, madam? You are young—comely—"

"Love me!" she exclaimed. "My husband has recently taken a new mistress, who is also young and comely—and with child. He is eager to wed her at once so that his son—for he is certain the child is male—shall be his legitimate heir. Far from loving me, my lord, he intends that some mischief shall rid him of me. There have been attempts—"

"Attempts?"

"Aye, my lord—at poison. A gift of sweetmeats. My little lapdog, always greedy, snatched one from the platter. And died in a frenzied agony. A gift of wine and one of the servants, a sly tippler, died within hours. We have learned to destroy all food and wine from the Earl's castle at Kirkwall—"

"Does not your husband live here—with you?"

"He prefers the more riotous company of his brothers and their retainers in Kirkwall, or in Birsay, rather than the sober quietude of Burray." She regarded him sadly. "The Earl killed my father, Erland St Clair—by torture—and sent him home to die merely because he refused to sign away his lands—as a gift. My poor mother has never recovered, for she loved him dearly, and I was allowed to return to take care of her, since my presence inhibited my husband's many lecheries. My maid, Inga, had her tongue cut out for trying to spread infamous rumours about the Earl. She tried to escape with her sailor sweetheart to tell King James how ill his half uncle used these islands. Alas, she confided her plans unwisely and now she will never speak again. You will notice many of the islanders lacking hand or foot, ear or nose—the Earl's punishment for those who offend him and are too poor to pay fine or tax—"

"But this is monstrous. Surely these islands are under the jurisdiction of the King of Scots. The Earl should be removed—"

"And who is to tell the King of his kinsman's infamy? Who is to risk maiming or death when the Earl's youngest son, Lord James, is Gentleman of the Bedchamber, his daughter Marie, wife to Lord Gray, the King's current favourite?" At his glum expression she continued, "I regret, my lord, that you will have as little chance of leaving this island as any of us. We are all prisoners—"

"But you tell me it is your husband's wish to be rid of you—"

"Permanently, my lord, with my tongue stilled. For I am pawn in a game of power whose details need not concern you," she added hastily. "Do not ask, for it is better you remain in ignorance."

"Madam, you have told me either too much—or too little." Her apparent frankness suggested evasion, that she was involved in some secret scheme.

"My husband requires a legitimate heir." Her face coloured and she looked away from him. "It appears that I am barren—or so Lord Henry tells me."

Felipe regarded her with pity. Barrenness, the curse of queens and fishwives alike and always, according to men, the woman's blame. "Could it not be your husband is at fault?"

She shook her head. "Not if the serving maids' evidence is to be heeded," she said bitterly. "My husband is desperate since his younger brother Patrick has taken wife and has several children, legitimate issue. The Earl has no lack of heirs—five sons by his wife, the Lady Jean Kennedy—and four daughters, some of whom have already married and left the parental roof." She sighed. "And besides his legitimate heirs, there are ten bastard children. A man with nineteen children needs land. Can you understand how eagerly he seizes upon every available acre, by fair or foul means? We believe the Earl has begotten at least another twenty by-blows about the island. And now his sons, legitimate and otherwise, also contribute regularly to the population." She laughed bitterly. "Soon everyone on the island will be able to lay claim to royal blood, seeing that we are already onto the second generation."

"An infamous Genesis indeed, madam."

She shrugged. "Should you meet them with their lawless bands in the narrow streets of Kirkwall when they are in ugly mood, beware, my lord. For there is no brotherly love. Each hates the other, jealous for the Earl's favour, jostling for a new piece of land, as each new wife or mistress grows large with child."

Felipe saw now her considerable danger. What chance had Sibella, a barren wife, in this vast family where fecundity was all?

She smiled. "Blackguards, scoundrels, my lord, are gentle words to describe the Earl and his progeny. Scoundrels do not poison their wives; such is the privilege of kings and rulers. Along with murder and beheading. The Queen of England's father, Henry the Eighth, set the fashion—aye, and one in multimarriage too." She paused.

"Nor are the Stewarts blameless; those who have occupied the Scottish throne have held it in hands red with their kinsmen's blood."

"If your own life is at hazard, lady, could you not pretend to love your husband?"

She laughed. "Surely, my lord, you are not simple enough to believe that love has aught to do with the begetting of children." She added bitterly, "Every day there are children conceived through rape. Do not tell me you believe that children are the will of God. I believe that the laws of nature hold no such divinity."

She was interrupted by the arrival of Inga, with candles and fresh peats for the fire. The two servingmen, John and James, followed carrying a table.

"As it is in our best interests to keep your presence secret as possible—" whispered Lady Sibella as meat and barley bread, fish and cheese were set before them. Aloud she said to the maid, "Our guest is still too weak to rise from his bed, and I will feed him. You may retire." As the door closed, she smiled with impish delight. "That should keep the tongues from wagging—not that poor Inga will contribute to any gossip," she added soberly, pouring wine into two goblets. "Will you take kale broth? You need have no fear of the viands upon this table. I do not intend that any shall poison you."

He was uncomfortably aware of her intent gaze.

"I shall return presently, my lord. I wish to see that my mother is comfortable before retiring."

When she departed, he left his bed and donned the furred and velvet robe placed at his disposal, washing his face and hands in the ewer of warm water. In the small steel mirror he was able to observe that the gash on his hairline had knitted together and that his countenance was otherwise recognisably his own. It was also, he thought, stroking the beard and moustache he had neglected to shave during the voyage of the Armada, considerably more like that of his late cousin, Amyas Lennox. His leg was mending fast, and he decided cheerfully that within a few days he should be fit enough to attempt an escape from this accursed land.

Sibella returned to find him sitting in the chair, an unexpected touch of domesticity and intimacy added by her late father's robe. With long legs stretched towards the fire, a goblet of wine, and that slow, charming smile to greet her, he made an exceedingly attractive portrait.

"I have found you some shoes, my lord." She indicated his bare feet. "I trust they will fit and that you have no objection to wearing those belonging to a dead man." At his startled glance she laughed. "I have found you a place in Burray for the present time, since you must be content to remain with us until opportunity presents a return to your travels."

"When I trust you will accompany me to freedom."

She shook her head. "Only if my family and household go with us. I will not leave them to the Earl's revenge. But we were talking of shoes—"

"So we were, madam. Who was the unfortunate owner?"

"A cousin by marriage to my late father, from the far side of the island. Hearing of our bereavement, a widower and a scholar, he begged the Earl that he might join our household and take us under his protection." She sighed. "We expected his arrival two days since; however, my mother tells me his body has been found, his neck broken. Apparently his horse took fright during the storm and bolted."

"An accidental demise?"

"Truly so, we believe. An inoffensive gentleman whom none would have wished ill." She regarded him thoughtfully. "However, you may consider it to your advantage, since he was of your height and build, a little older, and more serious. The role can be played in safety, since he had but recently returned after years tutoring a Scottish nobleman's family. Fortunately, he was unable to attend my father's funeral, owing to illness. If he met the Earl—" She shrugged. "But we must take a chance upon it."

"Did this scholarly paragon have a name?"

"One which may strike you as divine intervention since his name, my lord, was also Philip. Philip of Cleat." Seeing his doubtful expression, she added, "Perhaps you can learn to enjoy our rough-and-ready society. To one used to the civilised court of Spain, this nest of uncouth vipers must seem primitive indeed. This castle was not always bleak, my lord, before its treasures and everything of value were confiscated by the Earl." She paused, awaiting his answer.

"I would seem to have little choice but to accept, madam."

She looked wounded. "Do you find my society so disagreeable then, my lord?"

"You twist my words, madam. I find you charming, extremely so; it is the role of Philip of Cleat which prickles my scalp. I fear I will wear his shoes uneasily."

"But you will not mind remaining here with us? Even my husband cannot object to my late father's cousin."

He regarded her doubtfully. "If I can convince him."

"Then it is settled. You will take more wine?"

He shook his head. She had drunk three goblets of wine to his one, and already there were noticeable effects showing in her flushed countenance, her air of reckless bravado. He decided he would do well to remain sober and keep his wits sharpened.

"When will your husband visit you again?"

She played with the stem of the goblet. "We shall have warning. Andro the lookout tolls the great bell—my lord husband regards this as a welcome sign." She giggled, putting her hand to her mouth. "But it is far from welcome; the bell is a warning to everyone, myself included. However," she added carelessly, "only as a token that he is conscientious about his marriage vows to beget an heir does he sleep in my bed."

"This bed, madam?"

"Aye, my lord, this bed," she said softly. She stood up and, moving to his side, knelt by his chair. "This bed, which I would share with the lowest menial, the poorest peasant"—she stroked the velvet of his sleeve—"if he is well set up and can put a child in my empty womb—after all, the father's role is soon at an end."

He touched her cheek. "Would you bed with me, madam—is that what you want of me?"

Reaching up, she put her arms around his neck. "My lord, I thought you would never understand my message. And not only am I willing to bed with you for the child you might give me, but"—she touched his face lightly—"for your own dear sake. I have rarely met a man, Scotsman or Spaniard, who pleased me more—"

"Nor I a woman."

She stood up, hands primly folded before her. "I shall not thole you with false protestations of love, for this is a matter of business between us," she said sternly, "which I beg you think no more of afterwards than the stallion who serves a mare." Smiling, she held up the empty goblet. "My lord, I need more wine; come drink with me, let us first eat and be merry together. Before God, let us be friends, for we have fewer secrets between us than many who would be lovers."

Felipe had little heart for this bedding forced upon him. True, Sibella was comely; to any man who loved her, the white beauty of her body was dazzling. Possessing her in that ultimate moment of surrender, he expected fulfilment to yield the same ecstasy, the fusion of flesh and spirit, he had known with Maeve. He was disappointed, for when in that last instant she cried out, clinging to him, he found his mind detached from the scene, remembering another time Maeve's reluctance, the sad green eyes full of all the world's sorrow. Oh, dear God, why had he used the girl so ill?

Awaking next morning, he thought she was there again by his side, and knew that those hours of passion with Sibella had thrown his empty heart into disarray. With considerable anguish he recognised too late that it was Maeve who lived in his heart, his beloved Maeve, whose bones lay quiet somewhere in the sea off this island, but whose unquiet spirit would never cease to haunt him.

10

"The scholastic life well becomes you, cousin," said Lady Mary St Clair, "but then all my late husband's family are inclined towards religion and the arts," she added in approving tones.

Philip of Cleat smiled into his household accounts. In the passing weeks while summer days glided into the fruition of autumn, Lady Mary had accepted the fiction of his identity without question, asking soberly for the welfare of various unknown relatives and then proceeding tactfully to explain their kinship to him. "Now let me see —that would be your aunt by marriage," or "your second cousin from Stromness—"

"Lord Erland's death has thrown a shadow over her mind," said Sibella. "Fear and anxiety over Burray and the loss of her possessions —these are the only realities for her now."

Lady Mary also condoned the fact that Philip was Sibella's lover. Many mornings she came into the bedchamber unannounced, wild-eyed, distraught over some household tale of woe requiring Cousin Philip's immediate attention as Burray's new steward. She never questioned his presence in her foster-daughter's bed. Before Lady Mary, Philip and Sibella's relationship had acquired more than a touch of domesticity and staid matrimony.

Philip was to discover that Lady Mary's ready acceptance of his role in Burray came easily compared to the secret she had guarded for the past twenty years. He had a sympathetic ear and proved a willing listener who had not yawned over the story of the Earl's iniquities a hundred times before. Thus one day Lady Mary placed a document before him.

"Mark it well, cousin," she whispered, "for it cost my husband his life and drained our fortunes to the gate of penury. You should have seen this castle in the old days," she sighed.

Philip found that Lady Mary had not exaggerated. The picture of the tyrant of the Orkneys took on substance. Had the King of Scots been a strong, just, and experienced ruler, the document would have condemned the Earl. But to young James, harassed by intrigues, these distant lands with their quarrelsome barons were but names. Truth to tell the miserly king admired his half uncle's twisting the law's tail in order to gain the lion's share. His consequent inaction over the document had cost Lord Erland and the leading signators their lives.

Philip read a monstrous catalogue of iniquities. The Earl had altered the old laws of the island guaranteed by the Scots Parliament and added new enactments to suit his own purposes. His Sovereign Lord's free lieges who disapproved were banished, their property confiscated, or allowed to remain on condition they yielded up their heritages to him. Where these two methods of piracy failed, they were left to rot in prison without trial, despite the tears and entreaties of their families.

The Earl had further compelled lairds and lieges to entertain him and his household in a royal progress "to the number of six or seven score persons, with banquets and great cheer on their own expenses." Philip remembered Sibella's tale of nineteen children, each with a private army of retainers and followers. Even a short visit led to their host's immediate penury and the inevitable transfer of his desirable property into the Earl's hands, or whichever of his brood had cast a greedy eye upon it.

The diabolical list continued with misappropriation of "common moors and pastures," and refusing to allow the burgesses of Kirkwall to trade except by his leave and licence. Even churches were not exempt since the clergy were compelled to set their benefices to him. A more sinister form of subtle oppression was the increase of "bismer and pundler," the ancient Orkney weights, to his own specification, which ruined landowner and small tenant alike. The price of meat was raised so that none could afford to buy it.

The activities of the wreckers now appeared as a necessity for survival. There was no escape by death, since dead men could be charged with old crimes, condemned in effigy, and their goods confiscated. This left a margin for appropriating almost anything which took his fancy and showed a surprising depth of imagination, thought Philip. As for the live men, in which category he included himself meantime, "none should leave Orkney and Zetland in order to make complaint against himself." And this was further reinforced by stopping all ferries so that none might pass without his licence.

"You see what little chance of escape there is—for any of us," said Lady Mary as he handed back the document. "And if we do escape—what can we do, with our property confiscated and cries of 'Treason'? Aye, Cousin Philip, mark this well, for treason means death, as my good man suffered."

She wept, and he put his arm around her shoulders. Small, bird-boned, and frail, she could be little past forty but was already an old woman, grey and broken by her adversities.

"The great hall here," she said as they walked through the stone chamber of modest proportions, chilly and unwelcoming. "Gold and silver we had in plenty, tapestry and fine furniture."

Philip looked at the stools and benches, the worm-eaten scarred table. Even in its heyday it was impossible to imagine this as a hospitable room. The tiny minstrels' gallery near the table had stood empty for years, and frequent scufflings indicated the now forlorn haunt of rats and other creatures.

"All our fine things—gone. Not only goods, cousin, but bairns too went with him," she added in a whisper. "Some of them laughed, thinking it a great honour to be called to the Earl's service, surprised that their parents wept. It is no place for those with daughters—or sons—of presentable appearance. Maid-in-waiting or page at his court. Pah—they little guessed they were being procured for court prostitution. I have seen some of these maids-in-waiting, cousin. They start off in the Earl's bed, the *droit du seigneur*, then they descend to his sons, his sons' friends, and so down the line until they end up as army whores. As for those bonny pages—" She shuddered. "Parents prayed to be spared handsome children. Only the ugly, the deformed, escaped the Earl's pleasure. Aye, sir, it takes stronger flesh than these gentle Orcadian folk to disobey the Earl's pleasure—"

"You are not then from Orkney, my lady?"

"Cousin," she said slyly, "what a memory! You ken full well that I am from Fife—Orcadian by long marriage to my dear Lord."

"'Tis a long way from Fife to Orkney. How came you two to meet?"

She patted his sleeve. "You have forgotten? 'Twas at Lochleven.

My late husband was in royal service, King James but a babby, his sweet mother in prison. I was maid to her," she added proudly, "aye, with her when her twins were born and her own dear life near gone. Would that she had died then and not lived to see those terrible years ahead of her."

Unfastening the ruff about her neck, she drew out a long chain holding a gold cross, delicately wrought with rubies and sapphires. In its shaft a spring released an exquisite miniature of the Queen of Scots as Philip remembered her.

"This was her parting gift. I wear it always, hidden about my neck, where it is safe—" She stopped, looking beyond him towards the door. "Lady Sibella, will you not join us?"

And for Philip, turning to greet Sibella, framed by the dark shadows, the last piece of the puzzle slipped neatly into place.

Each time she smiled, he saw the resemblance more clearly, and his only surprise was that he had not observed it earlier. Added to the Queen of Scots' delicacy the quality of steel, of James Hepburn, Earl of Bothwell. In all probability Sibella had been conceived during the Queen's rape at Dunbar Castle. The ruthless child of ruthless, passionate parents. She deserved to survive, this Sibella.

Awaking before her next morning, he lay with his hands behind his head, considering his discovery.

Sibella opened one eye, saw him watching her, and stretched out sleepy childlike arms. "How does my sweet lord this morning?" Her smile was an invitation.

"Well enough. I have been thinking—"

"Of me, I trust."

"Not this time." He kissed her bare shoulders. "I have been thinking of your mother."

"You have brought her great comfort. She longs for a shoulder to weep on, poor soul." Leaning on one elbow, she regarded him solemnly. "You will not let this comforting become a habit—I do not wish my mother to be my rival for your love."

"Your mother, lady, was my very first love—"

She sat up, staring at him. "That is impossible—"

"But true. I was eight years old and she was Lord Darnley's bride— So there was naught between us."

Sibella stiffened. "You talk of the late Queen of Scots, sir. You are somewhat confused, I fear," she added coldly. "Lady Mary is my mother—"

"Lady Mary helped deliver the Queen's twins at Lochleven—and spread the rumour that they were premature and stillborn. But one survived—"

She leaped out of bed and seized a robe. "Sir, you talk like a madman. Everyone knows—"

Philip put his arms about her, held her gently. "Sibella, I remember the Queen of Scots, and you are her image. Have you not studied the miniature Lady Mary wears?"

Sibella sprang away from him. "You talk nonsense, my lord."

"God's grief, Sibella, will you not trust even me? Queen Mary and Lord Bothwell were legally married, so should any mischance befall King James, any man with royal Stewart blood—and you as his wife—might with good fortune and audacity lay claim to the succession."

She sat down on the bed, no longer angry. "It is not because I do not trust you, Philip. You carry my life in your hands as it is—" She seized his hands. "You would not smile if you knew the weighty burden of this knowledge. When it was known that Lord Erland's wife was pregnant at the same time as the Queen my mother, Lady Mary was engaged as wet nurse. Her child was stillborn—she was never to have another, poor soul—and two days later my mother gave birth to premature twins. The first and stronger—myself—survived. The other never breathed. Even then there were those who cast eager eyes upon the pregnancy, seeing interesting possibilities for ambition should a royal child of the marriage to Lord Bothwell survive. The Queen my mother was distraught. She had suffered greatly, was near death herself. All she could see was danger—imprisonment, perhaps murder—for her newborn babe. She implored Lord Erland to adopt me as his child until she could escape from Lochleven and claim me. And so the dead St Clair infant was buried with my twin. Those interested would be satisfied to see two bodies—

"The St Clairs returned to Orkney and thought their secret safe enough. The Queen had bestowed on Lord Bothwell the Dukedom of Orkney as part of her dowry to him. After the disaster of Carberry Hill my father fled here. He hoped for succour from this land, with its strong Norse influence, which he believed to be more or less withdrawn from the brawl of Scotland's politics. In their parting words they whispered that if all failed and the crown was lost, then my mother would ask permission to retire with my father in exile, passing the crown to my half brother James."

Resting her chin upon her hand, she looked at him with the eyes of a sad dreamer. "They were so much in love, neither could nor would believe that they parted for the last time. Lady Mary has told me how my mother cried bitterly for my father, pacing the floor like a caged tigress at Lochleven awaiting news of her lord. 'Twas well she did not then know of Gilbert Balfour's treachery. The erstwhile Master of her Household was now Sheriff of Orkney, and my father sailed to Kirkwall in good heart, with the certainty of taking sanctuary with his kinsman and onetime companion. He discovered that, far from welcoming him, Balfour had issued solemn orders that none were to give the Lord Bothwell succour or refuge under pain of death and confiscation of property. And so my poor father fled north again and on to a woeful pattern of disasters which ended for him in death at Dragshölm Prison.

"The secret of my birth had become known to Lord Robert Stewart, for the Queen my mother believed in her half brother's loyalty. From then on Burray Castle, instead of a haven, was a prison. At thirteen I was forced into marriage with the Master of Orkney, to become a useful pawn in the Earl's many schemes for ultimate power. Savage tribes in the Indes, I swear, have more delicacy and finesse than the life I endured with my husband at Kirkwall and Birsay."

At the window, she studied the rocks far below. "There have been many times when I longed to leap from this window and end it all. There were times when I wondered what unseen hands seemed to hold me back from that dread end." Turning, she smiled at him. "And now I think I know what my destiny held—"

Rapidly he reached her side, held her close, thinking that her parents, rare creatures in this sad world, would have been proud to own such a daughter, grown beautiful and gentle, treating with honour and respect the St Clairs, who had fostered her.

"Sibella," he whispered, "I have a plan for our escape. John and James discovered a boat swept ashore—damaged—but they believe—"

"I know all about your boat," she laughed bitterly. "And so does everyone in Burray." She shook her head. "I will never escape, and I am as sick of plans that come to naught as ever my poor mother was in her long imprisonment. There have been many plans—too many, believe me—through the years. Now I wish only to live—to survive in peace." She put her hands on his shoulders, regarding him solemnly. "I fear you do not love me, my lord, but I beg your compassion for my clumsy—my urgent—wooing. My survival depends upon you—

you are my only hope now. I must have a child—your child—and soon—"

The robe, loosely wrapped, slid from her shoulders, gleaming white with the burden of heavy auburn hair spread across them. He felt desire awakening as he took her once more into his arms.

Philip of Cleat was bored. Since his adoption of dead man's shoes he had found naught inside nor out of Burray Castle which did not depress his spirits. His daily activities were restricted to the cove where the half-completed boat occupied his attentions. As he shared with John and James the menial tasks of an unskilled labourer, he realised he had almost forgotten the pursuits of idleness which were a necessary part of courtly life at El Escorial. He thought wistfully of the library, the long days of hunting, the evenings of music and bright conversation.

He gathered from Sibella that Orkney had no time to spare for gentlemen or for idleness. What few lairds remained after Lord Robert's merciless culling wore the same clothes and ate the same food as their tenants. They worked equally hard. Few could read or write.

One day the brilliant golden weather vanished into storms rolling in from the sea. His two companions shook their heads but assured him, "The boat is well-nigh ready, Master Philip—two, three weeks more is all that is needed."

Philip stared at the worsening weather with a sinking heart, especially when the two calmly announced that if the boat was not ready "Then we will have to wait until spring."

Next year—oh, dear God, no, that was too much. He must leave—and soon, he thought in desperation, watching the rain stream down the windows in rivulets, eager to reach that cold leaden sea—invisible through a week's constant fog. The few servants, whose kelp-gathering took them down to the shore, carried on their tasks briskly, fighting back uphill against a fierce gale, whose dismal moan was the only music to penetrate the castle's battered walls.

The hours spent in Sibella's chamber were tinged with domesticity, but each night in her arms made the dividing line clearer between lust and love.

Their nights of lovemaking were far in excess of his brief interlude with Maeve, cherished by Philip as the epitome of ecstasy. And his working hours found him staring out to sea as he tried not to picture her bones picked clean, bleaching on the sea bed, her long black hair weaving lifeless through the waves like sea wrack. Tormented that he had ill-used the Irish girl and she had gone to her sea grave without granting him forgiveness, he was haunted indeed—

With much time to his own devices his thoughts penetrated the shallow, selfish Don Felipe Flores y Lennox de Montreuse, revealing some surprising facts about the new man who had been washed up on the shore at Burray.

His emotionless relationship with Sibella proved to him that he was capable of love and devotion to two people in his life only— Amyas and Maeve. And he had lost them both. Worse, he considered himself directly responsible for Amyas's end and indirectly for Maeve's. Had he insisted she return to Calais with the other women, she might still be alive—

Turning from Maeve, his mind presented a vivid picture of Amyas's family at Lennoxhoe, the house near Plymouth which he had never seen and knew only from Amyas's childhood descriptions. In imagination he followed the fortunes of the bereaved wife and children. Beside Amyas's unknown grave they wept, and he felt his throat constrict as he made a vow and a plan steadily grew—

Instead of returning to Spain's idleness he would go to Lennoxhoe and set himself up as the protector of his late cousin's family, as Philip of Cleat had done at Burray. For a while he rejoiced in such an idea—Kirkwall, a ship to London—he had no money but could work his passage—the rest would be simple. But what if the welcome he imagined was not forthcoming? However splendid his English, Amyas's family knew him to be a Spaniard, godson of wicked King Philip, the enemy of England. Surely someone on the *Warlock* had survived to tell the extraordinary tale of the Spanish commander who was Captain Lennox's double. It would not take them long to reach the shocking answer. They could only loathe and detest him, blaming him for his cousin's death—

Philip winced as from a blow at the memory he could not erase— of Amyas's limp body in the sea. He need not pretend that he could soothe his own guilt by succouring his cousin's family. His presence, so like in looks alone to the man they had lost, could only add to their distress. How could he comfort Mistress Lennox for her lost husband's love or inexperienced in paternity, take a father's place with her orphaned children? Besides, his whole plan was built on supposition that Amyas had been a man of family and substance.

What if he had been alone, like himself—a widower or bachelor? What penance would then acquit his guilt?

Suddenly his plans for the future came to an abrupt end. Those days of boredom appeared enviable beyond measure in the danger confronting Sibella and himself in Lord Robert Stewart's unexpected arrival at Burray.

They were awakened by the bell on Burray Castle tower. Three times, a pause, then three again.

Sibella sprang out of bed and ran to the window. "Lord Henry—he's coming to Burray. He awaits the tide on the opposite shore. Hush—listen—"

Another series of prearranged bells indicated that the Earl was with him. At such dire news Philip dressed hastily, and seizing his papers, he said, "In the hour of our trial may the Good Lord deliver us. I trust your dead cousin's shoes will not pinch too tight—to the extent of betraying me."

"We will soon know how well you have played your part," said Sibella sweetly.

"That remark lacks your usual charity, madam. I understood that your husband had not the pleasure of Philip of Cleat's acquaintance."

Smiling, she put her hands on his shoulders. "Sweetheart, I do but tease you. To my certain knowledge, they never met. However, it is exceeding fortunate that Cousin Philip was of your colouring."

"Fortunate indeed. And that his clothes are a tolerable fit. Are you sure he was not a spy? Perhaps the Earl suggested that he should enter the Burray household?"

"My dearest, you have a most suspicious mind. Poor Philip—I can assure you he had little of the attributes which would make a good spy." She regarded him, frowning. "I believe he also had some condition of the lungs. Consult Lady Mary if there were any habits—"

"Perhaps I had better add some faulty breathing to my role, for safety's sake."

She laughed. "A little wheezing, my lord, might serve. But pray do nothing which would bring yourself markedly to the Earl's attention."

"You forget—the Earl and I have met before."

She laughed. "A child of eight! You cannot be serious, my lord! Aye, feel fortunate that you—like poor Philip of Cleat—are of the

Scottish and Norse complexion rather than the Spanish." She regarded him, head on side. "You look like so many other people on the island."

"God be thanked then for small mercies," he sighed as she opened the door for him. His arms full of his possessions, she kissed him. "And keep well away from my side. Do not even speak with me if it can be avoided, for I fear we shall declare ourselves from our looks to be lovers."

Lady Mary met him in the corridor and bustled him into her room. "Your papers upon my table, cousin. We are at work on the household accounts."

Together at the window they watched the Earl and his followers ride up the steep winding path from the sea. As the jingle of harness grew nearer, Lady Mary helped him into scholar's gown and bonnet. Together they went downstairs and to the great hall, where Lady Sibella already waited, shivering, and not entirely from cold, to receive the newcomers.

Philip, bowing over his hand, was surprised to find the Master of Orkney both very young and very ordinary in appearance. For a man so unsavoury, he must have begun his infamy from the cradle. There was no feature to denote wickedness in a face that was beardless, comely although a trifle weak, with butter-coloured hair, marred only by eyes so close set they appeared to squint.

"The Earl my father will be with us presently." A high voice added to the youthful exterior, thought Philip, guessing that Lord Henry must be older than he looked. "Bring us refreshments, my lady, while we await him."

Wine, bannocks, and cheese were set before them. Philip bowed to Sibella, cold-faced, following her glance to the small plump girl at Lord Henry's side, who brusquely laid claim to the solitary armchair before the peat fire and was preoccupied in warming her hands.

Philip observed she was not ill favoured, a trifle bold of lip and eye —perhaps kin to the Stewarts rather than servant, seeing that Lord Henry paid her marked and anxious attention. Philip noticed how her eyes lingered admiringly on the one remaining tapestry. A question was clearly asked, and when Lord Henry announced an inspection of the castle apartments, she sprang eagerly from her chair to accompany him, all lethargy forgotten.

Who could she be?

"Cousin Philip will accompany us," said Lady Mary.

Up stair and along corridor the girl peered into each chamber, asked many questions, and received of Lord Henry in return some whispered comments.

Sibella led the party, her face paler than usual. Her nervous manner communicated her fear to him. His hands began to sweat. Was he about to be discovered?

Lord Henry fell into step by his side. "The Earl my father will pleasure you with his company later, Master Philip. Affairs take him to the other side of the island. He has questions to put to you." Philip swallowed hard, but failed to detect any grim knowledge in the smooth face before him.

Bowing, he hoped he appeared calmer than he felt. Was the Earl aware of suspicious factors about Philip of Cleat unknown to himself? Was there some connection in his "affairs"?

"I understand, Master Philip, that Lady Mary has put you in charge of the household and estate affairs at Burray. Mistress Crowe" —he drew forward the pouting girl—"Mistress Crowe here has a keen interest in such matters. Perhaps you will explain to her some of the household economies involved."

"Not now, Harry. God's grief—but I am weary and my feet hurt. My legs ache too," she added fretfully. "I must sit for a while." Her voice was coarse. "These hellish corridors are cruelly cold."

He saw Sibella's lips tighten, frowned a question in her direction. She looked away hastily.

"Have we a bedchamber, Harry?" demanded Mistress Crowe. "I trust it is warm—I want a good fire all the year." Then addressing Sibella, she said, "No doubt you will provide us with the best chamber in the castle." And taking Henry's arm in a possessive manner, she elbowed Sibella aside, whining, "I need to rest, Harry, I do truly."

As Sibella trailed behind the departing pair, Lady Mary seized his arm. "To bring his doxy here—under his wife's very roof. The effrontery of the bitch is beyond belief."

"And," whispered Philip later, suspecting from the frequent patting of her stomach that Mistress Crowe was with child, "I suspect looking for a nest in which to hatch her young."

Imagining that the passing years had turned Lord Robert Stewart into an ogre, Philip was surprised to find that the Earl of Orkney was still recognisable from childhood's memory and considerably more personable than he would have expected from his debaucheries. A strong, still handsome, middle-aged man, the hot darting eyes and loose sensual mouth proclaimed that he was also a virile one. Philip was impressed by the splendour of his robes—the predominance of silks, satins, taffeta, velvet, and fur, all lavishly bejewelled, marked the entire party as members of an old-fashioned royal court. The magnificent costumes served only to increase the shabby gloom of Burray Castle, whose inhabitants presented a sorry spectacle indeed. The formal gown worn by Lady Mary looked fifty years the worse for wear. Lady Sibella fared little better, her dress threadbare. The appearance of both noble women was remarkable for lack of jewels. If they possessed such, then knowing the Earl's "pleasure," they had sense enough to keep them well hidden during his visit.

"I have ordered food and wine, my lord," said Sibella, whose curtsey, Philip observed, lacked humility and whose expression was distinctly hostile.

Lord Robert pretended not to notice. "Ale, madam—I want ale. None of your pisspot fancy wines. Ale's a man's drink."

The dull morning had changed to drizzle, and the eye-smarting reek of the solitary peat fire hastily lit in the great hall did little in the way of adding warmth.

A man who enjoyed his food, the Earl cared little who knew—or heard. However, Philip realised it was discreet to laugh politely at his vulgar humour as Lady Mary dug him with her elbow and whispered, "Your face is glum enough for half a dozen funerals. Smile, Philip —for all our sakes."

Philip's eyes widened at the amount of food the Earl consumed. Never had he seen so much ale poured down a man's throat, and his frequent recourse to the garderobe, where the spectacle of a noisy performance of elimination could be enjoyed by all, declared that the Earl was not handicapped by modesty or sensitivity.

Listening to his loud lewd comments, Philip found it difficult to think of this buffoon as a monster of cruelty. Royal blood, however bastard, should have dignity, he thought, observing a resemblance about eyes and forehead to both the late Queen and her daughter. Cautiously he glanced to where Sibella sat rigid by her husband's side, her plate untouched.

"You do not eat, madam. Excellent food, it is," said the Earl, belching loudly to show his appreciation.

"I have no appetite, my lord."

"And why would that be?" The Earl paused, his embarrassed

glance in his son's direction denoting knowledge of certain activities among poisoned viands. "You are in good health, madam."

"Indeed, my lord, I trust so." The Earl's followers were doubtless aware of his heir's clumsy attempts to rid himself of this barren wife. In the small silence she turned to Lord Henry and, smiling, said:

"I believe, husband, that I am with child."

At the other end of the table, Philip choked upon his wine, but conscious of Lady Mary's steadying hand on his arm, made a rapid recovery.

"Do you hear that?" roared the Earl. "Our daughter is with child. Hech now, is that not splendid news, lad?" he added, digging his son in the ribs.

The noisy clatter of a falling goblet and a small scream indicated that one member of the company besides Philip was shocked by the news. Mistress Crowe seized Lord Henry's sleeve, shouted at him angrily that she wished to leave immediately, while her murderous glance at Lady Sibella should have been considerably more effective than any poisons directed from Kirkwall.

Lord Henry stared unhappily after his departing mistress. He made a feeble attempt to accompany her, but at his father's shouted command he remained by his wife's side. The possibility of a legitimate heir and grandson made the Earl doubly lewd, and while Sibella blushed and looked increasingly unhappy at his sniggers, Philip felt it was all Lord Henry could do to restrain his father from seizing, and taking out for all to admire, the member responsible for this miracle of paternity.

"Away to your bed, the two of you, for another go—hech yes, let us make sure that it is a bairn and not just wind."

Lord Henry left the table, Lady Sibella upon his arm, and Philip did not let his mind dwell upon what was happening behind the closed door of the bedchamber, or what might well be his fate should Sibella lose her nerve and confess all.

And the weather, upon which he had been relying for the Earl's speedy departure, let him down once more. A gale arose, heralding a storm.

The Earl and his party were therefore settled uncomfortably about the castle while, in his turret room, Philip made careful plans for rapid retreat should it be necessary. He preferred not to close his eyes that night. At every scuffle—of which there were a good many about, particularly accompanied by Mistress Crowe's shrill voice raised in anger—he waited with dagger at the ready.

He was thankful to see morning and calmer weather. However, his sense of relief was premature. No sooner had he set foot across the great hall than the Earl appeared, accompanied by several of his lustier retainers. Seizing his arm, the Earl said:

"Master Philip—I would have a word with you ere I leave. Where can we be private together?"

Heart hammering, Philip bowed. "May I suggest the garden?" He felt safer outside, where a watery sun brought cheer, but little else.

The Earl paced through the herbs and roses, which led a timid life behind the barmkin walls. Head bent, arms behind his back, he growled occasionally and stared balefully at the castle windows. Philip took the opportunity to gaze nervously at the Earl's five henchmen, walking a discreet ten paces behind.

The Earl stopped, smiling into his face, rotten teeth, bad breath and all just inches away.

"Well, my mannie, I'm waiting—we're safe enough here."

"Waiting, my lord?"

"Hech yes, waiting, man. Come on now, spit it out."

Philip bowed. "I do not understand—"

The Earl shook his arm, growling now like a bad-tempered dog. "Of course you understand, you nincompoop. What information have you got to give me?"

"Information?"

"Hech yes, man. Information." The Earl paused. "They told me that for a small—er—pension you would be willing to pass on certain information. Just any mortal thing that you think might be of advantage to me, in the—er—workings of the castle here. And of course, their leddyships—"

Philip swore under his breath. So much for deceased husband's cousin, he thought, and would have willingly despatched his unfortunate namesake then and there had not God seen fit in His infinite mercy to rid the world of a nasty, sneaky villain.

"You wish me to spy for you, my lord?" he asked coldly.

"Aye, to put the right word to it." Philip was pleased by the Earl's discomfort.

"You must forgive me, my lord. I did not understand that I was to spy upon my late cousin's family. I am afraid your informants were in error. I am no spy."

The Earl frowned. "A position not without its rewards, Master Philip. A substantial pension, do not let us forget that. I was not asking you to wag your lugs for nothing."

"My lord, I would be merely wasting my time and yours, and I must decline your gracious offer since I have never seen anything remotely suspicious in either lady's behaviour. Innocent and virtuous they are, like my own late wife, industrious and respectable." He paused thoughtfully. "Perhaps my labours would have been more amply rewarded among the servants."

The Earl spat. "Not a chance, not a chance. Hech man, you must have realised that the few servants have been with them for years. Lady Mary refuses offers of replacements, talks of dwindling needs requiring dwindling help." He laughed coarsely. "As she is at pains to point out, there is little finery to employ servants, scant silver, or furniture or linen. If I put someone new into that kitchen, he would be immediately under suspicion and would learn nothing. You were my best gamble, especially since there was the—er—matter of some wee dishonesties in the past—"

"I have confessed to Lady Mary my grievous fault," he said piously. "And I now wish to forget the past. I am grateful to my cousin for the shelter and the chance to earn a living at Burray." He sighed. "I do not know how long it will last, since my health is far from good." Tapping his chest, he coughed experimentally and was well pleased with the hollow sound. "I wish to spend my remaining years in peaceful meditation."

"The more fool you," said the Earl roughly, and then grinned. "Hech well, no spy is better than an unwilling spy."

"I assure you, my lord, you are wasting your time since none can arrive or depart from the island without your knowledge."

"True enough. On another matter. Keep your lugs flapping for news of this Spanish treasure."

"Alas, the ship was but an armed merchantman, not a true Spanish galleon. Besides, I understand that the ship was dashed to pieces—an immediate wreck."

"A pity, a pity indeed. I had high hopes that the Armada would yield us a king's ransom in gold, especially when Baubie Finn's a dab-hand at conjuring up storms. Hellish weather," he remarked, walking quickly in the direction of the castle as the rain clouds burst over their heads. "Hellish country too, with its warlocks and witches. Should all be put to the fire, damned lot of them."

As they shook the rain from capes and bonnets and the Earl tut-tutted over drooping feathers and muddy hose, Mistress Crowe rushed forth, pursued by a stammering, imploring Lord Henry. Staring after them, the Earl shook his head sadly. "Swears she is carrying his bairn too. Like enough, like enough, for they are at it most nights—aye, and a good part of the day—and I can never get the lad out of her bedchamber. Mind you, I took it upon myself to warn him, long since, that she had graced more beds than she has eaten hot cakes." He sighed heavily. "Hech yes, I am better pleased that Harry's lady wife is with child at last. We must have legitimate heirs, ye ken, to keep the stock pure," he added sedately. Preparing to depart, he gazed on the stony faces of Lady Mary and Sibella, and digging an elbow into Philip's ribs, he whispered, "Should you long for merrier company than this, we can provide better sport for you at Kirkwall. I will leave a pass for you to travel on the ferries. Have to make these rules, ye ken," he said sternly, "otherwise we would have no end of riffraff, beggars and all, fouling up our town. We would not be able to call the place our own. Why not return with us now?"

"My lord, I would gladly but there are matters with Lady Mary to settle first."

It was with considerable relief that he saw them depart, since Philip of Cleat's shoes were pinching dangerously.

He found Sibella already at work helping the servants clear the debris.

"In truth it looks more like a castle taken by siege than a peaceful visit."

Sibella shuddered. "Be grateful that neither Lord Henry nor the Earl comes to Burray more often than is necessary to maintain the appearance of a devoted family. They always depart richer than they arrived. You will have noticed the spare carts—in case some booty appeals to them."

In the great hall, Lady Mary wept beside a dustless patch on the stone wall where a tapestry had recently hung.

"The Earl?" said Philip, putting a comforting arm about her.

"Nay. This time it pleasured him to accept it upon Mistress Crowe's behalf. That little whore stole my tapestry," she added vehemently.

He was glad to return to his room in the turret. Although Sibella's announcement that she was with child had come as a complete surprise, he was glad for her sake and also for his own that the imposture of Philip of Cleat and my lady's lover were almost at an end. Even if the boat was not ready soon, he had the Earl's pass to visit Kirkwall. He would find a ship—he must escape from this cage without bars, where the door was constantly guarded by the Queen of Scots' daughter.

Ruefully he decided that as mistress she would behave in the same ruthless, reckless manner that had brought disaster upon her royal mother and the Earl of Bothwell. With such a heritage he need not expect any blessing on his departure or a few gentle tears.

In the little bed, seldom occupied by him, thankful to be sleeping alone, he closed his eyes.

His peaceful slumber was rudely awakened.

11

The Earl and Lord Henry had returned. He was betrayed, seized in brutal hands— The dream faded and he opened his eyes to find Sibella staring down at him, her face hardly less angry than those of his nightmare captors.

"What do you here, Philip?"

"I sleep—or try to," he said shortly.

"In the wrong bed surely?" Despite her honeyed tones she was in a tight-lipped rage.

"How so, my lady?" he asked wearily.

"You know well how so," she said, stamping her foot.

There was no possible avoidance of the storm about to break. "Did not your announcement to the Earl mean that your need for my presence was at an end?"

"You are jealous." She looked delighted.

Philip was prepared to humour her with such a presumption.

"Come back with me," she whispered, stroking his cheek. "I have not done with you yet, my lord."

"I am tired, Sibella. The Earl's presence was exhausting—"

"I shall be kind to you," she said.

"I would sleep, madam—alone."

She sprang from the bed. "What is this talk of sleeping alone? You mean to hurt—to humiliate me—"

"Nay, sweeting, I do not, truly. But since you are with child, need I remind you that such was our bargain—"

"Bargain, bargain—who talks of bargains, sire? We are but a man and a woman—and we are lovers."

Leaving the bed, he drew on his robe, put an arm about her. "Forgive me, Sibella. I had no thought of distressing or displeasing you. I shall return as you wish."

At dawn next morning she stirred in his arms and saw that he was already awake.

"What of this child we have made, Sibella?" he asked.

She shrugged. "It is too soon to know for certain that I am with child. I have missed my woman's sickness these past weeks. But I could not let that bitch of Henry's sit there crowing over me—and over my dear mother. Did you not see her? As if I were already disposed of."

"I think you have your revenge, love. Your piece of news means that she is certain to be disposed of by Lord Henry, with child or no, now that he believes he is to have legitimate issue. If he is reluctant, then the Earl will see to it."

"Serves the bitch right."

"How long before you are certain—of the child?"

"A short while," she said vaguely. "I believe the Earl invited you to visit Kirkwall," she added accusingly.

"Who told you that?"

"James overheard your conversation."

Philip realised he was dealing with experts and that had he in fact been a spy he would expect no more mercy from the inmates of Burray Castle than from the Earl, perhaps only the boon of a speedier parting with his life.

"Would you try to escape from me?" Although she smiled, her eyes were anxious. When he protested she clung to him, whispering, "I cannot bear you to leave me. I have become attached to you, my dearest—"

During the days that followed, he awoke in the early mornings to hear her retching miserably into the basin at their bedside. Her face, wan and white, told its own woman's story, that she was indeed with child.

As her nausea increased so did her dependence upon him, her desire for his presence. She was a petulant sickly child, wishing to be constantly amused and comforted, and his bored or restless looks brought forth immediate accusations that he wished to accept the Earl's invitation to Kirkwall, to sample its dissolute court. His daily absences at the boat were resented, yet he knew that within days, given good weather, the boat would be ready and he would have a decision to make. In his heart he knew he would rather go alone, but conscience tormented him. Had he really loved her, would he not have urged her to seize a cloak, fly with him—or die together in the attempt?

His brooding silences were suspect, as was any mention of the boat's progress—

"You won't leave me, my lord. Not now. You can wait until next year. You must see our son born."

Philip sighed. "That would be a mistake, Sibella—"

"How so—a mistake? Surely the mistake has already been made," she said angrily, and then throwing herself into his arms: "I love you —I want to be with you always."

Comforting, reassuring her, he thought this was a far cry from the arrogant woman who had warned him that once his part in the conception of her child was over they would go their separate ways. She looked at his sombre face. "You do not love me—that is why we quarrel, why you wish to leave me—"

"Sibella, I beg of you, do not complicate our delicate situation with such yearnings." He stroked her hair. "We both know that they can never be—"

She thrust out her chin in a manner that would have made her royal mother proud. "And why not? Find some means of escape—"

"I have one, Sibella," he reminded her.

"I cannot go across to Scotland in a fishing boat," she said loftily. "It is out of the question, but find some other means and I will come with you." She smiled wistfully, touching his mouth, "As my mother the Queen once said of my father, 'I will go with you to the world's end in only a white petticoat.'"

"And what of those you leave behind?" he demanded coldly.

"They have Lady Mary. She will take care of them."

"Sibella, Lady Mary is hardly able to take care of herself. Would you abandon her to the Earl's wrath? Make no mistake about it, lady, the Earl's methods of gaining information will soon reveal that the Master of Orkney has been cuckolded and that the child Lady Sibella expects is that of her lover, Philip of Cleat." The thought made him shudder, as did her seeming indifference.

"A pox upon those we leave behind," she said, stamping her foot angrily. Then seeing his expression, she clung to him. "I did not mean that. I love Lady Mary—and my Inga." He kissed her tortured face. "It is you I want in all the world, and it frightens me. Sometimes I don't care if the rest of the world—and Orkney in particular—sinks into the sea and rots as long as we can be together," she added. "Forgive me, Philip. I am only a woman who loves you. Please stay with me—I beg you—just until the child is born." She shivered. "I am so wretched with this sickness—"

"That will not last. In a few weeks—"

She seized it eagerly. "Aye, Philip—in a few weeks, when I am stronger, we will talk again about the future—"

Philip sighed. Hard to refuse her wishes, still harder to make a promise, knowing that he lied. For all concerned, including the unborn child, it would be better to fly, never to see her again. She would take his departure less ill, he argued with himself, once this new life absorbed her—

In his eagerness to escape reproaches and his own guilt, he spent more time out-of-doors, where a transformation had taken place in the weather. The brief summer he had thought vanished into autumn had stolen back with renewed vigour, warmth, and radiance, ignoring the months which pointed steadily in the direction of winter.

For Philip it became a time of revelation. At first appalled by the bleak landscape, he found himself wooed by the reluctant charm of wide vista of sea and shore, where cloudless blue skies brought long golden days, and even Sibella's humour was the sweeter for them. The sunrise was dazzling in its innocence, while sunsets hovered over a wine-red sea.

The constant traffic of seabirds, wheeling across the horizons, extended to awareness that in this apparently colourless vista kaleidoscopic shades abounded. The gentle winds and warm days had brought air fragrant with the perfume of innumerable small plants and wild herbs. An unseen army of stealthy insects in the grass and ditches over which he travelled emerged, winged in rainbow hues, filling the air with vibrant music. Overhead the birds of the air added their flute notes of joy. After the exhaustion of nesting and the rearing of young, they returned home to a happy celibacy—which Philip envied. Acutely aware of the mystic natural fulfilment of life, he listened to that inescapable music, night and day, storm and calm—the sea's song. He fancied he heard the whisper of creation, older than time itself, the power and the glory of God's almost forgotten plan for Eden—

His voyage of discovery revealed that it was man himself who walked the earth dun-coloured and drab, since every track and trail supported an infinite variety of shy creatures, splendidly apparelled and purposefully setting about their own highly individual and secret lives, hoping to escape the hunter man and beyond any hope of his understanding.

Walking back, along the shore, he met John and James carrying a bag of rabbits. And Philip knew guilt and sorrow for the unsuspecting pretty creatures lured to the cruel death of the snare. Luckily their anguish was short, for the two servingmen could crack their necks betwixt finger and thumb and carry on an argument at the same time. Philip averted his eyes from the small death as James warned him not to get lost in his daily wanderings and John added consolingly that in Orkney no one ever escaped from the sea's presence, that all paths and tracks eventually led to it.

"The sea is master over all humans. It commands lord and peasant alike—"

"Once, long before our time, the sea was God's highway. That is why there are kirks and kirkyards close to the shore—"

"Our parish church is more than four hundred years old," said James proudly. "Reverend Erasmus Flett would make you welcome. He could tell you things of the universe we are too ignorant to understand—"

They did not interrupt their talk to continue the grisly task of rabbit-gutting, skinning the animals as easily as drawing a glove from a human hand. As they finished their task, John told him glumly that there would be no work on the boat tomorrow. They had thought it seaworthy, but when they tried it for a peedie fishing, it had developed a slow leak. They had no notion of what was wrong, but work would have to begin all over again—in the spring.

Philip swore. "That it cannot. Is there no one who can help?"

And James told him there was one man—the minister's cousin Harald Flett, an expert boatbuilder—who would know what to advise. "But he lives in Kirkwall," he added as though that ended the matter.

Philip remembered the Earl's pass as a gift from heaven. "I will go tomorrow."

And I will never return, he told himself. Best for Sibella, best for the child—and, whispered guilty conscience, best of all for yourself.

He had one last pilgrimage, to where all trace of the *Black Duchess* had vanished long since. Moths rose like uneasy ghosts from the grasses under his footfalls as if they watched his progress from the sleepy banks.

He paced the shore. "Maeve." And he smiled at the glow of her name upon his lips. "Maeve." Her ghost would approve of how he winced away from the rabbits' deaths, his growing awareness of the unseen forces of nature. Amazed, he realised that in his sojourn in Orkney he had seen more naked earth and walked more muddy paths than in a whole lifetime in Spain. Don Felipe had led a velvet-slippered existence on El Escorial's marble floors or strolling through sheltered vine and orange groves where the sun-warm skins of oranges, lemons, or a ripe peach were his only associations with living nature. Even the route taken by the royal hunt was carefully selected, formalised as if laid down by skilled hands, with all matter removed which might offend the sight of his Most Catholic Uncle King Philip. Glimpses of mountains and wild country seen from travelling coaches left him uncurious, the miserable villages dust-bound and untidy, threadbare as some worn tapestry in which the weave of the land had rotted away.

Occasionally some mischance brought them to a halt outside one of the vile odorous hovels in which the peasants lived, procreated, and died. It was with surprise he raised his eyes to the rude crucifix upon a door, signifying that such animals worshipped the same God as the King of Spain in his well-appointed chapel. As for the peasants, black-clad, ragged, faces seamed as old leather, they were like some subspecies of the human race, far removed from the brilliantly clad huntsmen. Guiltily he recalled Maeve's insistence that the meanest of God's creatures was noble and possessed a soul. Never in his whole life had he enquired whether or not a servant was happy or well fed, for Don Felipe had closer communication with his pet dogs and horses. And now he had daily communion—aye, and comradeship—with two humble, ignorant servingmen. This vile land had stripped the scales from his eyes, made him aware of his own shortcomings and of the wonder of God's creation. Even God had become real, an approachable Father, instead of the remote deity of El Escorial, shrouded by ritual.

He reflected that Maeve would hardly recognise him. Not only had his appearance changed but the donning of the plain scholar's gown had also obliterated all that existed of his former self. It was not Philip of Cleat who had died, he thought with a shudder, but

Don Felipe Flores y Lennox de Montreuse who had perished with the *Black Duchess.*

Savagely he kicked a stone in his path. His love for Maeve was useless, a waste of effort. Maeve belonged to the past with Don Felipe. If only he could shed her as readily— The sun, descending, touched the world with the glow of blood, of unearthly beauty— Trapped in the purgatory of remorse, without hope of absolution, he cried into the dying fires of heaven, "God forgive me—let her rest in peace. But tell her, God, tell her that I love her—"

But the sky did not open, and he doubted if God heard his anguish. His only listeners were the dark and shining heads of seals which arose from the calm waters and stared at him.

Seals. He thought of the strange legends John and James told of these creatures who had the power to leave their "kingdom of coral and pearl beneath the waves" to take on human form and live among mortals for a year and a day before returning forever to the Seal People. He shivered, for they seemed to watch him with reproachful human eyes. His footsteps led him towards the rocks which had been his hiding place.

Trapped on a ledge by the tide, a piece of flotsam moved.

Heart hammering, he recognised the tiny cage made for the songbird Sweetling. Caught by one wicker strand, it swayed back and forth, back and forth. He knelt down, but the sodden withered black object in one corner no longer bore any resemblance to the bright ball of blue and yellow feathers whose cheerful singing had plagued him during his latter bouts of seasickness.

He touched the wicker cage, which he had last seen clutched in Maeve's hands as the ship broke upon the rocks and left him prisoner under the fallen mast. Sweetling's cage—Maeve's dearest possession. But the bird—poor wretch— He could not bear to put his hand inside and touch the corpse, recognisable only by yellow beak and pathetic sticks of legs.

Holding the cage to his heart, he rocked back and forth in an agony of despair. The songbird's death was the final rupture, the absolute proof that Maeve too was gone. It was as though she sent him a message from beyond the grave, from beneath this very sea, where her bones grew white and bleached and her hair drifted like sea wrack through his nightmares.

"Maeve, Maeve." Pillowing his head in his arms, he wept not only for her but also for himself and his grievous loss by that sad and empty shore.

Footsteps, a timid hand on his arm. "Maeve!" Blinded by grief, he turned expecting the miracle which had brought Maeve back from the grave; he found instead a small girl, pale-faced. Only the deepening sunset turned her dark hair into the sooty black he loved.

A second glance told him she was crying too. "Oh, Master, Master—I'm lost. It's getting dark and I stayed out too long. I'm scared— Baubie'll skin me alive—"

She was almost incoherent with fear once she had begun babbling a tale of following hogboys and talking to Seal People. With some difficulty he interrupted the flow of her childish fantasies and asked where she was from.

"Over there." She pointed in the opposite direction to Burray— "Baubie's place. Can you help me, Master? I'll never be home before dark, and *they* will get me—" She began to cry again.

"I'll see you safe home."

Smiling, she wiped her eyes. "Thank you, Master." Holding out her hand, she said, "I'll take that dead bird—perhaps Baubie can help. She's great at bringing peedie creatures back to life—"

"Not this one," said Philip hastily. The child's second glance confirmed that this resurrection was beyond even Baubie's ministrations. "Shall we bury it?" she asked respectfully.

"Of course." The child watched him approvingly. When he buried cage and occupant in a small grave, she folded her hands together and with eyes closed presented an angelic picture, he thought. Eyes, dark as violets, sprang open. "God says you are a good man. Come—" Trustingly he took the tiny hand into his— And so Jean Halcro came into his life. Thirteen years old, orphaned, from Stromness way, she had come to live with her uncle Magnus, married to Baubie Finn.

"You'll ken my aunty Baubie, everyone does. She is a most powerful witch—"

He listened to tales of the strange people, the Finnfolk, to whom Aunty Baubie belonged. And all the other strange people who had lived here before Jesus was born in Bethlehem. A bewildering array of the life and times of Seal People, trolls, giants, dwarfs, and fairy folk, all came vividly alive in the wild mixture of Christian belief and pagan ritual which he heard to his astonishment issuing from the lips of this small girl.

"They are to be feared because they have cloaks of invisibility and can't be seen by us mortals, only by animals. So if you have a dog, Master, who barks at empty air and a cat who spits into the dark, then they are seeing the fairy folk. So when we say our prayers at night we leave peedie offerings for *them* too."

At last, with Jean skipping at his side, he stared down upon a strange shore with a great round stone tower, which she told him was a broch. Close by a stone house nestling into the shelter of the cliffs was home. And a wisp of curtain moving against the dark oblong of window told him that they were observed.

Jean stopped. "Thank you, Master Philip, for bringing me safe home."

"My pleasure." He bowed.

Laughing, she curtseyed to him. "Shall I see you again?" she asked. So sad she sounded, he said, "Perhaps—someday."

She regarded him with infinite adult knowledge. "You are going away—and once you go the magic will be broken."

"What magic?" he demanded.

She shrugged and, staring at the tower, took his hand again. "You have been kind, and I have a secret—"

Philip laughed. "What is this secret?"

She touched her lips. "Baubie has a seal woman—whom she magiced from the sea. She has magic powers, we think—and you have been hurt—"

"Hurt? How do you know that, child?"

"By the pain in your eyes behind your smile, Master Philip. Would you like to see our seal woman? She is supposed to be a secret, but you have been good—"

But Philip had heard enough of the Queen of the Wreckers to realise that she was probably an arch trickster rather than a witch. He remembered that he had strayed far and that he was a trespasser in a dangerous kingdom among savage humans, as well as other unseen unhuman forces—

"You are kind, child. But I must go. If I return I promise I'll come and see your seal woman—"

"Oh, sir, I hope you will return, for you and Boy are the first real friends I ever had."

"Who is Boy? Your dog?"

She laughed. "Boy's an old man." And in farewell she stretched out her arms in a gesture almost womanly. Laughing, he caught her and swung her up into the air, then setting her feet on the ground again, kissed her forehead.

She watched him go down the path, and he turned, waved, and seeing for the last time the tiny figure of Jean Halcro as the road curved and carried her away from his sight, he realised that another thread had reached out to bind him with gossamer bonds to his new vision of this alien country. In that moment, staring after her, he knew that had she been but six years older—aye, less than that, he would have asked her uncle Magnus for her hand. Her long dark hair, her dainty shape, wide eyes, and gentle smile cast a spell that reminded him painfully of Maeve O'Neill.

Hurrying back to Burray, where the sky and sea had turned from wine to blood, he wondered would he ever meet a grown woman whom he might love, who would displace Maeve's reign in his doomed heart. He wondered uneasily, Was Jean Halcro the beginning of a lifetime taunted and tormented by wraiths in her image?

There was a light gleaming in Sibella's window. It did not warm his heart with a welcome, for he knew this to be an evening of endings. Wishing he were less of a coward and could face the storm, he scorned his self-righteousness, saw his excuses to be made of straw. The answer was simple—he did not love the Queen of Scots' daughter—

"Where have you been this long while?" Sibella demanded. "What kept you from me for so long, sweetheart?" she added reproachfully, burying her lips against his unyielding neck. "I have missed you—"

He had been busy, time had passed.

"Busy—sweet Jesu," she echoed, "there is no need for you to slave. John and James are capable of such matters without your assistance."

He felt his lips tighten. He would never tell her now about his discovery of Sweetling, for she knew naught of Maeve and he wanted no jealous scene to spoil their last hours together.

She was curious. John and James had returned hours since and did not know where he had gone. She had been anxious, afraid, so he told her about his meeting with the lost child.

"Jean Halcro? She came to Burray once with Baubie Finn. They had better enjoy her society, for I fear she will grow into a great beauty, that one. And if the Earl does not claim her, then every man in the parish will want her to wife—"

Philip surprised himself by the swift shaft of jealousy and anger.

"You look tired, my lord," said Sibella in changed tones, smoothing his forehead. "You work too hard on menial tasks that could be left to others—"

"I enjoy menial work. I like to breathe the fresh air, for there is little for me here—"

"There could be plenty, were you so inclined," she whispered. "You have your mistress to entertain—"

"How to entertain, madam? Am I a clown? A jester?"

She sprang from him, said angrily, "You know the matters to which I refer, my lord. While you gallivant with servants and ministers, I sit alone here waiting for you—"

He put his hands upon her shoulders, shaking her gently. "Sibella, love—Sibella. I was but teasing—"

"You tease a little too often for comfort these days, my lord," she said coldly. "And I am not in the humour for it."

"Then I promise not to tease again." When he smiled, patting her cheek, she came willingly into his arms, pressing her body against him.

"Your most important task is to be my lover. Do not ever forget that, my lord."

He kissed her, conscious that this night he would lie with his mouth upon a ghost's lips, with a spectre in his arms that was not Sibella's seductive flesh.

The peat fire glowed and the bed was turned down in readiness to receive them when they had finished their evening repast.

Taking the unemptied wine goblet from him, Sibella leaned back against the pillows. Down on the shore, the seals barked to one another, and Philip, listening to their strange calls, remembered Jean Halcro's secret.

"The child offered to show me a seal woman, a mermaid no less, for my kindness in taking her home—"

Sibella did not share his amusement. "Everyone on the island has heard about Baubie's seal woman—some new novelty, a sly trick to fool her gullible followers—"

"So I thought."

"Keep away from Baubie's domain, sweetheart. You are safe only here in Burray, where I can protect you. What if the Earl's troopers had come upon you and asked questions?"

"Then I would have told them I was from Burray—and lost."

"Aye. After curfew! And be carried off to rot in Kirkwall prison if you were lucky—or a musket butt and your brains dashed out if you weren't," she added grimly. "They don't waste time on prisoners—"

"I saw no one—"

"Did you not know you were also in the land of the wreckers? They would have killed you for that shabby cloak. You will not go there again—promise me—"

She still slept as he stole out like a thief next morning. Leaving explanations about the boatbuilder at Kirkwall with Lady Mary, he began his journey by rough road and uncertain ferry between Burray and the town of Kirkwall. He knew Sibella would suffer loneliness and terror, and all the pain of his rejection. But he intended never to return. He regretted also leaving Maeve's bones unburied and the child Jean Halcro, to whom he had promised friendship. Perhaps Sibella suspected and was more jealous of the emotions the child had aroused than afraid of his danger from the wreckers. The promise to stay away from Baubie Finn's domain had been easy—

"Rest assured, Sibella—no one saw me," he had told her.

But he was wrong.

Someone did see him. In the house by the broch, the seal woman whom Baubie had magiced from the sea had watched Philip and Jean's farewell with almost human interest.

12

Second only in power to the Earl himself, Baubie Finn was the most sought after and the most feared woman on the island. Baubie Finn was not her real name, and despite rumours, her nativity had been mortal. Long ago, as Barbara Wischart, she had married Magnus Halcro, fisherman. According to the handful of survivors who recalled the event, the old crone with gnarled limbs and huge twisted hands and feet had been young and bonny. To the less romantically inclined, Baubie Finn was the ugliest woman they had ever seen.

Her short stature amounted to dwarfism. The still black and luxuriant hair, which should have been a crowning glory, grew low on her forehead to well below her nonexistent waist and was merely grotesque, refusing to be confined to her head and wandering to less attractive regions of her face. Her nose was large, her eyes squinted abominably. Such hands and feet would have appeared excessive in a person twice her height. She looked like a troll, and enquirers bold enough would have found her gratified rather than offended by the fanciful kinship.

Her only son, Boy, was a simpleton, and Baubie had devoted almost forty years to magical means of imbuing intelligence to that bland and childlike face, and of breathing manhood's vitality into the youthful body. Her long search had accidentally revealed cures for sick cows, for making crops grow where none did before, and a lucrative trade in peddling fine weather and fair winds to pleasure anxious mariners. She had also stumbled on a particularly potent spell for luring distressed ships to wreck upon the shore, which she used sparingly, for she was a healer, not a destroyer.

A dark wooden barrel upon the shelf contained a yellowish liquid nauseous to smell and loathsome to taste which she dispensed in small dark green bottles, hastily corked. Its main ingredients were salts and asafoetida with other pungent but harmless herbs to purge the bowels and purify the blood. A sweeter medicine would have been equally effective, but Baubie pandered to her customers' belief that the nastier the taste the more effective the cure. Next to the barrel was a small stone jar, or "pig," of unglazed clay and ancient aspect. Baubie did not deny hints that it originated from the trolls, since the contents could cure anything, but however much was used, they never diminished. Baubie could have given the simple explanation for this mystery that she merely topped it up again. However, awe enhanced her power, and people came from far and wide to sample the contents of "Baubie's pig."

No trouble was too great for Baubie. She would patiently search out nine mothers whose firstborn were sons in order to collect food for a child at the gates of death. She wove black wool underwear for rheumatism sufferers and nursed a highly private recipe for locating buried treasure. But her main quest remained unfulfilled— She had still to discover the magic to cure Boy's idiocy.

Magnus Halcro regarded his wife's unusual occupation with an apprehensive eye. One never knew what she might conjure up or that the mysterious passing stranger seeking shelter might reveal cloven hooves and a tail. He had never known a moment's peace of mind while the *Book of the Black Arts*, the source of some of Baubie's favourite recipes, had been under their roof. This manual of magic, printed in white characters on black paper, gave to its owner unlimited power. However, as with all the Devil's gifts, there was a snag. The owner of the book, dying, would be carried straight to hell. Only for a smaller coin than was paid for the book could it be resold, and Baubie, young and inexperienced at the time, thought the peedie black man at Kirkwall Fair was giving her a great bargain. However, recently the rapacious Lord Robert had eagerly accepted it as a gift. Baubie shuddered, still remembering its opening page: "Cursed is he that peruseth me"; she wondered if the greedy Earl realised the potential load of destruction he had in his possession since she also placed him under St Ringan's Curse, used only by those who had suffered intolerable wrongs without other means of punishing their oppressors. Baubie felt he and his sons richly deserved the fate St Ringan offered: a family cursed to the second and third generation—at which juncture they died out.

Even Magnus trembled at the power wielded by his tiny wife. A man of peace—anything for a quiet life—he had in his time procured for her many revolting but not unusual specimens. In Baubie's cures the excreta of animal and human were in constant demand; fresh pig dung for bleeding noses, cow dung poultices for bruised limbs, sweetened urine for jaundice, and milk in which sheep droppings had been boiled for smallpox. Besides mice roasted for whooping cough and snails dissolved in vinegar for rickets, there were many others Magnus preferred not to dwell upon.

For Baubie could with considerable ease change into a shrew when thwarted, a transformation which Magnus did not care to witness. By giving Baubie her own way, life was not only harmonious, but even occasionally sweet. Baubie was rare company; she could make him laugh, and after some of her herbal remedies he forgot she was old and ugly as she danced towards him, alluring as the Barbara Wischart whom he had wooed and won long ago.

She could also bring joy and comfort to the island's many sad hearts. He had watched her exorcise a neighbour's toothache, a child's ringworm, and cure warts by placing stones in a bag and throwing them into the sea. He had seen scrofula cured by the placing of white money—a silver piece—upon the sore, and a bad eye cured with a gold piece. The money was of course then confiscated by Baubie to have its evils removed. Once he witnessed her treating a boy with the "doonfa-sickness"—epilepsy: she pared his nails and cut off a lock of his hair during one of his fits, and then buried the clippings and hair beneath the spot in the garden where he had fallen. He was apparently cured, and to many of their neighbours Baubie Finn's powers were nothing short of miraculous.

She cherished the islanders fiercely. However, shipwrecked foreign mariners fell into another category, and when she learned of their violent deaths she regarded them with less emotion than she felt at the annual seal culling, or for the occasional stranded whale. She had more than enough folk depending on her. Foreigners and their welfare were God's business, not hers.

Her compassion for the island's population extended to its birds and animals, none of whom feared her approach, for she talked to them constantly, and they would come right up to her large feet and sit waiting patiently for titbits. Doors were respectfully held open for wasps and bees to depart upon busy wings. She was not past wading out to bring back a seabird with a broken wing, or clambering over the rocks to rescue a sheep with a damaged limb or some old ewe distressfully bleating and like to die in the lambing. The old broch next door was full of cages and pens where sick creatures led a health-giving but raucous convalescence, packed full of Baubie's medicines and ointments, as their condition demanded, until the day they either expired or made noisy pleas to resume their own lives back in the wild.

Magnus was justly proud of Baubie's many skills, for when the huge cooking pot over the peat fire was not occupied by one of her rather odorous spells, then it was full of delicious fish broth and vegetables. Baubie could magic food out of almost nothing, as their poorer neighbours soon learned. The stone house was warm and cosy, superior to the usual island hovels outside, while inside were fine pieces of furniture, wall hangings, and curios from many strange lands whose existences were unknown to Baubie and Magnus—the fruit of the wreckers' activities. All things equal, Magnus considered himself a fortunate man, with a sweet house and—most times—a peaceful existence.

Thanks to Baubie's reputation and the superstitious terror in which the Earl regarded her powers, their only visits from the troopers were for magic potions to increase virility. In most cases this visit was soon followed by a request for another highly potent mixture, this time to rid the unfortunate victim of the French disease, an all too frequent result of his excesses. Other members of the Earl's vast household, less frivolous in disposition, merely sought cures for baldness or rheumatism. She had felt very important when the Master of Orkney came and requested a potion to cure his wife's barrenness, Lady Sibella—that fine well-set-up lady.

Aye, barrenness was the curse of fishwives and ladies alike.

However, Baubie shrewdly realised how easily she might be accused of witchcraft, and had every one of her clients sign a paper that the potions were medicinal, given by her in good faith. If the Earl intended a witch-burning, she would be in fine company, and several of the Earl's family would accompany her to the stake.

She looked with a sigh upon Boy playing cat's cradle in a corner. There was only one magic left for him. The Seal People. If a seal woman coul be lured from the sea and magiced into falling in love with Boy, then her touch would make him whole. There were irresistible ways of summoning her, like the eyes and genitals of a drowned sailor. With the right incantations Baubie could force even the Seal King to relinquish his own daughter for a year and a day.

Although there were frequent drowned mariners, most had island relatives or because of the currents were washed up away on Burray.

The spell required that the drowned sailor should be delivered within sight of her own dwelling. Baubie Finn had waited patiently for years, her spells in perfect condition. The day after the destruction of the Spanish galleon Magnus rushed breathlessly into the kitchen to inform her:

"There's a sailor—drowned—just by the shore. Must have drifted clean away from that Spanish ship. He is a foreigner by the look of him—gold in his ears—"

"I am not concerned with his ears," said Baubie, emptying the pot and propping up her book of spells. "You know what to do. And remember—I want *nice* pieces."

With a shudder Magnus departed to his loathsome task which took him longer than he had anticipated. When he returned, the storm that had threatened all day burst over their heads. He found Baubie dancing with joy.

"Know what this means, old man? An unruly sea—the Seal People are busy." Watching the contents of the pot reach the satisfactory bubbling stage, she nodded. "I think we have her this time. Here is a magic that no seal woman born could resist." And she sent Boy off to bed, forgetting to scold him for his untidiness.

They awoke at dawn to the barking of a seals' colony nearby, their excited cries almost human. Baubie raced to the shore, waded out seven steps, turned seven times widdershins, and elevating the pot to the compass point, murmured her incantation. To Magnus it seemed there was a sudden silence, as if the seals too had stopped to listen. Tipping some of the contents onto the sea, they waited. But only the waves rolled in with monotonous regularity, breaking on the shore with a languorous flutter of lace. Only the gulls greedily showed interest in the pot's toothsome ingredients, and had to be kept at bay by Magnus.

"We must be patient," said Baubie, clutching the pot. Together they sat down in the shelter of a large rock overlooking the sea. But they were ignored by the Seal King; only a fine drizzle descended from the heavens to reward them. Finally soaked and uncomfortable within sight of their own peat fire, Magnus managed to persuade the disgruntled Baubie to abandon the dreary scene.

"We have to give it time to work," said Baubie. "The spell doesna' indicate how many hours it might take. Magic doesna' take much note of human time, ye ken."

"Seems they work on a different system of telling the hours than we do, wife," said Magnus later, returning from his tenth visit to the shore and drying his garments yet again. "Baubie, d'ye really believe—"

"Of course I believe—you stupid old man. This is the best magic we've had yet; it canna' fail." She gazed at Boy thoughtfully, then filled a bowl from the pot. "Here, Boy, come and get this. Don't just look at it, eat while it's hot. This is your dinner—good, nourishing soup. No, Jean Halcro, there's none for you—"

The little girl did not seem unduly disappointed, although Magnus watched, appalled, and raised his eyes despairingly heavenward, while Boy greedily and noisily demolished the remaining contents of the pot. Magnus considered that such an activity on his son's part was little short of cannibalism, knowing, as he did, what had gone into that nourishing soup. Yet again he resolved to keep a sharp eye on kitchen arrangements. When Baubie was concentrating on some particularly exacting spell, she was liable to be absent-minded. God in His mercy knew what went into Baubie's famous soups, her delicious and strange-tasting meals.

The sun was swift falling to the horizon, Boy and Jean asleep long since when the 'cries of the gulls, the barking of the seals alerted the watchful couple. Baubie flung open the door and pointed a trembling hand.

"Look—look over there."

A naked woman had appeared in the sea—

Magnus stared, closed his eyes, blinked rapidly, and opened them again.

She was still there. A seal woman. She had arisen from the waves and was wading towards the shore with stumbling, uncertain steps.

"Ye've done it, Baubie—by Christ, it's a seal woman."

"I ken fine it's a seal woman," said Baubie placidly. "Don't stand there like the old ninny that you are. Go and get her. And remember, if she has her seal's skin with her, take it! She'll try to throw it back into the sea, swim away. Then all will be lost—lost—"

Magnus could not believe his eyes; wading through the waves, he blinked rapidly, but the creature remained. Neat breasts, a flat belly, long slender legs, her flesh was real enough. Stretching out to him were human hands, cold and empty, purple with cold, as was the rest of her body. Magnus was disappointed. He had expected a seal woman to be different to ordinary women—and a mite more interesting in her nakedness—

"Where's her skin?" demanded Baubie, throwing her cloak around the shivering creature. As if the garment were too heavy, or maybe she realised that she was captured, she gave a little moan and sank to the ground. They turned her over and she lay like dead, eyes tight closed.

Baubie knelt down, put an ear to her heart. "She's still alive. Pick her up and carry her to the house, old man. And don't let her run back to the sea. Do you hear?"

Magnus felt the warning was unnecessary as he carried the almost lifeless burden into the house. Baubie closed the front door, clapping her hands. "Thanks be to God all her parts look human. For a minute, with all that seaweed around her legs, I thought I might have conjured up a mermaid by mistake."

"They do say men mated with mermaids." Magnus regarded the seal woman thoughtfully. "I wonder how they got around the tail."

"Stop your lewd wondering and put her into the bedchamber next to ours." Baubie dried the creature's long wet hair. "You will be safe with us; fine silken sheets and white linen there is for you."

They laid the seal woman on the bed, and her eyes flickered open. Again they expected resistance, an attempt to escape. There was none; she looked with unseeing gaze upon her surroundings, then with a weary human sigh she closed her eyes once more.

Baubie signalled to Magnus and locked the door behind them. "She will take time to get used to us; it is only natural. After all, we must not forget that although she looks human she is a wild sea creature, this selkie. Aye, Selkie shall be her name—"

Like children with an exciting new toy, they could not remain away from the bedchamber for long and constantly sat by her bedside in case she should awake and steal away from them.

"If only we had her seal's skin," fretted Baubie. "She must have shed it to turn into a woman. We cannot rest safe and secure with her completely in our power until we have it."

"I will go and search when the tide's out," said Magnus.

His return at daybreak was triumphant.

"Look what I've found," he whispered. The seal's skin was real enough. But even Magnus could not believe that this withered object had sat with any grace upon the slender white shoulders of that still figure in the bed. By the look of her Selkie was going back to the Seal People whether they willed it or not, removed from her human captors' power by fast-approaching death.

Baubie thrust the somewhat odorous skin into his hands. "Wash it carefully, and I will find some place she will never think of. I'll not even tell you, husband, because part of her magic is in reading mortal men's minds. I'll use some of my magic so that she cannot read my thoughts," added Baubie proudly.

In the broch Baubie removed a loose stone on the wall and thrust the skin inside. Her appearance was greeted by noisy, excited cries from her charges, who believing this was feeding time were bitterly disappointed. Sharply commanding them to silence, she examined a couple of invalid seabirds and decided they were fit enough to leave their sanctuary. They had not the slightest desire to return to the wild, and resisted her shooing and chasing, eventually roosting upon the rooftop, where they regarded her shaking fists with disgust and reproach.

Baubie, comforted by the thought that the seal woman was unlikely to hear the skin calling to her, returned to the house. Carefully locking Jean's door on the still sleeping child, she rolled up her sleeves, dragged out a bathtub. Filling it with water, she called for Boy, whose instinct, so tardy in other matters, was swift to prompt him of bathtime's approach. He had left his bed and taken to his heels. She found his hiding place among the rocks without difficulty and persuaded him homeward, reinforcing her arguments with blows and shrill curses which turned Magnus' face pale and weakened his old knees with fear.

Boy's resistance to bathtime was a matter of principle. Once immersed in warm water, he solemnly splashed about in precisely the same childish fashion as he had done for forty years. Then shivering, he waited for someone to dry him. Baubie had to stand on a stool to accomplish this operation. However, she decided proudly that he was a fine figure of a man, and well endowed by nature too, as she hastily averted her eyes from his manhood.

"Aye, Selkie'll be proud to mate with a fellow like our Boy, who'll give her considerable pleasure," she said to Magnus, who was to preside over his son's nuptials.

"If he knows what to do with it," said Magnus sourly.

"All males, human and animal, know such things," sniffed Baubie, drying Boy's hair. "Remember Selkie knows nothing of mortals, therefore she will not know that her bridegroom is—well—different to other men. And remember, husband, once the mating takes place Boy will be a proper man, wise and strong."

"Boy—we cannot go on calling him that. He'll have to have a name like any other Christian," said Magnus. "I always thought Hakon—"

"Hakon Halcro," repeated Baubie. "That'll do. Come along now, Boy—we have a nice surprise for you."

Boy's eyes gleamed. Since nice surprises were associated with food, he made a dash for the cooking pot.

"Later—not just now, Boy. We have a companion for you—"

"A bride," added his father.

Boy frowned. He vaguely understood companion as cousin, the little girl who had come to stay— But bride? What was bride? However, he did know that going up that staircase meant bedtime. He resisted this idea strongly. His parents held him and cuffed him firmly, unaware that his dismay was natural. Having arisen from his bed not long since, he was wondering with sane logic where the day had gone. Where was the procession of tasty meals that punctuated so agreeably the slow hours? And why was he being punished by being sent back to bed in daylight?

Grumbling, hot and cross, his parents dragged him protesting into the guest chamber, where Selkie was still asleep. While Baubie tussled with Boy, Magnus patted the tiny hand which held clawlike to the bedcover.

Suddenly Selkie opened her eyes; their luminous green depths, her long, smooth black hair drying on the pillow reminded him of the many seal pups he had destroyed, all with that dying last reproach, staring unbelievingly upon his treachery.

He muttered, "You are safe with us."

Her expression did not alter, leaving Magnus a mite dubious about his wife's latest magic. Was he going to end up with two idiots to feed and clothe instead of one?

"Here, hold onto Boy; don't let him escape. I'm exhausted with his capers," said Baubie, and leaning over the bed, propped up Selkie against her best satin pillows. Magnus decided she was a delightful sight for any man, and felt a momentary twinge of envy towards his son, seeing that on the rare occasions when Baubie made demands upon him it now took him all night to perform once what once he could happily perform all night.

"Boy," said Baubie, "come here. This is Selkie—your new wife."

Boy frowned. Wife—what was wife? Where was the companion he had been promised? To his disgust and bitter disappointment, there was only a grown up woman in the bed. He had expected a small child like the ones who played with him and by some trick of time moved away into the world of adult folk and left him lonely, to throw stones into the sea alone. Perhaps she would stay—this cousin called Jean—

"This is your bridegroom, Selkie—your mortal husband," pronounced Baubie solemnly.

The seal woman stared at Boy without interest or understanding. Baubie Finn was disappointed. She had hoped at least that her eyes would gleam with natural desire and pleasure when Boy's robe was removed and he stood before her naked.

At her side, Magnus cleared his throat delicately. "Should we not leave them now?"

"In a while, in a while," whispered Baubie Finn. "We cannot trust Boy not to let her escape. Besides, you will have to show him what to do. That is your business, husband." When Magnus winced, she added soothingly, "Come now, it will not be much different to taking the bull to the cow. And you have done that plenty of times."

Magnus shuddered away from such a necessity, pleading, "Once we get him into the bed beside her, he'll soon know what to do."

Poor Boy was miserable. He was not used to being without his clothes except when he was forced to take a bath. He did not like what was going on, his mother's excited, flushed countenance as she urged him forward, indicating that he get into this bed without his night-robe next to a woman who was naked as himself. Embarrassed without quite knowing why, he hung back, shuffling his feet, hanging his head. Suddenly his parents grabbed him, pushed him forward so that he was kneeling on the bed, then they seized his arms so that he fell forward spread-eagled on top of the woman.

Beneath his weight, she screamed, a terrifying sound after all her stillness. Like a seal pup mewing it halted Magnus, whose accomplishments in farmyard mating were proving dismally unsuccessful when applied to a human male and a seal woman.

"You take his arms, I'll take his legs this time," said Baubie firmly.

Once again Boy found himself hurled down on top of the woman. He protested, and so did she. His parents, usually kind, ignored his pleas. Again and again he was seized, his body pressed down on the naked woman, who gave that thin eerie scream each time.

Even Baubie knew when she was beaten and gave up her clumsy attempts at forcible mating. Both she and Magnus were wearied and exhausted. Besides, Baubie could never bear Boy's childlike sobs from that great body.

Magnus was greatly relieved to return to the more mundane tasks in his daily life, especially as all the commotion had aroused Jean. Curious by nature and unused to finding her door locked except as punishment, she now hammered in a frenzied fashion, yelling, "Let me out—let me out. Aunt Baubie—"

Baubie released her and made soothing noises.

"Boy—has something happened to Boy? I heard him sobbing—it woke me."

"He was—frightened. You see, my dear, we—er—well, we've caught a seal woman—at last."

"Ohh—where is she?"

"Come with me—and be very quiet."

Selkie was, not surprisingly, fast asleep.

A finger to her lips, Baubie drew back the curtain fully, and Jean poked her head inside, withdrew it hastily, smothering laughter.

"Is that a seal woman?"

"It is."

"Aunty Baubie, I still don't believe you. She looks just like any ordinary mortal to me. She hasn't even got a tail."

"She's a seal woman, not a mermaid, you foolish child."

Jean merely shook her head, still laughing, and Baubie, on her mettle now, said, "All right—I can prove it. You wait here."

Baubie rushed to the broch and returned with the skin, the sight of which increased Jean's mirth. She turned up her nose at the skin, which unfortunately had improved neither in smell nor appearance during its short incarceration in the stone wall.

"Why, Aunty Baubie, that is a *real* seal's skin. I've seen many like it; the fishermen throw them away when they are not perfect during the culling."

"I don't think your seal woman is nearly as much fun as Boy," she said a week later, when she had tried in vain to get Selkie to talk.

Baubie admitted that she was baffled. "I would dearly love to ken what goes on in the creature's mind," she whispered, shaking her head.

"Perhaps she doesna' possess a brain like ordinary mortals," replied Magnus with sensibility, as the seal woman stared at them with less comprehension than they received from their assortment of birds and animals convalescing in the broch. It was faintly unnerving.

The seal woman did indeed have a brain. She was terrified of her three captors, the huge man whose naked body they tried to thrust upon her, the old man who smelt abominably, with his great granite slab of a face, both of them bowing to the will of their leader, the ugly old woman who looked less than human. As for the pretty little girl, she seemed to live in a fantasy world. They were strange, sinister creatures, out of a nightmare—the continuation of a pattern begun long ago, of eluding the clutches of her pursuers—

The sea—the sea—

"What's it like, the sea—where you came from?" The old woman repeated the question daily.

The sea—the sea—

But Selkie could not remember.

"What do the Seal People eat? How do they sleep?" asked the little girl.

Selkie's blank look was not surprising since she was as ignorant about that fascinating undersea kingdom as they were. She was a seal woman who had come to live on earth and be a mortal's bride—so she was told at frequent intervals. Selkie was surprised since she thought she was human; hopefully more human than her strange captors. She had two hands and two feet, like the folk gathering kelp beyond the windows, and the same bodily needs for food and warmth.

As for these Seal People? She did not like the fishy sound of them, even if Baubie insisted they were her close kin. Selkie had no memory of them, or of anything else for that matter apart from strange violent dreams which vanished the moment she awakened. She shivered. She tried to talk to Baubie and show her gratitude for being rescued from that terrible sea, but although she opened her mouth no words came. Speech was like memory; both were around the corner, just out of sight, and although she often awoke screaming she could never remember why she was afraid.

Except that terror was connected with the sea—
Always the sea—
As soon as she tried to shake her jumbled thoughts into some kind of order, the sea took over. Great rolling waves came pressing upon her mind, then as if by the closing of a giant eyelid, all memory was cut off. She trembled when storms threatened the house, expecting the sea to race upstairs, green and frothing, to carry her off in a foaming, writhing tide.

Yet most days the house was warm and secure. She liked being in her pleasant, peaceful bedchamber with the door closed, away from their questions, staring out at the breaking waves, trying to remember what it was she had lost. She was always hungry, and there was plenty to eat. A peat fire too, whose fragrance twitched at memory. Once the old couple stopped thrusting the man they called Boy into her bed, she was almost happy and daily growing stronger.

One morning she came downstairs and indicated by sign language a desire to help with the household tasks. Her progress pleased Baubie, and she soon had Jean at her side, chattering as they peeled vegetables.

Watching the days turn into weeks, Baubie felt she had been cheated of the legendary happy ending from the association of Boy and the seal woman. Selkie had not the slightest effect upon him, and showed as little desire for his presence as he did for hers. The only passion they shared was mutual antipathy.

One day Selkie was at work hoeing the herb garden, dressed in an old kirtle, the gift of a neighbour whose daughter had outgrown it, with her long black hair imprisoned by a ribbon.

"She looks quite like a normal person—does she no'?—apart from that vacant look on her," sighed Baubie.

Magnus kept his thoughts to himself. Useless to complain to Baubie about her hearty appetite, the extra mouth to feed. Baubie would only fly into a rage. Magnus valued his peace. But he watched the pair cynically. Boy was showing considerably more interest in peedie Jean Halcro than he had ever shown in Selkie. He would laugh and throw her into the air and roll on the shore with her. They played, splashing in the water like seal pups. Boy was a happy man; at last he had found someone who would throw stones with him. The seal woman had come too late. Even the neighbours no longer made excuses to see Baubie Finn's marvellous seal woman. They merely shrugged and hurried by about their business.

"The sea is all she cares about," grumbled Baubie.

In the beginning the sea had fascinated her. Hour after hour she would pace the shore watching the waves break, as if the tide's ebb could take away the confusion inside her head. One day from the clouds of darkness a face appeared, to vanish again before it could be identified or the voice understood. Sometimes the clouds rolled back to reveal other faces—voices. Gradually the past events became known to her—most of them—but she did not know her own name or the name of the dear one who had drowned or lay dead at the wreckers' command—

With knowledge came mortal danger. She must move warily, for she lived among wreckers. Safety lay in her magical identity of the seal woman—until her still slow-moving memory could make a plan—

To that daily perusal of the sea Selkie added another, more secret ingredient. She scanned the horizons now for escape. But where to?

Her foster-parents watched her activities with anxiety. "She wants to go back to her own people, I think," said Magnus.

"You think too much," said Baubie Finn.

"Why not let her go, wife? You can see she is unhappy. Give her back her skin." Magnus was weary, as the fish diet which the seals normally thrived on had suddenly ceased to agree with Selkie, who was constantly and unaccountably sick. Since the fish he caught was also their staple diet, Magnus felt resentful at coming home weary, only to set inexpert rabbit snares to coax their silent guest's appetite.

"If I didn't ken better," whispered Baubie, "I'd be wondering if Selkie could be with child, for she does not have courses like mortal women—only this terrible sickness."

"Now how could that be? How could she be with child?" demanded Magnus, "for Boy was never near her." Then conscious of his wife's brooding gaze, sucking in her lips, he added hastily, "Woman, woman, you surely dinna' think it could be me? Wife, you're mad. If she screamed at Boy, well set up as he is— I'm an auld man."

Baubie Finn shrugged. Of course such thoughts were wicked. And Magnus had been uninterested in such matters for long enough. The idea of his treachery with Selkie was ridiculous—

"If—and only *if*—Selkie were with child"—Baubie counted on her fingers—"by the Seal King's law she is ours for a year and a day, so it would be born before she returned to the sea. But what kind of bairn?" she added in awed tones.

"It certainly wouldna' be by man's begetting, for none has lain with her. A seal pup, like as not," he added, hoping that it wouldn't be his bad luck and a whale for him to feed. "Time will tell anyway."

When Selkie's bouts of sickness stopped, Baubie Finn accepted that it had been some fever or a change of diet from the seal kingdom that had upset her. She did not want to believe otherwise, especially as Selkie had adapted to mortal ways amazingly well. And she was still certain that given the right kind of magic, she could be persuaded to mate with Boy. Stranger than two ordinary mortals in their own separate ways, they needed time to get accustomed to one another, she told the disgruntled Magnus very frequently, adding, "Aren't you glad now we didn't put her back in the sea, husband? See how deft she is, and nimble-fingered too. Why, anyone would think she's been sewing all her life." She had developed a kindness towards the seal woman, especially when she watched her mending and baiting the fishing nets, a job which Baubie Finn loathed and for which Jean had no aptitude whatever.

One day Baubie thought her patience had been rewarded at last. She saw Boy smiling to Selkie across the table. Another morning, her heart bursting with pleasure, she rushed to Magnus, pointing a trembling hand towards the shore.

"Look—Boy is holding Selkie's hand."

As they drew nearer to the house, Boy was mumbling to Selkie, hanging his head forward in his shy, shambling way. And she was laughing.

Baubie seized her husband's arm. "We'll try them again—tonight."

Alas, the attempt met with the same spectacular failure as those which had preceded it. Both the silly creatures were frightened and began to cry and turned away from one another. With Selkie sobbing into her pillow on one side of the bed and Boy scrambling out of the other side, snatching at his robe. Selkie's cry of distress was almost humanly pathetic.

"Don't fret yourself," said Magnus, "and don't beat Boy," he added as Baubie became shrill and cross in her disappointment. "It is not his fault or Selkie's. They don't know what is intended of them. They're both shy creatures. When we meddle with nature we set them back, make them ashamed. Give them time, wife."

Meanwhile Magnus was keeping a sharp eye on Selkie. He did not share his wife's complacence about the seal woman's restorative powers on Boy. The creature was developing a very womanly shape, and the kirtle which had hung pathetically loose about her childlike frame now seemed to cling everywhere it touched.

When he pointed this out to Baubie, she said, "Let us hope that such curves impress Boy in the right way." Trembling with hope, she did not tell Magnus that her love philtres were responsible for this transformation. This new recipe was her last desperate resort, rarely tried upon anyone not under her personal supervision. Boy seemed immune to their calamitous effects. However, after seeing those smiles exchanged and the handholding, Baubie was afraid to experiment further upon Selkie, for fear she might take a fancy to some neighbour's man, returning from the fishing.

It was no neighbour's man that awakened Selkie's interest, but a stranger in the district. A young man in scholar's gown and cap staring up at the house, talking with Jean.

Selkie had been warned to stay out of sight when strangers appeared, especially men, who, Baubie hinted, might do her more lasting damage than Boy. The thought awakened old terrors. She needed no second warning.

From behind the curtain she regarded the tall fair man with some curiosity. She wanted— *She had to see him more closely*. A desperate need overwhelmed her. She must rush out, snatch the cap from his head—tear at the sober black gown—

With a sob of animal pain she sprang across the room and leaped down the stairs. Magnus, who had just returned from the fishing and was having a quiet rest by the fire, received a terrible fright, confronted by this creature with the shining wild eyes, growling and thrusting past him. Magnus realised she intended violence to someone or something outside, and with unaccustomed quick thinking he intercepted her flight as she wrenched open the door.

Shuddering at her screams as she clawed and struggled, he half dragged, half carried her upstairs and locked her into the bedchamber.

"She's quiet enough now," said Baubie, hearing the story when she returned home.

"You wouldn't have said that if you'd heard her. And seen her," said Jean, who had innocently entered upon this desperate scene.

"Aye, wife," said Magnus. "I could hardly hold onto her, not even with all my strength."

"What had she seen?"

"Not what, wife—*who* had she seen."

"I am waiting for you to tell me, husband."

"The scholar that is cousin to the St Clairs at Burray—" Jean explained that she had been lost. Kind Master Philip had seen her safe home.

"Philip of Cleat?" Baubie was mystified. "There was no one else? You're certain?"

Both heads were shaken.

"It was him she was after, Aunty Baubie."

"I canna' believe it," said Baubie, remembering Philip of Cleat. "That dull stick of a man." She regarded the now docile Selkie apprehensively. Those love philtres were to blame, and she resolved to remove them from Selkie's diet henceforth.

In the days that followed, Baubie was extra cautious. She took care to leave Jean in charge of Selkie and her door locked when she was alone in the house. Seal woman or no, Selkie was turning right bonny, and although Baubie enjoyed basking in her neighbours' awe and envy of her magical powers, she had little desire for news of Selkie's presence to reach the Earl's ears, to see her carried off to Kirkwall Castle as a curiosity.

She was too late. Rumour of the seal woman who dwelt with Baubie Finn had begun to filter around the island. In Burray Castle gullible servants believed every word, while Lady Mary and Sibella laughed and said you could get some people to believe any nonsense these days. As for Baubie Finn, she led a charmed life. If it weren't for her love philtres, which made her exceedingly popular among the Earl's men—and among the Earl's sons, about whom she knew too much for their comfort—she would have burned as a witch long ago.

Sibella thought of the seal woman as she looked out of her window that night. She touched her stomach fondly. Did the child she carried, Philip's child, already move, alive within her? When he returned from Kirkwall, perhaps he would take her to see Baubie's seal woman—

Sibella urgently needed an excuse to visit the witch, for with only a normal woman's intuition she guessed that she had no magic to hold Philip's dwindling interest and that it was going to be very difficult to keep him in Burray without supernatural assistance.

13

The Earl's pass, which Philip presented to the ferryman, received only a cursory glance, and brought second thoughts that reports had been exaggerated and leaving the island might be simpler than he had imagined. Throughout the cold and wretched crossing he encountered only his one old enemy—seasickness.

As he staggered weakly onto the quayside at Kirkwall, he found it well guarded by troopers in steel. They consulted all passes carefully and searched the ferry minutely. Watching them drive swords into bags of meal, which they could not be troubled with untying, he realised that in a tight corner he would have made a poor show of resisting anyone. Helplessly he watched them perform their inspection with a jeering arrogance which infuriated him, especially as the miller who had travelled with him mutely had to watch his precious grain trickling through the sword-thrust into the sea.

Staring into Philip's face, green with sickness, they asked his length of stay and business.

"I am expected by His Grace the Earl. My business is with him and no other."

This, at least, gave him respect and an easy access. His first glimpse of Kirkwall, a huddle of grey hovels merging imperceptibly into a grey sky, had not been encouraging. In the background, the grey shape of a castle and a tall and rosy tower, the Cathedral of St Magnus. In the foreground, the white flash of wings and hungry cries of seabirds crowding around the fishing boats returning with the tide.

He found the boatbuilder's exactly as James had described, but learned that Harald Flett was presently at the inn over yonder. Walking round the harbour, he made his way towards the noise issuing from a mean, shabby street, which was doubtless the inn.

The few ships at anchor were merchantmen of the poorer type. With one exception. And Philip found himself staring at a ship he had never expected to see again.

The *Rosie*. Memories came flooding back, of Maeve in his arms dying of the pestilence the ship had carried, of Mahmoud's disappearance with the chest of gold, his passport to Scotland. Its presence in Kirkwall could mean only that it had been captured by the Earl's ships.

He must have wine to settle his heaving stomach, whose condition was not improved by this encounter and the feeling of doom which shuddered through him. The inn's interior was dark and odorous, the smells of stale vegetables and staler fish were almost too much for him; however, he asked for Flett the boatbuilder and was directed to a table where a man of blacksmith's proportions declared his profession. His grey mane of hair, his fine blue eyes and whimsical expression also declared an honest man.

"You have business with me, Master?" His greeting was genial; his handshake made Philip wince.

In answer to Flett's technical questions regarding James's difficulties with the boat, Philip presented him with the sketch he had been given.

"I am testing out a new boat for Birsay Castle. Tell James that when I sail it to South Ronaldsay, I will try to visit them with the missing piece."

"When will that be?" At the impatience in Philip's voice Flett said gently:

"We take no heed of days, Master. We go by opportunity and the right weather. To test out a new boat's capabilities I need first of all the right sea."

Philip decided that he had no alternative but to trust this man with his own reasons for being in Kirkwall. Lowering his voice, he said:

"Would there be any possibility of leaving with a ship for the mainland?"

"There might be. See, over there—the man who has just entered. An Arab pirate, they tell me, who will stow away passengers."

Philip turned round joyously expecting to see Karim, but instead, seated at a table with two rough-looking seamen, was Mahmoud Ahmed—a very different Mahmoud to the ruffianly character who had stolen the *Rosie* and Philip's Spanish gold.

By his appearance, he had prospered; his clothes, bizarre no longer, but elegant and expensive although on the garish side, were at odds with the savage face beneath the plumed bonnet. Philip felt the bile rise to his throat at the sight of him. He longed to rush forward and enclose his hands about the man's neck, the villain he considered as author of the misfortunes that had kept him prisoner in Burray and had cost Maeve her life. If only he could still lay hands upon that gold—

"His ship is the *Rosie*," said Flett.

"I saw it in the harbour."

"He will take you, for a king's ransom, to Leith."

"I have no king's ransom," said Philip, adding to himself, But for that vile creature, I should have. "How came he to Kirkwall?"

"He sailed the ship into harbour one stormy evening seeking refuge, alone and barely alive. His story was that he had been taken out of the sea by the *Rosie* after his ship sank with the Armada. He had been forced at gunpoint to fight with the Spaniards—or some such tale—then a pestilence broke out on the *Rosie* and he was the only survivor."

Philip wondered what had become of the six men from the *Black Duchess* who accompanied Mahmoud and his stolen gold. Had they died natural deaths?

"As I told you, Master, he was so weak he could hardly stand, but when the Earl's men searched the ship they found a chest of gold, which he said belonged to him; he had rescued it from his Spanish ship. He offered it to the Earl in exchange for his life with information as to where there was more. The Earl spared his life and lets him come and go without too many questions in this quest for Spanish gold. I am told he is pleased to have the services of an Arab pirate since he is not above a little piracy himself, but his sailors lack the expertise in taking prizes. I fancy they will learn much from Master Mahmoud."

As Flett spoke, Philip looked up, aware that the Arab was on his feet and staring in his direction. He groaned, realising that he had been recognised. Mahmoud had stopped in mid-talk, a look of evil triumph vanquishing the frown on his ugly face.

Philip tried to rise slowly from the table, tried not to take to his heels and flee from this place.

"What ails you, Master?"

"We must leave at once. Ask me no questions."

Once outside, Flett took Philip's arm. "Master, are you sick? You look as if you had seen a ghost."

"And so I have, Master Flett. I trust you to be an honest man."

"I am that. And no lover of pirates or of His Grace the Earl."

"Then I put my life in your hands by telling you that Mahmoud and I have met before."

"That is unfortunate, Master. I can only suggest that you walk delicately while you are in Kirkwall, for the Arab would sell his own mother for gold." Walking briskly towards the quay, deep in thought, Flett said, "You asked about a ship to take you to Leith. In your present circumstances I feel an early departure would be advisable. I have a ship, the *Swallow*. I will show her to you. I am allowed to sail her to Leith and other Scottish ports for timber since there is scarce enough in Orkney for a house or two, let alone the ships which the Earl desires. I insist upon giving the matter of timber my personal attention, as ordinary traders might be cheated or bring back unsuitable material." He tipped Philip a large wink. "I sail for Leith tomorrow at five after noon."

Leith, the port of Edinburgh. Was this the hand of destiny? If only pointing to some other life than the emptiness awaiting him in the court of El Escorial, the sterile existence where King Philip would be eternally urging him upon the hopeless quest for a wife, persuading him against his will into yet another loveless political marriage. How could he face the intimacies of life with any woman who was not Maeve, irreplaceable, beloved Maeve, whose ghost would be but a head's turn from him for the rest of his life.

"Leith it is."

He decided he would put his visit to good purpose by seeking an audience with King James and throwing himself upon his mercy by pleading the condition of Orkney. He doubted that the islanders would receive much sympathy, redress, or comfort from their rapacious King, but at least it gave him an excuse, since it was unlikely that the Catholic lords under the Earl of Huntly would care any longer for his embarrassing presence now that the Armada had been defeated.

When he told Flett of his plan, the boatbuilder seemed surprised.

"You are a foreigner—I ask not from where, Master—and yet you have a kindness towards this land of ours, with its cold winds and, some say, colder hearts?"

"I have. Your people saved my life, and that is a debt which must be paid. If they seem uncharitable, then they have reason to be so, since the Earl has oppressed and tortured, stolen and murdered."

Flett cut short his defence. "Our survival is not your responsibility, Master. How can you care if the sea were to open and swallow these islands tomorrow? For they are not your native land."

"If I had reason, I could put down roots here as well as any other land. For I have seen enough of intrigue and sudden death of late. I long for peace."

Having spoken the words, he knew they were true. He would mourn the loss, the door forever closed upon this land which had seen his rebirth, whose wild beauty had left its mark upon his soul, whose haunting sad sea song would echo in his heart until his dying day. But he must accept what fate provided, knowing that the longer he stayed, the greater Sibella's growing love for him endangered them both. One day when the child was born, and her resistance to the pressures of the Earl and her husband, Lord Henry, was weak, she would find herself screaming the truth. She would turn to him again for the love that would destroy them.

Aye, when he quit this shore tomorrow on the *Swallow*, he would never return.

"I would give you shelter until we sail, Master, but I dare not. Not for myself, but for my wife and babes. I suggest you take the road north out of the town. About two leagues distant you will find a fisherman, Tom Croll; tell him you are a friend of mine. But whatever happens, Master, stay away from the inn."

They had to step smartly aside as a troop of men rode briskly past them, using their whips freely on whoever and whatever stood in their way. Despite the swiftly glimpsed Stewart livery, they had the aspect of desperados.

Flett sighed. "God help these Isles should they fall into the hands of that man. Lord Patrick—or Black Pate, as we call him—the Earl's second-born. The present Master of Orkney, Lord Henry, is vicious but weak. That one—" He nodded towards the fast-disappearing horsemen. "That one," he repeated, "has inherited all of his father's vices one hundredfold—and a thousand more just for good measure."

They had almost reached the boatbuilder's shed, and moored in the harbour was a handsome ship whose decks were packed with timber; the fragrance of fresh-cut wood filled the air.

"There is the *Swallow*. And for appearance's sake, I shall take you on as crew. Have you a pass from the Earl? . . . Good." Flett paused. "A moment, Master. I like not the look of this."

A band of troopers lounged near the ship. "Stay until I find out their business." Philip moved discreetly into the shadows of the yard while Flett strode towards his ship. Immediately the troopers clustered around him. Philip heard Flett's voice clearly.

"Aye, a man such as you describe talked with me. A spy, you say. Nay, he is no Spanish spy. I have known him since I was a boy; a servant he is from Burray Castle, here on Lord Henry's business."

So Mahmoud had betrayed him. Philip looked around. There was no escape. There was naught else he could do but put on a brave face and bluff it out. He strode forward as casually as his trembling legs would allow.

"What do you wish with me, gentlemen?"

They looked at him suspiciously and were silent so long he almost lost his nerve. "Your business, Master Scholar. What brings you from Burray?"

"Master Flett has told you. We need a fishing boat mended."

"Your authority."

As they examined his pass from the Earl, he saw suspicion fade and respect take its place. "My business is with the Earl."

"Then your footsteps are now pointing in the wrong direction, Master Scholar."

"I am merely taking a quiet stroll with my friend here, enjoying the fresh air," said Philip with an attempt at a friendly smile.

The troop leader frowned. "The air on ships about to sail is apt to be unhealthy—in case you should be toying with ideas of leaving us without the Earl's permission to sail. This pass entitles you to travel on the ferry alone."

Flett bid him a courteous but swift farewell and disappeared into the yard.

"Your direction lies over yonder, Master Scholar."

Philip had no alternative but to accept their advice and was grateful to escape since their mocking remarks, so near the truth, did little for his frayed nerves.

Until the *Swallow* sailed on tomorrow's tide, he had little desire to encounter the Earl or Mahmoud. He would heed Flett's advice and keep well away from the inn. Passing it circuitously, he decided to head north through the town. To the accompaniment of a fine drizzle he walked along narrow twisting streets where the houses, close set to one another, left little room to escape the muddy spray from a band of troopers who galloped through. Using whips with considerable freedom on those townsfolk either too old or infirm to step smartly out of their path, their leader yelled:

"Move aside for His Grace the Earl. Move!"

Staring ruefully at his mud-splattered cloak, Philip almost ended his association with Orkney that day.

"Move—I say—"

Above the captain's command, at Philip's side a young woman screamed as a tiny girl toddled after her puppy into the path of the second troop. Philip plunged after her, saw the dog escape unharmed. As he snatched the child and thrust her, into her mother's arms, he felt the troop captain's whip bite into his shoulders.

In that instant Philip of Cleat died and Don Felipe Flores y Lennox de Montreuse was reborn. A Spanish nobleman, the godson of King Philip of Spain, he had never been beaten even in childhood. Much less had he felt the indignity of being horsewhipped by a common soldier whose rank, birth, and breeding were so inferior as to be blasphemous to his person.

He wheeled about, seized the descending whip, and wrenched from his saddle the startled captain, who had never anticipated such a reaction. Forcing him to grovel face down in the mud while the horse reared and plunged above them, Philip applied the whip to his back with considerable satisfaction.

But not for long. Rough hands seized him. "You will pay dearly for this day's work, Master Scholar—and soon," said the captain, on his feet but much the worse for wear.

"What shall we do with him?"

"The usual." The soldier seized his arm, tore back his cloak, exposing his forearm. "Give me your sword," demanded the captain. "Now, Master Scholar, when you can write no more, you will have plenty of time to think—what it is to be without your right hand."

Philip struggled and cursed, but they held him firmly. He watched with horror as his wrist was held by one soldier while the captain unsheathed the sword. All around, the faces and stinking breath of the townsfolk, crowding for a closer look, with the ghoulish fascination of the mob for a fellow human's disaster.

The captain's face leered inches from his own. "Hold him fast."

"Let me go—damn you—"

"It's only a hand, Master Scholar. Next time it will be your life; remember that."

"What's all this? Why do we delay?" The voice was familiar.

Philip opened his eyes, saw above the raised sword the red and angry face of Earl Robert, who had ridden forward.

"This man assaulted me, Your Grace, refused to obey an order, and dragged me from my horse. He took my whip—"

"What for did ye do that, Master Scholar?" asked the Earl, clearly astonished.

"I was but trying to save a child from being trampled by the troopers—and this—wretch"—he pointed to the captain—"began hitting me with his whip."

"Hrmpph." The Earl frowned and stroked his beard, undecided in this somewhat novel situation.

"We were about to take off his right hand, Your Grace, as the usual punishment. Shall we proceed?" There was undoubted relish in the captain's request.

"Hech yes—er, but a moment, a moment." He was staring at Philip. "Have I not met you before—eh?"

Philip bowed. "Philip of Cleat, Your Grace."

"Hech yes—"

"Shall we proceed with the punishment, Your Grace?" The captain sounded eager.

"Release him, you idiot. This—er—gentleman is known to me personally." He leaned forward and whispered to Philip, "But unknown to our, er, somewhat narrow streets and the problems they present to those whose business is urgent and must travel at speed." Loudly he addressed the troopers: "We will say no more of the matter this time—"

"But I demand satisfaction," said the captain. "Look at my clothes—and my cheek. See, it bleeds."

The Earl looked at him coldly. "You will not demand satisfaction when I am present. You will remember that no one—not even my sons—demands satisfaction when my will is otherwise. You will be careful to remember that you, Master Captain, are but a cousin's bastard." Ignoring the man's furious face, he said, "Now, all of you, remount—I wish to have words with Master Scholar."

Waiting until they had ridden on, he told Philip, "Don't make a habit of infuriating my troopers, Master Scholar, or you may find yourself in some situation where my arrival will be too late to save your hand, or"—he grinned—"some more vital organ of your anatomy."

"I am grateful to you, Your Grace."

"Then behave wisely in future. My officers have touchy dispositions—they are readily offended." About to ride on, he turned. "Hey, Master Philip, have you a bed awaiting you this night?"

"I hope to find one—at the inn."

"The inn." The Earl laughed. "Yon flea-bitten, louse-infested, rat-chewed hostelry at the harbour? You'll come out richer than when you went in, Master Scholar—in more ways than one. There's better entertainment for a gentleman at the castle up yonder. Tell them you're my guest."

"Your Grace—"

"Enough— We have beds aplenty—and comely warmers to go with them," he added with a wink, "for those so disposed." He looked at his troopers, waiting impatiently, and sighed. "The presence of a man of culture at my table would pleasure me considerably this night. My command, Master Philip," he added sternly.

Philip bowed. "My thanks, Your Grace."

"You may regard that as a memento"—the Earl pointed to his muddied gown—"but have a care next time; my officers are apt to punish first and discuss the finer details afterwards."

As he rode off, Philip's gratitude for the Earl's arrival swiftly vanished. With scowls and murmurs the townsfolk, who had been deprived of the hideous spectacle of his maiming, advanced towards him. Someone threw a stone, and he waited no longer, feeling they might enjoy finishing what the troopers had started. As they screamed abuse at his undignified retreat, he felt badly treated indeed. Pausing for breath, he realised such was their gratitude for his saving one of their wretched children from certain death. The Earl's intercession had placed him firmly in the enemy camp.

He found himself in a maze of twisting, stinking lanes inhabited by wretched hovels, smelling strongly of human excrement, whose interiors defied his imagination.

Almost certainly someone in the Earl's household must have encountered the real Philip of Cleat. He shuddered to think of that denunciation. He could expect no mercy, not only for himself but for Sibella and Lady Mary.

If only he hadn't met the troopers—if only the Earl had not commanded his presence— He groaned.

With the tall cathedral tower as a landmark he eventually emerged beside the Earl's residence. Grim and ancient, intended for defence rather than relaxation, it was dwarfed by the half-built palace arising nearby. Scores of workers toiled with huge slabs of stone, urged on by cursing overseers very handy with their whips. Philip realised that he was witnessing the sorry plight of the freemen of Orkney, slave labour for His Grace. He saw the labourers, women included, and children, young boys and girls, all trying to escape the cruel lashes, and with murder in his heart he longed to launch himself upon their mindless savage oppressors. Sickened, he walked quickly away, realising the futility of such action; the blame lay not with overseers but with the Earl himself for giving such orders to them. He guessed that the young boys had started off with high hopes as pages, "to pleasure His Grace." As for the girls, God only knew what sufferings had led them to work like beasts heaving stones —rape, seduction, prostitution—

Restoring calm to his countenance with difficulty as a trooper asked to see his pass, he found himself within the castle walls. The loutish behaviour of the royal tenants had led him to expect a tawdry show of bad taste; however, the great hall was furnished with the considerable elegance and expense he remembered of the court of Queen Mary at Holyrood Palace. Watching the servants spread the tables, and warming his hands at the huge fireplace, in which reposed half a tree trunk, he realised that he was in the presence of a legitimised pirate hoard of treasures, the cream of many shipwrecks, the price of many lives. The rare tapestries, paintings, furnishings around him had been gathered from the despoliation of the great houses and churches of Orkney.

As the Earl and his men entered, he thought with sudden anger of the empty walls at Burray and of the labourers upon the new palace, for he heard the sound of stones being broken, of voices raised as they toiled by torchlight far into the night.

The Earl greeted him enthusiastically. Little remained of onetime beauty in his lady, Jean Kennedy, daughter to the Earl of Cassillis. The bearing of his nine legitimate children, constant exhausting competition with his many mistresses had taken a deadly toll. The jewels which extended from her gown ruff, sleeves, to every part of her person available for ornament were but a travesty of the Earl's vanished esteem. Seated next to her, Philip noticed that each finger carried several rings, holding her knuckles so rigid that she had difficulty using the new two-pronged forks which were now the rage in noble houses. Her magnificent red wig, heavily ornamented and coroneted, threatened to topple into the meats each time she bent over her plate. Philip hid a smile. The Countess of Orkney would have reduced the legendary flamboyance of the Queen of England to modest insignificance.

A never ending tide of progeny of all ages followed their parents, jostling and shouting over matters of precedence. Above the din Philip murmured his thanks for being invited to sup.

The Earl grinned. "One more doesna' make a ducat of difference. What is one more mouth among this mob, eh, Master Scholar?" he asked proudly.

Sons had brought wives, daughters had brought husbands, all had brought children able to sit at table. At a decent interval behind the legitimate brood followed the Earl's bastard sons and daughters, and where applicable, their adherents.

"We are fair cramped for room," the Earl continued. "You'll have seen our new palace when you came in. Hech yes, one of the greatest in Christendom when it's complete. We have great hopes—"

Philip hardly listened to his hopes, trying to forget the wretched spectacle of human suffering involved in this architectural marvel.

"But labour being what it is these days, another year at least. Hech yes, folk are so unreliable—driven they have to be—no pride left in their work," the Earl added with a sigh.

There were two notable absentees from the noisy meal—Sibella's husband, Lord Henry, Master of Orkney, and the Earl's second son, Lord Patrick, on an "inspection" of the island.

As the Earl talked, the Countess ate with the single-minded dedication of those whose lives contain few interests in life beyond the gratification of appetite.

Philip observed that issue, lawful and unlawful, were extremely handsome. The young wives and daughters, richly attired and bejewelled, all fell short of the Countess's magnificence, and none was very clean as a forest of grubby hands waited to pounce on each dish before it came finally to rest upon the table. At least four Venetian glass goblets of exceptional beauty and delicacy were shattered in the fray. Philip had hardly time to mourn such a loss while fish dishes, florentines, wildfowl, game pies, roast coney, beef, pork briefly appeared and vanished as if by magic, since the diners were not content to take a modest portion and second helpings were unknown. Plates were heaped to overflowing, fish and fowl mingling indiscriminately—

Philip remembered the frugal kitchen at Burray as he ate a capon leg and, hopeful for game pie, saw that the depleted savoury courses had been succeeded by sweetmeats, greeted by a hush of expectancy from the younger members of the family at the sight of marchpane, sugar bread, gingerbread, tarts of divers hues, conserves, suckets, quince marmalade. Shrieks of delight soon became screams of anger as the smaller children not quick enough were elbowed out of some delicacy upon which their young hearts had been set. The Earl and his wife, impervious to the resulting furore, did full justice to a groaning platter of sweetmeats.

Goblets were emptied and refilled. Several musicians of depressed appearance took their places in the minstrels' gallery. There they gave determined vent to lute and gittern, their efforts barely audible above the din of family life. Among the younger members, with their own vicious quarrels to settle or their own small authority to assert, constant screams rent the air, pots and plates were upset by accident or by deliberate assault. No attempts at chastisement were forthcoming since the wine's effect was evident in a marked deterioration in the behaviour of their elders. Coarse ribaldry was exchanged between sons and servants, while wives averted eyes from husbands whose hands strayed relentlessly into the serving wenches' bosoms.

Noisome eating, drinking, the ineffectual minstrelsy, and the discordance of family life made Philip's head ache. The Earl's voice droned on—and on—

The Earl was aware of his guest's inattention and irritated by his lack of gratitude and subservience. His rare impulses of generosity were entirely for his own self-gratification and his almost childlike desire to impress superior brains by the display of superior wealth and power. He enjoyed fawning courtiers, especially those who were either in his debt or anxious to secure his favours. Master Scholar was neither, and he gazed upon him with contempt. What a life for a man still young and virile. Dry as old boots—yet, at a closer look, that tight chin, firm mouth, unwavering eyes, steel-bright, were not those of a scholar. The Earl had seen eyes like that too many times, cold and hard, not to recognise the eyes of a bowman—or a duellist. His gaze dropped to the long hands, the fine slender fingers, tip-touching. Noble indeed. Looking into the scholar's face, he glimpsed distaste hurriedly veiled into a bow.

The Earl rubbed his chin thoughtfully. The face and body of a fighter. Put Master Scholar into silks and velvets—and into steel. Hech yes, he would be a rare man indeed, worthy of any royal court.

The thought made him quiver like a hound on the scent. His nose twitched. There was a quality about this young man which might bear further investigation—

He saw that his wife ate less than usual, hanging upon every word Master Philip spoke. He caught her languid smiling glance in the scholar's direction. That silly old bitch hadn't looked at a man in such womanly fashion for years.

The Earl shook his head, wishing he were less wine-fuddled that he might set some sort of a trap for this unwilling, ungrateful guest who was not what he seemed—

At that moment a disturbance near the door announced the arrival of Lord Patrick.

Philip saw that he bore no resemblance to Sibella's husband, the pale, delicate-looking Master of Orkney. Lord Patrick was the image of his father. Thick black hair grew low on his forehead, above a handsome, dissolute face, which suggested acquaintance with debauchery at a remarkably early age. The fine Stewart eyes were already tarnished by greed and lust.

He bowed acknowledgement of his father's introduction. "We might have met ere this, Master Philip, had I reached Burray a day earlier."

"And how was the Lady Sibella?" asked the Earl, sniggering and indicating a great belly with his hands.

Patrick shook his head. "Nay, Father, it is early days yet. But she is tolerable well."

"Taking her food?"

"Aye. And with more eagerness since she was told that by your orders Harry has taken Mistress Crowe back to Caithness. She informed me that she has no wish to be further humiliated by her husband's flaunting such low persons—"

The Earl laughed coarsely. "Hech yes. Our fine Sibella so closely resembles her own mother that I fear it will be the worse for her. I should not be surprised should she end her life in violence. Blood will out."

"As you say, Father. But not, I hope, until she has served her purpose to us."

"Queen Mary and the Earl of Bothwell, the best and worst of two dynasties, created Sibella. Let us never forget that, Pate. And this grandchild she carries is strengthened by a further dose of Stewart blood. By God, Pate, we will yet hold the throne of Scotland in the palm of our hands—" They turned their heads and paused to look at Philip, who was snoring gently, his head sunk in his chest. He felt the pretence of sleeping might bring forth a more interesting conversation. He was not disappointed.

"A harmless fool," whispered the Earl.

"True. But you talk unwisely. Even to think such matters is treason."

"I talk treason—I, the Earl of Orkney, half uncle to the King of Scots? Now *you* talk nonsense," he growled, adding peevishly, "More wine—I want more wine. And what saw you on your travels that might be to our advantage?"

"Poor spoil, Father, alas. A few tapestries and pieces of furniture that might be of interest, in the carts out there. And some miserable pieces of silver and gold produced from hiding, under the usual threats." Patrick sighed. "These people never learn a lesson, it seems. We travelled far as Stromness for evidence of the Spanish treasure, but found nothing. I fear the Arab lies."

"He brought us rumour of a Spanish spy, one of his comrades from the Armada who, he claims, had a chest of gold for delivery to Scotland."

"*Another?*"

"Aye, he states that there were several, and that this Spanish spy knows where they are hid. Doubtless he's sniffing about your hidden treasures. But he cannot escape, for we are having all ferries and departing ships checked minutely. He cannot escape us."

"If he exists," said Patrick. "I fear this is another of the Arab's devices to keep himself in your good favours after his failure to locate the gold."

"Then he is running out of time, as he will find to his cost. No man lies to Robert Stewart and lives. He had better be speaking truth about his Spanish spy and we had better catch him and squeeze the whereabouts of this treasure out of him," he added with a laugh that was not a pleasant sound on Philip's ears.

He was sure that his face had turned pale. He had left his prison in Burray for Kirkwall and freedom, to find himself a prisoner again on this accursed island. How could he possibly elude them with ferries and ships being searched? He groaned.

Jesu, he thought, I was never made to be a schemer, and I have little courage to be an adventurer, either.

The Earl was sighing. "I had my heart fair set on that gold, Pate. Hech, well, what else *did* you pleasure us with?"

"Some girls who have left childhood since our last visit and are now nubile enough to be taken into our service." He smiled. "And a trio of handsome boys to appeal to those who care not for wenches—"

"What did you with these wenches?"

"Sent them to the kitchens to be prepared for their new tasks."

The Earl rubbed his hands, good humour restored. "Something for us to look forward to, eh, Pate? You are a good lad. But what of this mermaid? Did you bring her back?" the Earl asked eagerly.

Patrick shook his head sadly. "I let her remain where she was."

"And what for did you do that? Did she have a tail?"

Patrick sighed. "No, Father, she did not. Nor was she a mermaid, as we had been told. She was a seal woman."

"Pity. I would rather have a mermaid. However—a seal woman—what was she like?"

Patrick laughed. "Like any other woman. She had two eyes, two breasts, two legs—and, I imagine, all the relative parts between. Comely too—"

"What for did you not bring her back to us then?" The Earl sounded disappointed.

"Because, Father, she dwells at the house of Baubie Finn."

"The old witch? Och, hech no, we wouldn't want to trouble Baubie," said the Earl hastily. "Maybe we can ask Master Philip here to keep an eye out for a mermaid, eh?" he added with a dig at his ribs which had the desired effect. Philip, opening his eyes, yawned tipsily as the Earl repeated his request.

"I shall certainly inform you if I encounter a mermaid." Refusing another goblet of wine, he swayed to his feet as though still half asleep and more than a little drunk. Bowing clumsily, he said, "Your Grace must pardon me. I left Burray at dawn and I am a wretched sailor. In addition to sickness I sleep poorly at the best of times. I also rise early, a habit from former days of tutoring." He bowed. "With Your Grace's permission, I would be excused—"

Long, dark corridors and winding staircases, ominously chilly, were depressingly like a giant rabbit warren. Philip shuddered to think where so many people found a place to rest their heads. Pleasantly surprised by the comfortable bedchamber with its peat fire and handsome bed, he was grateful indeed that his couch was not a crowded bed in the troopers' quarters.

He had removed his boots and was stretching his feet to the fire when the door opened and a girl with butter-coloured hair entered, curtseyed, and immediately began to unlace her bodice with barely a glance in his direction.

"A moment, wench. I think you mistake the bedchamber."

The girl shrugged and continued to undress without looking at him. "You are the scholar, Master Philip."

"I am—but there is some mistake."

She turned, removing her bodice and revealing soft rounded breasts. "There is no mistake." And her expression was pure hatred. "The Earl had me sent to you. I am to warm your bed."

She was little more than a child, despite the bitter harlot's eyes.

"What would you have me do, Master? Do you wish me to——?"

Her explicit troopers' talk shocked him, even from that young-old face.

He shook his head, and taking her bodice, draped it gently around her shoulders while she stared at him in amazement. "I am not needing my bed warmed tonight. Go in peace."

She curtseyed, relief flooding her face with childlike pleasure. At the door she turned, ran back to him. "Master, you will not tell the Earl you were displeased with me?"

"I promise."

"Why, thank you, Master—thank you."

Under his old enemy's roof to his surprise he slept without dreams and awoke to the clatter of hooves in the courtyard directly below his window. He watched a troop of horsemen ride in and retired gratefully once more to the warmth of his bed, deciding that the urgent travellers were Lord Henry and his men. In no hurry to encounter his mistress's husband, he lay for a while, planning how he would fill in his day until it was time to join Flett on the *Swallow*.

Alerted by the sound of mailed feet thumping along the corridor and voices raised in excitement and hoping that the Earl would not be in evidence, he made his way down to the great hall, where Lord Patrick swaggered over to him, goblet in hand. "Doubtless you have heard the news, Master Scholar." His wine-flushed face was excited and pleased.

"Alas, I have just arisen," said Philip, yawning.

Patrick seized his arm. "Then you do not know? We have just heard that my brother Harry is dead. You realise what this means? Unless the child Lady Sibella carries is a son, then I am Master of Orkney and my father's heir." His grin shocked Philip as he looked in vain for some modest vestige of grief and found only callous delight in the new role for which Lord Henry's misfortune had cast his brother.

Philip found himself murmuring condolences, adding, "It was sudden, surely. I did not realise that he was in poor health."

Patrick laughed. "Nor was he. Some seafood disagreed with him at Mistress Crowe's. She too is dead. Both of them gone within the hour," he added cheerfully.

Philip thought of the poisoning attempts at Burray Castle. He remembered Lord Henry's bold-faced mistress, whose child would never be born, and how she must have whispered to her lover, urging him on to dispose of his lawful wife. He felt little grief, recalling her rapacious behaviour at Burray, the departing tapestry which had "pleasured" her greed.

"You are for Burray, Master Philip." Patrick jabbed a finger in his direction. "To bear the news to Lady Sibella, ahead of the Earl my father. A troop will escort you for a speedy arrival."

As they rode unchallenged through the soldiers vigilantly searching the quayside for Mahmoud's Spanish spy, Philip kept his bonnet well turned down to hide his face—and his wry smile at this most ludicrous deliverance from his enemies.

14

"Poisoned."

Sibella sat down upon the bed, still clinging to his hands. "Harry dead," she whispered. "Oh, Philip, I cannot believe it." Then springing to her feet, she clasped him in her arms. "Philip—my lord, you realise what this means. I am free—free of the Earl. Free of all of them."

"So thought I when first I heard. Then I remembered the child you carry. The child whom the Earl believes is Harry's—and," he added carefully, "whose mother is the Queen of Scots' daughter." Quickly he told her of the conversation between the Earl and Lord Patrick, overheard at the supper table while he pretended to be in wine sleep.

Sibella wept. "And it is all my fault—fool that I was. If only I had not been so enraged at that bragging bitch—God rest her soul—I need not have told Harry. None would have known that I was with child." Wringing her hands, she looked at him. "I was not even sure myself then. Oh, my lord, as a widow—you see what it means—I could have married you," she whispered.

"Aye—and will." He drew her close. He did not love her but he was grateful to her. He also feared for her future.

She looked at him in wonder. "So you would marry me, my lord," she whispered.

"If we can find means of obtaining the Earl's permission without arousing his suspicions—about the child." Philip was not hopeful.

"We can escape"—her voice was no longer forlorn—"take Lady

Mary and the servants— Aye, my lord, we are for Scotland, where we two can be wed. I have made up my mind." With chin tilted proudly, her eyes glowing with pride, in that moment she was the undoubted child of Queen Mary and Bothwell. Regal, demanding, expecting obedience, here was the Stewart hauteur, the resemblance to her mother intensified in that moment.

"I shall tell the Earl that I miscarried," she continued. "Look, I am still flat-bellied. Come, my lord, why so glum? Is it not a splendid idea?"

Philip put his hands on her thickened waistline and shook his head. "It is not an idea but merely a fantasy. You do not yet look *enceinte*, but another few weeks—" He shrugged. "The Earl has experienced matrons and midwives in his household. They will soon discover that you are lying."

Philip's suspicion that the Earl's speedy arrival at Burray directly concerned the future of Sibella and her unborn child proved correct.

Lord Patrick was to be given Burray, Sibella and Lady Mary removed immediately to Kirkwall under the Earl's care and protection to await the birth, and in due course Sibella was to be found another husband.

Timidly Philip suggested that he might fill this role—after the requisite period of mourning. The Earl gave a roar of lascivious mirth at the idea. "Ye canna' be in your right mind, Master Scholar. Wanting to wed a mare in foal? Hech no, that's poor sport, ploughing another man's furrow—" He nudged him painfully in the ribs. "Aye, and encountering his seed."

Philip made a bleak bow. "I am a widower and have given some thought lately to possible remarriage. I am of a sickly humour"—he coughed hollowly—"I pine for a wife's comfort." Seeing the Earl's brow darken, he added hastily, "I mean no harm, Your Grace, wishing only to make seemly my protection of the ladies of Burray."

The Earl's eyes narrowed. "They are under *my* protection, so find your comfort elsewhere. The Queen of Scots' daughter is not for the likes of you." He rubbed his chin thoughtfully. "I have plans for her future and for that of my grandchild, who, if male, will be Master of Orkney. Mind ye, Pate is praying that the bairn—if born at all—will be a lass." He laughed. "Aye, a son will fair put his nose out of joint again. 'Tis best he comes to Burray—I would not wish aught to befall Lady Sibella. I have a great affection for her, as I had for her mother the Queen," he added sentimentally.

Philip knew he lied, and coldness stole over him as he deliberated upon the future of Sibella and the child, particularly the survival of a son. Accidents were remarkably easy to arrange among the Earl's scheming sons—

"I ken fine what you're thinking, Master Scholar," said the Earl, wagging a finger at him. "But she will be safe enough. I am the law and order at Kirkwall; even my sons disobey at their extreme peril. Should they incur my displeasure, I would as soon take *their* heads as look at them." He thumped his hands on the table. "Hech yes, the rule of these islands is mine while I live—and let none forget that. Even Pate will be satisfied with Burray meantime," he added significantly. "What he doesna' see will keep his ambitions in check."

Summoned by Philip to attend the Earl, Sibella sighed. "I had great hopes, my lord. However, I shall pretend to be scornful of your proposal and contemptuous of your person." She added tearfully, "If the Earl has suspicions, your life would be in danger—"

"We would both go to the block, make no mistake, madam. See to it that you act well the part of rejecting the advances of a poor relative."

She kissed him. "If only we had more time together, my lord. If only—"

"If only," he repeated, the saddest and most oft used words in the entire world—

"You will come to Kirkwall and see me?"

"Yes."

"And our babe?"

"As often as I can." But Philip knew this would be a promise hard to keep with his own plans for the future. Now that marriage with Sibella was out of the question, he intended to leave Orkney as early as he could, but he had no wish to add to her grief with such cruel information.

They were joined by Lady Mary, who, weeping, clasped them in her arms, holding them close.

"My dearest daughter—and my beloved friend—what is to become of us?"

"Philip has asked the Earl for my hand—and has been refused," said Sibella proudly.

"What did you expect?" asked Lady Mary bitterly.

"You shall come to Kirkwall with us," said Sibella. "After all, Master Philip is part of our household."

"No. You do not know what you ask, Sibella." Lady Mary's face was stern. "Consider the danger you would plunge Philip into by such a request—and yourself too."

"But he must come and see us." Sibella stamped her foot angrily. "I insist."

Lady Mary put an arm around her waist. "But the fewer times, the better, my darling. Surely someone at the Earl's court must have known Philip of Cleat. Have you thought of that? If his real identity should ever be revealed, there is another precious secret," she whispered. "Aye, and one for which it will not take people long to count up on their fingers to connect the two events. There will soon be tongues wagging about how Lady Sibella's barrenness was speedily cured by Master Scholar's arrival at Burray." She shook her head. "You, my lady, must be content with the lasting memento of his presence you carry in your womb—" Suddenly embarrassed, she clung to Philip, crying, "God knows, my lord, I shall miss you as sorely as a son of my own flesh. But I have something for you ere we part." From the placket of her gown she took a parchment. "These are the deeds to the land of Cleat. You have done much for us, and I wish you to have them. Here also is a bag of gold—take it, I shall have no need of it now. We can never repay you for what you have brought into our lives."

"You are kind, Lady Mary, but if I cannot marry Sibella, nor accompany you, then I should leave the island, stow away on board some ship in Kirkwall—"

"Leave if you can, but if not, then the lands of Cleat are yours."

"You cannot leave us—you cannot," cried Sibella, clinging to him. "I forbid you to leave me—"

Over Sibella's head Philip exchanged a helpless look with Lady Mary, who said firmly, "Come, my dear, we must not enrage the Earl by keeping him waiting."

The troopers were carrying out the furnishings, tapestries, and household goods, thrusting them into waiting carts. Lady Mary sighed. "I have seen some of the Earl's requisitioning. My days at Burray are over. Lord Patrick's wife will be chatelaine from now on." She watched the departing goods sadly realising she would see little of her treasures once they fell into the greedy hands of the Earl and his family.

"It is outrageous," said Sibella. "I shall complain."

"You will not, my lady. We have our lives, and after struggling all these years to keep you safe, that is all I ask, that we should survive. And the babe you carry."

At last they were ready to depart, and before the Earl's astonished gaze Lady Mary stood on tiptoe and kissed Philip. Philip watched the amused faces of the troopers as she wept, clinging to him. Better to have their lascivious sniggers over this parting as the older woman's passion for the younger man than that any should remember how Lady Sibella had also cried.

"Take care of her," he whispered.

Inga alone of the servants accompanied her mistress into exile. John and James had decided to return to the fishing or make a living kelp-gathering, although the Earl had offered that Lady Mary might bring with her a "handful of body servants."

Lady Mary had declined politely, saying it was her wish that the servants return to their own families. To Philip she whispered, "In truth, I am fearful for all our safety should too many servants who have tongues to wag do so at Kirkwall. For there are always ways for those who were good and faithful here with us in Burray to be corrupted by the Earl's household and others"—her face darkened—"whose tongues could be loosened by torture or fear."

He did not trust himself or Sibella for that final farewell.

She made it an easy one for him. With a quick curtsey she hurried to the litter and sat far back from sight. He had one swift glimpse of her pale and tearful face before the leather curtain was drawn.

"God keep you—"

At that moment he was thankful he did not have to mourn her loss as a lover or he would have been riding hard after the troopers at the harbour. Into his death—and hers.

Upon Dainty, Sibella's parting gift to him, he rode towards Cleat, on the far side of the island, a landscape bleaker than Burray, softened by few undulating fields and fewer trees.

Here all life was at the mercy of the sea.

Wild, windswept moors with bog asphodel in an eternal dance before a carping fretful wind, the sky above steel-grey, empty but for the hovering flight of hen harriers and hawks. Lady Mary had warned to walk warily on these moors since the birds were known to attack man for trespassing on their domain.

The journey was slow. Several times the track vanished and he had to retrace his steps. The mist came down, and suddenly the sky above him was ripped open by a jagged streak of lightning. From the lost horizon growled a thunderstorm which promised considerable volume and violence.

As the first drops of rain spattered like coins upon the ground, he saw the only shelter offered was the church he had observed earlier. Swiftly he rode across the field, taking a chance upon finding it empty, since this was an unlikely hour of the day for services in the Protestant faith.

Pushing open the ancient scarred door, he found the church of St Peter was dark and gloomy. It smelt depressingly of age, damp wood, and lichened stone. The effigies on the tombs lining the walls dated it from the thirteenth century, and as the rain battered the roof and a gale hurled itself like demons upon the closed door, he discovered the elegance and grace of a fine east gable and stained glass windows continued in stone pillars which supported the roof. The evidence of the faith in which the church had been founded remained in the now empty niches which had once housed sacred relics, holy water, and Communion vessels.

Waiting for the storm to cease, Philip wished he could have seen it furnished with saints and holy statues, with banners and fine vestments. He decided that he must find a priest to confess him, although he felt the remote deity of the Mass in El Escorial, shrouded by ritual and available to heed men's cries only through the intercession of the saints, had little connection with this savage land. The God of Orkney, to whom he owed his survival, was another Being.

He was saved from further heretical thoughts by a pale sunlight streaming under the door. He let himself out, and leading Dainty from her shelter by the doorway, he walked through the dripping kirkyard, where he suspected from the large number of tombstones the parish supported more dead members than living ones.

Before a monument of weeping angels his steps faltered.

"Here lieth the body of Margaret St Clair, dearly beloved wife of Philip of Cleat, departed this life August 8, 1578."

An odd coincidence which sent a shiver down his spine. Eager to escape, he turned and found a black-clad figure bearing down on him.

"I am Erasmus Flett, minister of St Peter's. You have come some distance, sir, and the weather is inclement. Allow me to offer you refreshment. I have ale and bannocks I would share with you."

Philip was about to politely refuse the invitation, but found the minister already striding ahead towards the small house overlooking the kirkyard. In a parlour sparsely furnished but with books in plenty, he took the seat offered in a high-backed cane chair and warmed his hands gratefully at the glowing peat fire.

Producing the refreshments from a press, the minister settled himself upon the bench opposite. Philip decided that they must be near in age if not experience, for this youngish man with a long face and receding hair had the penetrating pale eyes and almost transparent skin he associated with fasting and visions. Murmuring a grace, he raised his head and, pouring a goblet of ale, asked:

"You are from Burray Castle? Master Philip, is it not?"

Philip sighed as, buttering the bannock and accepting a large slice of cheese to accompany it, he realised that his new identity had successfully passed its second test. He began to enjoy the repast set before him. Barley bread, with fruit cooked in honey. At last he said, "No more, thank you, sir. A delicious repast, and you are most kind to regale a passing stranger to such hospitality."

"I live alone and am always glad of an excuse for company. The parishioners, my little flock, take good care of their minister." Laughing, he indicated the food remaining on the table. "I lack naught that they can provide." Sighing, he added, "My good wife died in childbed four years since. Are you on your way to Cleat?"

This was dangerous ground, thought Philip warily, and said:

"Aye, now that Lady Mary and her daughter travel to Kirkwall to take residence there with the Earl."

Deciding that there was probably little in Burray or elsewhere that the minister did not know about, Philip had no wish to prolong his departure to the extent of answering the many questions he felt sure he was bound to be asked. Indicating that he was anxious to resume his journey while the weather held, he thanked the minister graciously.

Accompanying him across the kirkyard, whose stones now glistened in shafts of sunshine in token of the resurrection promised to those who lay in patient waiting, the Reverend Flett said:

"Should chance take you to Kirkwall to visit Lady Mary, I have a cousin Harald, a boatbuilder."

Here too was dangerous ground. Philip decided not to mention his almost disastrous meeting with the minister's kin.

"I hope you will call upon me again, now that your destiny has led you to Cleat."

"I would like that, sir," said Philip, bowing politely.

"I understand from Lady Mary that you worship in the old faith."

"Yes, I am a Catholic."

"You must find it difficult to practise your religion in Burray."

Philip nodded politely with little desire to be drawn into any detail concerning his life there.

"If you should ever go to Kirkwall, go to the Church of Our Lady, which stands high on the hill to the east of the town. Tell Father Thomas that I sent you." He laughed. "You are surprised? No doubt you expect a Lutheran minister and a Catholic priest to be continually at daggers drawn."

"Nay, sir, I find it pleasing that amity can exist between two men of different faiths."

The minister smiled. "We do but sharpen our wits upon each other over a game of chess or an interpretation of some aspect of the Gospels. Father Thomas is a fine, good man; would that we had millions more like him. For all our differences we both agree that the main duty of a Christian is to love God and serve others instead of arguing which is the right way to do it."

"But that is—that is—"

"Heresy? Aye, perhaps so. But I can assure you that our needs upon this troubled island go deeper than any ecclesiastical argument can settle. However we worship, we are bound together against a common foe, and God knows we all need Him and each other. In His mercy he sees fit to send us an occasional wreck to help us survive the starvation imposed by the Earl of Orkney's tyranny."

"A wreck with sailors to murder and rob, Master Flett?" Philip's voice was stern.

The minister's brow darkened. "Nay, I would not permit such actions. I do not preach murder, but a rich wreck, without survivors, can keep these poor folk with clothes upon their backs and food in their bellies—aye, and give them hope. What use is a rich wreck rotting at the bottom of the sea, or falling into the Earl's greedy hands?" He laughed. "I can see by your expression, Master Philip, that you find me a strange parson, who approves of the spoiling of wrecked ships and does not hate Catholics as he should. I would go to prison for the former and to the stake for the latter. Fortunately, for me, Earl Robert is too busy following the lusts of the flesh to consider his immortal soul or the deadly reckoning that awaits."

"Which is scant consolation to those he cruelly misuses upon this earth."

"God will avenge, Master Philip."

Philip said nothing, and he continued, "Our story goes back a long time, a catalogue of iniquities. Over two hundred years ago these islands were pledged by a needy Norse king as his daughter's dowry to the Scottish prince who became James the Third, and since that time the Scottish noblemen who have held the earldom have found our islands a splendid opportunity for plunder, while the islanders, helpless before avarice, have watched their land change hands between powerful landlords, like dogs fighting over a large and juicy bone, to provide for parasites such as the Earl and his family. Whoever won, the Orcadians were always the losers since Scottish laws had little in common with the Norse way of life which was their heritage." He paused. "I trust you are the honest man you look, Master Philip, and not a spy in the Earl's pay, or he could have my head on this."

Philip smiled grimly. "I am my own man, Master Flett. I too despise the Earl, but I am glad this is a sermon which you are not tempted to preach in public," he added, moved by the minister's tale of a ravished land.

"Nay, sir. I am a coward and, alas, not of the stuff of which martyrs are made." He sighed. "God knew my limitations when He made me. He intended only that I should be a faithful servant and do the best I can for His people."

They stood by the tombstone where they had met, and Master Flett smiled, holding out his hand. "I am glad you came."

Philip nodded respectfully towards the grave with its inscription. "I was but passing by."

"And thought to pay your respects to the departed. We do not see you here often. I realise that I do not know your name."

"Philip of Cleat."

The minister shook his head. "Nay, sir—your *true* name. For you cannot be Philip of Cleat." Seeing Philip's startled look, he smiled. "Your secret, whatever it is, is safe with me. I buried Philip of Cleat weeks since." And following his glance at the tombstone, Master Flett continued, "Nay, not there. In the St Clair vault, by the wall over yonder. By Lady Mary's command. She thought it would be less public and more—er—expedient since his resurrection was already in hand." The pale eyes stared into his with their penetrating gaze. "In faith, although I know naught of your reason for taking Master Philip's place upon this earth, I wish you God's mercy, for you have about you the look of an honest man. And I am seldom wrong. There was rumour lately of a Spanish sailor who escaped the wreckers. Perhaps you have heard it," he added casually. And then respectful of his visitor's reluctance to declare himself, he bowed.

"Come whenever you are in the area or feel the need for talk. If you are a reading man, then there are books which might interest you. God keep you."

Philip watched him striding back the way he had come, and had plenty of thoughts to occupy him on the remainder of the journey while the sun set in rose and lavender flames upon a looking-glass sea.

The waves were breaking soft and gentle as a heartbeat on the shore when at last he reached his destination. A tall, narrow house stood dark against the headland, approached through a tidy garden where two stories, narrow-windowed, modestly set one upon the other, suggested fortress rather than yeoman's dwelling.

He pushed open the door. The house was gaunt and a trifle chilly. Alone like himself, and forsaken, he thought, a fitting place for one who had lost his place in the world and was in the slow and painful process of self-discovery.

The real Philip of Cleat had not been an extravagant householder, and the stark pieces of furniture pointed to a frugal existence. A twisting narrow staircase emerged at two bedchambers, each containing beds built into a walled recess, shuttered for privacy. A threadbare tapestry was the sole furnishing of the larger room, whose solitary window stared over the rosy sunset sea. The window of the smaller chamber faced down into a muddy backyard. However, Philip returned from his inspection well satisfied, feeling that a bond was forged between himself and his new home. Under a woman's hand it might still blossom into a fine proud place for any man to dwell. But not for him—

Dainty stabled and fed, he lit a fire and rejoiced to find a modest cellar below the spiral stair; wine accompanied his meal of bannocks and cheese, the candles he had also brought from Burray burning bright against the walls.

Sighing, he stretched out his legs to the blaze, at home and almost content with the firelight throwing warm shadows upon the walls, touching the scholar's books, and a decanter of wine on the table. The house looked cared for, and was infinitely more comfortable and less draughty than Burray Castle. Even the wind which had arisen did not trouble him, for the walls were thick, secure—

Turning the pages of Virgil, he felt his eyelids grow heavy, and with the remaining candle he retired upstairs to the box bed, a place of considerable warmth and security.

Like a return to the dark womb, he thought. Lying with his hands behind his head, enjoying his solitary couch and regrettably not missing Sibella's head nestling against his shoulder, he wondered if the Catholic earls would make him welcome without King Philip's gold. Tomorrow or the next day, he resolved to begin careful plans. Before the *Swallow* returned again to Kirkwall, he would have plenty of time for plans—

When he awoke, the bedchamber was full of sunshine. From the window, he looked beyond a garden neatly tended to a long silver stretch of sand where seabirds strutted with airs of importance, pecking anxiously. In the far distance, a round tall tower. Was this the same tower to which he had escorted Jean Halcro, the child who had reminded him of Maeve?

Maeve. He bit his lip, frowning. Would she never let him be? Even here would her restless ghost never allow him the balm of forgetfulness? Firmly he decided he must exorcise her dead presence from this temporary sanctuary before he journeyed on into a future where only violent death seemed certain. Dismally he remembered how her ghost had clung about him at Burray, how even in the act of love Sibella's embraces became those of his lost love, their very bedchamber changing into the creaking cabin of the *Black Duchess*. Even his walks upon the shore were haunted by her, the day he found Sweetling's cage and the drowned bird—

Cursing himself for his inability to thrust her face away from him, he hurried downstairs to discover the answer to the house's well-kept appearance.

He blinked before a room transformed, in which a peat fire glowed, the furniture gleamed, and the mouth-watering smell of freshly baked bread pervaded the air. A woman entered briskly, and curtseying, she set before him a bowl of kale soup on which to break his fast.

"My brother James from Burray told me of your coming. I trust you slept well."

She wore the dress of a middle-aged peasant, although looking closer, he saw that she was comely, with brown curling hair and rosy cheeks, a spirited lively countenance, as her dimples testified.

Her name was Alys; she was a widow, and he learned she had looked after Master Philip after his wife died. "James tells me that he left his inheritance to you," she added carefully. Head on side, she smiled, regarding him. "Aye, sir, your late cousin was fair-coloured like yourself. I can see there is a look of kinship about you. He too had the Viking strain—that's what we call it here—though he was not so handsome as yourself." Colouring slightly, she added hastily, "Of course, he was an older man."

She seemed eager for conversation. Her two sailor sons had escaped from the island. "Thanks be to God, for I would not want them here, under the way we have to live," she added in a whisper, as if the very walls were listening.

"James tells me you are from Edinburgh, sir. What is it like there?"

He had no difficulty filling in details of streets and houses, and markets too. She listened delightfully, chin in hand, as if the story of the court riding down from the castle to the Palace of Holyroodhouse were exotic as ancient Cathay. At the end of her questions and his answers she sighed:

"Why then did you ever leave such a paradise to come to this hell the Earl has made of our land?"

"I arrived in ignorance," he said truthfully. "Moreover, I was wearied with my tutor's life and thought a pleasant inheritance with a little land would be an inviting prospect." Not knowing how much James had told her, he tapped his chest significantly. "I hoped the change of sea air from Edinburgh's reek might be beneficial."

Alys was immediately sympathetic. And his dry cough, summoned with difficulty but conviction, had her returning from her neighbouring house with a bottle of syrupy medicine. "This has soothing properties—I made it myself, Master Lennox," she added proudly, and he started at the name he had given at short notice.

He had a distinct feeling that he had impressed Mistress Alys favourably, since she eagerly offered to take care of his house. She lived alone. It would be no trouble to provide him with hot nourishing meals each day, which would be fine for his ailing condition. Philip was well pleased with this arrangement.

Finally she warned him not to go abroad at night alone.

"Over there—" She pointed in the direction of dark and heathery moorland perched against high and sinister rocks. "Over there is the land of the wreckers. And down by the shore too, one must take care at night for there are gloups—open pits into which the sea enters at high tide by an underground channel. Sometimes in a storm you can hear the roaring, like a captive giant, from miles away."

Finally she assured him that only the stranger was in any danger from the wreckers. They would not harm any of the inhabitants, but there was an unwritten law that they did not trespass upon the moor. When he indicated the distant tower, her face darkened. "The old broch, Master Lennox— Before even the Norse folk came; it belongs to the times when giants and dwarfs ruled these isles."

"Do any live there now?"

"Aye, Baubie Finn the witch owns it. Baubie can do anything. Why, just recently she got herself a seal woman to do her bidding. Captured her and hid her skin, so that she is enslaved to Baubie. Magiced her from the sea, she did."

Philip watched her putting out his supper upon the table. Food and a comely woman, what more could a man ask for? Perhaps he should forget the *Swallow*'s voyage to Leith, his vague and uncertain future. Why not stay at Cleat, settle down? He could do worse than wed Mistress Alys—

"I heard talk of this seal woman in Kirkwall," he said, taking a spoonful of soup. Delicious it was too. She dimpled when he complimented her. "Have you seen this strange creature?"

"Aye, that I have." Hands on hips, Alys sniffed contemptuously.

Amused, he asked, "Well, has she two heads and a tail?"

"Not she, Master. She looks exactly like any other mortal woman. Mind you, she canna' talk—though there are those men who say such a disability is no disadvantage. Impudent creatures." She dimpled again; her sly glance told him that Mistress Alys would not find his advances unwelcome—

He smiled. "Why, are there no other differences?"

Alys frowned. "Well, she has a wild look about her, right enough." She shook her head. "Nay, Master. There's trickery afoot. She looks too womanlike. I could swear, sir, that there's naught magical. Young and bonny, she is, long black hair. Only her eyes are strange, green—green like the sea she is supposed to have come from. Right bonny, Master Lennox, but there's many like her you would see every day in the streets of Kirkwall—"

Alys looked up and saw that she was talking to the empty air. Master Lennox was standing by the open door, staring at the headland, his spoon clattering unheeded from his hand. He was perfectly still, and his face was awful, frightening, as he turned slowly to face her.

"When did the seal woman arrive? Can you remember?" His voice was brittle, as though the words needed effort in the saying.

"I canna' rightly tell you, Master, since Baubie kept her secret for a while."

"Then think—think hard."

Alys frowned. "It would be well before the harvest—"

Philip took down his cloak from the peg behind the door.

"Now, Master Lennox, finish your breakfast, do."

"Not now, Mistress."

"But it will spoil—"

"Not now." His voice scared her too. What strange devil had got into the man, what had she said to change him, so handsome and smiling a few minutes ago? "Tell me how exactly do I get to the house of Baubie Finn?"

And as she explained, he hardly listened to her instructions, so eager was he to be gone.

Dead, dead, long since, whispered the breakers as he rode fast along the shore, trying to pretend it was just curiosity, idle curiosity which had led him to leave a pleasant woman and excellent food in order to see the seal woman.

She cannot possibly be Maeve. Maeve is dead, said Reason. Mistress Alys has told you there were many girls in Kirkwall with black hair and green eyes. Your Maeve is dead, eaten by the sea creatures long since, and you are the greatest fool who ever lived to cling to such a fantasy as this. You deserve the misery and disappointment awaiting you at the house of Baubie Finn. After all, had Maeve lived, would she not have searched for *you?* Conscience argued that there were no words of love exchanged. Had it not been for Sibella, would he have known that his love for Maeve was irreplaceable, or why she was so different from one wife long dead, one betrothed, and a succession of mistresses whose names and faces he had forgotten? Remembering her wounded eyes, her avoidance of him—he had no reason to believe that perhaps Maeve loved him too—

Dainty was galloping fast now, a little upset by her master's urgency.

Fool, fool, hammered the turf. Too late—too late, echoed the tide's boom. Now he was almost there, house and tower growing closer. Just idle curiosity brings me, he told his racing heart.

Idle curiosity, laughed Reason, your love is a dead woman, her bones bleaching, unrecognisable, as was little Sweetling in his cage washed ashore at Burray— Now, *there* was a sign before God that Maeve too was gone. So what are you doing here, Philip of Cleat, as you now call yourself? You should be at home concentrating on a plan to escape from Kirkwall, or if you want to settle on this accursed island and make the best of a bad bargain, then you should be thinking in practical manner of choosing a wife. You have already decided that Mistress Alys would fill the role splendidly. An attractive, comely woman, the right age for you. A good housewife, a better cook—what more could any man ask for?

"Love," he said aloud. "Love is what I could ask for and love is what I will never find again."

Idle curiosity, that was all. Here was the broch, the stone house where Jean Halcro lived. In the garden, a girl working with a hoe—a girl who wasn't Jean—

Her back was towards him. She had long curly hair, and occasionally she stopped to lift her hand, wiping her nose upon the sleeve of a rough country gown.

Long hair, dark but not black. And even as she turned to look across at him, he saw that she was just an ordinary pretty girl, watching him with great round frightened eyes, pale they were—either green or blue. He no longer cared which— He must have been mad—

"I wish to speak with Baubie Finn. Where is she?"

The girl stared at him, hand trembling on the hoe.

"Where is the child then?" Again she shook her head, bewildered, scared. "You are the seal woman? Answer me!"

Her eyes widened in terror, and hurling down the hoe, she rushed towards the house.

"Wait," he called. "I mean you no harm. Wait—"

His answer was the door banged shut, the bolt rammed into place.

Helplessly he stood looking at the house. All was silent but for a curtain twitched at the upstairs window. He waited for a few moments, then turning on his heel, gathered Dainty's reins and rode away.

Fool he had been. A fool to hope, gulling himself with false dreams. Would he never learn to accept that Maeve was dead?

A beautiful seal woman indeed. He laughed bitterly. An ordinary girl in an ordinary garden.

Weak with disappointment, he rode slowly back along the shore. He would put an end to this folly this very evening. When he got back to Cleat he would bury the last vestige of Don Felipe, godson to Philip of Spain and incompetent spy. In that grave he would also shut away forever the memory of Maeve O'Neill—

Aye, he would ask Mistress Alys to be his wife, build a life for himself and her on the island—a right practical end to his fantasies. Mistress Alys would keep his feet upon the proper path, he had no doubt of that.

15

In the house of Baubie Finn the girl ran upstairs and opened the door of Selkie's room. Magnus was fishing, and Baubie had been called away to attend a sick child in the abode of the wreckers. She had taken Jean with her, leaving her neighbour's lass Meg sole charge of Selkie. Even Boy was absent with his father since he was becoming more amenable to a day's toil of late and showed mysterious signs of wakening intelligence.

The Selkie had been very poorly lately, and Baubie Finn was worried about her future. Most days she rarely left her bed, hardly eating or stirring. Or—what Baubie found more unnerving—sitting motionless by the window, staring out across the sea.

The sea seemed to be drawing her life away, thought Baubie, and there were times when Magnus almost persuaded her that Selkie should be given back her skin and allowed to return to the Seal People. Magnus had his own reasons for urgency; if the seal woman was carrying young, then he didn't want another mouth to feed, seal pup or human.

Meg found Selkie's bed empty. She sat far back in the chair at the window, almost invisible, and hardly stirred at Meg's approach.

"There's a man down there, Selkie—look, in the garden. He was asking for you. Wanted to see the seal woman, he said. I doubt he's one of the Earl's sons, educated and well set up he is." And as Selkie peered out of the window, she added, "Keep out of sight now or Baubie'll flay me alive—"

But when Selkie gazed down at the man, it was as if a stone in her mind rolled away.

"Something strange happened to her," wept Meg later. From her description of the stranger both Baubie and Jean realised with relief that he was Philip of Cleat, whose first appearance had also affected Selkie adversely, thanks to Baubie's overdose of love philtres. Terrified of the punishment in store, Meg continued, "She screamed something—I never heard her speak afore—and dashed past me. Oh, the strength of her, Mistress Baubie—I never felt anything like it. I couldna' stop her. Away out of the house and along the shore, she went after him—"

Philip had not ridden more than a hundred yards from the witch's accursed house when he was aware that Dainty had gone lame. A solemn judgement on those who would traffic with the Devil, he thought as he dismounted and inspected her fetlocks. A fine rain began, and he cursed himself for this fool's errand which would have him walking all the way back to Cleat—

Before God, he was sick—sick with misery and disappointment. He longed for Mistress Alys' comforting—

The cry he heard seemed to echo from the depths of his own heart. Turning, he saw a tiny figure with long black hair emerge from the garden he had just left and stumble out of the gate, running along the shore as fast as the pebbles would allow.

She was racing towards him. Even at that distance he recognised her. Tears of joy streamed unbidden as he recognised too that miracles do happen. Straight as an arrow she came into his arms.

"Maeve."

"Philip—"

And the words lost on the wind became a whisper of the rain and one with the wild seabirds' call.

Huddled with him in the shelter of the rocks, protected by his cloak from the worst of the drizzle, she shivered no longer. Bound to him by the warmth of his body though her thin gown, she sighed with content, touching him with shy unbelief.

"I believed you to be dead."

"And I you," she sighed again.

He told her that Mahmoud still lived and he had seen the *Rosie* in Kirkwall. He asked her what had befallen Karim.

"He leaped overboard, to try to reach you. He never returned."

She shook her head. "I cannot recall anything until much later, finding I was about to drown in a leaky boat. I had no memory of what had happened to the ship—to you—nothing but that terrible sea. Then I saw the shore not far off, and the house. As I waded in Magnus was waiting for me. Suddenly I was warm and safe again; that was all I cared about. But when the world came back to me, it was as if a great stone had rolled into my memory and I could not see past it. Then there was Boy—" And she told him of their clumsy attempts to get her to mate with their idiot son. Angrily he cursed and held her closer.

She laughed for the first time, pleased to find him jealous. "Sure, and there is no need for that. He was but a child despite his man's body—an idiot, and scared of me as I was of him. Once I understood he needed a child like himself to play with, we became friends. Magnus' niece, Jean, was good to me—" She was suddenly conscious of his arms, and moved a little away from him. "What of you, Sir Captain? You have the look of a man who has prospered."

He smiled, the slow beguiling smile she had carried in the sad requiem of half-remembered dreams. "Sir Captain," he repeated, "a long time since any called me that. I never expected to hear those two words again." And he told her that he had survived the wreck and had been befriended by Lady Sibella Stewart and her mother, without any details—which, since she was a woman, her ready imagination soon supplied—telling her only that he had taken the place of a dead relative, Philip of Cleat, as steward at Burray Castle.

Watching the sunlight and shadow crossing her face when he mentioned Sibella, the slight tensioning of her arms— Could it be, he thought, wondering, could it be that she *was* jealous—that perhaps she loved him a little?

"Her mother, Lady Mary, gave me the deeds of Cleat. I now have a house and some land. I will take you there, if you'd like to see it," he added shyly.

"I should indeed, but first I must tell Baubie Finn. She will be anxious, for she never heard me speak—"

"Don't go back. Surely you want to escape the old witch's clutches."

She laughed. "No. Baubie was kind to me; she brought me back to life with her herbs and simples. And Magnus too, who is an old grumbler, but kindly at heart—and Boy—and Jean." She looked at him solemnly, as if realisation had just dawned. "I now have a life here, Philip."

"Oh" was all he could say. He had found her, but she did not need him. She was happy, and did not want his rescue or to be carried off to Cleat with him.

He told her he had heard that the Armada was a total defeat— there would be no uprising of the Scottish earls under Huntly now— no march to London to dethrone the Protestant Queen Elizabeth.

"Do you intend to return to Spain?" she whispered.

He shook his head. "Nay, even if I could escape without money or being taken for a spy, I have little desire for my former life or for His Majesty's attempts to find me a rich heiress. Too many things have happened to me. I am happy to be regarded as lost with the Armada."

She could hardly believe that he was here beside her, unchanged apart from the beard, which became him. There was a new gentleness besides that smile which she had not expected to see again this side of paradise.

"So Don Felipe is dead?"

"Aye, and buried. Hail to Philip of Cleat, Orcadian crofter." He laughed. "If only we had wine, we could drink to that."

But drinking wine brought memories, and a shadow of embarrassment touched Maeve's face. Looking into his eyes, she saw that he too remembered their overindulgence in Karim's gift, Philip's broken promise, and the loss of her virginity aboard the *Black Duchess*.

"I have taken a fondness for this wild and stormy land," he continued hastily, eager to change the subject. "I think I should settle here, perhaps take a wife from the island." Maeve was very still. "What do you think of the idea?" he added gently.

"Sure, I think you will be happy with your house," she said lightly, "for there was always much of the scholar about you. And we shall be neighbours."

They were both silent, with only the sea sound and the rain. "Are you no longer to return to Ireland and your cousin the Earl of Tyrone?"

She laughed and shook her head. "I have to confess that I deceived you, Sir Captain. My powerful relative was a ruse to keep me on the *Black Duchess* and under your protection."

"Isn't your name O'Neill then?"

"It is, but my father was just a simple peasant on Tyrone's estate until he went in for soldiering and developed ideas of grandeur. Sure, I expect we are related to Tyrone like many of his tenants if we traced their by-blows back far enough."

"So you have no bonds holding you to Ireland?" he said shortly.

"None." He was silent. "Do you forgive me for telling you a lie?"

He was frowning. Before God, she thought, he is angry with me. I have offended him. Does he not realise dishonesty was necessary? Humble birth would have thrown her to the crew with the public harlots—or sent her back ignominiously to Don Diego and the hateful marriage.

"Of course I forgive you." He was smiling again, the cloud had passed. She felt weak with relief.

"I am happy here," she repeated. "I have no thought of leaving—"

"Not even for a rich husband?" he reminded her slyly. "Ripe for picking in London—or at the court in Edinburgh—as once you told me, if you failed to reach Ireland."

"Nay, Sir Mariner, a rich husband is not for me, I fear," she said sadly.

"Why not? You have youth—and beauty."

It was true. Despite the ordeal of the Armada and the last months, she was more rounded in shape; difficult now for her to fool any man into believing that she was a youth, with a ribbon tying back her hair. Could it be— The thought came unbidden with such suddenness that he felt as if he had tumbled from the cliff top far above them and left his stomach on the way down. His arm tightened around her shoulder. Ashamed of his sudden desire for her, he felt his body stir, quicken—

She said sharply, "As you doubtless also remember, I am no longer a maiden and so have lost the bargaining power for picking a rich husband."

Before he was allowed to recover from that crushing accusation, she added, "So I had better return to Baubie Finn, who loves me and has given me a good home. Magnus will be pleased that the Selkie is human after all. I am grateful to you, Philip," she added primly. "If we had not met again, perhaps my memory would have stayed full of clouds and I'd never have learned that I wasn't a seal woman in the world of man for a year and a day—"

"What will you do?" he interrupted.

"Work and pray, I expect."

"Pray for what?" he insisted.

"As I was taught to pray long ago. And to give thanks to the Good Lord that He spared us and gave some purpose to our new lives—our separate lives—"

"How separate?"

"You have said so, have you not? You to be a crofter and seek a wife, myself to look after Baubie in her old age."

"But I need you, Maeve—"

"How so, need me?" she asked lightly, leaving the shelter of his cloak, for the rain had ceased. With a hand shading her eyes she stared along the shore towards the broch. "How so, Master Philip—to keep house for you?"

"Nay—" He was about to say, "Because I love you," but the words remained unsaid, for at that moment Maeve pointed towards the witch's house.

"Look—I see Baubie, and there is Magnus' boat. I must go; they'll be worried about me. Poor Meg too will be waiting, wringing her hands."

"Stay with me—for a while. We have much to talk about—"

"Nay—you come with me. If that is your wish," she said, and sounding as if she cared little one way or the other, she walked a few steps ahead of him back along the shore.

Philip thought Baubie Finn was quite the ugliest woman he had ever seen, while she thought him the most divinely handsome young man she had ever encountered. She was prepared to forgive him for luring Selkie away when the seal woman, taking her hands, surprised her by having her speech restored. And once Selkie began to talk, it seemed that the words would never cease, while Jean, her romantic heart stirred by such marvels, held her friend Philip's hand and smiled up into his face encouragingly.

Baubie Finn did not expect to be astonished by any of this life's dealings, but nevertheless was intrigued by the first part of the story which Philip and Maeve had agreed upon at the garden gate. Both captives of the *Black Duchess*, trying to escape, she to Ireland, he to Scotland— Better that even Baubie Finn and her family did not know the whole truth in case it tumbled out and fell into the ears of the Earl of Orkney, for there was still Sibella to be protected. Their secret would be safe with Baubie Finn—

"So you have the house at Cleat, Master Philip? And you intend to stay with us?"

"Aye, Mistress, that is my intention."

Baubie Finn glanced at Maeve, then turning back to Philip, nodded in her direction. "Then you had better take her with you."

Maeve sprang between them. "Baubie, I will not be thrust upon Philip like a sack of oats." As Baubie opened her mouth, she swung round to face Philip. "Please, I wish to speak to her alone. Will you wait outside?"

When the door closed behind him, she said, "I meant that, Baubie. I will not be thrust upon Philip like a sack of oats—"

"A sack of oats," repeated Baubie with a sniff. "Which is what you are going to look like in a short while."

The girl's face reddened, and she held out her hands as if to thrust the truth away from her. "Oh, Baubie, please don't—*don't* tell him—promise."

Baubie brushed her protests aside. "You had better find yourself a husband—and quickly."

"Nay, Baubie—"

"Don't 'Nay Baubie,' me. Is it not true that he is your bairn's father?"

Helplessly Maeve watched Philip pacing the garden. Baubie continued, "Aye, from the moony looks that passed between you both, I guessed there had been more stirring matters than glances in that cabin you shared—"

"He doesn't know—how it is. He doesn't even guess." She grasped the old woman's hand. "Baubie, I cannot bear that he should wed with me out of duty, a sense of honour—I would rather stay with you." She held the worn hand to her cheek. "Let me stay with you," she whispered. "I can learn your spells—help you—"

"We will have none of that," said Baubie sharply, then smiling, she stroked the girl's hair. "Aye, you would stay with me, my Selkie, and break your heart every minute of the day longing for him. At least go to Cleat—see what you think of it. It's a fine house."

Perhaps the witch had enchanted Dainty, for once Baubie extracted a small pebble from her hoof, she was frisky as ever. So with Maeve behind him, Baubie, Magnus, Boy, and Jean waving from the door, Philip rode up the hill to his new home, where Maeve ran from room to room, exclaiming with delight over a chest she had found full of materials which would make into fine garments or curtains, pillows, and spreads. Her enthusiasm took him back to an earlier scene on the *Black Duchess* when wearing his second-best shirt, she had made a similar discovery. Now she held up handsome dresses, cloaks too, which must have belonged to the former mistress of Cleat.

"I fear they are a trifle old-fashioned now, but they are still wearable," she said wistfully.

"Have them," he said.

"Oh, may I—may I really?" And narrowing her eyes, she pursed her lips over a tuck here, a flounce there. Following him downstairs, explaining what might be done to improve his house, while in the garden she showed surprising knowledge about the waywardness of hens and beasts.

"Don't look so amazed, Philip. From when I could first toddle, looking after the hens was my responsibility on the farm back in Ireland."

They were aware that day had gone and the first stars hung bright in the sky.

"My apologies," he said, "to have kept you so late—"

"So much to see—" she smiled. "I'll be safe enough; the wreckers will not touch the seal woman. I have magic for mortal men, remember."

At the door she paused, staring wistfully back into the house, as though she might not see it again.

"Have you forgotten something?" he asked, uneasy at her departure.

She shook her head. "May I come and see you sometimes—that is—" She paused.

"Go on."

"—*if* you decide not to marry Mistress Alys."

Philip's neighbour had arrived soon after she had seen Dainty tethered. Bearing dishes of pie and other goodies, she was put out of countenance by the sight of another woman occupying the hearth at Philip's side. She had recovered quickly but the observant Maeve was the recipient of reproachful glances and sharper, although smiling, remarks.

"Why should I marry Mistress Alys?" asked Philip, wondering guiltily if Maeve had learned to read men's secret thoughts during her stay with the witch.

"Because she is half in love with you already."

"But I hardly know her," protested Philip. Maeve merely smiled.

Here was a man on whom the wiles of womankind were completely lost.

She breathed deeply. "Is this not superb air?"

Philip cut short her remarks. "I am not in a mood to discuss the merits of the night air—"

"Then what—"

"I should like to return to where we were earlier this day." He took her hands, held them tightly. "When you decided that you loved Baubie Finn so much and would stay with her, I was about to ask you something."

Maeve stared at the ground, and with a groan he seized her in his arms. "I was about to ask you to wed with me. I have waited all day for this moment, and I will not be deprived further—"

"You might have—"

"Be silent." She was surprised by his authority still, and by a sudden return to the Don Felipe both believed had died with the *Black Duchess*. "I am asking you to be my wife, Maeve O'Neill—and you had best say yes, because it occurs to me that a husband might soon be necessary—"

Angrily she sprang from him, reminding him with a rush of sweetness of their stormy passage as lovers—and before—

Hands on hips, she surveyed him. "Sure now, I suppose Baubie Finn has been after you with her daft remarks and suppositions."

"Daft remarks and suppositions—about what?" he enquired innocently.

For answer she scowled and turned her head away.

Very gently he brought her chin round, so that her face was inches from his own. Her face, and the soft seductive lips he had known. "Nay, sweeting," he whispered, "Baubie has no need to tell me what I can see—for I have eyes in my head and they tell me you are more —rounded—than you were during our voyage. Remember, I have been a married man—and have known such—expectations—before. The child you carry is mine."

It was not a question, but a statement. In answer she nodded. "Aye, it is."

His hold upon her tightened. "Then we have reason for rejoicing and for a speedy marriage. There is a priest in Kirkwall—"

Again she pushed him away. "Now you hearken to me, Master Philip. I will not wed with you, or with any man, for *that* reason alone."

"What reason then? What reason is good enough for you to consider being my wife?"

She was silent, biting her lip, and again he took her hands, gathered them to his heart. Gently he whispered:

"Will you accept as good enough reason that life without you has been intolerable and to lose you again would be final as death itself?"

With a small moan of pleasure she went into his arms. Words were for the uncertain, he thought, those who read each other's hearts had no further need for words.

He led her across the threshold, and as he closed the door upon their homecoming, a meteor crossed the sky like a promise of joy.

16

Inside the house of Cleat, as the days folded into weeks and Maeve became the wife of Philip's heart and his body, time itself seemed vanquished and he dreamed of a child laughing in its cradle. A child whose springtime birth would be speedily followed by that of a half brother or sister, borne by the late Queen of Scots' daughter.

Sibella. What of Sibella? He thought of her often as autumn vanished in fierce winter storms, hurling themselves upon the shore, the seabirds, outraged, screaming high above the cliffs and all life at the mercy of a wind, hissing, moaning, day in day out across the desolate shore. Then with the perversity Philip had come to expect from this accursed land, winter disappeared in a blaze of sunshine and cloudless skies which had them racing out-of-doors in December, to walk hand in hand along silver sands, lapped by the calm of an azure sea. With this fair tranquility came such sunsets that painted the heavens in purple and scarlet and turned the sea to blood. The land, dour and sodden in yesterday's storms, became alive with opalescent shades, the dark blue shadows outlining the fine tracery of winter hedges.

Shadows. Sibella was the only shadow in his life. The greater his happiness with Maeve, the greater his guilt about Sibella. Far from erasing her from his mind, Maeve's love made him bitterly aware of Sibella's loneliness, her rejection. Sometimes he thought his burden would have been easier had Maeve known the truth, or if he could have talked to someone about it. However, when Sibella's name was casually mentioned, he discovered that as well as gratitude for the high-born lady, she also showed a woman's instinctive jealousy. Philip had lived with the Lady Sibella all that time. What had they talked about, what kind of person was she? Maeve wanted to know. This gentlewoman who had saved his life.

And Philip, groaning inwardly, thought of the life he had given her in return, plagued by remembrance that as Maeve's pregnancy advanced, so in Kirkwall did Sibella's.

Kirkwall. He tried to thrust from his mind her day-to-day existence there among the rapacious Stewart wives and mistresses, the Earl's searching questions, her terror of discovery. Only in Maeve's arms did he forget for a while. With Maeve he had everything he wanted in life, and even the unlikely role of crofter he felt would suit him someday.

Although there were no more fearful episodes like the end of the *Black Duchess*, winter storms deposited an occasional modest wreck on the shore, and Philip had no qualms now about taking his share of dead men's spoils, this gift from the sea which threatened and held them hostage.

Erasmus Flett became a constant visitor, attracted by a companion for chess, an argument about books. He was impressed by Philip's knowledge of languages, since he spoke fluently French and Latin—and Spanish. As they talked together, Philip remembered wistfully the library at El Escorial, which had been part of his daily life, and all that he missed of his former existence.

One day Erasmus came to him with a proposition. "It has long been in my mind that our parish should have a teacher. I doubt whether the older folk would be interested, but the young ones should know their letters. The more knowledge we have," he added in a whisper, "the more weapons at hand to fight Earl Robert and his clan. What think you of a village school, here at Cleat?"

The children came slowly at first to the Scholar's house, as they called it, but by the end of the year Philip was gratified to have twenty pupils most days in the parlour of Cleat. If numbers increased at this rate, he decided that next year he would turn the barn into a schoolroom proper.

Erasmus was delighted by his parishioners' response, and Philip found this new exercise for his mind and intellect more gratifying than simple crofting or fishing, especially the latter since any close dealings with the sea brought a speedy return of his old enemy, sea-sickness.

He discovered he need no longer rely upon his croft for a living. His pupils could not pay him for their lessons, but they paid in kind, and so the larder was never empty and there was always cloth for Maeve to sew, especially as she had become skilled at weaving.

At first Mistress Alys adopted a maternal attitude to Maeve, but found Baubie Finn regarding her jealously. Baubie came often, just to sit silent and admire Philip. The very sight of him pleased her, for he was a beautiful man, she thought, handsome as a painting.

Before her pregnancy made it impossible, Maeve would walk along the shore most days to Baubie's, to see Jean and Boy. However, her absence worried and frightened Philip. He could hardly bear to let her out of his sight even when he was teaching, and so to please him she stayed at home and cultivated Mistress Alys' friendship as well as her instructions in housewifery.

In due course Father Thomas arrived from Kirkwall on his twice yearly tour of the island, to attend to the spiritual needs of those who still adhered to the Catholic faith. There were not only confessions to hear and Masses to be said, but also couples to marry and babies to christen.

"If he does not arrive soon," grumbled Philip, "he will have both offices to perform for us in the same hour."

Philip had no strong feelings about being married by the priest. Erasmus Flett would have served this purpose just as well, since his religious feelings had also undergone considerable change and he would have readily changed his faith to match his new image. The faith in which he had been reared in Spain, the pomp and ritual of the Mass at El Escorial, seemed inappropriate to the life of a simple scholar and crofter. Although Erasmus never tried to convert him, he could see good sense in many of the concepts of the Reformed Church.

Maeve, however, clung passionately to her Catholic upbringing, the only stability and comfort in the wretchedness of her early days in Ireland. She argued with Philip that it was through her prayers to the Holy Virgin that a miracle had occurred and Philip had been restored to her.

And so, one windy day in March 1589, they were wed in the parlour of Cleat, with Erasmus in the role of first witness and Mistress Alys sighing sentimentally, despite the bride's advanced state of pregnancy. Baubie and Magnus, Boy and Jean Halcro were there. Baubie, with the tears streaming down her old ugly face, stood on tiptoe to kiss the bridegroom, who, laughing, swung her up into the air as if she were no more than a doll. Hugging, kissing her, he told everyone of his gratitude, for she had brought his beloved Maeve safe back to him from the sea for this perfect day.

Baubie thought this was the happiest hour of her life, so proud she was. Even Boy, she noticed with satisfaction, seemed to understand a lot more of late. He was smiling happily, holding Jean's hand.

The ceremony over, everyone wanted news of Kirkwall. The tidings Father Thomas brought were of Earl Robert. A mysterious accident while out hunting had thrown him from his horse. His heavy overindulged body had apparently suffered little damage, but one day he began to wither down his left side, and it was also noticed that he was no longer quite right in the head. Such infirmity had not improved his temper, and when for several days at a time his senses left him and he lay as one dead, it was clear to everyone that his days as ruler of Orkney were numbered.

"Black Pate is already taking over the iniquitous cloak that his father sheds with his earthly shell," said Father Thomas, shaking his head sadly. "As well as jubilation there is also caution that we should not rejoice too soon, since we are perhaps changing one tyrant for another of equal wickedness."

And Philip, having met Lord Patrick, was inclined to agree. Mistress Alys too. After all, folks had only to see him in his excursions about the island, those excuses for theft and abduction, to know that Father Thomas uttered a timely warning.

Gloomily they remembered that he was young and strong, with a whole lifetime's tyranny ahead of him.

Despite his concern for the future of Orkney, Philip was at that moment more deeply concerned about Sibella. But he had to wait patiently for the news he longed to hear. Father Thomas had to leave immediately after the ceremony since his flock were widely scattered, but gratefully accepted the hospitality of Cleat on his return journey a week later. There Erasmus Flett joined them at supper and Philip asked idly:

"What news of Lady Mary St Clair and the Lady Sibella? How fare they with the Earl's son?" He was conscious of a sudden silence, and his heart hammered so loudly at the mention of Sibella he was sure Maeve heard it too, for she paused with her hand poised above her plate. Her look in his direction was frankly accusing.

Father Thomas shook his head, spread wide his hands. "Gone," he said.

"Gone?" croaked Philip, his knife clattering unheeded to the floor.

Now both Maeve and Erasmus stared at him, the latter's whimsical expression hastily concealed. Before God, thought Philip, am I so transparent; can all of them read my thoughts? He touched his face, sure that it had paled.

Father Thomas was unaware of the catastrophe his one word had created. "Aye, gone to Edinburgh—long since," he said, helping himself to another bowl of broth.

Philip tried unsuccessfully to suppress a sigh of relief. "I am surprised that Earl Robert allowed them to leave the island, for I fancied that they were little more than prisoners until—er—" He wished to say "Lady Sibella's child was born." But the look on Maeve's face changed his mind and he said, "You know that the Earl had some plans for the lady's future as the late Master of Orkney's widow?"

What had befallen his child soon to be born? If only he dare ask that.

The priest sighed. "Aye, there was rumour that the Lady Sibella was with child at the time of her husband's death. After the lady had been barren so many years," he added in a sympathetic aside to his audience, and Philip was painfully aware of Maeve's eyes upon him, still and watchful. "However, if child there was, then it came to naught. Black Pate, with his inheritance at hand, so to speak, and a wife who tends to be a peedie bit parsimonious." The priest shook his head. "I know not the details, my son, only the rumour that they were packed off to Edinburgh."

"Did any see them depart?"

"Aye, a fair number of folk watched the ship sail away with envy in their hearts, wishing they too could be free." He saw the strange expression in Philip's eyes and added, "Why do you ask—did you fear that they had been put away by more wicked means?"

"I did."

Father Thomas smiled. "You have nothing more to fear, my son."

But Philip stared at the plate Maeve thrust, somewhat sharply, before him. Nothing more to fear, eh?

"Have you heard that we are to have yet another tax—" the priest was asking. But Philip heard no more; he toyed with his food, his eyes unseeing.

The child—his child—had come to naught.

What of Sibella? What of her agony of mind and body? Oh, dear God. If only he could have been with her, to touch her hand and tell her he was sorry. Sibella—where was she now?

At that moment, Sibella sat by the open window of a handsome house in Edinburgh's High Street, breathing in the warm brightness of a spring evening. She looked at Lady Mary engrossed in a tapestry and Inga lighting the candles. Her gaze travelled contentedly, following panelled walls, glowing peat fire, and handsome furniture. How superb to live in a modern house after two draughty ancient castles! The house she now occupied was the King's property and used for special visitors who required their own establishment. Though it was just five years old, its original shell had existed in her mother's reign. Fine glass windows had been added, and a balcony overlooking the street.

Sibella sighed. Sometimes she had to pinch herself quite severely to believe all this good fortune had come her way, that the horsemen clattering up and down the Royal Mile between Edinburgh Castle and the Palace of Holyroodhouse were impersonal, going about King James's business and unconcerned with her. At the sound of troopers no matter how innocent she still went rigid with fear, her safe, happy Edinburgh insubstantial as a dream from which she would awaken again to the nightmare of Burray, with the Earl's men thundering up the hill and the warning bell sounding in the tower.

She knew that her foster-mother suffered similar nightmares and on occasion wept without reason. Questioned, she shook her head, saying it was naught, but Sibella guessed that she too was afraid that their present security and comfort were ethereal as fairy gold which must somehow desert them in the end.

But Lady Mary and she still marvelled that after all their devious and tortured plans to escape from Orkney, in the end it had been easy. The door of their prison opened and they had been positively bustled out by Lord Patrick to board a ship for Leith, where His Gracious Majesty King James the Sixth of Scotland had announced himself pleased to offer Lady Sibella a small house and income on condition that she sign certain documents.

The documents presented by the cautious young King were to sign away her birthright as the legitimate surviving issue of Mary Queen of Scots by her marriage to James Hepburn, Earl of Bothwell.

The fact that Lady Sibella was agreeable, grateful, and showed not the least desire personal or political to be known as His Majesty's half sister, endeared her further to the King's eternally suspicious heart. Since he lived in constant terror of rivals, of assassins, and plans to steal his throne, her attitude towards giving up even her title pleased him beyond measure. He had regarded her existence in Orkney with superstitious fear, and decided that for the well-being of his realm, now that she was widowed, he should take her into custody. Besides, rumours from those unhappy Isles had been reaching him with some regularity of late, and he decided that his late mother's half brother, Lord Robert Stewart, was becoming all too powerful and wealthy. The persecution of the Isles did not bother him as much as the unequal balance of monies and treasures so obtained. Had a little more of the profits been directed towards himself, he would have been prepared to turn a blind eye and a deaf ear. However, a great believer in fair shares, as long as he got the largest portion, he thought it was time to act, and the case of Lady Sibella gave him the perfect excuse.

On reading the terms of the agreement Lady Mary was tearful, but Sibella remained adamant. "I have suffered long enough. I will be happy to be a private citizen of Edinburgh, with a comfortable home for us both provided by His Majesty. Do not weep, dearest; my birthright has brought us nothing but misery and danger, and I will be happy indeed to be quit of it forever."

King James was curious to see this half sister, and invited her to an audience at Holyrood. He had hoped for an impostor, but one look confirmed that she was indeed a Stewart; she even resembled the portrait of his late mother, and what was worse, some of his other less pleasant but eagerly ambitious relatives. Such a pawn she would be, should she fall into the powerful hands all around him.

The King closed his eyes, gulped convulsively. Fortunate indeed that she had been so willing to immediately relinquish any royal rights. If she had not, he thought grimly, then more permanent means would have been needed to dispose of such a lady. He was glad she was no fighter, as their mother had been. He was tired of fighters; they unnerved him.

The documents signed, the audience at an end, he said, "I gather, er—um—there wasna' issue to the marriage, was there now?"

"None, Your Majesty."

"Never?" His voice was sharp. There had been rumour of a bairn on the way. He did not want the same situation over again. He had been told that the twins his mother had borne Lord Bothwell were safely at the bottom of the Loch of Leven—and here was one of them before him. And in Scotland history had a nasty way of repeating itself. Nay, he must have proof positive.

"Never?" he repeated.

"Never, Your Majesty. Lately I miscarried of a son." He knew that, she thought.

The King scratched his head. "Would that be about the same time your late husband was—er—met with his unhappy end?" He knew he had been poisoned with his mistress, an ending not unusual for similar royal indiscretions. He searched her face for guilt or sorrow, found neither.

"A little later, Your Majesty." It had been three months later, but never mind.

" 'Twas doubtless due to the shock of—er—um—"

She agreed with a modest lowering of eyelids. "I had, alas, a series of such miscarriages and had failed to provide my late husband with an heir. I fear I am barren, Your Majesty."

The King beamed. A barren Stewart cheered him more than anything, and they parted on the most cordial terms, with His Majesty making her an even more generous allowance than he had first intended. Afterwards he gnawed his lip and paced the floor, pained by such unseemly extravagance.

The document safely signed, Sibella was happy. Each day she lived through carried her further from the grief of losing Philip's child, further from the memory of that perfect son, a waxen doll who had never breathed. She had snatched him from them, hugging him to her breast, trying to shake life into the tiny body with her own warmth, her passion and tears. For a day and a night she had held him in her arms, refusing to sleep or eat. Only when at last she slept through weakness and exhaustion did Inga gently take him from her. When she awoke and found him gone, she wanted to die, her prayers and cries ringing through the chamber.

Lady Mary had despaired of her reason, certain that grief would drive her mad, or that she would betray Philip and they would all lose their lives at the Earl's displeasure. Now she looked at her in amazement. Never had she thought to see her smile again, let alone hear her laughter.

As for Sibella, her deeply unhappy marriage to the Master of Orkney had destroyed much of her natural desire for children. Philip's child she recognised as the fulfilment of her love for him rather than as an individual being. She was glad she had loved Philip and had his precious memory, for she wanted no other man and was certain none in this world could replace him. But wisely she realised that had their child lived they would both have been held prisoner, the Queen of Scots' grandson another pawn in the Earl of Orkney's power. The little time she had spent with King James made her see clearly that with such an inheritance and a child, she need not have expected much more than imprisonment at his hands. She observed that the young King was a very frightened man.

As for Lord Patrick, he had also been eager to be rid of her since rumour had reached him from Edinburgh that the King was considering a tightening and reorganisation of the government in his far-flung Isles, which were somewhat impervious to his rule. Especially in the matter of this late Spanish Armada. Rumour had it that there were wrecks in plenty, treasure ships and the like, but not even the sniff of one had come in his direction. The Earl of Orkney kept on denying that he had seen so much as one Spanish doubloon.

Black Pate kept on denying it too. However, he was anxious to create a good impression upon the King without relinquishing his father's grip upon the land. He did not wish to be dispossessed, and when His Majesty requested the protection of the widow of the late Master of Orkney, his brother, he was eager to accommodate his monarch's wishes.

If Sibella suspected sometimes that she was a prisoner in the house on the High Street and that the servants he had so thoughtfully provided were royal spies, she did not mention this to Lady Mary. At least the house was comfortable and furnished with luxuries unknown in either Kirkwall or Burray castles. Besides, Lady Mary was happy. A dozen times a day she commended to the wistful-eyed Sibella the virtues of her royal half brother.

"Please do not call him so," said Sibella. "I entreat you."

"Not even when we are alone?" whispered Lady Mary.

"Nay, dearest. Not even when we are alone."

And so the early weeks of 1589 passed agreeably well. The High Street was occupied by handsome houses and towers, the residences of noblemen and rich merchants, and there were invitations in plenty for "the Lady St Clair and her Widowed daughter, Lady Sibella Stewart." Sibella met many men who made plain to her that they desired more than a mere acquaintance. But Sibella remained true to Philip, for there was not a man among her admirers whom she desired in the least. When the month came wherein she should have borne Philip's child, old wounds reopened and she missed him intolerably.

She wept, clinging to Lady Mary and crying why was she different, why could she never hold a child of her body and her love in her empty arms? She was that despised creature of the Bible, a barren woman, accursed.

One day she visited Lady Drummond, and while they refreshed themselves with a cup of muscadel, for the day was uncommonly warm, and gravely discussed the matter of gowns for Lady Haddington's Masque, the door flew open and Sibella's maid, Inga, rushed in unannounced.

Lady Drummond was appalled at the interruption, for the creature seemed unable to speak, with only strange animal sounds issuing from her gaping mouth.

Inga seized her mistress's arm.

"Will it not wait awhile?" asked Sibella, her tone gentle despite her exasperation, for Inga did not normally behave so strangely.

"You must excuse my maid, Lady Drummond, for she cannot talk. This, I fear, is important. You will excuse me? Perhaps my lady mother is taken ill—"

Inga shook her head vigorously, indicating that she had left Lady Mary in the best of health and spirits.

Lady Drummond, unable to restrain her curiosity, followed them to the door and watched Lady Stewart descend into the street, with her maid gesticulating in that frightening fashion.

Inga's pointing hand, the excited grunts, stirred memories of Orkney for Sibella, and she saw emerging from the merchant's house opposite a sea captain whom she knew traded between Leith and London. With him, a man. They were deep in conversation.

"What is it, Inga?" There was nothing in the least familiar about the cloak he wore, the bonnet, or the young man and girl at his side.

"Who is he?" What had taken possession of Inga about these strangers? She frowned, shaking her head, about to return to Lady Drummond, who watched them from her balcony.

But Inga would not release her. She clung to her arm imploringly, dancing up and down, making rasping noises in her throat as if she sought to form a name.

At that moment, the man turned and Sibella found herself staring into that well-loved face she now encountered only in dreams.

He had found her. In answer to all her prayers, he had come for her—at last.

"Philip." Regardless of the horsemen trotting briskly over the cobblestones, she rushed across the street.

"Philip—oh, Philip," she cried.

The horses reared, whinnying. The onlookers rushed forward, yelling a warning. Lady Drummond screamed and closed her eyes against the horror taking place beneath her balcony.

No one could save Lady Sibella from being trampled to death.

17

He had been taken from the sea by a damaged merchantman trailing far behind the rest of the Queen's ships, crippled at Gravelines. He had survived their rough surgery, which had removed the musket ball, and had lain like death in the swaying cabin until at last the ship limped into port some days behind the main fleet.

There, by the merest chance, the unconscious man on the litter was recognised as Sir Amyas Lennox, and the humble mariner's house where he was lodged visited by Elizabeth of England herself, who insisted that Sir Amyas be taken to the Palace at Greenwich and there nursed back to health—if such was God's will. Which to any looking at him seemed a pious hope indeed, taking into consideration the man's fever and weakness from loss of blood.

The royal physicians fought for his life, and a rider was despatched to Lennoxhoe, where Barbara and Francis, hastily summoned, began a vigil at their father's bedside. When he opened his eyes and saw them there, his first words were a whispered:

"How goes it with thy mother and the babe?"

Neither spoke. His glance took account of their sombre attire, and even before Barbara's first sobs broke the silence, his face turned to wax, for he knew that his beloved Jane was dead.

It was an ill time for him to receive such tidings, and for a while, they feared for what little remained of his life, his slow recovery thus set back.

Barbara, whose dearest wish to be at the Queen's court had been dourly granted, now wished to see only the inside of her father's bedchamber. She refused to leave him night or day, clutching his hand as if by so doing she could hold him into the life that apparently drained hourly away.

Francis maintained that it was Barbara, whose imploring face penetrated the darkness of their father's despair.

Amyas could have told a very different story, but he never did. Through his fitful consciousness the world of reality flickered, and he stood upon a vague threshold, perilous and disagreeable, where it seemed he had many conversations with Jane. Though they were of considerable length, afterwards he could never remember their content or whether they belonged only to his fevered imaginings. Could it have been Jane who wept, saying Barbara was young and needed a father's love and care? And so too did Francis. To both of their beloved children, the fruit of their love and their happy marriage, Amyas owed a duty still. And while he pleaded to go across the divide and return into the darkness with her, she rebuked him sternly, and pointed the way back to the world he longed to leave. She cried that she would never forgive him should he abandon her precious darlings to the life of orphans, even the life of wealthy orphans under the Queen's patronage. Now weeping too, he watched her draw away from him, back into that place behind whose veil there was no time, but only God's promise that they would meet again—

He opened his eyes, smiled upon Barbara, returning a steady grip to her clutching hand. From then on his progress was remarkable. Within the following week he sat up in bed and talked with Francis of matters at Lennoxhoe, and in the next month the three of them returned home.

For a moment, confronted by that empty threshold with no beloved welcoming figure rushing out to greet him, Amyas felt his courage fail him. He hesitated, and leaning his head against the harsh and cold stone wall, he turned his face from them and silently wept. Inside, he could hardly bring himself to inhabit the chamber in which Jane had died, and their once happy bride-bed.

Then one morning he found the windows ablaze with the golden light of autumn and remembered that thus it had been on the day when they were wed. This annual resurrection was like God's promise renewed that he and his beloved Jane would meet again. For a brief moment the sunlight was a benediction, bathing him once more in the radiant illusion of youth that had gone forever, buried with his wife. Now Barbara and Francis observed sadly that the first frost of age had tarnished the head, once bright as the autumn wheat fields about Lennoxhoe. The wound of a sorrowing heart would pain him longer than the wound of battle slowly healing. The scars of both he must carry to his grave, but before that he had much to live for, his children, his home, and the *Warlock* although she must sail without her master until he was fit enough and his affairs at Lennoxhoe were in order. And so in the warmth of loving family and loyal servants, he who had thought never again to smile heard himself laughing out loud at the capers of his two children, chasing a hound pup who had run off with one of Bessie's garters. Barbara, returning breathless with the pup in her arms, whispered to Francis:

"I believe Father is healing."

She wrestled with her new role as mistress of Lennoxhoe under Bessie's expert guidance and cast only occasional sighs towards Greenwich when couriers arrived with messages of the Queen's goodwill. Francis, determined to forget Oxford, took upon his young shoulders the heavy responsibility of their vast estate, under his father's guidance.

One day a messenger, mud-bespattered and weary, rode in. They listened to his strange, uncouth accent and learned that he had come from the far north, from Scotland, where their grandfather Thomas Lennox lay sick and like to die. He wished to be reunited with his only son, Amyas.

Such were the events which led them to Holyrood Palace, where an old man in the last days of his life reminisced over the past, recalling the boyhood days of Amyas and Felipe, marvelling over the marriage of twin brothers to twin sisters, which had produced cousins each the mirror image of the other.

Amyas then told his father of destiny's strange meeting with Felipe during the battle of the Armada.

"Aye," said the old man, "'twould be Felipe right enough, for he was godson to the King of Spain."

"What, your cousin fighting for the Spaniard, aboard a pirate ship?" demanded Francis. "An incredible tale."

"Does your wound trouble you, Father?" whispered gentle Barbara, concerned for the look of pain on his face.

"No more than usual, child." He patted her hand. "Besides, I am grateful to God for the miracle of being alive this day." Which was more than he could vouch for Felipe, lost forever in the holocaust of

Gravelines. And yet in those minutes in the sea before his rescue he thought that Felipe leaped overboard after him, held him afloat. Sadly he shook his head; he had so many delusions during those lingering days between life and death. Good sense told him to dismiss Felipe as another fantasy, but he thought of him often in Holyrood, this scene of their happy childhood days.

In fact, he had been telling Francis and Barbara only that morning about poor unhappy Queen Mary's wedding to Darnley. That very morning, when a madwoman rushed out of Lady Drummond's house to scream at him and throw herself under the horses' hooves. He had discovered that, for a cripple, he could still move uncommonly fast.

"Philip," Sibella whispered as she opened her eyes.

"Nay, my name is Francis," said the boy before her, who bore only a very fleeting resemblance to the man she had seen outside Lady Drummond's. Now a girl came forward, sweet-faced, bonny. She curtseyed, smiling. "And this is my sister, Barbara," said the boy. "Your mother told us we might look in and see you."

"We have been most anxious for you," said the girl.

"'Tis a miracle you were not trampled by the horses," the boy reminded her sternly.

"Where is Philip?" she demanded impatiently.

The boy shook his head. "Philip? 'Twas our father saved you."

She saw the frowning looks they exchanged.

"Do you not remember?" asked the girl gently.

Philip. Oh, Philip. So it had been a dream, a fantasy that she saw him, she *really* saw him in the High Street. How could it have been Philip, far away in Orkney, how could he come to Edinburgh and find her? Sick with disappointment, she turned her face away and wept.

"Please do not weep," said the girl. "There now—see, Father has come."

She opened her eyes to the vision who had appeared framed in the doorway. From the shadows emerged that well-beloved face—

"Philip," she cried, and tried to sit up.

He approached the bed rapidly and took her hands. "Nay, Mistress. My name is Lennox, Amyas Lennox. But I have a cousin. He is my image. Perhaps it is he you take me for. A Spanish gentleman, Don Felipe?"

Miserably she nodded.

"Then he lives?"

"Aye—in Orkney."

The man looked delighted with this news, and his children exchanged smiles.

The man who looked like Philip wanted to hear all about his cousin, and Sibella answered his questions dully, her heartache almost intolerable, for now that she saw Amyas Lennox close, she wondered how she could have been so mistaken. He looked older than Philip, his voice was quite different, deep, with an English accent, his face was broader. He had the look of a man who spends most of his life at the mercy of elements. The compact strong body proclaimed a man of action. He had none of Philip's delicate grace of movement, and that gilt-coloured hair was sadly tarnished, even streaked with white. His face was scarred too, and lined with suffering.

But he did look kind. A warm, tender man, easily hurt by the misfortunes of others. A caring man, more caring, she thought, than her oft chilly Philip.

"And so my cousin lives. That is good news indeed, Mistress. How came he to Orkney?"

"He was shipwrecked from the Armada." And Sibella told him the story of how her servants had rescued him and that he had served in Burray Castle as steward to her mother, Lady Mary St Clair. And when her husband, the Master of Orkney, died, she had come to live in Edinburgh. She was careful to omit any hint of her royal parentage.

Her recent widowhood was a bond with Amyas. They had both suffered irreparable loss, he thought, looking at her sad young face, a sadness only the bereaved could ever understand. He doubted not that she mourned her dead husband as he still mourned—aye, and ever would—his sweet and gentle Jane.

Amyas had met many beautiful ladies in King James's court at Holyrood, but although he hopefully searched each new face, he looked in vain, for none could fill his heart with longing or his body with desire. Strange, he thought, that this unhappy woman fleetingly touched a chord. What was it? Did she remind him of his Jane? Not in looks, but in the turn of her head, a smile, a gesture, that was all. In the days that lay ahead while he awaited the ship that would take him home to Lennoxhoe, he came often to the King's house on the

High Street. He told her that having buried his father, there was no longer matter to keep him here in Edinburgh. He had that very day they met been making arrangements to sail when she had leaped across the road into his life. His barren life, he thought, and she smiled as if she understood. Her smiles troubled him, for it was as if Jane's ghost stared out at him beseechingly from Sibella's eyes. Uncomfortably, he shrugged such an idea aside, but it refused to be banished.

He discovered he was not alone in enjoying Sibella's company, telling himself that she was young enough to be his daughter. She was also young enough for Francis to be captivated by her.

Aye, thought Amyas sadly as the day of their sailing approached and he found his son making more excuses to walk past the King's house. One day he said:

"Father, I intend asking the Lady Sibella to return with us to Lennoxhoe."

Amyas hardly needed to ask the question. "As your wife, Francis?"

"Aye, sir, if she will have me. And if it pleases you."

It did not please Amyas in the least. A shaft of pure agony consumed him at the thought of Sibella becoming his son's wife. Was he only jealous of Francis' youth, he tried to reason with himself as he lay sleepless that night? After all, he was no longer young. Since his injuries fighting on the *Warlock*, his long submersion in the sea, he was a crippled bad-tempered old man on bad days, and even on good days scarcely ever free from an aching head. How dare he presume a young and beautiful—aye, beautiful—woman should find his graying head more attractive, more to her taste than his handsome son's? He must put all thought of her from his mind and not only allow Francis to court her, but also give the union his blessing.

But Sibella turned her face away from Francis. When Amyas made an excuse to visit her later that day, she stared at him with wistful Jane-eyes, as though willing him to say words that he could never find.

Francis took his rejection to his sister. " 'Tis not I she loves," he said.

"She is too old for you."

"She is not."

"Then she has suffered too greatly," said Barbara. "That makes people older than the year in which they were born. Look at Father."

She thought privately that her brother was a babe, innocent and guileless.

Francis continued to glower and to sigh. "If I am not to marry Sibella, then I shall go to sea on the *Warlock,* for that is my ambition since Father is now well enough to take care of Lennoxhoe."

"That is a splendid idea," said Barbara encouragingly. "Although we shall all miss you sadly."

Francis straightened his shoulders. "I shall enjoy the life. Perhaps we shall get another chance to fight the Spaniards, or I may sail to the New World."

Although Barbara smiled, she thought men never learned anything if they wanted to throw away their lives fighting when there was so much beauty at Lennoxhoe to love.

"I shall miss home, of course. But it would irk me to have such an inactive life, for I was never meant to be a country squire."

When Francis told his father of his plans and that he would not be marrying Sibella after all, Amyas tried not to feel guilty relief at his son's disappointment, his hurt pride. He said, "Do not grieve, you are young yet. You have many years to find a wife."

"So all tell me, but you were married and a father when you were my age," said Francis sourly. He did not want consolation, and the old seemed always to refer to youth as if it were some deadly affliction.

"Take it not ill, son. The lady doubtless still mourns her late husband."

"Did she love him?" asked Francis. "For she never speaks of him."

Amyas shook his head sorrowfully. "Perhaps it pains her too greatly."

"You speak constantly of our dear mother."

"For different people, different ways of grieving."

When Francis repeated this conversation to Barbara, she laughed. "What fools men are, brother dear, not to see what is under their very noses."

She refused to explain further, but when she was alone with her father, helping him pack Grandfather's few treasures for return to Lennoxhoe, she asked, "Have you spoken to Lady Sibella?"

Amyas frowned. "Upon what matter?" What now, dear God? Was he expected to intercede for his son?

"Upon the matter of returning to Lennoxhoe with us."

So that was it. "I will most willingly be Francis' ambassador if he has spoken to you. He could have asked me himself." His face was bleak.

Barbara shook her head. "Nay, Father, I do not mean that at all. You should go to Sibella—as your own ambassador," she said gently, and standing on tiptoe, kissed his cheek. "Dear Father, look not so astonished. The lady loves you. She will not have Francis when it is you she wants."

Amyas disentangled himself from her arms. "What foolish talk is this, daughter? How could she love me? I am old and a cripple."

"You are lame, but you are not old. I wonder if you *are* blind though, not to observe how she sighs for you."

"Sighs for me? Never. 'Tis her late husband she mourns—and quite rightly so. You mistake those sighs." His laughter had a hollow sound.

"I mistake nothing. I am with her often, and she shows all the signs of loving you—I would swear to that."

She saw hope on his face, hope which turned him into a young man again, eager and gallant. His shoulders, which had stooped of late, with defeat rather than a bad back, straightened wonderfully at Barbara's words. Now he questioned her closely, keenly, as Francis had done. How did she know, did Lady Sibella ever speak his name?

Barbara sighed. "Father dear, she talks of naught else but you when we are alone together. She seeks my company with her sighs and pounds my ears with questions about you, about your ship and your bravery and how you came to be knighted by Queen Elizabeth."

" 'Tis just polite conversation, a touch of hero worship for an older man."

"Hero worship—polite! She asks all manner of other questions too, about your life at Lennoxhoe. Nay, it is ungallant of me to divulge the lady's confidences thus. You must discover for yourself."

"I cannot." Amyas sat down, having discovered that his legs were trembling.

"You must, Father dear." And Barbara knelt by his chair. "For in truth, you are both lonely and in need of love."

"You would not—mind, Barbara?"

"Off you go, make haste and bring the lady back with you."

At the door, he asked again. "You do not mind—you are sure?" He remembered how dearly she had loved her mother. "You would not think I was bringing a usurper to your dear mother's place?"

Barbara smiled and a tear glistened on her cheek. She shook her head. "None can ever usurp our dear mother, for the love we have for her is changeless. She took it intact to the grave with her. What I feel for Sibella is a new kind of love which will not detract in the least from those memories. She will be more sister to Francis and me than stepmother. But to you, I swear, dear Father, she will be a true and loving wife."

And so on the morning before the ship was due to leave for England, Amyas visited Sibella for the last time. He fancied that her hand shook a little as he greeted her and that her eyes were suspiciously red.

"Has aught distressed you?" he asked anxiously.

Shakily she replied, "Naught but some fearsome herbs I was helping Inga prepare in the kitchen when you arrived." But her laugh was false and he saw Lady Mary dart her a reproachful look before curtseying and tactfully vacating the room.

"Will you be glad to return to Lennoxhoe?" asked Sibella.

He said he would, and she asked him casual questions about his home, and he asked her casually whether she would care to see Lennoxhoe for herself.

She whispered that if she ever found herself in the neighbourhood she might call upon him, for she would love to meet him again. Tears sprang to her eyes, and Amyas dropped on one knee before her. Seizing her hands, he said:

"Sweetheart, then come with me to Lennoxhoe—do."

"Oh, I will, Amyas, I will. Nothing in this world would please me more." And tearfully she added, "For I cannot bear to lose you."

"And I cannot bear to let you go."

They kissed and sighed a great deal, and Sibella wondered how she had ever thought him in the least like Philip. The thought of that ghost threw a shadow over her new happiness.

"Amyas, sir—there are many things you should know before you take me to wife. I fear I am of barren stock, and will not bring you babes. I did but recently miscarry—"

"Nay, no more—that is in the past." He shook his head sadly. "I lost my dear wife in childbirth. I long not for babes, and would be happy to have only you to love." Then laughing, he added, "Besides, we have Barbara and Francis. Love them well and you will please me."

"That I do already."

And so Sibella went to Lennoxhoe, taking with her Lady Mary and Inga. King James was delighted that she should be gone from his kingdom and that an expensive house and pension should revert to the royal coffers. His joy that she should become an English squire's wife and live in distant Plymouth extended to a small wedding present, a jewelled miniature of his mother which he had never liked. When the ship sailed taking away the happy couple from his kingdom, he decided that was one less in the complicated family tree bequeathed him by his grandfather's overindulgence in seed-scattering outside the bonds of wedlock.

In Lennoxhoe, Sibella had found her niche at last. Even Bessie, Jane's faithful servant, after the first shock was prepared to take her new mistress to her bosom. One day Sibella recognised what she had hitherto refused to see.

Henry of Orkney had never loved her. Philip of Cleat had never loved her. Although she had carried his child, his heart had never been hers. But Amyas loved her with all his heart, as she loved him.

For neither would it have the glory of first love. For neither would there be the bitterness of disillusion. Knowing the sorrows her royal parentage had brought, Amyas never enquired about her life in Orkney. He was interested in Philip, but not excessively so, relieved that after surviving the Armada he had landed safe in Burray. That was all. And Sibella realised that Amyas had meant a good deal more to his cousin than Philip had ever meant to him.

Sometimes Sibella wondered if she should tell him the truth of her life with Philip. But reason always prevailed. By confessing to a situation that was over and done with and therefore unchangeable, she would merely burden Amyas with her own guilt and perhaps sour their marriage.

For they were a perfect match. Each passing day saw their happiness grow like the great oaks in the park at Lennoxhoe. She had brought him new life and love, which he thought had gone forever. When she remembered Philip, she also recalled the fable that truth lies at the bottom of a well, and decided that too often in life more harm than good can be done by disturbing those muddy waters. The past had no place in their joy of each other, and she did not need Barbara and Francis to tell her that Amyas Lennox was a new man these days, or that they had all laid aside their cloaks of sorrow since she came into their lives.

What goodness or honour would be served by bringing a shadow into the serenity of their lives, a sadness into her dear husband's eyes? Why tell him what he really did not want to hear?

And so she never did.

In Orkney, Earl Robert survived until 1591 in increasing imbecility. His death brought little call for jubilation since Lord Patrick's rule was already well steeped in tyranny.

To Cleat, Harald Flett the Kirkwall boatbuilder, visiting his kinsman Erasmus, brought a strange story. Two years since, while he was in Leith, he had seen a family take ship for Plymouth. And he could have sworn that the man he watched was Philip of Cleat.

Philip smiled and shook his head. "I daresay there are other Lennoxes in Scotland. Perhaps there is a strong family resemblance."

Amyas was dead. He had died at Gravelines, and Philip had long since ceased to torture himself with dreams and hopes of his miraculous resurrection. He was happy now. Amyas belonged to the past, with Sibella.

Sibella. He had not thought of her in ages. Now, as a former servant of Burray, he asked:

"Was there news of Lady Mary?"

"She left Edinburgh some time ago with her daughter. Their departure was abrupt—there one day, sailed for England the next. I understand that Lady Sibella married an English gentleman, after a swift courtship."

Maeve had brought in the baby Erland during their conversation and was standing very still, listening intently. Erland cried at this inactivity. He was a strong, handsome child with prodigious energy. And Maeve tired easily these days.

Sometimes Philip found her motionless, staring out towards the horizon with its passing ships. Often he surprised an expression of infinite yearning and melancholy, swiftly banished by his presence. Although he never doubted the endurance of their love, he did wonder if she was truly content with the harsh demands and uncertainties of their future on Orkney. After Harald and Erasmus departed, Philip brought out his books to prepare the morrow's lessons, but his mind wandered constantly as thoughts of Latin verbs jostled uneasily with the significance of Flett's visit and the old ghosts summoned at the mention of Amyas and Sibella.

"What was that about the Lady Sibella?" Maeve demanded as if she read his mind, an accomplishment he considered well within her wifely capabilities.

"She has remarried and gone to England."

And suddenly Philip put aside his book. Supposing Amyas *had* lived. Supposing, for instance, that the man Flett had glimpsed *was* Amyas—and that Sibella had married Amyas. Narrow-eyed against the glare from the cold bright sea beyond the window, he watched a tiny ship rock gently towards the horizon. Amyas—

"What are you thinking about?" Maeve was frowning, looking hard at him.

"Nothing in particular." He seized his book again.

"Oh? Then why do you smile so secretly?"

With a sigh, hoping that the sharpness in her voice was prompted by weariness rather than suspicion, he pulled her onto his knee, cursing inwardly that a man should be so plagued by dreams when his wife was truly all in the world he wanted or needed.

"I smile because I am happy for us. And with good reason," he whispered, for that morning she had told him she was with child again.

Now she closed her eyes and held him tightly, as if she had glimpsed his dream and was afraid it would tear him from her side. That night, with Maeve asleep in his arms, Philip lifted the corner of his mind to admit Sibella.

Sibella. The one secret he still withheld from Maeve.

In the early days of their marriage he had been tortured by guilt, longing to tell all and be forgiven. Now he wondered even after all the time that had passed whether Maeve would understand. Some instinct told him to remain silent, that even when they were so happy she would not. That she would forgive and understand more readily the real reason for Harald Flett's visit than his lost love for Sibella Stewart.

Aye, Flett had brought news that day which swept even Sibella and Amyas from Philip's thoughts. News he had long dreaded, warned by Erasmus that the plan to overthrow Lord Patrick—Black Pate, as he was known—was almost ready, for the Orcadians had called a halt to patient resignation and submission. They were not prepared to tolerate the rule of another Stewart. A tougher generation than their elders had emerged with voices which cried out against tyranny, and when a painful death silenced them, others took their places until they too were silenced. An endless tide of martyrs, they ebbed and flowed, carrying their call for freedom against all tyrants across the Isles of Orkney and Shetland.

Flett was one of their leaders, but he told Philip that he needed other leaders, not only men who had passion and dedication and were prepared to die uselessly but gloriously as patriots, but also men of education, who could teach others. Men like Erasmus, like Father Thomas—like Philip of Cleat.

When Philip first listened to his plan, he seethed with inward anger. Why me? Ask someone else. Why should I risk my neck and the lives of my family for this land? I am not an Orcadian.

But he bit back the words, for when Flett had gone and he walked by the shore, the sun dipped into a sea of blood and the land called out to him as it had done one evening long since when he had found the drowned songbird Sweetling and had thought Maeve was dead. The land had taken pity on his agony and the sea had given back Maeve to him. The land had supported them, given them happiness together, and a son. Now he knew its ancient spirit rose again and cried out to him, its voice crying across heath and from the solemn brochs whose builders were lost in time. Now the wind clung to him like a lover, while the rain turned into a ravished woman's passionate tears.

He turned, cursing. "Leave me alone, leave me alone, damn you."

But he was beaten and he knew it. He owed this land a debt and he must pay it, even with his own blood. Or live on in the knowledge that he was forsworn that the honour of the two noble houses which had given him birth was besmirched. To his land he owed his rebirth and that of Maeve.

As though in obedience to his command, the storm died, the sea was at peace. Next morning the sun shone, but the disquiet in his heart remained. In the days that followed he told himself over and over that if Flett's plan failed, Maeve and Erland, the babe unborn, would be in mortal danger from Black Patc's revenge. But conscience mocked his excuses. Whatever happened to him, Baubie Finn would defend Maeve and her children like a lioness. They would be safe, for Baubie Finn had hiding places where no man dare enter.

And so the vigil began. One day soon without warning, Flett's boat would appear and men would follow him to the wild secret haunts north of the island. There Philip of Cleat would train them in the use of arms. The erstwhile commander of the *Black Duchess* had known nothing of sea warfare despite his imposing title. But he did know about arms. In common with all Spanish noblemen, he had been trained in arms from his earliest days at El Escorial. Again he thought of Amyas Lennox. If only Amyas had lived, for he too was a fighter. With men of his calibre, ridding the world of creatures like Black Pate would have been a glorious adventure. But Amyas was dead and he was alone.

He did not have to go. He could ignore the signal flying from Flett's boat, pretend illness. He looked at Maeve's sleeping face. He could close his eyes, bury his face in her hair, go on pretending there was no other world than this one they had created together.

He could. But he would not. For already, as if that fatal dawn had lightened the sky, he saw himself telling her that he must go. He saw the proud tilt of her chin, belying the fear and desolation in her eyes. He knew then that he had won his first battle, the most important one of all, for it was the victory a man won over his own heart.

And even as Harald Flett's boat stole out from Kirkwall upon the tide, absolved and at peace, he fell into a deep and dreamless slumber. But in the soul of the scholar Philip of Cleat, who was after all a king's godson, the ghost of Don Felipe Flores y Lennox de Montreuse, so long asleep, stirred and held patient vigil against the morn.

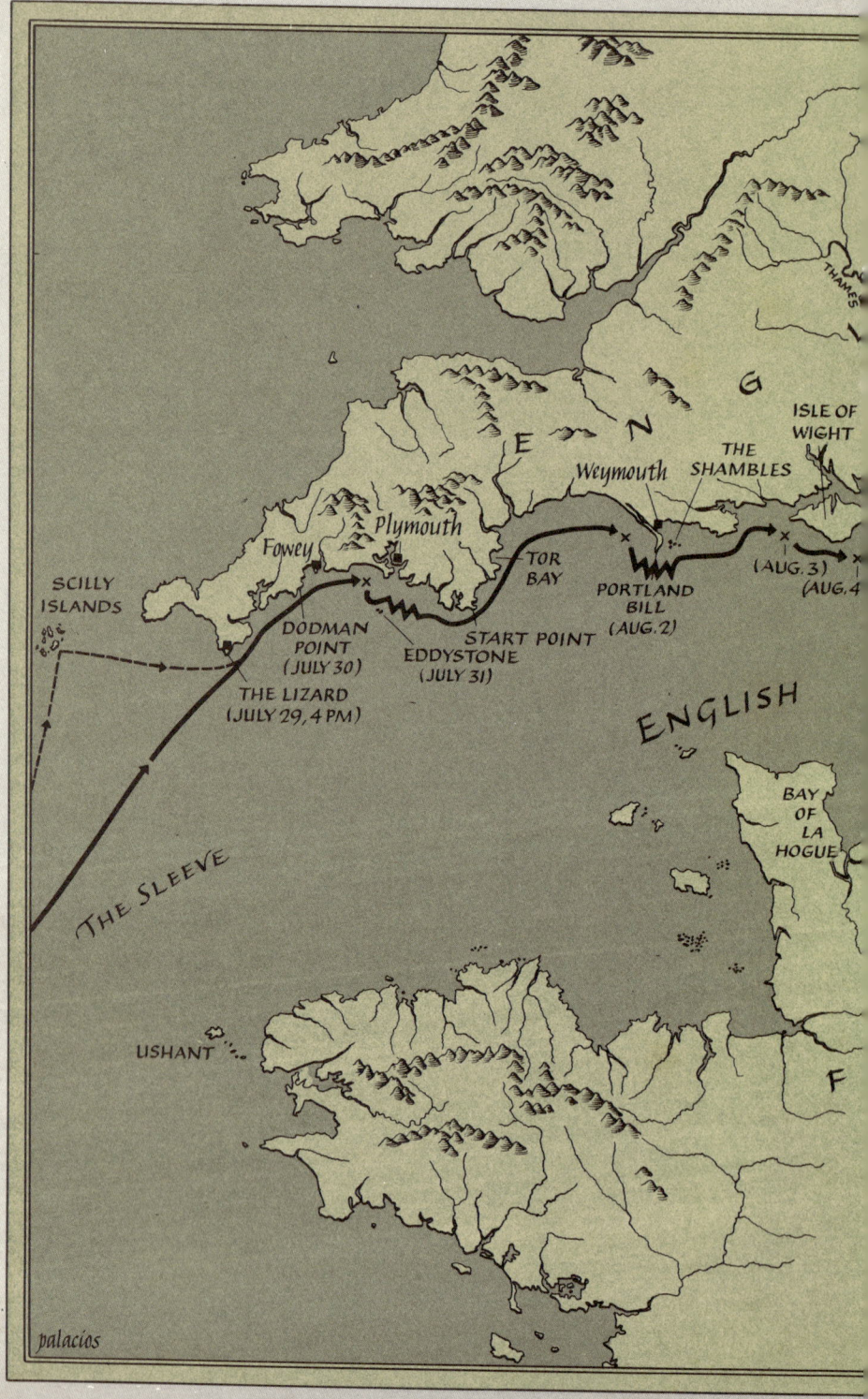

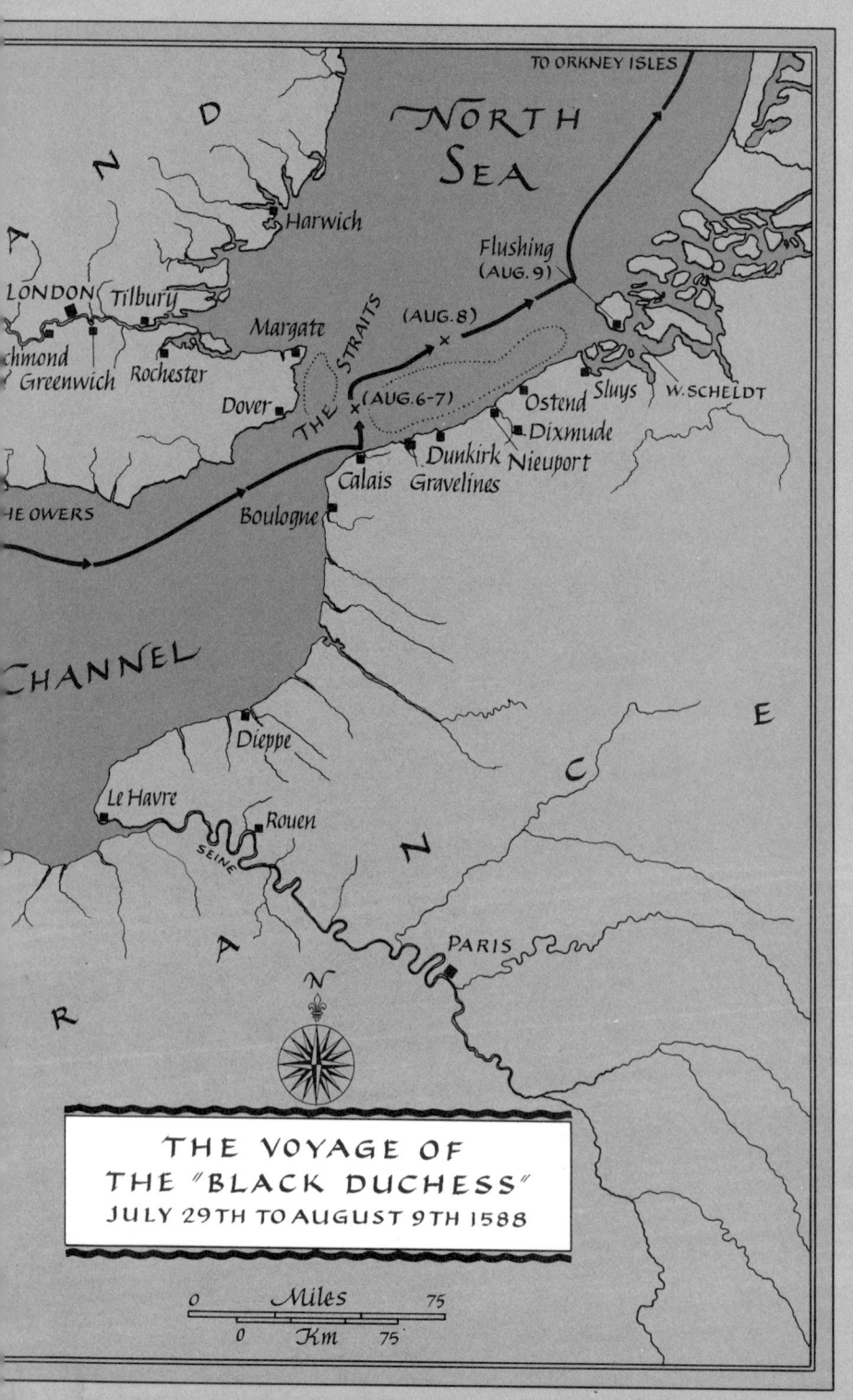